C000144303

Denise Barnes in several cou events have fo her stories, b In 2008 she self-published *from* ... *Wurst: Bavarian Adventures of a Veggie Cook*, a light-hearted travel memoir.

Denise ran her own chain of eight estate agents for 17 years and in 2005 sold (unwittingly!) to two conmen. She wrote her nightmare story *Seller Beware: How Not To Sell Your Business*, as a warning on how easily one can be conned (Biteback Publishing 2013).

Denise writes under the pen-name Fenella Forster for her fiction. The Voyagers trilogy is a saga stretching from 1913–2012. Book 1: *Annie's Story* (2015) and Book 2: *Juliet's Story* (2016), are both set mainly in Australia in 1913 and 2005 respectively. Book 3: *Kitty's Story* (2017) is set mainly in Cairo 1941. Each novel is a standalone although they are linked.

Annie's Story achieved the American award, BRAG (Book Readers Appreciation Group) Gold Medallion. The trilogy is published by SilverWood Books.

She contributed to the USA best-selling 'Chicken Soup for the Soul' series in their anthology *The Joy of Less* (2016). Denise's story, 'The Challenge', was a featured highlight of *Good Morning America*.

Denise is currently writing a new series set in WW2 for HarperCollins under the pen-name Molly Green. The first is *An Orphan in the Snow* (November 2017).

Visit Denise's website at www.denisebarneswriter.com, and you can follow her on Twitter @denisebarnesuk.

Praise for *Kitty's Story*

'*Kitty's Story* is a captivating romance with
well-researched period detail.'
– Jean Fullerton

'Fenella Forster takes readers on a breath-taking journey full
of stunning period detail from Blitz-torn Britain to the deserts of
Egypt, weaving a captivating love story in which passion
wars with duty and courage defies betrayal.'
– Joanne Walsh

'I lapped up this book. At its heart is Kitty, courageous, a little
outrageous but, at just seventeen, quite innocent. It is 1941, and
from her home town she's off to London in the hope she'll learn
to sing, see the world and help the war effort...probably in that
order. What follows is not only a roar of a story, but something
that warms the heart. At the end, Juliet, who we meet in book 2
of Fenella Forster's Voyagers trilogy, has finally tied up the
pieces of her past. A remarkable feat and a must-read.'
– Nina Milton

THE VOYAGERS

Kitty's Story

FENELLA FORSTER

SilverWood

Published in 2017 by SilverWood Books

SilverWood Books Ltd
14 Small Street, Bristol, BS1 1DE, United Kingdom
www.silverwoodbooks.co.uk

ISBN 978-1-78132-637-4 (paperback)
ISBN 978-1-78132-638-1 (ebook)

British Library Cataloguing in Publication Data
A CIP catalogue record for this book is available from
the British Library

Page design and typesetting by SilverWood Books
Printed on responsibly sourced paper

*For my mother who with my father went through the Blitz.
Her favourite film at the time was* Dangerous Moonlight *starring
Sally Gray as a beautiful American reporter called Carol.
Pregnant when she saw it, Mum named the baby Carole
(though with an 'e'), who became my older sister.*

Also by the Author

Prologue

Rome

Juliet, September 2012

Juliet snapped the empty suitcase shut and stood it in the corner of the gloomy space on the top floor of one of Rome's oldest hotels. She had no time for sightseeing. She had to concentrate on her main purpose for coming here – to find out about Kitty.

Strange how her father had mentioned Kitty only the day before he died. He'd lost touch with her, he'd said, so he didn't know where she lived now or even if she was still alive. When Juliet had questioned him he'd closed up, saying he was tired and would try to remember more about Kitty on her next visit. A few hours later he'd slipped into a coma.

Juliet set out her toilet bag in the shower room, her mind racing with possibilities. The lady would probably be in her eighties by now and might be reluctant to dredge up what could be painful memories to a complete stranger.

Kitty was obviously someone important in her father's life or else he wouldn't have kept her letter for more than fifty years. One that he'd never opened.

PART I

Leaving Home

1

February 1941

A roar vibrated through my body as the train thundered into King's Lynn station through a fog of belching steam and smoke. I stepped back to avoid the smuts and several other women did the same. But smuts were not the only things to avoid. I was terrified Dad would suddenly appear and haul me back home. I pressed into the crowd, trying to make myself invisible. The platform heaved with soldiers who were talking, shouting and laughing, showing off with their mates to their wives and girlfriends. What with the train screeching and the row everyone was making, I probably wouldn't have heard Dad yell at me to come home if he *had* appeared.

'Don't fret, Katy,' one of the soldiers behind me said. 'I'll be home before you know it.' For a split second it sounded like "Kitty". I whirled round, but the soldier was pressing his girl close and kissing her. I envied her their romantic parting. She had someone who loved her even though he was going away and she might never see him again. I'd never had a boyfriend. Never been kissed even.

Screaming kids were darting everywhere, no doubt picking up the silent screams of their mothers who were being left behind. Then a line of heads poked out of the train windows as the great beast clanked to a stop with a hiss. I watched as a row of hands fumbled for handles on the outside of the doors which then swung open simultaneously. A smattering of civilians and hundreds of exhausted soldiers spilled out. On the platform several people knocked into my side or pushed into my back in their frenzy, terrified the train might leave without them.

'Do you mind?' I spun round as somebody's suitcase banged into the back of my leg for the second time.

'You should watch where you're going,' said its weasel-eyed owner.

I gave him a glare and climbed up the nearest steps of the carriage marked Second Class, using my foot to push my suitcase along the packed corridor, stepping over people, determined to find a seat. If this was Second Class, heaven knew what Third Class conditions were like. I came to the last compartment. It was so full people were bursting into the corridor. I must have looked desperate because one of the soldiers standing in the door grabbed my arm and practically dragged me in. He took my case and swung it up on the rack of kitbags as lightly as if it had been a bunch of flowers.

The acrid smoke caught in the back of my throat, almost choking me. I glanced round. Three uniformed men, cigarettes dangling from their lips, stood between the two rows already occupied. I'd have to squeeze in between them all the way to London.

'Give the lady a seat,' the soldier who'd taken my case instructed one of the half-sleeping soldiers.

The young man immediately rose. I felt terrible as he looked as though he hadn't slept for days. I mumbled a thank you, and he smiled, though it seemed an effort.

Making myself as comfortable as I could in such a tight space, I tried not to look at the grey-haired man opposite in a pinstriped suit. Stray threads hung from the collar of his shirt which I itched to snip off, though it was an expensive one if the glinting cufflinks were anything to go by. He shook out the newspaper in front of him, but instead of reading he looked over the top of the pages at me and smiled.

'Where are you travelling to, young lady?'

'The Smoke,' I answered.

I'd heard one of Dad's friends call it that, and feeling incredibly sophisticated just saying the two words, I watched his reaction. His smile deepened.

'No less? And where are you staying in The Smoke?'

He emphasised the last two words. Was he was making fun of me?

'With friends,' I answered, squirming. Dad had drummed it into me often enough not to get into any personal conversation with strangers, especially men.

'I hope your friends will look after you.' He sounded concerned. 'You need to keep your wits about you. And keep your eye on your handbag. There are too many unsavoury characters roaming around London. I wouldn't like to see you get robbed.' He went back to his newspaper.

More soldiers piled in and blocked him from my sight.

Was he trying to frighten me? But I quickly forgot him as the train wearily pulled out of the station. I peered out of the grime-smeared window watching the smoke curl past, remembering my last moments with Mum.

'I wish you weren't going.' Mum's voice trembled. 'The only reason I'm allowing you to go is because I trust Helen to look after you. Because if anything should happen...what with the bombing, and you only seventeen...'

'You went off to Australia when you were only a year older,' I reminded her.

'Yes, but that was different. I was with Dad. And there wasn't a war on.' She gazed at me long and deeply with those incredible navy blue eyes, the exact colour of mine, as though she was trying to imprint my face upon her mind forever. 'Promise you'll write every week...' She shook her head and gave a sigh of resignation.

'I will.'

'And telephone me as soon as you get a chance.'

'I will.'

'And give my best to Helen.'

I nodded and gave her another hug. She seemed to shrink in my arms.

But I hadn't said what I really wanted to say to her, though she would have understood. She knew me so well. London was my only chance to live my life, war or not. I wanted to be a proper singer and no one was going to stop me.

I tried to read my book but I couldn't concentrate. Mum's anxious face swam in front of me and I snapped my book shut. Time dragged. The fug of smoke and trapped air and being so squashed began to make me feel faint. *Must get out of the carriage.* I half stood, heart thumping in my ears, but there was not an inch of space for me and I was forced to sit down again. Sweat trickled down my back. If I could just get my coat off I'd feel better. Frantically, I wriggled from it, then desperate to stand up and stretch my legs I worked one leg out in front. Immediately it came into contact with the nearest soldier's legs. A ginger head gazed down at me.

'Okay, you've got my attention,' he said, grinning.

I blushed and glanced away. One of the standing soldiers bent down for his matches which he'd dropped, leaving a gap. My eye fell on a woman who had tucked herself into the opposite corner. She wore a khaki skirt and jacket, the polished golden brown belt matching her shiny brogues, light brown hair swept off a high forehead. She had a strong face, firm jaw...she caught my eye and I sent her a feeble smile. She nodded. The gap closed as the soldier straightened up.

I will get to London, I will get to London. The refrain repeated in my head, over and over, in time to the rhythm of the train's wheels as they hurtled along the track.

'Poor old Lofty.'

My attention locked on the ginger-haired airman who was standing, head bent, talking to the fair-haired one sitting beside me.

'Yes, he was a good chap. Bloody bad luck.'

'He didn't bloody deserve it. Best gunner we had.'

'Excuse me, there are ladies present,' said the man opposite, putting down his newspaper and glaring at the two young men.

'Sorry, love.'

'It sounds as though you've had bad news about your friend,' I said, looking up from my book.

''Fraid so. He's bought it.'

'I don't understand.'

'Plane shot down. He was only nineteen...our age.'

In spite of the heat a chill slithered down my back. It was the first time I'd heard anyone speak about someone who'd been killed in such a matter-of-fact way. I stared up at him in horror, my stomach churning. Until now, when I'd heard of soldiers killed it was numbers in a newspaper or announced on the wireless. Faceless men. But the boy they were talking about was a real person, their friend, and only two years older than me.

The grey-haired man briefly closed his eyes as though to shut out the image, but said nothing.

'I'm sorry,' I said, realising as soon as I spoke the words how useless they must have sounded.

'Don't you be,' the fair-haired one said, turning his head and giving me a long look. 'Pretty girl like you don't need to worry about nothing. Leave all that to us.' He grinned, then leaned his head on the soft back of the seat, sinking into the small comfort it provided.

I glanced out of the corner of my eye. Even with his eyes closed he had a nice face. As though he knew I was watching him he opened his eyes and slowly winked at me. My cheeks grew hot again and I couldn't help wishing I was wearing something brighter than my Sunday grey skirt, white blouse, and one of Mum's fawn cardigans which was a size too small, making me feel self-conscious. I felt drab and older than my age.

15

The only colour I wore was a dab of pink lipstick that I would never have dared to wear around Dad. I resolved that when I got to London I would buy some pretty clothes. How I was going to pay for them, Lord only knew. But that was the least of my worries. I just hoped the Lord had somewhere in mind for me to rest my head for the night. He, and He alone, knew there would be no Helen at the station to meet me.

2

London

After the first hour we kept stopping, and much as I squinted out of the window every time we approached some town, I had no idea where we were and asked the grey-haired man.

'That was Cambridge. They've taken all the signs down on purpose so as not to help the Germans,' he explained.

His words made me go cold, as though the war was getting closer. Once we stopped on a deserted platform; some of the passengers got out to stretch their legs and light up a cigarette, but I didn't dare leave my seat, terrified the train might suddenly start moving. Now I had more space I managed to pour a cup of tea from my flask without it spilling, and devour the beef and mustard sandwich Mum had packed.

'It's always like this,' he continued. 'I go to King's Lynn once a month to see the parents, but since the war started the trains are rarely on time. And we're never given any explanation.'

'I suppose they're doing their best,' was all I could think of to say, but my remark was drowned in a boom like thunder over our heads. The soldiers on the platform shot in and for a moment I thought it was a bad storm. There was a terrific bang followed by an explosion. The train juddered. Gripping the flask between my knees I put my hands to my ears. Everyone went dead quiet. Had we crashed into another train? My heart thudded so loudly I thought they would all hear it. Then all the lights went out.

'That one was a tad close.' The man opposite crackled his

newspaper. 'Never even heard a siren.' There was a pause. 'Are you all right?'

I gulped. My whole body was shaking. My ears were so painful I could hardly hear what he said. I didn't trust myself to speak. It was the closest I'd ever heard a bomb and I was petrified.

Finally, after nearly four hours of stopping and starting, we were on the outskirts of London, the city of my dreams. I'd been eagerly watching to catch the first glimpse of The Smoke, but as the train began to slow we heard another bomb explode. Everyone jumped and I ducked my head, heart hammering again. I'd have to get used to this. When I'd calmed down a little and looked out of the window, all that welcomed me were lines of washing in people's dreary backyards, gathering smuts, no doubt, they were that close to the railway line. The sky looked as grey as the washing.

Then came a sight which shattered my dream of London as surely as the bombs shattered the lives of the people who lived there. Out of a street of houses there were only a few rooftops here and there with great gaps in between. People were stumbling around the rubble, their necks straining skywards. Some were shaking their heads in bewilderment, some crying. One woman shook her fist at the sky. Ambulance and fire engine bells clanged in the distance. We ground to a halt under the station roof where clouds of dust rose from the platform. Fear clawed at me, knowing I had to leave what I'd come to think of as my safe little corner in the train.

The grey-haired man stood up and retrieved my suitcase. 'I'll take it down the steps for you,' he said.

'You're very kind, Mr—'

'Raymond Glover.' He looked at me with sharp grey eyes. 'You're sure you have your lodgings sorted out?'

'Yes, sir,' I said, my eyes steadily meeting his. 'They're expecting me.'

The lie came as easily as the one I had told my mother. I had no idea where there might be a hostel.

'Hmm.' Mr Glover looked at me, his eyes narrowing with suspicion. 'I think you'd better take my card and telephone me if you ever have the need.'

He handed me a business card which I stuck in the zipped compartment of my bag without giving it even a cursory glance, then he grabbed my case and was first off so he could help me on to the platform.

I took the case from him, thanking him for his kindness. He raised his hat and strode away.

I don't know how I stopped myself from rushing after him, telling him I had no idea what to do or where to go. Shaking with nerves I turned my head to see the others from my carriage coming down the steps, the three RAF boys bringing up the rear, joking and laughing as though they'd never had the news of their poor dead friend on their minds. They swaggered by, proud of their uniforms, wishing me good luck. The fair-haired one turned and winked at me before his friend grabbed his arm.

My case felt as though it was about to pull my arm out of its socket as I struggled along the platform towards the exit. After fifty yards or so I stopped and set it down to change hands. Someone banged into me.

'Excuse *me*,' I said crossly, twisting my neck round to see the same uniformed woman, her mouth tight with annoyance, who was in my compartment.

'How was I to know you were suddenly going to stop right in front of me without any warning?' she demanded.

Her voice was well-bred but with an irritable edge.

'I'm sorry,' I mumbled, stretching up. 'I wanted to give my arm a rest.' I turned to face her.

She hesitated. Then she said, 'Do you live in London?'

'No, it's my first time here.' I tried to keep my voice from wobbling. Everything was so strange. The oily smell of the station. The crowd of men and women in different uniforms, gabbling and laughing and patting one another's arms and shoulders, oblivious to anyone around them. It was unnerving but I was determined not to show it to this woman with the firm expression.

'Where are you going?'

I started to tell her the same lie but her cool blue eyes swept over my face and I knew she missed nothing.

'Um, I don't have...that is...I need a room for a few days,' I stuttered, 'just till I find my feet.'

'How are you going to find this room?' she asked.

'Someone told me you can get into a hostel or something.'

The woman raised her eyebrows as though she was trying to work out a puzzle. Then with a tiny shake of her head, presumably so her peaked hat had no chance to fall off, she said:

'I think you'd better come with me. It's not safe to be roaming around London with a suitcase. I'll take you to where I'm staying. The landlady can probably give you a room for a couple of nights.'

Gratitude and relief pulsed through me. I gave a genuine smile of thanks, but to my horror I heard myself answer her in words which surely I couldn't be saying:

'It's very kind of you but I'm perfectly capable of making my own way.'

The woman's lips parted with astonishment. 'Don't be a fool, my dear,' she said, after a moment. 'Haven't you heard there's a war on? You need all the offers of help you can get. And you'll be called upon to do your bit as well, sooner or later.'

'Sorry, I didn't mean to sound rude, but I don't even know your name.'

'Diana Hamilton.' She thrust out her hand.

The skin was dry but warm. There was something about her I could trust. I'd had the same feeling when I'd first set eyes on her in the train. She was a figure of authority, used to telling people what to do. I stared at her, feeling ridiculous.

'And,' she said, an amused glint in her eyes, 'who are you?'

'Kitty Bishop.'

'Well…are we going to stand around here for the rest of the afternoon, Kitty Bishop?' She flashed me another of those piercing looks. 'Why don't we go and have a cup of tea? I think we both need one after that journey.'

I nodded, picked up the suitcase and followed her. She had a purposeful walk and had no need to push through the crowd; they seemed to melt away at her approach. We walked past the poster of a soldier's stern finger pointing at us, asking if our journey was really necessary. The man standing at the platform gate took our tickets and moments later we were out in the thick damp air.

I trembled on the edge of the pavement. Miss Hamilton nipped over the road, zigzagging between the horses and cars, leaving me terrified on the opposite side. She waved for me to go and I stepped out and was almost hit by a man on a bicycle going full tilt. He shouted something at me and I stumbled backwards, too scared to make another attempt. I'd never seen such traffic.

Finally, I managed to get across the road accompanied by neighing horses, shouts and horns of cars so close to my ear I thought my eardrums would burst, and bells impatiently jangling from men on bicycles. I slammed my heavy case on the pavement for a few moments, perspiring more with fear than exertion, holding on to my hat which threatened to fall off at any moment. Reluctantly, I picked up the case again; it felt twice as heavy as it had when I'd started out. Miss Hamilton took hold of my arm and propelled me along the pavement for what seemed like miles. A painful ache ran up and down the arm holding the case, but I couldn't have stopped even if I'd wanted to, her grip was so tight. We passed some huge department stores and I longed to look in the windows at the mannequins but Miss Hamilton marched purposefully on.

Finally, we came to a rather beautiful building with J. Lyons & Co. written in curly gold writing above an arch. My heart did a little skip as Mum had told me about these tea rooms in London where you could have tea and cakes and lunches. It had always sounded so sophisticated to go with a friend to Lyons' Corner House for tea. 'Rather different from Annie's Tea Rooms,' Mum had said, laughing. I began to feel better and if I hadn't been holding my case I would have pinched myself.

Inside, the place was far bigger than I'd expected. It reminded me of a photograph I'd seen in a newspaper of one of the dining rooms on the *Titanic*. Lyons' tea rooms couldn't have been more different from Mum's modest little place if it had tried. There were rows of tables and pillars soaring up to a fancy-looking ceiling with chandeliers dangling down, and a hum of a hundred voices. My mouth watered as we swept by a long counter where there were more varieties of cakes than I'd ever seen in my life, and the smell of fresh bread was tantalising. A waitress in a black uniform with crisp white collar, and cap and apron, found us a table for two by the wall. It was heaven to drop my case down. I took off my hat but Miss Hamilton kept hers on. Had I breached some rule? But she didn't say anything. Soon the warmth in the room began to penetrate my bones and I unbuttoned my coat and draped it over the back of my chair.

Miss Hamilton ordered tea and told me to choose a cake. She asked me where I lived. I didn't want to let on exactly where so I just said it was a village near King's Lynn. When I asked her the same question I wasn't prepared at all for her reply.

'You might have heard of it,' she said. 'It's also near King's Lynn...on the outskirts of Bridgewater. Hatherleigh Hall.'

I almost passed out, right there in Lyons' tea rooms. Hatherleigh Hall was where Dad had worked as a footman. I was just about to tell her how I knew Hatherleigh Hall when something made me stop. Of course. Lord and Lady Hamilton. Dad occasionally mentioned them. Diana must be one of the daughters. She would have been a child when Dad knew her.

'Mmm, I know it,' I muttered.

Miss Hamilton threw me a sharp glance. 'Really?'

'Well, I don't *know* it exactly,' I said, feeling flustered. 'But it's not far from where my parents live...in Bonham.'

'Ah, yes, Bonham. There's another lovely country house outside the village – Bonham Place.'

'Yes, that's right.' I hoped she'd change the subject. That was where Mum had worked as head housemaid.

'So what brought you to London?' Miss Hamilton asked.

'Oh, I, um, well, that is...' I knew she'd laugh if I told her my dream was to be a singer. Those boys on the train – and other soldiers like them – they'd be going to unfamiliar places and I wanted to be there with them, singing the new wartime songs. I could impersonate Vera Lynn and Peggy Lee and Judy Garland (who I secretly thought my voice most resembled) and couldn't wait to sing their songs and hear the applause.

Miss Hamilton waited without speaking and I felt I had to answer her question.

'I don't feel able to do much to help the war effort while I'm living at home,' I said feebly. 'I thought I might be more use in London.'

It sounded very childish to my ears but Miss Hamilton's eyes were curious.

'And your parents don't mind you coming here?' She didn't wait for my reply. 'It's far more dangerous than King's Lynn, and you're so young.'

'They'd prefer I stayed in King's Lynn, which is natural, I suppose.' I hoped she wouldn't press for more and looked round the café, wondering how to change the subject.

Where on earth was our tea? My stomach was rolling and my mouth dry. We'd been waiting ages to be served. I could see one waitress doing the work for three. She was flying from table to table trying to calm down people who were demanding to know what had happened to their order.

'We're short-staffed today,' I heard her explain to a couple on a nearby table. 'I'm doing me best.'

'But how can your parents allow you to come here when they don't know where you'll be staying?' Diana Hamilton demanded.

The arrival of our tea saved me from having to go into any detail, and as we sipped – well, I gulped – our tea, and I began on the first of *two* lemon-curd tarts, she began to tell me about her work.

'I'm in a corps called the FANY.' I must have looked completely blank, as she continued, 'That's F-A-N-Y – stands for First Aid Nursing Yeomanry. It's a voluntary service.' Her lips formed a smile. 'And we're always looking for more volunteers,' she paused a moment, her eyes penetrating mine, 'provided they come from the right background, of course.'

Her words cut into me. Presumably she meant the *approved* background. Miss Hamilton certainly didn't mince her words. A flicker of annoyance twisted through me. I wouldn't be grand enough to join this FANY, whatever it was, with having a mother and father who'd been in service. I wondered if the FANYs wore a nurse's uniform, and whether it would suit me, until an image flashed through my mind of wounded soldiers, blood pouring out of heads and limbs, and me bending over them in my crisp nurse's uniform, whispering words of encouragement. Then fainting.

'I could never do that,' I laughed nervously. 'I can't stand the sight of blood.'

'Oh, it isn't all first aid,' came the surprising answer. 'We run a multitude of sins.'

As far as I was concerned she was talking double Dutch.

'FANY was set up before the Great War,' she went on to explain, as she cut her scone in half and buttered one of the pieces. 'In those days it was very much a first-aid and nursing branch loosely attached to the army, though they were often treated with derision.' I didn't know what derision meant but it didn't sound very complimentary.

'Nowadays,' Diana Hamilton continued, 'one of the main things the girls do is transport work...driving ambulances...which can be pretty dangerous sometimes, especially for those that went through the Blitz. Even worse is ferrying unexploded bombs to safe places.' She must have seen my startled expression as she laughed. 'But if one's lucky one can chauffeur the officers.'

Singing went right out of the window as I imagined driving a handsome officer to wherever he had to go. It definitely sounded a lot more fun than cleaning up blood or getting blown apart by an unexploded bomb that had suddenly decided to explode after all.

Eventually, she looked at her watch.

'Oh, my goodness, it's getting late.' She stood up and gathered her belongings. 'We should go. Mrs Parker's expecting me...to stay, actually,' she added with a contrite expression. 'But I've got to push off after supper.'

'Who's Mrs Parker?'

'My landlady. She might be glad of your company, though she does have Barney.'

'Is he a dog?'

'Who, Barney?' Miss Hamilton gave a throaty laugh. 'No, he's a soldier who was wounded. Mrs Parker looks after him. But don't worry. He's perfectly harmless.'

I tried to take this all in but everything felt muddled. All I wanted was for Mrs Parker to give me a bed for the night.

3

Every door looked exactly the same as all the others in the terraced street, but Miss Hamilton trotted up the steps of one of them and put her key in the lock. She beckoned me to follow.

'Is that you, Barney?' a woman called.

Even from the hall I could hear her wheezy voice.

'No, it's me, Diana.'

Almost scraping both sides of the narrow hall, a middle-aged woman waddled through, the smile on her heavy face vanishing as she caught sight of me behind Miss Hamilton.

'Who's this? Who've you got with you?' Her tone was accusing.

'This is Kitty Bishop,' Diana explained. 'She was on the same train as me and doesn't have anywhere to stay. I couldn't leave her in the middle of the street.'

I watched the sour-faced woman but there was no trace of sympathy.

'Don't take any notice,' Miss Hamilton said under her breath as we followed Mrs Parker into the sitting room. 'She's always a bit funny at first with people she doesn't know.'

'I expect you'll be wanting a cup of tea.' Mrs Parker tossed the words over her shoulder. They would have sounded welcoming from anyone else.

'Thanks awfully, but we stopped at Lyons' Corner House to have one,' Miss Hamilton said cheerfully.

'All right for some,' Mrs Parker grumbled as she heaved herself into one of the easy chairs. 'You're staying for supper, I hope.' She didn't look at me but kept her eyes fixed on Miss Hamilton.

Miss Hamilton nodded. 'Yes, please. I'm looking forward to your cooking.' She removed her hat, hooking it on the back of one of the chairs, then cleared her throat. 'Mrs P, Kitty needs a room for a few nights until she gets her bearings.'

'Well, I've no spare room here.' Mrs Parker made frantic faces – she thought I couldn't see – at her paying guest.

'What about the attic room?' Miss Hamilton ignored her landlady's sour expression. 'Didn't you once say there's a bed up there and a wardrobe?'

'The room never gets cleaned.' Mrs Parker's tone was triumphant. 'It's sty-baked. I wouldn't put a dog in there.'

'I expect you're exaggerating as usual, Mrs P.' Miss Hamilton turned to me and smiled. It lit up her face. One of her pins was falling out of her hair and she shoved it back. 'Come on, Kitty, let's have a look at it.'

'Well, I'm not going up there.' Mrs Parker's lips tightened into a thin line.

Miss Hamilton led the way up a flight of steep stairs, and through a bedroom to what I thought was a cupboard, but it was a door with narrow winding steps leading up to the attic.

Mrs Parker hadn't exaggerated. The room reminded me of Miss Haversham's in *Great Expectations*, which I'd read in my last year of school. Cobwebs draped over the small filthy window like a grey net curtain, clinging to every surface and across every beam like miniature hammocks. The room smelt damp and musty and in the corner I heard the clicking of small claws on the lino. Mice, probably. Or rats. A wave of dread swept over me as I pictured Mum's spotless rooms. I felt sick. Luckily, Miss Hamilton seemed to have the same revulsion as me.

'No, of course you can't stay up here,' she said, turning to look at me in the cramped doorway. She gave a short laugh. 'You've gone quite pale. We'll have to think of something else.'

All my worries came flooding back.

'Well?' Mrs Parker (or Nosy, as I'd privately renamed her) stood with her hands on her hips at the bottom of the stairs, waiting for us.

'You were right, Mrs P.' Miss Hamilton hesitated. Then she said, 'Couldn't Kitty have *my* room? No one's in it at the moment.'

'Where will *you* sleep? It's only a single.'

'I'm away for the next few days so you could let Kitty have it. The room's paid up to date. And she'll be company.'

Nosy's face screwed up. 'I've got extra food in for you. And that's not easy, neither, as you well know.'

'I'm sorry, Mrs P, but I've told you before – we don't know ourselves until the last minute. But as I say, it will be nice for you to have Kitty in the house. And I'm sure she'll help you eat the extra food.' She turned to me with a grin.

'I'm all right as I am,' Nosy snapped. 'And I'm not alone, as you well know. I've got Barney...not that he's much use,' she admitted.

Miss Hamilton explained. 'Barney's only been out of hospital a couple of weeks and doing all right. But not well enough to go back into the fray just yet.'

I couldn't care less about Barney as I silently begged Mrs Parker to let me stay.

Nosy scratched her head and looked at me. 'All right. But no more'n a couple of days. I can't be looking after no one extra, what with Barney and the NAAFI and everything I'm trying to do for the effort.' She threw me a warning glare. 'You'll have to help out with the washing-up and suchlike. I won't be waiting on *you*, if that's what you're thinking.'

I bit back a retort and sent her a smile. 'Thank you, Mrs Parker. Of course I'll help. And I promise I won't get in the way.'

'Humph. See to it that you don't.'

I wondered what Barney thought of his lodgings – more to the point, his landlady. I was relieved, but if Nosy was going to treat me as a skivvy I wouldn't be able to hold my tongue. Miss Hamilton caught my eye and a miniscule movement of her head warned me not to say anything more.

Miss Hamilton took me up to her room which turned out to be the one with the staircase running up to the attic. The stairs had taken up a good piece of the room leaving it tight for much furniture. A narrow bed was overshadowed by a mahogany wardrobe and matching chest of drawers. I stepped over to the window and looked out on a small yard enclosed by a wall at the bottom and a fence to one side. Deflated, I turned my back on it, used to seeing our lovely garden at home, and the trees and fields surrounding us.

The only colour in the room was a faded blue and green rag rug placed by the side of the bed. That was all except for one picture – a seascape with a ship in the foreground. Coming from the grandeur of Hatherleigh Hall, Miss Hamilton must have noticed a big difference in her lodgings, though it was perfectly comfortable for me. But I didn't intend to stay a minute longer than necessary.

I squeezed my suitcase between the bed and the window and followed her downstairs.

'I'm off now,' Miss Hamilton announced, as she carried the dishes out to the kitchen. 'Thanks for supper, Mrs P.'

'But I thought you were staying at least tonight.' Mrs Parker drew her eyebrows together. 'Your waif can sleep on the couch.'

I wasn't pleased to be called a waif but Miss Hamilton merely said, 'Sorry, Mrs P. You know I would, but it's work. I've got to report in this evening.'

'And you don't know when you'll be back,' Nosy said as she ran some water into the washing-up bowl, then swished it around with stubby fingers.

'You'll be the first to know.' Miss Hamilton winked at me. For some reason I wanted to giggle.

'I'd just like to know what you're doing,' Nosy grumbled. I was gratified she was living up to her name. 'All this secrecy nonsense.'

'You know no one's allowed to talk. It costs lives.'

'So they keep saying.' Nosy looked put out. 'I'll see you when I see you, then.'

'That's right.' Miss Hamilton picked up her bag and gave Mrs Parker a kiss on her fat floury cheek. Why she seemed so fond of her, I couldn't see.

'Good luck, Kitty,' she said, patting my arm as I walked with her to the front door. 'I'm sure you'll find a job now you're in London. And there's always the opportunity to join up. In fact, I wouldn't leave it too long. There are rumours women are to be conscripted, and then you won't get a choice.'

My throat felt as though it was closing up, making me speechless. Not because of what she'd said – I'd been thinking of joining up anyway when I was eighteen, even though I didn't much like being told what to do. No, it was just that I couldn't bear to be left alone with her ill-tempered landlady.

'It's Mrs Parker, isn't it?' Miss Hamilton said, her blue eyes alight with mischief. 'She's a bit of a battle-axe but the way to deal with her is to ignore her remarks. At least you'll be fed well. She's an excellent cook. And something will turn up sooner or later.'

'Miss Hamilton, could I—'

'You can call me Diana.'

'Diana,' I repeated, 'is there anything I might do where you work?'

'Not in my department without another language.' She thought for a moment. Then she looked at me with a hopeful expression. 'I didn't ask if you could drive.'

'No, but I'd be willing to learn.'

'Hmm. I'll have to have a word in the right quarters – they're always looking for drivers. I'll see what I can do.'

I watched Diana Hamilton's neat figure begin the long trek down the street. Soon she became a blurry outline. I brushed the tears away as Nosy's voice rang out.

'Shut the door, will you. You're letting the heat out.'

Nosy grumbled without stopping for breath. Her droning voice wove a cage around me, pressing me in. After only one day I was desperate to escape. But if I left, where would I go? And if Diana *did* come up with some job or other she wouldn't know where to find me. I had to stay until Diana returned in a few days' time.

The second day I met Barney.

He was feeling his way down the stairs as I wanted to go up, so I waited for him. A glance told me he was probably in his early twenties though he looked older, very tall and thin and slightly hunched, as though he was ashamed of his height. He didn't say a word of greeting. Just looked in my direction through glasses so thick I could hardly see his eyes.

'Good morning,' I said, determined to get a response.

'Is it?' he snarled, and stumbled by me as though I wasn't there.

I looked after his retreating back. What an unpleasant man. Then I felt guilty thinking what he must have gone through to be injured and sent off to recuperate, though he'd picked the unlucky straw when he was sent to Nosy's.

Uppermost in my mind was getting a job. I went out that morning, and the next, walking miles. Dad had insisted I go to shorthand and typewriting classes but I left halfway through the course. Surely no one would complain if I was a bit slow, I reasoned. I was wrong. Though the city was in shambles it seemed as though any prospective employer wanted me to do a test. I failed every time; even a dull man interviewing me for a dull job in a smoke-filled insurance office turned me down. I'd have thought they'd have more important things on their minds as to whether I could do forty or fifty words a minute. I could barely do twenty but I told myself it was because my heart wasn't in it.

Was Diana right about being conscripted? I wanted war work, but *singing* war work – if that counted. And I couldn't see joining the army or one of the other forces being the way in. All I wanted at the moment was a fill-in job until I could find out more about singing to the troops. Then finding another place to stay.

As I'd seen from the train window, London didn't look anywhere near as glamorous as it had been in my fantasies. Each day the streets looked worse than the night before, and the heels of my shoes kept getting caught in the debris as I walked and walked. How eerie to see the insides of people's homes, those that were sliced in half by the bombs. I tried to imagine our house in Bonham being ripped to pieces for all the world to see. Mum would have hated it. You could even see the choice of wallpaper in some of these houses. Women's clothes scattered like litter, mattresses blown out of the windows and spread out in the road, children's toys flung in the street as though they'd been tipped out of nursery windows, and people and cats and dogs wandering in and out of the debris. Everyone, including the animals, looked dazed.

That second day I saw something even more shocking. Something which made me nearly sick. A hand poked out amongst the rubble which had once been the front of someone's home. I watched a man pick his way over to have a look and carefully pull away some of the bricks from around it. I stepped a little closer, hating myself for not helping and instead just looking. I bit back a scream. It wasn't attached to a body. Just a hand. Dear God. I'd made a terrible mistake coming to London. I wasn't prepared for this. No wonder Mum had been so worried. I swallowed the bile that caught in my throat, turned my head away and dragged on, telling myself it was too late – there was nothing I could do.

I'd sent Mum a letter with Nosy's address, writing that I had taken temporary accommodation for a few days as Helen had gone away on a family emergency. But I still had no idea where there was a hostel. Nosy could turf me out at any moment. Besides, Diana might need her room sooner than she'd thought.

'When do you think you'll see Miss Hamilton again?' I asked Nosy that evening at the supper table.

'You know as much as I do,' came her caustic response as she ladled out the fish pie.

The pie was delicious even though my portion only had four or five pieces of fish the size of a sixpence. Nosy had layered the meagre fish with plenty of carrots and peas mixed with sauce, and topped it with mashed potato. I tucked into it with gratitude. Her cooking was almost as good as Mum's.

Barney was sitting at the table. Usually, Nosy confided, she took him a tray upstairs, but maybe she didn't want the smell of fish to waft into the bedrooms.

'A little more, Barney?' she questioned in a loving-mum kind of voice.

'No, thanks,' he said. 'It was very good, though.' He rested his gaze on me. 'I'm Barney.'

'I know,' I replied. 'Mrs Parker's just called you that.'

His mouth went up about a millionth of an inch at one corner and he pushed his glasses up to the bridge of his nose with his forefinger.

'And you are...?'

'Kitty Bishop.'

'And what are you doing in London, Miss Bishop?'

Before I could answer, Nosy piped up, 'She's a friend of Miss Hamilton's.'

Barney looked puzzled but didn't pursue the conversation. He and I passed the rest of the meal tucking into Nosy's apple crumble in silence.

4

I still hadn't found a hostel, or even a room in someone's house, and whenever that thought crossed my mind – only a hundred times a day – my stomach churned. Who would take me in when I didn't have a job? And who would give me a job with no address?

I could do nothing without money. I couldn't even afford bus fares to go looking for work. Just as I was almost ready to give up I thought of Dad and gritted my teeth. No. I would not go back with my tail between my legs.

Then it came to me.

I counted the last few shillings I had and started walking towards Liverpool Street station. Once I was outside I tried to imagine when I'd first arrived and met Diana. It was difficult as everything had looked so strange and the traffic was so noisy that afternoon. I crossed the same main road, picturing myself trotting behind Diana, my suitcase heavy as I swapped hands every so often. I remembered turning left.

There was nothing I recognised. I'd have to ask someone. The nearest person was a well-dressed woman carrying a shopping bag.

'Excuse me, could you please...?'

The woman glanced at me, stony-faced, and hurried by.

Why couldn't she at least have let me finish what I was saying? A spurt of anger bubbled up inside me but I pasted on a smile as I approached a kind-looking elderly lady. Minutes later I was outside Lyons'.

It was the same one. Same curly writing over the door, although I remembered Diana saying Lyons' Corner Houses were springing up over London like mushrooms and maybe they all looked similar. I pushed open the door and the warmth and chatter enveloped me.

It was definitely 'my' tea shop, and even more crowded than that first time. I threaded my way through the tables, looking this way and that, but I couldn't see even one empty seat. I'd just have to stand outside and wait until someone came out. As I made for the door a couple rose from a table to the side of me.

'We're just leaving,' the man said, with a smile.

The woman nodded and left her chair pulled out. Gratefully I took it.

It was as though I was invisible. There were only two waitresses in the packed room, one who had served Diana and me that first day. They were overwhelmed with far too many tables to cope with. Several times I tried to catch one or other of their eyes, but it was as though they ignored me on purpose. A few people began to leave but whether they had finished or were fed up that their order hadn't been taken, I couldn't tell. Then a woman with bright red lipstick and hair to match, wearing a beige coat with fur collar, came in, paused to take in the scene, and waited for a few heads to turn before sitting down at the now vacant table next to mine. She shrugged off her coat, and raised her jewelled fingers. One of the waitresses immediately came running to take her order. My temper flared.

'Excuse me,' I called over, 'I was here before this lady. I've been waiting ages.'

Both waitress and woman stared at me.

'Can't you see I'm busy?' The waitress jerked her head to no one in particular.

'It's just that—'

'I'll be with you in a minute.' Her voice had lost its irritability and just sounded weary. She focused on the glamorous red-haired woman.

True to her word she came back swiftly. 'What can I get you, miss?'

'Beans on toast, please, and a cup of tea, and I'd like to speak to the manager.'

She took a step back and regarded me with alarm. 'I didn't mean no harm, miss. It's just that we're so short at the moment.'

'I can tell,' I said quickly. 'In fact that was what I wanted to talk to the manager about. You see, I need a job.'

Relief washed over her face. She smiled. 'I'll put your order in, love, and have a word with Miss Rushton. She's the one in charge.'

No sooner had I finished eating when a tall bony lady appeared.

'I understand you're looking for a position,' she said, unsmiling. 'If you're ready, come with me.'

I followed her to the back of the restaurant, through a swing door, down a short passage and into her office.

'Sit down.' I did what she asked. 'Now, tell me about yourself. Let's start with your name.'

I felt a little in awe of her but I wasn't going to let her see I was nervous.

'Katherine Bishop.'

She nodded. 'And what experience do you have, Miss Bishop?'

'My mother has her own tea rooms near King's Lynn. I used to help her after school and at weekends.'

'How many covers does your mother have?'

'Um...'

'How many people can she seat?' Miss Rushton's voice was impatient.

I was tempted to lie. To make Annie's Tea Rooms sound much grander than it was. But the last thing I wanted was to be found out.

'Oh, yes, I'm sorry. There are seven tables,' I began, trying not to be put off by the contemptuous curl of Miss Rushton's top lip, 'and when it's fine weather she puts three or four outside in the garden.'

'Covers, child. How many people?'

'Um…I'm not sure. Maybe thirty, maybe forty, if you include the garden.' It was an exaggeration, but I looked at her steadily.

Miss Rushton's expression never moved. 'Where was your last employment?'

'It was something temporary until I found the right job.' Miss Rushton kept her eye on me as though wanting to trip me up. 'I'm a hard worker and I get on well with people,' I added.

'How old are you?'

'Eighteen.' I had to keep to *that* lie. By now I almost believed it myself.

'Why did you come to London?' Miss Rushton's mouth was pinched in disapproval. 'I'm surprised at your mother and father allowing it. Don't they know how dangerous it is here?'

I mumbled that my parents knew, and that I was staying with a friend, and that I'd always wanted to work in London. Miss Rushton raised an eyebrow.

'We need another pair of hands,' she said finally, looking me up and down. 'I suppose Babs could show you the ropes. At least you've had some sort of experience.' She drew a breath as if to give herself time to think. After a minute she said, 'When can you start?'

I couldn't believe it. She was offering me a job. I was so excited I forgot to ask her what my pay would be. And how I'd get the uniform.

'Would tomorrow be all right?'

'We'll expect you at eight o'clock, prompt.'

With that, she showed me out.

Barney shook his head when I told him about my new job.

'It's bloody hard work on your legs all day,' he said, chewing his lip. 'Well, we'll see how long you stick it.'

I wasn't daunted in the least. I'd helped Mum in the tea rooms often enough. The best thing was that Nosy said I could stay on a bit longer until Diana came back.

*

'Dresses and aprons and hats are in that cupboard.' Babs pointed to a recess with a flowered curtain pulled across. 'You should find something to fit. And buck up. There's a gentleman in the corner who's been waiting more'n five minutes.'

Everything was neatly stacked on shelves labelled with the sizes. Dresses, aprons, caps. No shoes. Presumably you wore your own. I struggled into one of the dresses that looked about my size, but the person it was intended for was shorter than me. I looked round but the other dresses were much too large. Well, I was sure Miss Rushton would soon speak up if I didn't look right.

I plonked the cap on my head, wishing I had a couple of kirby grips to fix it into place, grabbed a tray and hurried over to the podgy gentleman in the corner.

'I'll just clear the table first,' I told him, glancing at the array of dirty cups and plates.

'You do that, my dear. Then you can get me eggs on toast. Not powdered. I hate that muck.'

'Yes, sir. Would you like anything to drink?'

'You can bring some tea with the food.' He looked up and gave me a huge slow wink.

I couldn't get away quick enough. Who did he think he was? I didn't relish the idea of going back to him, but of course I had to.

'Here you are, sir,' I said, holding the tray and setting the plate and cup of tea in front of him.

He grinned up at me showing a row of cigarette-stained teeth. I nodded but as I turned away his horrible fat hand squeezed my bottom. Furious, I swung round, my arm flying out, knocking over the cup of tea which spurted like a cascade down the front of his suit and dripped on to his lap.

'Now look what you've done, you stupid girl!' He half rose in anger, his hands gripping the edge of the table, his voice shrill. One or two diners looked our way.

Damn him. He deserved it but I couldn't risk my job when I needed every penny. I attempted to mop him up with one of the napkins but he roared at me, 'Stop it, you stupid girl. You've done enough damage.'

'What's going on?'

It was Miss Rushton. My heart plummeted to my shoes.

'This clumsy girl,' the man spluttered, 'spilt a cup of tea down me.'

'I do apologise, sir,' Miss Rushton said in a put-on soothing voice. 'I'm sure it was an accident. It's her first day.'

At least she'd stuck up for me. I almost threw my arms around her.

'I'm not interested in whether it's her first or her last. She did it deliberately. Boyfriend trouble, I expect, and now she's a man-hater.' I opened my mouth to deny such nonsense but he beat me to it. Glaring at me, and then at Miss Rushton, he said in a loud enough voice for the whole room to hear, 'I'll be sending you the bill.'

With that, he snatched up his coat and hat and marched out.

'You will clear and wipe down the table,' Miss Rushton said, very quietly and pointedly, 'and then you will pack your things and leave.'

'But, Miss Rushton, he—'

'I'm not interested in what you have to say,' she said, her eyes like needles. 'I should have listened to my instincts. I want you out of here in ten minutes.'

She turned on her heel.

Numb with fury I grabbed the tray with his untouched eggs and toast and the almost empty cup of tea. I'd have to come back with a cloth to clear up the spill and wipe down the salt and pepper pots. Swearing at both of them under my breath, I picked up his newspaper and tucked it under my arm, tears blurring my vision as I stumbled towards the kitchen. I chucked the newspaper in the bin, then on impulse retrieved it and stuffed it into my string bag which hung underneath my coat. I tore off my uniform and threw it on a chair. I was not going back in that room after all to wipe down any table. I glanced up at the wall clock. My job had lasted all of twenty-five minutes. I slunk out of the back door.

That evening I went to bed early. There was nothing really to stay up for. I didn't want to tell anyone I'd got the sack on my first day.

Still smarting when I thought of Miss Rushton believing the lies of that horrible man, I suddenly remembered I'd kept his newspaper. At least it was something to read. I propped the pillow behind my head but it didn't give me much comfort as I could still feel the iron bed-head digging into my back. The dim overhead light flickered and I supposed the bulb wouldn't last much longer. I shivered and fetched my coat, wrapping it around my shoulders.

The headlines in the newspaper were grim. I read a couple of articles about the war but when I turned the page a different headline caught my attention: WHAT'S ON TODAY? Underneath the article was a photograph of a man – a Mr Peter Sellers. He was a comedian and the picture was taken of him entertaining the troops in France. With racing heart I read on. It mentioned he was with ENSA but didn't explain what the initials stood for, and there was no address or telephone number. It was just a notice saying when the next show would be performed.

Wild excitement ran haywire over me. That slimy customer in Lyons' might have done me a favour after all. I was determined to find out about ENSA. It must be the name of the group. For the first time since leaving home my heart lifted. If Mr Sellers could do it, then so could I.

5

The next day I decided to ask at the local police station if they knew of any cheap lodgings, when a poster outside a cinema caught my eye. It was advertising their latest film, *Dangerous Moonlight*, starring Sally Gray. I'd never heard of her. The poster showed Miss Gray and the leading man. They looked as though they were smiling straight at me. I don't know how long I stood outside the cinema looking at that poster. It would have been hard for anyone to take their eyes off her; she was so pretty with her beautiful blonde hair. I looked in my purse. Four shillings and sixpence. And I still had the five-pound note I'd tucked away in Diana's bedroom. The cheapest seats were a shilling. I didn't hesitate.

It was the most thrilling film I'd ever seen, and all the way through they played this wonderful piano music. By the time I came out I'd made a decision.

I found the nearest chemist and told the thin-faced man in a white coat that I wanted a bottle of peroxide.

'What do you want it for?'

'To dye my hair,' I said, feeling embarrassed. Then I thought, why should I worry? I'll never see him again.

'Why do you want to do that?' he asked as I was thinking all this. 'You've got lovely hair. You'll ruin it.'

I didn't bother to tell him I was going to be a professional singer and that I needed to look glamorous. He was a man. He'd never understand.

'If you're determined, you should see a proper hairdresser,' he said, studying me with his robin's eyes.

'I can't afford it. I'll have to do it myself…at home.' In Nosy's bathroom, I thought. Just hope she doesn't catch me.

'If you're set on it.' Reluctantly he reached for a dark brown bottle from the shelf. 'That will be sixpence, please.'

Half the price of the film. One-and-sixpence could change my life. Scarcely breathing I watched him wrap the bottle in a piece of brown paper, twisting it round the top as he handed it to me.

'Be sure to dilute it,' he said. 'I don't know how much. Ask at the hairdresser's. The young one's nice. Called Joyce. She'll know.'

He came outside the shop with me and pointed diagonally across the road.

The peroxide stung my scalp and brought tears to my eyes. But I couldn't have been more delighted with the stranger who stared at me in a sultry manner in the hairdresser's mirror. Instead of Sally Gray I was more Veronica Lake, with a low side parting and a curtain of hair which hung over one eye.

'I can't see a thing,' I said jokingly.

'That's the whole idea.' Joyce, the girl who'd dyed and cut it, laughed. 'You've got to look mysterious.'

'So mysterious I'll probably end up on my behind.' I tossed my head and the curtain of hair lifted before falling over my eye again. We both giggled.

'You look really sophisticated,' Joyce said, tucking in a strand here and there as she clearly admired her own work.

'Do you really think so?' I still needed reassurance even though I loved it.

'I know so. It's just perfect for the new you.'

Joyce had carried out the transformation after the shop closed, threatening me with death if I told anyone, and wouldn't charge me a penny. It was only afterwards she admitted she was still an apprentice. But I didn't mind. She'd turned me from a girl no one would give a second glance at, to this glamorous blonde woman.

And I'd found a new friend in Joyce.

'I still can't believe what you've done to your hair,' Nosy said at breakfast the next morning.

I wondered what Barney would say but he was nowhere in sight. He hadn't been down to supper last night either.

With my brightest smile I said, 'I felt like a change.'

'I'd box your ears if I was your mother,' she retorted.

Just as well you're not, then, I felt like saying. 'Don't you like it?' I asked innocently.

'Makes you look like a tart.'

'I'll be leaving soon,' I said, stung by what she'd called me, but nothing anyone said could dim the thrill I felt every time I caught sight of myself.

She remained silent; just sat staring at my hair in disbelief.

'Nos...Mrs Parker,' I said, 'I'll be leaving here soon.'

'I heard you the first time,' she grumbled. 'Just as I was getting used to having a bit of company around. Well, what do I matter? All I'm good for is to find a few scraps to turn into some kind of halfway decent meal and then clear up after everyone. And Barney's no good. You get nothing out of him.'

I had to agree with her there.

'Where is he this morning?' I asked her.

'Gone for a newspaper.'

Maybe this would be a good time to have a word with her.

'It's not that I'm ungrateful, Mrs Parker,' I told her. 'It's just that I came to London to do something – make something of myself. Help the war effort. I shouldn't have stayed as long as I have, but I kept hoping Miss Hamilton would think of something I could do.'

'She can't be relied on,' Nosy said. 'She—'

But I never found out why Diana couldn't be relied on. A warning siren screamed overhead. We stared at one another in horror. Then I came to my senses and shot up from the table.

'We've got to get into the shelter!'

Mrs Parker just sat there. All the blood had drained from her face.

The siren went again, and this time it was louder.

'Come on, Mrs Parker, we've got to get to the shelter.' I was screaming, even though she was only a few feet away.

'I'm not going in,' she whispered. 'I hate them shelters. I'm clorsterphobic, I am.'

Swearing under my breath I grabbed hold of the nearest part of her and without thinking somehow shoved her heavy body underneath the table, throwing myself alongside. Pressed hard against me, I could feel her shudder with fear as we listened to the drone of enemy aeroplanes. She began to sob but I didn't have time to comfort her as there was an almighty flash, making a fairground of the little kitchen, followed by a roar. Instinctively, we both put our hands up to shield our ears. Moments later I put my arm around her, more to comfort me than her. She was still shaking as though in a fever. Dear God, was this the end? Not even eighteen. My life hadn't begun. I— Then a noise smashed through me. Every bone rattled. Please, please. I want Mum. Another bang. I screamed, drowning out Mrs Parker who was weeping in between gasping out the Lord's Prayer. Plaster fell around the table like an avalanche of snow. Surely the ceiling would collapse on top of us. I could feel the table vibrating with the tremor of the bomb as though we were in an earthquake. Another bang. Even louder. Where had it hit? More plaster and then the sound of water gushing. A pipe must have burst. We waited in silence for what seemed like an hour but was probably no more than a few minutes until we heard the all clear. Gingerly, I crept out.

'Mrs Parker,' I said, bending under the table to talk to her. 'I'm going outside to have a look. I think it's over now, but maybe you should stay there a bit longer – to be on the safe side.'

'All right,' she stuttered. 'Don't be long. My nerves aren't what they were.'

'I'll be back in a jiffy,' I promised.

I let myself out of the kitchen door and picked my way through the fallen debris down the side path to the front. Neighbours were rushing out, like me, to inspect the damage. I looked around. I couldn't take it in. It was like being dragged into some science-fiction film. Thank God Mrs Parker's house was still standing but her neighbour's on the end had taken a direct hit. Tables and chairs and beds and pots and pans were strewn over the pavement. A tin bath was upside down on the front patch of gravel, a wardrobe had tumbled down a broken staircase, and a thin black and white cat wandered in and out of the shattered building, mewing.

A baby was crying.

I rushed to a group of women further along the pavement who were bent double, making soothing noises to something or someone, though the circle was so tight I couldn't see what. When I reached them I saw it was a little girl, not more than four or five years old, sobbing her heart out. I'd seen her playing with some other children in the street only yesterday.

'Where's her mother?' I put my hand on the arm of the nearest woman who looked at me with soulful eyes. She shook her head.

One of the other women turned round. 'It's Doreen's kid, Milly. But she's in hospital having another one.'

'Who's looking after the little girl?' I asked.

'Doreen's sister's supposed to be. But it looks like the little'un was on her own. Heaven knows where the sister is. Thank the Lord Milly ran outside. She could've been killed.'

The brick dust made me cough as I tried to take in what the woman was saying.

'Are you all right, dear?' the woman asked me. 'That cough sounds nasty and you look white as a sheet. You've not been hurt, have you?'

'No, no,' I mumbled. I couldn't trust myself. Then I remembered. 'Was a baby crying a few moments ago?'

She looked surprised. 'I didn't hear nothing. Maybe it was a cat mewing.'

'No,' I said. 'I'm sure it was a baby.'

I looked around, my head weaving this way and that, trying to peer through the rubble, but all I could see was a doll, blasted from the house. I looked again. And froze. I saw its fingers curl. Then I snapped to and flew over. The baby's neck was at a peculiar angle, its mouth ready to make another howl. Gently, gently, I picked it up, supporting its head in the crook of my arm. It was the first baby I'd ever held. It looked like a boy baby and couldn't have been more than a few months old but I was surprised at how heavy he felt. As I looked down at him he let out a thick gurgle. 'Shhhh,' I whispered. 'You're safe now.' His surprised blue eyes looked up into mine. Then he sighed, a long sigh, his cheeks puffed out with the effort. He closed his eyes. And then I felt him go limp in my arms, like the rag doll I'd first thought he was. Oh, dear God. My heart thumped in my chest as I looked at him, tears streaming down my face. Poor little mite. He didn't have a chance. What should I do with him? Where should I put him? I heard running footsteps.

'All clear!' a warden called, then spotted me. 'Are you all right, miss?'

I felt sick. I tried to pretend the baby was still a doll. That it had never looked up at me with such innocent clear eyes.

'Take him, oh, please take him,' I sobbed, pushing the baby into his unsuspecting arms. I hung my head over the gutter where I brought up the contents of Mrs Parker's breakfast.

'Dear, oh dear,' the warden said, coming over to where I was clinging on to the gate post, my whole body shaking. He awkwardly patted me on the shoulder. 'We really caught it this time. Jerry don't usually come out until dark.'

'Where's the baby?' I asked him. He helped me straighten up and I noticed his eyes were full of concern.

'Don't you worry about him. He's in the right place. He'll have a proper burial. One of the women knows the mother. She's gone to break the news.'

How would you do that? How would you tell a new mother her baby has died in a senseless bombing attack? I shuddered. I'd wanted to be part of the action. Do my bit. Now I couldn't stop trembling.

'There's nothing more you can do,' the warden told me. 'Did you live in the house that was hit?'

'No,' my voice sounded flat. 'I'm staying next door, at Mrs Parker's, but I don't know what damage there is. I haven't been back to look.'

'At least she still has her home,' he said, with a thin smile.

'I have to go and tell her it's over and she can come out.' I brushed the filth off my skirt and glanced towards the gutter. 'I must clear that up,' I said, desperately embarrassed what I'd done.

'I'll see to it, miss. Don't you worry. You go and see Mrs Parker. She'll be wondering what's happened to you.'

I shot off, back down the side path and through the kitchen door that I'd left wide open.

'Mrs Parker,' I called. 'It's Kitty. The all clear's gone.'

Her legs were still sticking out from under the table. She wasn't going anywhere until I told her she could.

'It's safe, Mrs Parker. You can come out now.'

There was no reply. She must have dropped off. I couldn't help smiling. Only Nosy could sleep through a bombing raid. I bent down and shook her arm. Felt her hand. Pulled back, knocking my head on the edge of the table as I did so. Diana's landlady wasn't quite so warm as when I'd left her.

The raid had been close but not close enough to kill poor Mrs Parker, though I'd heard of people literally dying of fright. My heart beating wildly I didn't have the foggiest idea what to do next except to telephone the police. It was a long walk as the first 'phone box I came to had been blown up. The policeman I eventually spoke to was very kind and told me not to worry – they'd deal with everything and take Mrs Parker's body away. I came out of the 'phone box and was sick again at the side of the road.

There was no way of letting Diana know what had happened to her landlady, so wasn't I glad when two days later, in the afternoon, the doorbell chimed and there was Diana on the step.

'Whatever made you put that muck on your hair?' Seeming not to expect an answer, she marched by me in the narrow hall, saying over her shoulder, 'I almost didn't recognise you.'

I followed her into the kitchen.

'I'd give anything to have lovely dark hair like yours,' she said, as I lit the gas ring under the kettle, 'so why on earth did you do it?'

'I just fancied a change, that's all.' For once I didn't want to talk about me.

'Hmm,' was all she said.

I busied myself making the tea, my back to her, wondering how on earth I was going to tell her. Tears gathered as I thought of poor Mrs Parker and the horrible thoughts I'd had about her. I wished I could take them all back. I wished I'd never called her Nosy.

'Anyway, what's been going on since I left?' Diana asked, biting into her biscuit. 'I saw the house next door caught it. Must have given poor Mrs P a terrible fright. Where is she, by the way?'

'She died in the blast,' I told her flatly, feeling sick at the memory of poor Mrs Parker's lukewarm hand dropping from my own.

I told her what had happened. Diana's eyes widened as she gasped.

'It was terrible,' I managed. 'I told her I wanted to have a look at the damage. She was alive then because she answered me. "Don't be long," she said. It was such a shock when I got back to her and she was gone.'

'She once told me she had a weak heart.' Diana quickly became her usual practical self as she patted my arm. 'And she's been in a bad state since her husband died. At least she's at peace now.'

Suddenly I missed my mother with such a yearning. I wanted to be held in her arms, cry it all out, have her put me to bed with a mug of hot milk. Filled with misery I cupped my head in my hands.

'Don't upset yourself,' Diana said, and the concern in her tone made me feel even worse. 'You didn't know her that well and she could be a real battle-axe, believe me. We rarely saw eye to eye.'

My head shot up. 'It isn't just Mrs Parker,' I told her, tears flowing down my cheeks, 'but Milly, the little girl—'

'Yes, I know Milly,' Diana interrupted. 'Good heavens. Don't say something has happened to her.'

'No. Thank goodness she ran out of her house. It took a direct hit. She was hysterical as her mother isn't there. Doreen's having another baby in the hospital.' I looked across the table at Diana. She looked fuzzy to me and I found my handkerchief and wiped away my tears. 'Bringing another baby into the world.' I couldn't keep the anger from my voice as though this was all Doreen's fault.

'Life has to go on.' Diana sounded surprised at my outburst.

'It didn't for the baby down the road,' I shouted. 'I found a baby. A little thing...not more than a few months...he was crying like a kitten...he died in my arms.' I broke down completely, sobbing my heart out.

'You poor kid,' Diana said, coming to my side and holding me. I was grateful her matter-of-fact tone had changed to sudden warmth. 'Here, you go upstairs and have a nap. I'll bring you up a couple of Aspros.'

'What room?'

'Where you've been sleeping – in my room. I'll go in Mrs P's tonight.'

I was too tired to argue and tottered up the stairs to Diana's bedroom. It would do for the time being, but I wanted to escape as soon as I could. There wasn't even Mrs Parker's food to stay for now.

'How are you feeling?' Diana appeared with a cup of tea and two digestive biscuits.

'Better,' I admitted. 'What's the time?' It was dark with the curtains pulled to, and I had no idea.

'Half-past six,' Diana said. 'You must be hungry. I've found some food in the larder – cold, I'm afraid. I'm not much of a cook.'

She left me and went downstairs and ten minutes later I followed her.

'Good,' she said, looking at me approvingly. 'You've got a bit of colour back in those cheeks. With that pale hair you looked quite washed out. Anyway, I've set the table. Let's eat. And decide what you're going to do.'

I felt relieved that she thought I was the next problem to tackle. We ate Mrs Parker's leftover vegetable pasties and Diana had found some cold potatoes and fried them. I felt sad thinking how Mrs Parker had never known it would be the last pastry she'd make.

'A brandy would go down well now,' Diana sighed, as she put down her knife and fork.

I immediately felt all grown up. 'Yes, please,' I said. 'I'd love to try one.'

Diana laughed, a kind of horsey neigh. 'It would go down well,' she repeated, 'if only we had some – which we don't.'

The warmth rushed to my face and Diana laughed again. 'One day we'll have a glass together,' she promised. 'But for now, it's only more tea.'

We talked about why I'd bleached my hair and how good the film was which had inspired me to do it. Diana didn't say anything about her work.

'Tell me about your family,' she suddenly asked. She looked

younger. She'd put a bit of colour on her lips.

It was the question I'd been dreading.

'I have an older brother and sister. They both joined up. Harry's in the army and Frankie's in the WRNS.'

'You must miss them.'

'Not really,' I said truthfully. 'They're older than me with different interests, and now they've both left home...' I didn't bother to finish the sentence.

'But you've not joined up yet?'

I shook my head. I didn't want to tell her my age.

'What about your parents?'

I didn't want to give Diana any details about them either but it seemed rude not to say something. 'Mum has her own tea rooms in Bonham,' was all I could think of.

'Not Annie's Tea Rooms?' Diana sounded surprised.

I gave a start. 'Yes, that's right. You know it?'

'I've been in there. I was curious. A woman with her own business. My mother told me it was quite the talk of Bridgewater when she opened up.' She looked at me. 'Now I realise who you are.'

I squirmed.

'Your mother used to cook for us. After your dad took off to America, wasn't it?'

Whatever was she talking about?

'You must have the wrong person,' I said, blushing furiously.

'Oh, no. I remember her quite clearly. Slim little thing. Not so tall as you. Beautiful dark chestnut hair. And her eyes...they were so unusual. Such a deep blue. Almost navy. In fact, they were exactly like yours.'

My heart did a flip. Diana's description fitted Mum to a tee. But what did she mean about Dad taking off to America? Is that where he'd gone all that time ago? He'd been away for a long time though I don't remember missing him at all. Mum would never tell me where he'd gone, even when I'd grown up. I longed to know more and was about to question her when Diana said:

'And in case you're asking, that's all I know. Mother didn't discuss that sort of thing with us girls.'

Biting back my disappointment I told her about the article in the newspaper I'd picked up in Lyons'. 'Do you know what ENSA is?'

She nodded. 'It's a group you belong to if you sing or dance or play an instrument and want to entertain the troops. I forget what it stands for but the nickname is "Every Night Something Awful".' She threw back her head and gave her horsey laugh. Then she sent me a suspicious look. 'Why are you interested?'

'Because I want to be a singer. It's what I've always dreamed of.'

'Do you think you're good enough?'

'I-I think so,' I faltered, 'though I've never had lessons.' Diana looked rather doubtful. 'I won first prize for singing when I was twelve. And Vera Lynn is my idol,' I rambled on. 'She goes all over the place singing to the troops. That's what I want to do.'

'Well, you need to find out if you're any good. I've no idea how you get hold of ENSA. But I do know it's the group your Vera Lynn is part of.' She put my empty plate on top of hers. 'How old are you, Kitty?'

'Eighteen.'

'You'd probably have to be eighteen to get in,' she said, scrutinising me. 'Which you don't look.'

I felt my cheeks redden.

'But that shouldn't matter, so long as you've got your birth certificate.'

6

King's Lynn

I had to go home and ask Mum for my birth certificate. Risk seeing Dad, risk him stopping me from coming back to London. If only I'd thought about this – but it hadn't occurred to me I might need it for singing.

Dear Diana lent me the money for my fare back to King's Lynn. She told me I could stay in her old bedroom for the next few weeks when I came back; that one of the other girls would be returning from abroad at any time, and Barney was still there, so maybe I could be useful.

Not to wait on him hand and foot, I thought, like Mrs Parker used to, but I didn't say anything, except how kind Diana was and how grateful I was.

Mum opened the door to me about ten days after I'd left. For a few seconds it was as though she was looking at a stranger. She gasped.

'Kitty! What have you done to yourself?'

I'd forgotten about the hair. I put my hand up to pat it, and beamed. I still loved being blonde.

'Do you like it?'

'Your lovely hair.' She looked upset, as though I was telling her in a roundabout way I wasn't satisfied with the looks I'd inherited. 'Why would you want to change it?'

'I want a new life, Mum. I'm going to be a singer and I need to look the part. That's what you're always saying. If you want anything in this world you've got to look the part.'

Mum sighed as she ushered me through the front door and into the kitchen where we always congregated to do our talking.

'Tell me the truth, Kitty,' she said, as she poured me a cup of tea. 'How bad is it in London?'

I didn't let on what a terrible state it was in, that we had daylight raids as well as night ones, but I did tell her about the one which killed poor Mrs Parker. Mum went pale.

'You should have come straight home,' she said. 'I would have worried to death had I known.'

'I was all right, Mum.' I laid my hand over hers. 'I can look after myself.'

She didn't look convinced. I spared her the overflowing hospitals, the women queuing for hours to get a couple of chops or a bit of liver, or a few eggs; things we used to take for granted but were now hard to get; my sleepless nights with the noise of the bombs. But Mum always listened to the wireless. She probably had a good idea of what it was like.

'But you're home now, thank the Lord. And I've been thinking about your singing. Why don't you join the church choir. They're—'

'Mum,' I interrupted her, 'I need my birth certificate.'

A tiny flicker of unease crossed my mother's face. Or was I imagining it?

'Why do you need it, darling?'

No, I wasn't imagining it. Her hand was trembling as she poured me another cup of tea. I'd just told her I didn't want a second one.

I plunged in. 'I'm planning to join ENSA, but they want proof of my age.'

'ENSA?' Mum's eyebrows shot up. 'Isn't that the people who entertain the forces?'

'Yes,' I said, a little surprised she knew about it. 'I'm going to sing. I've already had an audition and they've offered me a place.'

It was all a lie, but I had to assure her I had something definite. All I could think of was getting into ENSA, and even though I hadn't spoken to anyone there, to me the contract was as good as signed.

'So you're going away again?' Mum said quietly.

'Not necessarily,' I answered, trying to soften the blow. 'Not at first, anyway.'

'I've heard they send entertainers away.' Mum pulled her top lip in as though to stop herself from crying. 'Even abroad.'

'I think you have to volunteer.' I didn't really know if that was the case, though if they sent me I'd go like a shot. 'But I do need my birth certificate.'

Mum closed her eyes and I could hear the rush of air in her nostrils as she took in a deep breath. She let the air slowly escape as though to will herself to do something she didn't want to do. I noticed her hands folding and unfolding.

'Kitty, I have something to tell you.' She looked directly at me. 'Something I should have told you before now.'

Her voice shook. An invisible veil shielded her eyes which now looked the colour of a stormy sea.

'First I'd better go and find your certificate.' She coughed and rose to her feet, using the edge of the table for support. She was only in her forties but suddenly she was acting like an old woman.

The tea was cold and tasted sour, but I hardly noticed. Mum was nervous and upset, and it was obvious my birth certificate was the cause.

All my old fears that I was adopted tumbled through my mind while I waited for Mum to find it. I'd once tackled Frankie about my birth. She merely said that children always go through a stage of thinking they're adopted, which I didn't think was much of an answer. I studied Frankie as she spoke. Golden hair which I supposed was like Dad's before he turned pepper and salt; bright blue eyes, again like Dad's, with a hint of Mum's bumpy nose. She was definitely theirs. My brother hadn't been part of this conversation so I got hold of him that evening when he'd come to help me clear away the dishes.

'Was I adopted, Harry?' I asked him. 'Tell me the truth.'

'Have you looked at yourself in the mirror lately, Kitty Cat? Take a look at your eyes, for instance. They're exactly like Mum's.'

'Loads of people have blue eyes.'

'But not dark, like yours,' he said, his own sky-blue ones teasing me. 'Yours and Mum's are a navy blue. And when you have a tantrum they look black.'

'I don't have—'

'You do,' Harry cut in, chuckling, 'when you go all fierce – like now.'

I threw a tea-cloth at him.

'Hate to disappoint you, Kitty Cat,' he said as he deftly caught it, 'but you're stuck with us as your family.'

That could have meant anything.

I was lost in my own thoughts when Mum appeared a few minutes later, looking flushed, pins falling out of her usually neat hair. Although she was a slight woman she sat down heavily in the kitchen chair opposite me.

'Read this first,' she said, handing me a thickly folded cream paper, 'and then I'll try to explain.'

I caught her eye but she shook her head and nodded for me to open it. My cup made a clattering noise as I clumsily set it on the saucer. Heart beating a little faster, I spread it out. My birth certificate. The first time I'd ever set eyes on it.

A girl, Katherine Alexandra, born 23rd December 1923. Mother, Annie Elizabeth Bishop. Father, Dr Alexander Townsend.

My stomach turned over. What was going on? I looked at her and this time her gaze never wavered. I peered at it again. Yes, it was as plain as my hand which held it. Father, Dr Alexander Townsend. In the space where Ferguson Percy Bishop should have been.

'Don't you think I deserved to know this a long time ago?' My voice grated as I rushed on without waiting for a reply. 'Do Frankie and Harry know this? Do *they* belong to Dad?' I glared at her. 'Tell me, Mum. Is it only *me* who's the odd one out?'

Mum was silent for a few moments. Only her eyes told me how distraught she was. I couldn't bear it. Hated myself. But I couldn't get up and put my arms around her either, because it suddenly dawned on me that this was much worse than being told I was adopted. Mum's unspoken words were that she'd had a *lover*. She must have had a love affair and I was the product. Did Dad know? Did he suspect he wasn't my real father? If so, it certainly explained why he didn't treat me the same as Harry and Frankie. Or had she pulled the wool over his eyes the way she had mine?

I watched her and I knew she could tell what I was thinking. Then her eyes drifted from mine, and a strange faraway look crept over her face. I couldn't really take it in. Mum with a lover? And by her expression she still had him. When did she meet him? Where did they meet? Did he know he had a daughter? What was this man like? Did I look like him? Did I take after him? Had he ever seen me?

I couldn't stop the stream of questions fighting for answers in my head. Would Mum be prepared to explain? Whether she wanted to or not, it was her duty. I was coming up eighteen, for goodness' sake. I had a *right* to know. Anger bubbled up from nowhere and swept through me, making me almost keel over in my effort to force myself to sit quietly and listen to what Mum would tell me...about *him*...about her lover...about my real father.

And then it all poured out.

'I met your father going to Australia,' she said, and I could see she was trying to bite back the tears. I hardened myself. 'He was the ship's doctor. There was a smallpox outbreak and the nurses hadn't been vaccinated. I had. So when he asked if I would help him I agreed. He saved many lives on that crossing.' Mum stopped and cleared her throat. Then she said, 'I got to know him a little.'

'But you were newly married,' I broke in, my eyes wide with shock.

Mum held up her hand. 'Please let me explain without interrupting, darling. This is difficult enough for me as it is.'

I flushed, and she covered her hand with mine but I snatched it away.

'I only got to know him on the ship as a doctor.' Mum gave me a challenging glance. 'I never dreamed I'd set eyes on him again. Then when I was going to have Frankie in Melbourne I went to the doctor, and it was him – Dr Alexander Townsend. I was so homesick for my father and sisters and he was kind to me. He was one of the few friends I had, but he was always professional. He delivered Frankie, but when I was about to have Harry...'

I noticed her face crease in such terrible lines of pain it frightened me. This time I didn't interrupt her.

'...he was away on an emergency and another doctor...someone I didn't know...delivered H...Harry...and...'

To my horror, Mum broke down in tears.

'Mum.' All at once I stopped being angry and rushed round to her, gathering her in my arms. 'Don't go on if it upsets you too much.'

She stiffened, and felt in her apron pocket for a handkerchief. She blew her nose, taking in gulps of air. I waited.

'No, darling, I've wanted to tell you about your father so often. Where was I? Oh, yes, I had...Harry...and then we left Melbourne soon after.'

They'd come home because Mum was homesick. But the way Mum looked, I had a feeling there was more to it.

'Didn't you plan to go to Australia for good?'

'Yes, but it didn't work out as we thought.' I opened my mouth to ask her why, but she cut me short and said, 'I don't want to talk about that part of my life.'

It sounded as though it was simply too painful. Did that mean there were more secrets? But I just said, 'And then?'

'After we'd been back in England a few months Dad announced he was going to America and he'd send for me and you children when he was settled with a job.' Mum looked up, and even though her face was streaked with tears her chin was stubborn, her brow clear. It struck me again what a strong woman she was. She went on, 'I told him I was not going to upset the children with yet another move – Frankie was happy in her new school – and he'd have to go without me. So he did. Finally he wrote to say he was going to stay out there, and it was best for Frankie and Harry that they remain with me.'

I sat there, stunned. So Diana was right about Dad going to America. I swallowed hard. 'Do Frankie and Harry know Dad went to America?'

'Frankie remembers it. She was heartbroken. Harry was too young.'

But he'd have been old enough to remember when Dad came back.

'Then what happened?' I prompted. I had to know the truth now.

'About a year later I had a letter from Alex who'd found out Dad had gone. He was due for a holiday and wrote to ask if he could come and see me. I was in two minds. I was still married, you see, and living with your Aunt Ethel. What would people say?'

'How did he find out about Dad living in America?' I asked.

'Your Aunt Ruby told him,' Mum said.

Oh, yes, Aunt Ruby. She'd stayed out in Australia, though I knew very little about her. Her name was rarely mentioned in our house, and we hardly heard from her except a card at Christmas, though Mum still loved her because her eyes would fill with tears if Aunt Ethel mentioned her, or anyone in town happened to ask after her.

'And then Dad wrote and said he'd met someone,' I heard Mum

say. 'And that we should all stay where we were. It was a black day when I got that letter and realised our marriage was over.'

I thought of Mum being left with two children while Dad went off to seek his fortune. I thought of her getting a letter from him saying he wasn't coming back. That he'd met someone else. How humiliating it must have been.

'And when you saw Dr Alexander – Alex – again…?' I said more softly, to encourage her to continue.

'We fell in love,' my mother said, simply. 'He stayed a fortnight and went back to Australia but he promised he'd return. And he did. They were the best years of my whole life. You were born at the end of our first year together and he was the proudest man alive, though he was always a loving dad to Frankie and Harry as well. They called him "Dad" and loved him too.' She looked at me. 'Don't you remember him at all, Kitty? You adored him. A real daddy's girl. You used to make up songs together.'

And when she said that, something clicked inside my head. I could remember a tall dark figure coming home from work, and I'd be in bed but I'd call out to him and he would come upstairs and read me a story. And it must have been on Sundays that we used to sing songs together because I'd have him to myself for an hour or two before Frankie and Harry got bored and demanded to be taken somewhere.

'Are they his records – the ones we listen to?'

'Yes, darling. He loved his music. It was his passion. He and I used to listen to them together and I was so happy that you and I could enjoy them. It somehow helped.' Her eyes were moist. 'Frankie and Harry were never particularly interested but you always loved listening with me.' She reached for my hand and gave it a gentle squeeze. 'I wanted to tell you so many times who the records belonged to. I'm so glad you know now.'

'What sort of a person is he, Mum?'

I badly wanted to meet my father, to see what he was like for myself, but I needed to hear what Mum had to say.

Her face lit up. It was as though a light was burning inside her. She turned to me. 'The kindest, dearest, most loving man in the world. He used to tell you how much he loved you. He called you his little jewel.'

'Then Dad came back and ruined everything,' I said, more as a statement than a question, but it came out all wrong. Mum didn't seem to have noticed.

'Not until Alex had gone. Then I heard from Dad that things hadn't worked out in New York and he wanted to come home. To be with me and the children, he said.'

'So Alex had already gone back to Australia?' It didn't sound true to form after he'd been so happy with Mum and had a little girl.

Mum looked puzzled.

'You said Alex had already gone,' I prompted.

More tears sprang to her eyes.

'He died. My darling Alex died of TB. I loved him so much. But thank goodness I've got you. And you remind me of him every day – you're so like him.' Then she smiled her lovely smile. 'That is, you *were* before you went blonde.'

For a split second we looked at each other. Then we burst out laughing and clung to one another. And then we were crying.

'I'm sorry I didn't tell you before, darling,' Mum said, drawing away at last and brushing the tears with the back of her hand. 'But I had my reasons.'

Dad. But I didn't press her. What would be the use?

'I'm glad I know now.' I kissed her smooth cheek and she hugged and kissed me back. 'I wish things had worked out differently for you.' I hesitated. I didn't want to upset her any further but I wanted her to understand what an effect Dad had had on me.

'Why did you take him back?'

'I thought about it for weeks. Maybe months. Dad said he'd

61

missed us all. That he'd made a terrible mistake. He loved us and would try hard to be a better husband and father. And you see, darling,' she looked at me with tear-soaked eyes, 'he *was* Frankie and...' she gulped, 'and Harry's real father. I would never have forgiven myself if I hadn't at least given him a chance. Besides,' she put her hands over her face, 'he promised to love you the same as the others.'

'But he didn't,' I said bitterly. 'There's always been something awkward between us—'

'What the braddy hell have you done to your hair, Katherine?' Dad loomed in the doorway, scowling. Mum looked up, her face flushed.

'Hello to you, too, Dad,' I said.

'That's enough of the sarcasm.' He glared at me. 'You look like a washerwoman.'

'Thanks, Dad.'

'Leave her alone, Ferguson,' Mum said.

He ignored her and plonked himself down opposite the two of us and jerked his head towards the teapot. 'Any tea for me?'

'No, there's none left.' Mum rose up to clear the dishes.

Dad looked a little taken aback, then regarded me with more interest than usual. 'What's the matter? You both look as though you've been crying.'

'Kitty's been offered a singing job with ENSA, and she's accepted it. It was out of the blue and I was a bit upset, that's all.' Mum went over to the sink and made a clatter as she piled up the crockery.

'Some romantic notion of entertaining the troops, no doubt.' Dad's voice had an edge of contempt as he glanced at me, then at Mum's back. 'There's no need for you to be upset, Annie. Katherine can forget it. Annie, did you hear?'

Mum turned around. 'I heard.' She came back to the table.

'I'm not going to forget it,' I told him, braver than usual with my

62

new hair and new-found knowledge. 'I'll be eighteen by Christmas. And I'm going with them, whatever you say. It's all settled.'

Somehow I had to convince both of them that I had a definite job.

'How dare you cheek me!' Dad glared. 'You'll go over my dead body.' His voice rose and his face grew pinker. 'And you can get that stuff off your hair. No daughter of mine is going on the stage looking like a tart to sing to a load of strange men.'

'That's where you're wrong,' I said. 'You'll just have to get used to it – seeing as I'm not your daughter.'

There was a terrible silence.

I broke it.

'Mum's just told me who my real father is,' I said, heart racing against my ribs, trying to gauge his reaction.

'Oh, yes?' Dad's tone was harsh.

'It wasn't a great surprise,' I said, pretending a calmness I didn't feel. I wasn't sure how much to say, but then I decided I had nothing to lose. He already knew the truth anyway. 'Apparently I wasn't quite four when my real father died so I can't really remember what he looked like. But when I was older something didn't add up.'

Dad's eyes became steely. 'What do you mean, Katherine?'

'My *real* father loved singing,' I told him with feeling. 'We'd make up songs together. I remember him whistling and singing around the house.'

I didn't remember the whistling bit, but he sounded like the kind of person who would. I watched Dad curiously. I was probably telling him more about my father than Mum had and he was beginning to look annoyed.

'My real father was always telling me he loved me,' I went on, warming to my theme. Dad frowned even harder. 'Then he got ill, and I couldn't stop crying.' I didn't remember that either, but I'm sure that's what I must have done. 'Mum said he'd gone far away for a long time. So when you came back I thought it was funny how you'd changed. You didn't act the way you used to. You never kissed and hugged me. And you didn't encourage me to sing. In fact, you refused to let me have singing lessons. But of course you were a different person. You weren't my father.'

All this time Mum had remained silent. Dad looked at her and she held his gaze.

Finally, she said, 'I should have told Kitty sooner. It wasn't fair to her.'

'We'd agreed not to.' Dad's face was tomato red. 'You say it wasn't fair to *her*, but you didn't think of *me* – my feelings.' His voice rose. 'Trying to provide for everyone all these years.'

'I've always worked,' Mum cut in, just as sharply. 'But I don't want to argue, especially as Kitty is going back to London.'

'What do you mean?' Dad swung from Mum to me. 'We're not letting her out of our sight again.'

7

I begged and stormed and threatened, but Dad was adamant. He made Mum promise to keep a strict eye on me. After three days I thought I would go crazy. And the more I thought about it the more I needed to know about my real father. Mum had loved him and I wouldn't be here if she hadn't.

'Mum,' I said when Dad had left for work and we were clearing away the breakfast dishes, 'will you tell me more about my father?'

This was going to be painful for her. And me, too, I thought, a spurt of anger erupting at the deception. I pressed it down. Mum had had a rough time. But I needed to ask her what was on my mind. 'Did he have any family?'

My mother hesitated, then vaguely shook her head.

'It's important to me,' I persisted. 'If I don't have my father, there might be an aunt or uncle or a cousin somewhere. Didn't he ever say anything about his mother and father – where they lived?'

'He didn't tell me much. His father – that is, your grandfather – died before Alex. Thank goodness he never knew his son was so ill. Alex's mother went back to Italy. To Rome. That's where she came from. I often think about her. She must have been heartbroken with first her husband, then her son. Poor woman.'

'Was she Italian?'

'Yes. Your grandfather was English. They met in London and moved to Italy when they married. Your father was born there.'

An Italian grandmother. That would explain my dark hair.

So different from Frankie who had taken after Dad (I couldn't stop myself from calling him that, it was such an ingrained habit) and was golden, and Harry who was bright auburn, after his Aunt Ruby, everyone always said. For a brief moment I felt disloyal to my real father for dyeing mine blonde. But a half-Italian father...how did I feel about that? Even though he was dead, the Italians were our enemies. Not as bad as the Germans, some people said, but our enemies nevertheless. My poor mother had given me the worst news now we were fighting them.

'Alex and the family went to Australia when he was twelve,' Mum went on, 'so he lost his Italian accent and from then on became Australian. He took Australian citizenship when he was twenty-one.'

'What did his mother and father say when he told them he was leaving Australia for good to live with a servant?' I blurted out. Oh, God, why couldn't I keep my mouth shut?

'It must have been a shock for them,' she said, not seeming to mind my reference to her being a servant, 'though we never really talked about it. I did ask him once or twice, but he said his mother and father were sorry he'd decided to live in England, and that was that. He didn't have any brothers or sisters so there isn't really anyone for you to look up.'

'They don't sound as though they were a very close family,' I said, flinging some knives and forks into the cutlery basket. 'I wonder if his mother is still alive.'

'Don't you go having any ideas,' Mum said, looking at me suspiciously.

I gave a hollow laugh. 'We're at war with them, in case you've forgotten.'

Mum's shoulders drooped. 'It would break his heart if he could see this,' she said. 'He often used to talk about Italy, especially Rome.'

'So you never met his parents?' I asked. 'My grandparents?'

'No…no, I didn't.' She sat down and closed her eyes briefly, then opened them and looked up at me. 'They were both still in Melbourne when I left, so when Alex came to England they were much too far away for us to visit. Besides,' a shadow passed over Mum's face, 'he wouldn't discuss it but I had the feeling they didn't approve. I wasn't a Catholic, don't forget. And, of course, we were living together by then but not married…I was still married to Dad and had two children. They saw all the bad things and none of the good. It was very complicated.' She looked at me as though asking me to understand. 'They must have been terribly sad that they might never see their son again. And then his dad died and his mother went back to Italy.'

I could tell by her anxious expression that she hoped I wouldn't pursue the conversation. But I couldn't help it.

'Didn't you ask him if you could both go and visit them?'

'No.' Mum shook her head. 'The answer wouldn't have been what I wanted to hear, and your father,' she looked at me with pride shining from those amazing eyes, 'would never say anything to hurt me. So we rarely spoke about it.'

'Did they ever write? Did you write to them?'

'I know Alex wrote to them several times and he did get a couple of letters from his mother but nothing much.' She looked at me, her eyes full of sadness. 'He sent a photograph of you shortly after you were born, and one every year on your birthday.'

'Did they reply? Or send a card for me?'

'No…oh, I think once. To say they were glad he was happy, and another to congratulate him on his baby daughter. That was about it.'

'But no mention of you?' I was like a dog with a bone.

'Not really, darling. But I didn't mind too much. In many ways I understand the hurt I must have brought them.'

'Well, I don't,' I burst out. 'You wouldn't hurt a fly. They didn't even give you a chance.'

'There's no point in getting upset, Kitty.' She rose to her feet. 'You sit down. I'm going to make some tea.'

That was her way of changing the subject.

I watched her busy herself and felt guilty knowing she would get into trouble with Dad when he discovered I'd disappeared for the second time in a fortnight. To even it up I decided to come clean with Mum about Diana.

'You'd like her, Mum,' I said. 'And you'll never believe it but her name's Hamilton.' Mum's eyes widened as she brought the tea tray over. 'Yes,' I nodded, 'she's one of Lady Hamilton's daughters. She knew all about you and Annie's Tea Rooms.'

I told her I'd never found Helen but met Diana who'd lent me her room. That I'd borrowed the train fare from her and must pay her back. If Diana never heard from me again she'd think I'd scarpered.

'Not the kind of behaviour she would expect from my daughter.' My mother looked at me, and to my surprise I saw a glint of amusement. 'Before I forget, I have something for you.' She went to a drawer in the kitchen cabinet and took out a brown envelope. 'You'll need this.'

I opened it. There were several five-pound notes inside.

'Mum...'

'No need to say anything, Kitty. I always save a bit out of the tea rooms when we have a good week. Just don't mention it to Dad.'

I jumped up and hugged her tightly. 'You're the best mother anyone could ever have but I must go back.' I held her a little away. 'You do understand, don't you?'

She nodded. But her eyes filled with tears.

'You'll have to give Dad some excuse as to why you left me for half an hour to give me time—'

'I'll think of something,' she said quickly.

I don't know what Mum said to Dad, but she didn't tell him any lies or make any excuses. She must have worked on him in some other way because the next day he said:

'Your mother's told me you don't want to miss your chance to do your bit. Why you think singing to the troops is going to help, I don't know, but far be it from me to stand in your way.'

Was this really Dad speaking? Maybe he couldn't wait to get rid of me mooching around the house, thoroughly miserable. Maybe Mum had threatened to leave him too. I didn't know.

But I didn't care. I was off.

Barney opened the door to me, a flare of relief in his eyes. I told him Diana had said I could come back and stay in her room for a while, then asked him if he'd seen her lately.

'She wrote me a letter,' he admitted. 'Said if you didn't return I would have to find other lodgings.'

'Just as well I'm back then,' I answered, brushing past him.

I stopped at the kitchen door, horrified. Dirty cups, plates and glasses were jumbled on the draining board, and even from the doorway I could see the sink overflowing with soapy greasy water. The kitchen table was piled high with papers, saucepans, spectacles, matches and a paraffin lamp, and a foul smell of stale cigarettes completed the total neglect of the room. Mrs Parker would have not just turned but somersaulted in her grave. I threw Barney a look which I hoped showed my disgust. He cleared his throat.

'It's not the same with Mrs Parker gone.'

'It certainly isn't,' I agreed. 'But we're going to clean this place up before we have supper. And you're going to do exactly what I tell you.'

I ignored his surprised expression. He looked as though he was about to argue, then seemed to think better of it.

'What do you want me to do first?' he asked.

That evening we shared a tin of tomato soup. And a large bottle of cider Barney found in the pantry, which made him loosen those tight lips of his.

He didn't relate his whole story – that would have been too much. But he did tell me how he'd got wounded. It was seconds after a mate of his was killed. He was running with him, heard a colossal bang, glanced for a moment to the left to try to tell where it had come from, and when he looked back, his friend was no longer by his side. He'd been blown to pieces. Poor Barney. His face crumpled and tears dripped behind his glasses and down his cheeks. I put my hand on his for an instant, hoping he would know I understood – but of course, I didn't. How could I? I hadn't lost a friend or a relative. But I'd had a flavour of the horror when Mrs Parker's neighbour's house had been demolished, and Mrs Parker had died. And the baby. I bit my lip as I remembered the baby's innocent expression in his clear blue eyes. Moments later he'd gone. It had dawned on me at that exact moment there was nothing glamorous about war, as I'd stupidly thought when I lived in King's Lynn.

Barney poured us another glass of cider and in spite of his awful story I started to relax for the first time in weeks.

'I barely had time to realise what had happened when *I* got shot.' Barney took a long swallow of cider. 'Ended up in hospital with a pretty serious leg wound. After the doc had patched me up and I started to feel stronger, all I wanted to do was get back to the front and shoot every Jerry I could lay eyes on as revenge for Chris. But the doc had other ideas. He told me I had to recuperate in hospital so it had a proper chance to mend. Said I was lucky he didn't have to amputate it.'

'How did you find out about Mrs Parker?'

'After I came out of hospital I was supposed to go to one of those rest places, but they were full. One of the chaps had known Mrs Parker's husband. So here I am. And although Mrs P was a bit of a dragon she was always all right to me...and, of course, she was a first-class cook. She kind of mothered me...said I needed feeding up.'

I felt ashamed of myself for ever thinking bad thoughts of poor old Nosy. She'd been kind to Barney and now she was dead. But I wasn't that keen to stay in her house with only Barney for company. Admittedly, I'd been quite happy to order Barney around this afternoon, with him not even arguing; we'd got the kitchen cleaned up and it had taken my mind off things, but now I wanted my mother. I was frightened. Frightened of being blown up like Barney's poor friend, frightened of being on my own, frightened of not having any money, frightened of having nowhere to live in London, frightened of strangers, frightened of not getting a job, frightened that I had a father who, if he'd been alive, would be the enemy...

My eyes began to sting, and I cupped them with my hands to stop the tears from flowing. But they seeped between my fingers and my whole body shook with my sobs.

'Please don't cry, Kitty.' Barney came round the table to me and laid a hand on my shoulder. For a few moments it felt comforting but when he didn't take his hand away it began to feel embarrassing. 'Here, have the rest of the cider.' Barney handed me his nearly full glass. 'It'll make you feel better.'

I gulped it down as though it was a glass of water.

'I'll clear the dishes away,' I said, scrambling up, more to get away from his hand still on my shoulder. It was a mistake. My head swam. I lost my balance and fell heavily to the floor.

Barney hauled me up. The next moment I was in his arms.

'Kitty, will you let me...?'

I froze.

'Don't be scared,' he said, pushing away a strand of hair from my forehead. 'I promise I won't hurt you. But I've had some news. They want me back on the front and I don't think...' I watched his Adam's apple jump as he swallowed. 'To tell you the truth, Kitty, I don't think I'll make it.'

He was telling me he'd never come home. I looked closely at him. There were no lines on his face, only raw pain in his eyes. He couldn't be more than twenty-one or two. A horrible vision came

71

into my mind of him lying in some foreign field, wounded, then dying, with no one to give him any words of comfort.

'And I've never done it before.' He stared at me. 'I don't suppose you have, either.'

I didn't know what to say.

'I just don't want to die without knowing what it feels like to make love,' he said, seemingly oblivious to my silence. 'And I'd love it to be with you, Kitty.'

I felt sick with fear and probably too much drink, which I wasn't used to. And I felt desperately sorry for Barney.

'May I kiss you?'

I nodded feebly. He put his mouth on mine but it felt as soft as a girl's. I eased my head away, hoping he wouldn't notice. He took my hand and I followed him upstairs…into Diana's bedroom. Mrs Parker would've killed the pair of us, no doubt about it. Somehow I managed to push that thought to one side.

'You didn't tell me if this *is* your first time,' he said matter-of-factly, as he helped me undress.

'It's not,' I lied, already embarrassed that I was standing before a man in my underclothes. Why couldn't I just tell him the truth? That I shouldn't let him do whatever he was about to do. That you were supposed to be married. That I was scared of the pain. But I was also curious. I wanted to find out. All I'd heard were whispers from friends about what a man did, and how painful it was…and there'd be loads of blood the first time. You couldn't fool a man for that reason alone, they said.

Barney looked doubtful.

'I'll be as gentle as I can,' he said, as though to reassure me. He obviously guessed I was a virgin. 'And I'll put something on so you don't have a baby.'

When he said that, I nearly got dressed again. The thought of Barney's baby filled me with alarm. Then I imagined him getting shot, writhing in agony all alone. Never coming home. His life cut short. Tears sprang to my eyes and I took his hand and led him over to Diana's bed. I had no idea what to do next.

Barney undressed and sat with his back to me for a few moments. I smelt rubber.

It was over as quickly as it had begun. A searing flame of pain which practically split me in two, a few strange thrusting movements from Barney, which felt as though he was stabbing me with a broom handle, then a shout from his lips which pierced through my head, and finally his lanky limbs flopped on top of me like a Norfolk seal. As he rolled off, leaving me with the marks of his sweat, he gave me a hug.

So that was it. A man thrusting his private parts into mine. I'd forgotten how I'd once vowed I would never let a man do that to me. So why had I let Barney? It wasn't as though I fancied him. I didn't know what to think...what to feel about what I had let him do. I hadn't enjoyed it one bit, and if I was honest, it had felt like an invasion. Where I should have felt shame I was only aware of the soreness between my legs, and a stickiness I supposed was the blood they'd warned me about. I slid him a glance. He had his eyes closed but his breathing was uneven so he wasn't asleep. His hair was sticking out all over his head like a porcupine.

'Barney?' I whispered, not knowing what I was going to say.

'Did I hurt you?' He sounded anxious as he hugged me to him again. I tried to edge away. 'They say it's not so bad the next time.'

There wasn't going to be a next time.

'Thank you, Kitty,' he muttered, not waiting for my reply. 'I'll never forget you.'

No words of love, the kind I'd read in books, but why should there be? Barney didn't love me any more than I loved him. But he was a nice man when you got to know him better.

It was then that something struck me with such force: I didn't know what it was to be in love, but I'd found out what it was *not* to be in love. And Mum had been passionately in love with Alex, my

73

father, and he with her. It must have been unbearable to try at first to deny it. And how wonderful it must have been when they finally told one another of their love.

I was glad Mum had eventually found true love and happiness.

As for me, I was now a woman. For that, I was grateful.

When Barney came back to life the next morning he was all for repeating it, but I told him I had a headache, which was perfectly true, on all that cider.

From that moment on I swore when I gave myself to a man it would be because I loved him.

8

Rome

Ruggero, February 1941

Ruggero Andreotti frowned as he buttoned his jacket, ready for his meeting with *Il Duce*. The war was going badly for Italy. Had been, right from the start. For the hundredth time he wondered why Mussolini couldn't see Hitler's admiration for him had already faded into contempt.

In Ruggero's opinion Mussolini wasn't as clever as he thought he was. He couldn't see that the Germans would never give any power to Italy if they won the war. Italy could say goodbye to its independence. Ruggero's clean-cut lips pulled into a hard line. Would the people of Italy really be prepared to give up their freedom to be led by the nose by Germany? Once upon a time it would have been unthinkable where their national pride was concerned. But soon it would be too late – they wouldn't have any choice.

Today he felt even more depressed than usual with the news that relentlessly poured in from Berlin; rose-tinted reports Mussolini would *want* to hear rather than hard facts. And he would have to translate these fairytales. Many times he was tempted to alter the tone, slip something in, leave something out...but what good would it do? He'd be lucky not to be shot. He'd certainly be out of the door and never get another position translating. No, he needed to tread carefully; stay close to Mussolini.

It was difficult these days working out who was trustworthy and who might go against their nature. Ruggero had heard of people betraying one another, colleague to colleague, neighbour to neighbour, even brother to brother; turning a blind eye to Hitler's atrocities; believing in Mussolini's propaganda. Where was their backbone? Where was their integrity? He could feel the anger rising. Yet he knew he shouldn't judge them so harshly. Many of his colleagues had families – children – they were trying to protect at any cost. For Christ's sake, he himself was in a precarious position. If Mussolini had any suspicion...

And then there was his brother, Lorenzo, who had gone to fight a year ago when Italy first entered the war, while Ruggero had been helping his frail father to run the estate. Lorenzo had called him a coward because he hadn't joined him. There was nothing he could say in defence until he'd achieved what he'd set out to do. Fortunately, his older brother was delighted that Ruggero finally appeared to be working for the fascists. If Lorenzo even suspected what Ruggero was planning, he knew full well his brother would turn him in.

With a grimace he strode from his office, thoughts of the Italian Army spinning through his head.

It was already under the control of the German Army by sheer lack of military planes, tanks, weapons and personnel. Why on earth hadn't Mussolini prepared the country? Begun building up supplies as any leader should have foreseen? Instead of that they'd had to rely on Germany to supply them with most of their emergency needs. Ruggero reluctantly admitted that Germany usually responded quickly. But that's only because they prefer to have us as friends rather than enemies, he thought grimly, as he ran down the marble stairs. Trouble was, the pay-off was selling your very soul. Unpalatable to every true Italian.

Mussolini had sent for him unexpectedly – not always a good sign. Ruggero made his way along numerous corridors of the ugly but undeniably powerful fascist building, to Mussolini's office, thinking how all the propaganda had paid off. Even the Church supported Mussolini. That had been *Il Duce's* trump card, to have the Church behind him, as though it was actually hand in glove with the dictator. What a mockery it made of the Roman Catholic faith. Ruggero shook his head in despair.

Yet there was a time when he, too, had admired Mussolini even though his own father had done his best to point out that *Il Duce* was a dangerous man and would one day lead the country into war. Admitedly Ruggero had been young – barely fifteen – when he and his friends from the same wealthy background had listened to Mussolini's fanatical speeches of how he intended to make Italy great again. At the time it had caused quite a frenzy amongst his classmates and led to many of them jeering the socialists.

Everything changed in October 1935 when Ruggero had finished his final year at Bologna University studying languages. His faith in *Il Duce* had been broken when Mussolini attacked Ethiopia, saying he was going to teach those barbarians a lesson, and that it was only "right" that Italy should have a "place in the sun". *Dio mio,* what the hell was he on about? As if everyone didn't swelter under Italy's burning skies every summer. Mussolini had persuaded the people that the war would be over quickly because the Ethiopians would be taken by surprise and the country would become part of the new Roman Empire. Most civilians were taken in and only a few of Ruggero's friends had questioned it but Ruggero was determined never to be sucked into such propaganda. He hated Mussolini and loathed Hitler and everything the two tyrants stood for.

Ruggero's stomach had tightened into a solid knot when the rumour flew round that the army had begun to use bombs of chemical gas to drop on innocent people. What a cowardly method to win a war. What would ordinary Italian people think of such wickedness if they knew? But the rumours were quickly hushed up. Even when the soldiers themselves came back from Ethiopia and told their families of the terrible massacres and cruelties, civilians murmured that *Il Duce* couldn't possibly know such things were going on else he wouldn't have allowed it. And when it became clear that the Jews were being persecuted in Germany, most people still refused to comment, and any mutterings were only that it was a pity but it seemed a necessary evil.

So Ruggero's plan had been to infiltrate Mussolini's inner circle. He'd had to pull strings using his father's aristocratic connections to persuade the great man that he was quite capable, at twenty-four, to be a valuable asset in translating the stream of messages and reports which flowed daily from Nazi Germany.

To his surprise Ruggero had been offered a position as one of Mussolini's translators in early 1938, thanks to his degree in German and French, and subsequent year working for Daimler-Benz in their correspondence department in Stuttgart. He'd applied to a German company on purpose to perfect his fluency, realising Germany was highly likely to go to war with France and his languages might come in extremely useful. "Know your enemy" had been his motto, as it was obvious Mussolini was sympathetic to Hitler's ambitions. Now, working closely with Mussolini, Ruggero made it his business to persuade the man of his loyalty to the fascist cause – all part of his plan to help sever the future relationship of the two dictators. And to eliminate them.

He knew he'd have to bide his time for Mussolini to completely trust him. By the second year of the war, Ruggero had become more and more alarmed and sickened by Mussolini, who jumped whenever Hitler ordered him to. It was only a matter of time before *Il Duce* obeyed the Führer's instructions to get rid of every Jew in Italy. If that happened they'd have sunk as low as the German scum. A few years ago, if anyone had told Ruggero what the Italian people were capable of, he'd have laughed in their faces.

As he approached Mussolini's office he rolled his eyes before he knocked on the closed door. How could the man work in a clean warm office while his soldiers were dying in frightening numbers in unfamiliar, hostile places for their beloved Italy, most of them too young to understand what they were fighting and dying for.

Ruggero's pulse raced in anger as he tried to arrange his handsome features as mildly as he could before stepping inside, praying that time would prove he was right to gain the trust of Mussolini and be privy to his documents and private papers.

'Fucking race of sheep,' Mussolini was swearing as Ruggero entered. 'All this art nonsense has made them flabby.' He jabbed a finger on the top of a handful of papers he was holding. 'Opera-singing buffoons. They're not proper fighters, none of them. Fucking disgrace to the nation. They need a spell in Hitler's army. That would sort them.' He gave a snort of disgust.

Ruggero's stomach clenched. He hated to admit it but unfortunately there was a grain of truth in *Il Duce*'s venom. He stood, waiting to be told to take a seat, knowing he wasn't expected to make any comment. Mussolini flung his arm impatiently towards a hard visitor's chair.

'Cast your eye over this, Andreotti.' He tossed the sheets across his desk. One fell on the floor. Ruggero stooped to pick it up, certain he'd dropped it on purpose to make sure his junior knew his place. 'I've got the hang of most of it,' Mussolini paced back and forth, his hands behind his back, his brow furrowing, 'but I want a final check. We don't want to make any slip-up where the German High Command is concerned, do we?' He gave a short mirthless bark.

To *Il Duce* the term "cast your eye" really meant "translate extremely carefully word for word" as Ruggero had once learned to his cost in the early days. Mussolini had threatened to get rid of him if he ever slipped up again. Ruggero's blood raced as he turned over the cover page. *Dio mio*. It was from the Führer himself. Obviously the self-important Duce didn't know his German as well as he made out or he would never have passed a Top Secret file from the great German leader to a junior aide. Dr Schmidt normally had this job but he was away. What a stroke of luck.

Ruggero skimmed this latest report, his eyes shrewd as he mentally translated the words. Then his heart leapt. It was what he'd been waiting for. Hitler mentioned paying another visit to Italy next month. So far he'd only put in two appearances even though Mussolini had invited him many times; Hitler had always given an excuse. Ruggero flipped over to the third page with a practised movement and quickly scanned the page, looking for a definite date, though he knew from various conversations and reports of Hitler's sadistic enjoyment in keeping Mussolini on his toes until the last minute. Hitler didn't always let his Italian counterpart know what he was planning until it was done, causing *Il Duce* to fly into a temper.

Yet things, Ruggero was sure, were about to change.

'It looks as though Herr Hitler is planning a visit to Rome.'

'Yes, yes, I understood that,' Mussolini answered impatiently, but Ruggero noticed a triumphant gleam in his eye. He hadn't understood at all. 'But get the translation done immediately.'

'Right, sir,' Ruggero said, his head lowered a fraction, careful not to let Mussolini see his flash of excitement. 'I'll have it ready first thing tomorrow morning.'

'You'll have it on my desk in one hour,' Mussolini barked. 'I want confirmation of the details. So get on with it.'

The puffed-up little man would almost be laughable if the situation wasn't so serious, Ruggero thought grimly. The burning question flew across his mind for the hundredth time: how could just two men cause such chaos and misery to hundreds of thousands of innocent people? Looking at Mussolini's unblinking eyes, Ruggero was certain the man was too far under Hitler's spell to worry about God or what it was like to be a human being who didn't fit in with the Führer's ideal. A wave of disgust ran down Ruggero's spine.

'I don't want to rush it, sir, as that's how mistakes are made,' he said. Mussolini's square jaw hardened at such impudence. 'But I'll get on to it right away, and see that it's back on your desk in, say...' he glanced at his watch, 'two hours.'

His boss nodded a dismissal.

For once he'd had the upper hand.

Back in his office Ruggero relaxed and took off his jacket. He picked up the papers and began to read the closely-typed German report. The first part referred to Hitler's planned visit to Rome, but there was a second report. This one was interesting. Ruggero lit a cigarette and narrowed his eyes as he read. The Germans had got their eye on an American destroyer, the *USS Reuben James* in the Atlantic. It was important to the British, the report said, as it was to be used to deliver goods to Britain. The German U-boats would be deployed for the job. Ruggero frowned. If only he could get this kind of information into British hands. They would be in close contact with America and it probably wouldn't be long before the Americans declared war on Germany and Italy, if Churchill had anything to say about it.

Before Ruggero started to pen the translation he made two copies of the original report: one for the file, the other tucked into a secret pocket in his briefcase.

It had taken months for him to find out exactly where his colleagues and friends stood; if they were true fascists or making a pretence, the same as himself. Except his one close friend, Piero Lavori. He'd made it clear to Ruggero at the start, blurting out Hitler's arrogance and paranoia, which if Mussolini had overheard would have meant instant dismissal or possible imprisonment. Even so, one or two colleagues had narrowed their eyes and Lavori had had to be quick to convince them his loyalty lay with Mussolini.

But Ruggero knew different. He knew his friend's secret. Lavori had admitted to him early on that he was half-Jewish, his wife full. So far, he said, their false papers had held, but luck could run out at any time. Everyone knew the Führer expected Mussolini to implement the racist laws that he'd introduced – that Jews in particular were only sub-human. Ruggero shook his head in despair.

Well, this evening he and Lavori would finally get a chance to talk.

They'd deliberately chosen a bar where the owner was a fascist sympathiser so the customers wouldn't guess the thrust of their conversation, but they were sure no one could overhear anything in the cacophony. As it was, they could hardly hear themselves, though they were careful not to raise their voices.

'Do you have a plan?' Lavori leaned forward and practically tipped the words into Ruggero's ear.

'Yes.'

Excitement flashed in Lavori's eyes. 'So what is this plan?'

'It's simple. So simple I'm hoping it can't go wrong. I only want to use four who are willing to put themselves in danger.' Ruggero casually raised his glass and took a swallow of beer. 'They need to be crack shots. Do you have any suggestions?'

'Yes,' Lavori answered without hesitating. 'And they're ready for anything.' He lit the stub of a cigarette and drew in a few puffs.

'They'll need Nazi uniforms – ones that fit.'

'Nazi?' Lavori raised his eyebrows so they almost disappeared into his hairline.

'They'll raise the least suspicion, as the fascists won't recognise them or dare to question them. They'll assume they've been placed by The Screamer himself.'

Lavori smirked on hearing Hitler's nickname, given to him by his rescuers when he'd been severely injured in the last world war and had screamed his head off for someone to help him. 'I'll see to it. Just give me a few days.'

'Be very careful.'

'That goes for you, too,' Lavori said. 'If anything happens to you, our main source of information would dry up. The further away you are from all of us, the better.'

Ruggero gave his friend a tight smile and a nod to two giggling girls at a nearby table as though they were just a couple of chaps having a drink and trying to chat up women.

'Don't say any more.' Ruggero made a small gesture to a group of German soldiers nearby, one who was paying far too much attention to the pair of them.

A week later, in a different bar, Ruggero outlined the plan.

'Our aim is to get both of them at the same time.' His eyes met those of his friend's. Ruggero saw the same fever and spike of fear he himself was feeling. 'The Screamer is arranging to visit our great man in three weeks' time and they plan to give a dual speech in the Piazza Venezia. Our four friends,' he paused to emphasise the last word, 'will be amongst the crowd, near to the front and a good distance apart. At a given sign, which I'll make as I'll have his speech pretty well marked out, the shots will be fired. Two birds killed with one stone, I believe the English say.' Ruggero laughed, but there was no humour.

It would be dangerous, no doubt about it, and several similar attempts had failed. But with the two leaders together in one small space it was too good an opportunity to miss.

'You have the four volunteers?' It was a big question and Ruggero felt every cell in his body tense, waiting for the answer.

'Yes.'

'Who are they?'

'Best if you don't know,' Lavori said, 'though I'll be one of them.'

'No.' Ruggero shook his head. 'You have a wife and children. Get someone without ties. It's safer. If you get caught you'll spill the lot if they threaten your family.'

Lavori clenched then unclenched his fists. 'I *want* to do it. Besides,' he added slyly, 'I shan't need a uniform.' He gulped down his beer, leaving a film above his top lip. 'We'll need to practise the timing down to the last second.'

Ruggero nodded. Lavori was short and wiry, and it always amazed Ruggero how he'd become one of Mussolini's bodyguards.

But he was intelligent. And apparently fearless.

'If you're determined. I suppose you would arouse the least suspicion being one of the known guards,' Ruggero said reluctantly, 'though you'll be assigned to stand somewhere *they've* chosen. But that shouldn't matter. Just be ready. The Screamer is likely to settle on a date, and then come a few hours early or late. It can even be a day out. He has some kind of antennae that always outwits any whispers of a plot.'

Lavori wiped his forehead with his handkerchief. 'Well, this time he's in for a surprise,' he said grimly, glancing at Ruggero. 'I told my lot we could count on you, even though one or two hinted you might be playing a double game.'

'I don't need to answer that nonsense.' Ruggero's words were quiet as he rose up and placed his hand on Lavori's shoulder, unwittingly echoing one of Mussolini's gestures. 'We'll meet in five days. At café number three.'

9

Kitty

That morning I decided to go to the library to see if I could find out more about ENSA. Mum always said they were good places to find information. At least I would have a definite place to start. I asked Barney where the nearest one might be.

'I'll show you,' he said, looking pleased to be doing something at last.

But I wanted to go on my own, and said so.

Before I left the house I looked in my purse, checking to see how much I had. It looked so little I was too worried to even count it. Mum's five-pound notes were gradually being used up for food and fares. Then I felt something in the zipped compartment of my handbag. I pulled out a small white card and eyed the gold script. It was the business card Raymond Glover, the man on the train, had given me. What had he said? *Telephone me if you ever need any help.* I didn't hesitate. You could only receive calls on Mrs Parker's telephone, so I decided to make for the nearest 'phone box and go to the library afterwards.

The one down the end of the road had lost most of its glass but at least the telephone seemed to be working. I dialled the number and a woman's voice answered.

'Wandsworth 2932.'

I couldn't tell whether the voice sounded like a housekeeper's or a wife's. For a second I didn't know what to do. I'd been so sure that Mr Glover himself would answer. Should I hang up? Then I told myself to stop being so ridiculous, and pushed in the coppers.

'Is Mr Glover at home, please?'

'Who's speaking?' Her voice sounded suspicious.

'Katherine Bishop.'

'Is he expecting you to ring?'

'Not…not exactly,' I mumbled, staring down at the little white card.

'I'm sorry, he's not home at present.' The voice had cooled down several degrees. 'Can I take a message?'

I just knew this was an outright lie. If not, she could have told me that before I said my name.

'No, but—'

'I'm sorry,' she repeated, and I heard the receiver click.

It's a good job she didn't see the childish face I pulled. I stood for a few moments wondering if I should try again and explain who I was, but a knock on the only pane still intact stopped me. A middle-aged woman was gesturing at me to let her in. I picked up my bag.

By now it was pelting with rain and when I arrived soaking wet at the library it was closed. The notice on the door said Wednesday was their closing day and it wouldn't be open until nine o'clock Friday morning, with no explanation as to why they wouldn't be open tomorrow. I could have wept with disappointment.

I put off going back to the house as long as possible to avoid seeing Barney. But when I eventually went back, to my surprise he was quite cheerful when he opened the door. He was wearing one of Mrs Parker's aprons and the smell of cabbage wafted from behind him.

'There you are,' he said. 'I'm making supper. And though I say it myself, I think it's going to be all right.'

'That's good.' I threw my hat and coat over one of the dining chairs, and shook out my wet hair. 'Can we have it early because I didn't have any lunch?'

Barney's meal consisted of corned beef, overcooked cabbage, and boiled potatoes with Bisto gravy, which I wasn't really sure went with the cold corned beef, but I suppose it added some flavour. For sweet he'd done a baked apple with a few currants. My stomach was rolling and I ate it up with enthusiasm. It was surprisingly good and I told him so.

'What are you planning to do now?' he asked, after I told him about telephoning Raymond Glover.

'I'm going back to the library on Friday,' I said, 'when it's next open. They should be able to tell me how to get in contact with ENSA.'

'You're probably too young anyway,' Barney said. 'And they may be looking for professional singers.'

Barney always looked on the bright side of everything.

'Well, if you don't have any luck at the library, why don't you telephone that chap again at a different time?' he suggested. 'If she's the housekeeper you could try this evening – she'll have gone home. If she's his wife, at least he'll be home from work and you'll have a better chance to speak to him.'

It made sense. But I wasn't going out again this evening. It was still pouring with rain and my shoes were sodden. Or was I just making excuses?

'I'll come with you,' Barney said the next morning, as I was squeezing my feet back into the still-wet shoes. 'At least it's something to do.'

But I told him I'd be perfectly all right and nipped out before he could argue. Thankfully the rain had eased a little. Someone was already occupying the 'phone box and to my delight it was Joyce. She waved and smiled at me, mouthing that she wouldn't be long and for me to wait.

'Do you still like your hair?' she asked immediately she emerged.

'Everyone was shocked,' I told her, giggling and putting my

hand up to tuck some stray hair underneath my hat. 'But I love it.'

'What're you doing this early?' Joyce fished in her bag for a sou'wester.

'I need to call someone.' I wasn't sure how much to say. Joyce was nice and I was glad to have her for a friend, but I wanted to keep Raymond Glover to myself.

'Well, go on then, but this evening d'you fancy a drink at the Black Lion?'

Should I admit that I'd never gone into a pub before? Much less had a drink since that night I got tipsy on Barney's cider. Joyce was watching me with a twinkle in her eyes.

'Go on,' she said. 'I bet you've never gone drinking. Well, now's the time to have a go…and get to know some people.'

'I don't have the right clothes for an evening out,' I protested, but she took no notice.

'You'll be okay, if I know anything. Go on, be a devil.'

I hesitated at most for three seconds. 'All right. Wait a moment while I make my phone call. Then we can arrange the time to meet.'

The same woman's voice answered. I pressed the button to get my tuppence back.

The Black Lion was packed. Joyce and I forced our way up to the bar and she ordered two gin and oranges. I couldn't wait to find a table and instead took a big gulp of my drink which ended with a coughing fit. Joyce asked the barman for a glass of water.

'Looks as though it's your first proper drink,' she said laughing, handing me the water. 'Let's go and sit down.' She propelled me through the crowd and magically found a table.

I tried the gin and orange again, only this time I was ready. It was quite pleasant, but I didn't realise how what I thought was such a small amount of alcohol (unlike the full glasses of cider I'd drunk when I was with Barney that time) would affect me. I drained my glass far too quickly.

Joyce's eyes darted this way and that. A man whose hair was plastered with hair cream strolled over and asked if he could buy her a drink. Joyce looked at me and I nodded. It was the last I saw of her until the barman called for final drinks.

'Sorry I've been gone ages,' Joyce said, sliding into one of the seats.

The pub had begun to clear and I was feeling tired and more than a little annoyed with Joyce leaving me alone all evening. I felt sick and wanted my bed.

'I'll see you home,' Joyce said, looking contrite, but I told her not to worry – I'd be perfectly all right. She looked doubtful, but when the same man who'd bought her a drink came up and slipped his hand round her waist, she turned to him and smiled.

'Can I give you girls a lift?' he said. 'I've got a car – well, it's a van, actually.'

'Oh, that would be lovely,' Joyce answered before I could speak. 'Kitty?'

I quite wished she hadn't spoken my name but I reluctantly agreed. I didn't particularly want to wander the streets on my own as I had an awful tendency to get lost, and the blackout made it particularly lethal.

The man, whose name was Peter, asked us where we lived.

'So I'll take you home first, Joyce,' he said, and I had to bite back a smile when I noticed her mouth turn down at the corners. 'Then Kitty, as it's on my way.'

His van turned out to be a butcher's van. It reeked of meat and blood. I already felt queasy with the gin and tonic and the stench was so overpowering I felt my stomach heave. Joyce didn't seem to notice.

We dropped Joyce off and she promised we would do it again sometime soon. I nodded, but wasn't at all sure I wanted to go through another evening on my own, watching Joyce have a good time.

Peter knew Mrs Parker's road, and five minutes later he braked outside her door. Some instinct told me to say goodnight and make a fast exit, but before I could grab the handle, Peter had grabbed *me*. Although I struggled it made not a scrap of difference. He clutched a handful of my hair and pulled my head back, then bent over me, and forced my lips apart. The next moment I felt this thing whirl round the inside of my mouth like a piece of raw tripe. The back of my throat filled up with his tongue and I gagged and coughed, partly by a real physical revulsion and partly to dislodge him. But he held on, his other hand now violently rubbing my breast.

I managed to twist from under him and slapped his face so hard his neck snapped right over to the side. He looked at me, his expression one of surprise. Then he chuckled.

'I like a girl who plays hard to get,' he said, his mouth curling. 'You've been wanting me to do that, even though you pretended you didn't.'

I couldn't believe my ears. I'd done absolutely nothing to encourage him.

'You're the last man on earth I'd want to kiss.' I spoke clearly, right into his face. 'Besides...' I gathered courage, 'your breath stinks as much as your disgusting van...and you could fry an egg on that greasy hair of yours. You must have used half a jar of Brylcreem.'

His eyes hardened as I said the words, and his hands tightened on my shoulders.

'You fuckin' prick-teaser.'

A ball of saliva had formed at the left-hand corner of his mouth. It made me feel sick, it was so white and frothy, yet I couldn't take my eyes off it. A shiver of fear pulsed through my body. I should have kept calm...even pretended I liked him...anything to get out of his car.

'You'll wish you'd never—' he started.

'Let me out of here. This minute,' I ordered, but my trembling voice didn't quite match the confidence of the words.

He hesitated and I was sure my heart stopped. Then he leaned across me, trapping me with his arm, and grasped the door handle. He flung the door open, and with his two oversized hands shoved me out on to the pavement where I went sprawling. Then he slammed the door behind me and he and his horrible van roared off into the night.

10

I slunk into Mrs Parker's house, thanking my stars she wasn't there to see me. She would never have let me in looking such a wreck. Luckily, Barney had left the door on the latch as I didn't have a key and hadn't thought to ask him if there was a spare one.

I raced up the stairs and brushed my teeth hard. And then I brushed them again to make sure.

In bed that night I couldn't sleep. Everything kept jumbling over and over in my mind. Had I done anything at all to encourage Peter? But I couldn't think of a thing. What on earth had Joyce seen in him? Should I tell her what had happened? If I did, would she stop being friends with me? I didn't want to upset her. Besides Diana, Joyce was the only friend I'd got unless I counted Barney. Oh, well, at least I had the library tomorrow.

I looked at the clock. A quarter to three. I must get some sleep. I snuggled down and pulled the blanket over me and closed my eyes. The next breath I shot up in bed, heart pumping madly. Five seconds later Barney flung my door open without knocking.

'Kitty, are you awake? Did you hear the air-raid warning?'

'Yes, I heard it and I'm staying right here.'

'No, you're bloody not,' he said as he came over and grabbed me. 'Get dressed! We've got to get to the shelter at once!'

That dread of being buried alive. Perspiration beaded my forehead, and I tried to swallow the lump of fear which had glued to the back of my throat.

'No, I—'

'Don't be a fool. We have to go NOW! Grab a blanket and your bag. That's all. I'll be outside.'

I didn't want to be ordered around by Barney but he was right. Half tumbling out of bed I dragged on my clothes which I slung over the back of the chair every evening, then snatched up my handbag and ran down the stairs.

'C'mon, we've no time to lose.' He grabbed my free hand and we rushed out of the door and along the street to the Underground.

The sour odour of sweating bodies and beer and stale cigarette smoke hit me as I stumbled down the escalator which had either stopped working or the officials had deliberately switched it off, giving me a peculiar feeling it was still moving. The platforms were already heaving with bodies. By the time I'd slanted a few curious looks, Barney had disappeared. Some people seemed perfectly at ease, as though being down in a smelly tunnel was their normal home. They'd staked out an area and arranged pillows and blankets, picnic baskets with cups and plates, toys for the children, clocks – anything they must have thought they would need, trying to make themselves comfortable for the night, determined to ignore however many sirens went off.

Everyone was pushing and elbowing into me as I tried to fight my way through to find Barney. Where had he disappeared to? He was tall so I should have been able to spot him straight away. There didn't seem an inch of space around me and my lungs felt they would burst for want of air. Then a peculiar warm sensation filled my head. My heart seemed to slow right down. I couldn't breathe. I blinked…tried to focus. The next moment people in my vision froze into a yellow mist, until they all slipped into nothingness.

'She's coming round.'

Dimly, I heard a man's voice.

I swallowed a couple of times to moisten my mouth, and ran

my tongue over dry lips. Where was I? Who were all these people?

'Here, drink this.' Somebody bent over me and gently lifted up my head. My vision cleared and I saw a middle-aged woman dressed in a baggy brown skirt and what looked like her husband's jacket. She put a beaker of liquid to my lips and I gratefully took several gulps. Orange tasting, but like nectar to me.

'How do you feel now?' she asked.

'A bit dizzy.' Someone had rolled a coat underneath my head and I lay back. 'What happened?'

'You fainted,' said the same man's voice. No, it wasn't Barney's. This was an educated voice. And strangely familiar.

I tried to struggle up but his hand pressed me back down.

'Just wait a minute or two,' he said. 'Make sure you're all right.'

I lay there feeling light-headed but calmer and felt, rather than saw, him looking down at me.

'I know you.' He leaned over more closely. 'You're the girl who came down from King's Lynn. It's Raymond Glover. We met on the train.'

Of course. Well-educated, well-dressed, well-spoken Raymond Glover. What a coincidence that I'd been trying to reach him.

'I've been wondering how you've been faring,' he said.

This time I managed to sit up. He looked so out of place down here in this damp hole with his pinstripe suit and crisp white shirt, even with its frayed collar.

'Come on, I'm getting you out of here.' He pulled me to my feet with capable hands which I doubted had done any rough work. 'Take my arm.'

'I should tell Barney,' I said. 'He'll be worried.'

'Who's Barney?'

'A wounded soldier where I lodge. He brought me here when the siren went. I have to find him.' My voice rose with anxiety.

'You'll never get through this crowd. I'm sure he'll be there when you get home.'

He crooked his right arm and as I took it the all clear sounded. He smiled at me, and together we battled up the lifeless escalator and out of the Underground.

He shot me into the nearest café.

'I did try to telephone you,' I told him, after he'd ordered coffee.

'You did?' He sounded surprised, but pleased.

'Twice. But I hung up the second time because I thought it was useless asking the same woman to pass on any message when she hadn't bothered the first time. I was hoping you'd answer.'

'When was this?'

I told him the day and that the woman on the other end didn't sound particularly friendly. He went a bit quiet, then frowned.

'Did you say who you were?'

'Yes. But she didn't tell me who *she* was.'

'It was Lilian, my wife.'

'No wonder—' I began.

'Oh, no, she's used to strangers calling. New clients.' He must have noticed the puzzled look on my face. 'Didn't you read my card?'

I had to admit I hadn't bothered to study it when I'd telephoned him. For one thing, it had been difficult enough to make out his name with that curly writing. I ferreted in my handbag and pulled out the little white business card. There it was: *Raymond Glover: Private Detective.*

'I see,' I said, not really seeing at all. 'So if she's used to new clients, as you call them, why didn't she pass on my message?'

He shifted in his chair, not catching my eye. Then he said, 'She's always suspicious of any new woman who telephones asking for my services. Sometimes she accuses me of having an affair with them.' He gave a nervous laugh.

We talked of other things. Raymond, as he asked me to call him, had to work from home as his office had been bombed the year before. He said jobs had almost dried up because people had more on their minds these days than to worry about infidelities, which is what he seemed to specialise in. Besides, most of the men of that age were away fighting. It was becoming harder for him to make ends meet.

I told him how badly I wanted to sing, and I'd read about ENSA but didn't know how to contact them.

He studied me for a few seconds. 'You're not eighteen yet, are you?'

I shook my head. What was the use of telling a private detective a lie?

'I've heard of girls in ENSA as young as fifteen and sixteen,' Raymond said. 'But they weren't singers – they were in some pipe band. I'm not sure what the entry rules are for an individual singer but I'm pretty sure it'll be eighteen – maybe even twenty-one. You'll need your birth certificate, no doubt.'

My face must have fallen because he looked at me curiously. I certainly wasn't going to tell him I'd never seen my birth certificate until recently, and the shock of what it contained.

'First I need to find out how to contact them,' I said. 'Then I'm sure they'll tell me how old I have to be. I'm hoping the library can give me the information.'

'You don't need any library,' he said, his smile showing good strong teeth. 'I'm not Raymond Glover, notorious private detective, for nothing.'

As Raymond had predicted, Barney was back at Mrs Parker's when I eventually arrived home, my head full of ENSA and birth certificates. A young girl had fallen when she'd rushed down the steps, he explained, and he'd stayed to help until an ambulance came. He was a kind man. I bit my lip, sad that I couldn't feel anything special for him.

Raymond had told me to telephone him that evening. I still carried out my plan to go to the library in case I didn't hear from him again, but they couldn't find any address for ENSA. I'd looked in the telephone directory but it wasn't there. If Raymond couldn't help me I was up against a blank wall.

This time when I rang, Raymond answered.

'If you're an entertainer, such as a singer, you're supposed to have some proven experience. Have you any?'

I chewed my lip. Barney was right. Somehow it made me feel all the more determined to get into this ENSA.

'Yes,' I said. 'In King's Lynn. I've sung at the theatre.'

He laughed. 'I said "proven", Kitty. So it's no good telling me porkies.'

'All right, then, I haven't.' I swore softly, disregarding the image of Mum's disapproving face. 'So what happens now?'

'I was expecting that answer,' Raymond said in a most irritating manner. 'I've spoken to a friend of a friend, a Mr Bertwhistle, and he's prepared to give you a try-out. Then if you're any good he'll recommend you for an audition.'

'Will I have to pay anything?'

'It's just for him to hear your voice and see whether you're good enough to arrange an audition. You don't pay anything. If you need singing lessons that's another matter.'

'I wouldn't be able to afford them,' I said.

'Well, just make sure you get through the audition.' Raymond sounded impatient.

'Where do I have to go?'

'It's in his house. I'll give you the address.'

My heart plummeted. Why couldn't it have been in a proper studio? 'Is there a Mrs Bert—?' I began.

'He's perfectly safe, if that's what you're thinking,' Raymond interrupted. 'His wife died at the beginning of the war. Bertwhistle's one of the best, so I'm told.'

I drew in a deep breath. For the first time I became giddy with hope. This Mr Bertwhistle was actually offering me the chance to prove what I said I could do.

'Did he say what I should sing?' I asked, frantically trying to work out what was my best song.

'He didn't say. I think he's happy if you choose.'

'What about "I'll Never Smile Again"?'

'I'm sure that would do very nicely.'

11

Mr Bertwhistle's house in Charlwood Street was a long way from Nosy's but Raymond said there was a bus service and to take an early one in case there were any delays. He handed me the address and said to ask the conductor to put me down at the nearest stop.

'Bertwhistle's slightly deaf,' Raymond said, 'though it doesn't seem to affect his playing. Make sure you knock loudly.'

It was a house like countless others I'd passed by since I'd lived in London. Four storeys high with a basement and a neglected patch of front garden, but it did still have its iron railings. I was surprised as Barney told me Mr Churchill had ordered all iron railings to be removed for the war effort. Everywhere you looked there were spaces and stumps where the railings had been. But I had other things on my mind besides railings.

I looked at the slip of paper again. Yes, this was the right number. I grasped the door knocker, held it for a second, before letting it crash down.

A minute or two passed and just as I was about to bang the knocker again the door swung back. An old man, about as tall as my shoulder, stood outlined against a dark narrow passage.

'Yes?'

'I...um...' I was a little taken aback by his abrupt tone and I wasn't sure who he was. He certainly didn't look like any singing coach. 'I think Mr Bertwhistle's expecting me,' I gathered courage. 'My name is Katherine Bishop.'

'Ah,' he said. 'You must be the young lady my friend mentioned.' I nodded. 'I'm Bertwhistle. Well,' he looked me up and down, 'you'll have to change your name if you want to be a singer. Katherine Bishop sounds like an authoress.'

It was a strange conversation to be having on a doorstep.

'I'm usually known as Kitty,' I said defensively. I thought quickly. My professional name was important. 'And...my father's name was Townsend. Would that do?'

He put his head on one side. 'Kitty Townsend,' he repeated, rolling it over his tongue, trying it out. 'Not quite right,' he said. 'Vera Lynn...Gracie Fields...needs to be something easy to remember. Short and sweet.'

'I'd like to keep to Kitty Townsend,' I said, feeling bold and hoping being obstinate wouldn't annoy him.

He looked at me and nodded. 'All right. Kitty Townsend you shall be,' he said in his odd formal voice, and his face cracked into something resembling a smile. 'Come through, won't you?'

He stood to one side, pressing close to the wall. I edged past him, feeling a little strange with the new surname. I looked at him over my shoulder and pointed to a door.

'Shall I?'

'Please do,' he said.

A quiver ran through me, as though something important was about to happen. I opened the door, not knowing what to expect... and gaped.

The room beyond looked nothing how I'd imagined a real studio would be. Musical instruments littered the floor or were propped up against their cases; brass instruments, looking like golden monsters, were drunkenly set against one wall, one leaning against another; there were flutes and other wooden instruments I didn't know the names of jostling against two sets of drums. A piano stood at one side. How could Mr Bertwhistle make his way through all those instruments? I looked round the room again and spotted a microphone standing a few feet from the piano. My heart went wild with excitement. I was going to be a real singer. Songbooks were slung anywhere in any kind of heap, stacks of them. My breath caught. It wouldn't be an exaggeration to say I'd stepped right into heaven.

'What do you think?' Mr Bertwhistle asked, with the faintest smile.

'Oh, it's wonderful,' I said. My smile couldn't have stretched wider.

'Go on in,' he ordered, 'and take off your coat and hat. Have you got your sheet music?'

My face must have fallen several feet.

'Well, never mind,' the old man said. 'What are you going to sing for me?'

'"I'll Never Smile Again",' I said, watching his expression.

The watery grey eyes sprang into life, then faded. 'Aren't you a bit young for that song?' he asked me.

'I never think it matters what age you are to like a song,' I said, hoping he wouldn't think me rude. 'Or sing it.' He lifted a grey eyebrow and gave another hint of a smile. 'Anyway, it's the only one I've prepared.'

'Luckily for you, young lady, I think I've got the music here somewhere.'

He disappeared under a mound of papers. After what seemed like ages he emerged, triumphantly waving a songbook.

'Right' he said, plopping down on the piano stool. 'Stand over there.' He stretched out his arm and waggled his fingers towards a spot on his left, near the microphone. 'You should find it's the right key. Just listen to the introduction, then off you go.'

All my bravado blew away and I felt suddenly shy. I'd only ever sung at school when we'd put on a concert, or around the house when Dad wasn't there, trying to harmonise with the singers on Mum's gramophone. But I wasn't going to tell Mr Bertwhistle that.

I stood where he'd asked. Was I supposed to use the microphone?

'Do you want me to use the microphone?' I asked, praying he would say yes. In my nervous state I thought it might make me sound more professional – or at least louder.

'Not at the moment,' he said. 'I want to hear your natural voice first. Maybe later. Not today.' His short stubby fingers poised a few seconds over the keys. He glanced over to me and played a few notes, then nodded for me to come in.

The only good thing about my performance was that I remembered all the words. Nerves made my voice thin and breathy, and once or twice I noticed him looking up at me. I made myself get through to the end but it was useless. He'd never recommend me to anyone in ENSA. I'd ruined my chances. All my dreams would remain just that. Tears stung the back of my eyes, and my voice wobbled even more.

'I'm sorry,' I said, when the last note feebly died away. I brushed a tear from my cheek, hoping he wouldn't notice. 'I can sing it much better than that. I don't know what's the matter with me today.'

'Sing it exactly the same,' he said, surprisingly, 'but with the microphone.' He glared at me. 'Ever used one?'

'Yes,' I lied.

'Good. Don't think about your voice – just think about the words. Right. When you're ready.'

I sang it again, doing my best to make my voice behave how I wanted it to. It was even worse the second time. Either I was too close to the microphone and my voice sounded unnaturally loud and distorted, or I stood too far away and any soldier more than ten feet away would have been hard-pressed to hear me. Tears of frustration poured down my cheeks, but this time I didn't bother to wipe them away. My voice cracked once on the repeat but out of sheer terror I kept going. And Mr Bertwhistle showed no sign of stopping me.

At the end he gave a little flourish of notes and a final chord.

I just stood there, red-faced, miserable, wishing the ground would swallow me up. I turned to pick up my coat.

'Where are you going, young lady?'

'Home. It's obvious I'll never be a singer.'

'That's what you think. *I* think different,' he said.

'But—'

'No buts, Kitty. You'll have them bawling their eyes out.'

I looked at him sharply. Was he being sarcastic? But he looked perfectly serious. Did it mean he thought I was all right? That I was good enough to sing to the troops?

'You've never used a microphone before, have you?' he demanded, his eyes flashing. 'The truth now.'

There was no point in pretending. I shook my head.

'We're going to get on famously,' he told me, 'so long as you speak the truth. And that isn't just inside these four walls. It's a rule for life. Nothing good ever came of lies.'

That all sounded very nice and proper but Mr Bertwhistle was wrapped up in his world of music. It was easy for him. He'd probably had two normal parents who gave him the same name, and he'd chosen a career to earn a living doing something he loved.

'And you're going to practise,' he went on, 'every day, with or without the microphone, to build up your confidence. No matter how long it takes. When I decide you're ready – and not before time – I'll introduce you to a friend of mine in ENSA. She'll look after you.' He looked at me sternly. 'Think you can do it?'

Heart thudding in my ears, I nodded. I left my coat where it was and looked across at him. He was smiling.

'And you're coming to see me twice a week for lessons.'

I opened my mouth to protest that I had no money to pay him, but as if he knew what I was about to say he waved his hand.

'Now what else are you going to sing for me?'

12

Rome

Ruggero

'I want the ringleader found and arrested immediately!' Benito Mussolini roared. 'And everyone associated with him.' He flung down the papers that had been delivered from Hitler's private office and Ruggero had translated in an untidy heap on his desk.

Really, the man was behaving just like his hysterical German idol. But Ruggero couldn't stop the hairs rising at the back of his neck. He couldn't begin to imagine Mussolini's outrage if he only knew the man he was looking for was standing right opposite him. Ruggero shifted the weight off one of his feet which was beginning to rub in the new boots. Didn't Mussolini realise how much his countrymen hated Hitler? That there was bound to be some resistance? The man was completely out of touch with his people.

Ruggero tracked *Il Duce* as he stormed over to his office window, his heavy jaw tight with fury. In truth, Mussolini's reaction was nothing less than Ruggero had expected, but all the same he wanted to get this over with and get the hell out before Italy's leader asked any awkward questions.

'All the key people are on the case, sir,' Ruggero replied, forcing his tone to sound urgent. 'Hitler's people, too. Naturally, it's been put on high alert.'

'What exactly has been done so far? I want details. Now!'

'Patrols are at all the borders and airports. All trains are being searched. Everyone possible will be questioned. They'll be going through all the usual procedures, sir.'

'It's not enough,' Mussolini barked, his back still to Ruggero. He continued to look out of the window, though Ruggero doubted he was seeing anything, his temper was so high. Abruptly, Mussolini swung round. 'This should never have been allowed to happen.' His hard eyes blazed and he stamped his boot hard down on the wooden floor. 'What were the fucking bodyguards doing?' Before Ruggero could open his mouth Mussolini shouted, 'Picking their fucking noses, that's what.'

'I'm sure what happened could never have been anticipated.'

'Really?' Mussolini's tone was now ominously quiet. 'You suppose no one had ever thought what a coup it would be to get Hitler and me in one blow?' His voice rose again at the word "Hitler". 'I was made to look a perfect dolt in front of him. I doubt he'll ever show his face in Italy again with our security so lax. Thank God the bullet only scraped his bodyguard's arm or I'd never hear the last of it.'

Ruggero lowered his gaze, not in deference, but to hide the gleam of triumph in his eyes that *Il Duce* must now realise he was not as popular as he had thought.

When Ruggero had discovered how far Mussolini was prepared to go for his imperialistic aims, he'd been sickened by the level of atrocities. His first instinct had been to resign immediately. But he couldn't think of an excuse which would satisfy Mussolini. Why would he be giving up a position that dozens of Italians would give their fascist-raising arm for? And if he did give Mussolini a plausible excuse, his own life and that of his family would be kept under surveillance. He'd never be free. Never be able to do some good for his beloved country. But the more he knew what was in Mussolini's mind and what his plans were, the more he needed to find an opportunity to filter it through to the Allies. The only real risk he'd taken so far was to copy any document he thought might be useful to them. But if he delayed, the information would be useless. And if he was caught, he knew without any doubt he'd be executed.

His heart plummeted as Mussolini's rage gave full force. The last time anything like this had happened, the top-ranking officers had been executed – without a proper trial. Even though Mussolini was not yet as maniacal as Hitler, Ruggero knew that Hitler would insist his Italian counterpart follow the same rules he was implementing with any Germans involved. Ruggero knew several of Hitler's bodyguards, two or three of whom, he suspected, felt the same way as he did about their leader, but had families and like their Italian counterparts dare not say anything. However, it was Piero Lavori he was most worried about.

'We've arrested three of them,' Mussolini smirked. 'Some fucking partisans, dressed up as fucking Nazis, no less. And with a little encouragement one of them said it's one of the bodyguards who's involved. Refused to give a name. I'm not convinced. There's someone else – someone far more important at the bottom of it. Maybe more than one.'

They must have tortured the poor bastard, whoever he was, for him to have told his interrogators about bodyguards, as that would surely lead to Piero's demise. Ruggero's heart sank further.

'It may not have been anything to do with the bodyguards,' Ruggero said, his expression and voice as neutral as he could make it. 'We shouldn't jump to conclusions. There's sure to be others involved and we could miss them if we only focus on the bodyguards.'

'You may be right.' Mussolini's eyes seemed to slice through Ruggero's brain. 'Most of them are thick as planks. But they've been closely vetted for their loyalty – by me – though I've always had reservations about Lavori. And he's not to be found anywhere.' He snapped his eyes on Ruggero's again. 'Is he a Jew boy?'

'No idea, sir,' Ruggero said, his heart thumping. This was getting close. 'We're too busy to discuss our private lives. But

I doubt it. It would be too dangerous working so close to you. You'd have found out immediately.'

He hoped he had appealed to Mussolini's ego.

'Mmm.' Mussolini stroked his jaw thoughtfully. 'If he is, Hitler will have no compunction in forcing me to arrange his execution. No, it's someone more clever than Lavori. Someone more cunning, more subtle, who's planned this. Any idea who it might be?'

'None, sir.'

'You need to think, Andreotti. That's why you work for me. Advise me.' Mussolini's voice dripped with sarcasm.

Ruggero flushed, but he was not going to be intimidated.

'You've said yourself I'm too young to be one of your advisers, sir. Besides,' Ruggero desperately tried to play for time, 'I have a stack of reports to go through and translate. I must keep on top of them. That's where I'm more valuable to you.'

'Not in this case,' Mussolini snapped. 'Not when I know what a *close* friend you are to Lavori.'

Ruggero felt his stomach lurch on his friend's behalf. He shrugged. 'Not more than any of the others, sir.'

'That's not what I've heard.' Mussolini gave him a penetrating gaze.

Ruggero longed to shift his position but he forced himself to stand quietly.

'Well?'

'Yes, of course, sir. I'll do my best.'

'Well, I'm sure Lavori will enlighten me with a little persuasion. I want him found. *Pronto.* I've spoken to the other guards. They know what to do.' He glared at Ruggero. 'Do you hear me?'

'Yes, sir.'

'And if I find you have the *slightest* knowledge of this murderous attempt, whether you've condoned it or not, I don't envy you what lies in store.' Mussolini's mouth twisted. 'But I'll tell you this – you'll never be the same man again.'

With all the concentration he could muster, Ruggero forced himself to ignore the prickle of fear running over his scalp. He barely managed to say, 'You won't need to worry about that, sir.'

'Let's hope you're right, for *your* sake.' Mussolini's mood suddenly altered. He put his hand on Ruggero's shoulder. 'You still lack experience, Andreotti, but you're an astute man all the same. I'm counting on you.'

PART II

ENSA

13

Kitty

I'd never worked so hard as I did for Mr Bertwhistle. True to his word he gave me a lesson twice a week.

I'd sing the whole song and he wouldn't normally stop me, but when I finished he'd take it apart line by line, even word by word.

'Your breathing's all wrong,' he'd say, and we'd go into breathing exercises.

And another time, 'Your posture is bad. You're stooping. It's probably because you're tall and didn't want to stand out from your friends at school. But for a singer, creating space in the upper body is essential and you can't do that if you're not standing properly.'

Then I'd have to hang my head low so it was almost touching the floor and come up very very slowly, pulling back my shoulders but still allowing them to relax.

Or, 'When you sing a high note, put your head down, rather than up. Looking up constricts the throat.'

So I'd put my head down.

'Not that low. And relax your jaw. Now waggle your jaw up and down, making a ya-ya sound – keep it really loose.'

I would sigh as I tried to do all the things he said simultaneously.

'It's like driving a car,' he said. 'There are so many things to do at the same time and you think you'll never get the hang of it… when suddenly you do it without thinking. Same with singing.'

As I couldn't drive, his comparison didn't really help.

'You need to get into good habits,' Mr Bertwhistle went on, tenderly fingering some notes as a kind of background to his instructions. 'It will make a tremendous difference to your breath. You won't run out at the crucial moment. And it will add richness and depth. But you must practise every day. Even with no piano. Do the scales and exercises. Take your voice seriously. It's got the potential for being absolutely captivating, but you need to work on it.'

Absolutely captivating. I hugged the compliment to myself.

After the third lesson I said, 'I should pay you but I can't afford it.'

'I wouldn't dream of taking any money from you, Kitty.' A shadow passed across his face. 'I had a daughter,' he said softly. 'Lily. She was about your age. Such a lovely girl.'

That hateful word "had". He looked at me with such sadness I wanted to put my arms round him and give him a hug.

'She could sing too. And compose. She was killed in the Blitz. On her way to the hospital. She was a nurse there.' He blew his nose loudly. 'You remind me of her. So don't speak of payment again,' he added gruffly. 'It cheers me up to see you, and hear you sing. I look forward to it. It makes my day.'

Poor Mr Bertwhistle. I was determined not to let him down.

It was already April and Mr Bertwhistle finally had something to tell me.

'Jennifer Long is willing to see you.' He must have seen my puzzled expression because he added, 'She's in charge of new recruits in ENSA. Here, I'll write down her address and you can go and see her. I told her you'd be there at noon tomorrow.'

I closed my eyes for a few seconds. Could it really be true that I was on my way to living my dream?

*

Jennifer Long lived in Kensington – what Mr Bertwhistle called the posh part of London. It was a large detached house in a street which looked untouched by war damage. Jennifer Long's had a deep recessed porch with iron steps leading to the basement. I thought she must be terribly wealthy and for a minute I wondered what on earth I was doing. I didn't belong here. Then I told myself not to be so silly. If I lost this chance I'd never forgive myself.

I pressed the bell with "J. Long" against it and heard running footsteps. Scarlet nails appeared round the edge of the heavy door and I heard her give a grunt with the exertion. Finally, the door opened and Jennifer Long stood there.

I'd never seen a woman like her. And dressed in such a way. Everything about her was tiny: small nose, mouth which looked like a bud about to open, and even her eyes, the colour of conkers, were small, though she'd outlined them with some sort of brown pencil. Tiny marks like kitten's whiskers feathered the corners. The only thing she had an excess of was her hair. It was long and thick, and what Mum called strawberry-blonde, tumbling to her shoulders. Her slight body was drowned in a man's white shirt which she wore over a pair of grey trousers. I'd never seen a woman in King's Lynn wearing trousers so I couldn't stop staring. She gripped a cigarette between a red-tipped finger and thumb.

We looked at one another. I lowered my gaze, my heart sinking. I would never be able to sing to someone who scared me so much. Why didn't I just drop the idea and find another waitress job? Then to my relief she smiled.

'You must be Kitty. Come on in.'

I followed her up what seemed like a dozen flights of stairs.

'I'm at the top,' she said, looking over her shoulder at me. 'They had the devil of a job getting the piano up these stairs.'

She flung open a door and ushered me in.

Were all musicians so untidy?

The room was even more disorganised than Mr Bertwhistle's.

For a few seconds I actually thought it had been hit by a bomb. Pictures leaned drunkenly against walls, books and newspapers were piled on every conceivable surface, dirty cups and plates were stacked on a dresser, too exhausted to find their way into the kitchen, and the room stank of smoke.

'Sorry about the mess,' Miss Long said apologetically. She gave a half-hearted attempt to push some sheets of music on one side of what had probably been built as a coffee table but no longer served that purpose.

'The piano's in another room,' Miss Long laughed as she saw my expression. 'Dear girl, did you really think I would make you sing in here?'

I didn't know whether she was teasing me or if she was serious, so I just smiled.

'Here, let me take your coat,' she said, and threw it over the back of a chair.

The next room was much smaller and was as tidy as the first one wasn't. In one corner the upright piano gleamed like ebony.

'Let's get started straight away,' she said, sitting down on the stool. 'What would you like to sing?'

I thought I'd play safe. '"Dancing With Tears In My Eyes",' I said.

'Oh no, not that,' she said. 'Far too dismal. The men need to be cheered up, not ready to commit suicide.'

I felt my cheeks burn. Of course. How could I have been so thoughtless?

'I'd like you to sing something in a lower tone. Do you know "The Very Thought of You"?' She flicked over the pages of her music book, not bothering to wait for an answer. 'Ah, here it is.' She drew in a breath and let her shoulders fall.

'I'll try.'

Miss Long gave me a few chords but when I opened my mouth, to my horror, I hit the wrong note. I was way too high. She tutted and sang the first bar, and when she sang I could hardly breathe. There was nothing tiny about her voice – it was magnificent: warm, rich, mellow.

That's how I want to sing.

She glanced at me and seemed to take delight in my astonishment.

'Now, do you think you can do it?'

This time was better but not much.

'Mr Bertwhistle highly recommended you.' She sounded disappointed. She couldn't have been more disappointed than I was.

'He liked my songs,' I said defensively, heart pounding against my ribs. 'I like songs that tell a story, even if they're sad.'

'Well, you'd better sing something you're more familiar with,' she said. 'What else do you know really well?'

Judy Garland. I knew her song back to front but I'd never had any accompaniment. Just so long as I reached that top note without wavering.

'I'd like to sing "Somewhere Over The Rainbow." Would that be all right?'

Miss Long nodded. 'I'll have to play it by ear.' She picked out the introduction.

I drew in an almighty breath in preparation for that second note. She stopped me after the first phrase.

'Too much breath,' she said sharply. 'Let it all out. You don't need to start like that or you'll run out. And don't bellow.'

She came over to me and tilted me forward, pressing my head down to my chin.

'It's not an easy song to sing,' she said, and though I couldn't see her face, by her tone she was frowning. 'But that's all the more reason to sing it with depth – with feeling. *Feel* the dream of what lies over the rainbow.'

I began again, even more nervous than before.

'Too quiet,' she snapped, her hands cupping her ears. 'You'll have them asleep in no time.' She took her hands away from the piano and I caught her brown gaze. She seemed to be weighing me up.

'Tom Bertwhistle says you're eighteen,' she said. 'Is that right?'

From someone so slight in frame, the question was like the yap of a small dog. How could her singing voice be so different?

'Yes,' I said, my eyes not wavering from hers.

'Again.' She gave me my note.

This time she didn't stop me. I felt I had given it everything I could. When I'd finished that last high note I just stood there, my eyes not leaving her face.

'We're short of singers,' she said finally. 'We've got plenty of comedy acts and dancers, and male singers, but it's women our boys want to see. To remind them of the girlfriends and wives they've left behind.' Her eyes flicked over me. I held my breath. 'Very well. But I'll need to see your birth certificate.'

Tears sprang to my eyes. It was no use. Everything was against me whatever I tried to do. I might as well tell her the truth.

'I'm not *quite* eighteen,' I said. 'But I will be at the end of the year. Oh, *please* Miss Long, don't make me wait. I'll be exactly the same person I am now.'

I saw Miss Long's mouth curve in amusement. She seemed to think for a few moments, then said: 'Well, perhaps we'll overlook it this once. I'll draw up the contract. You can collect it next Tuesday. But you need a few more lessons. Probably best to get Hal to help you. He's our pianist and coach.' She came across the room and stood in front of me, her hands stretching up to my shoulders. She looked me up and down. 'You have a voice, my dear. It just needs a bit of polishing. But it's there.'

I left Miss Long's house on clouds.

I went to collect the contract the following Tuesday, as Miss Long had requested. There was no answer. I stood for ages not knowing what to do, ringing the bell every few seconds and beginning to feel foolish. Just as I turned to leave a lean man with a shock of shiny brown hair opened the door. He was maybe in his thirties, tall, his horn-rimmed glasses slipping down his nose.

'Are you Kitty?'

'Yes. I'm expecting to see Miss Long.'

'Sorry, I was in the garden and didn't hear you. Jennifer's given me an envelope for you.' He held out a brown envelope and I noticed how long and slender his fingers were. So Miss Long hadn't forgotten.

'Are you joining us?' he asked.

I presumed he meant joining ENSA. I nodded. I didn't feel like making conversation. I just wanted to sign the contract.

'I'm Henry,' he said. 'But call me Hal. Everyone does.'

He voice sounded like an American film star.

'All right, Hal. Pleased to meet you.' A little embarrassed from his green-eyed gaze, I said goodbye and made for what I now called home.

14

I caught the bus to Miss Long's street again the following morning. *This is going to change my life.* My heart beat furiously as I rang her bell. The thought made me smile. I'd felt the same when Joyce turned me into a blonde. Again, Hal came to the door.

'You've signed it then,' he said. 'I'll take it. Jennifer's out.'

Oh, how I envied the easy way Hal called Miss Long "Jennifer".

'I had some questions to ask her,' I said, disappointed not to see her.

'You can come in if you like,' Hal said. 'I can probably answer most things.'

His room was the exact opposite of Miss Long's. Tidy, clean, organized. He, too, had a piano, though a shabby one compared to the one upstairs.

'Do you sing, too?' I asked him, as I sat on one of the sofas.

'A bit,' he grinned, and I liked the way his eyes crinkled. 'I compose a bit, as well.' He ran his hand through his thatch of shiny hair.

A composer. It sounded very grand. I looked at him with more interest. His long legs curled round one of the dining-room chairs as he leaned forward, pulling me into his world. Or at least that's how it felt to me.

'I have to say, you look very young,' he said. 'You don't look any more than about fifteen.'

'I'm almost eight—'

I stopped myself in time but he laughed.

'I think I've caught you out,' he said, green eyes twinkling, and at that moment I knew this man would always be on my side. 'Well, Kitty, what is it that you want to know?'

'The main thing is, when will I start? And where is the first place I'll be sent? And how many in the group? And—'

'Enough!' Hal put the flat of his hand in the air, but his smile told me he was only teasing. 'I can't tell you anything definite. Jennifer has the details. But be prepared – we'll probably be going abroad next month.'

Abroad. I'd never dreamed…well, people like Vera Lynn went abroad but I didn't think they'd let me do that without first getting some home experience.

'Hope you're pale with excitement and not shock,' Hal grinned, 'but in any case, I'll go and make a cup of tea.'

'That should calm you down,' he said, a few minutes later, noticing my hand shake with excitement as I took the cup from him.

We turned as we heard the front door open.

'Are you around, Hal?' Miss Long's voice sang out.

'I've got Miss Kitty with me,' Hal said, as she appeared at his door.

'Have you brought me the contract?' Miss Long threw me a glance and a nod.

I handed her the envelope and she cast her eyes over the first page, then flipped it over.

'It looks okay,' she said, after such a long pause I thought she was going to find some problem. 'We're leaving for the Middle East three weeks Friday. Can you be ready?'

The tea definitely didn't have the power to keep me calm when I heard those words.

'Whereabouts in the Middle East?' I had pictures of belly dancers and camels in my head.

'Security won't let us say. I shouldn't be telling you this much.'

Miss Long regarded me sternly. 'But you might like to look at your school atlas. Acquaint yourself with the area – which is huge.'

My atlas was in my bedroom in Bonham.

'You'd better inform your parents,' Miss Long went on. 'You could be gone several months – even as long as a year. But bear in mind that an ENSA contract is only good for one particular tour.' She gave me a hard stare. 'Do you foresee any problems?'

'No,' I said, too quickly. A year. Oh, how marvellous. A real adventure. My life was just about to start.

She gave me another sharp look. 'If you do, let me know immediately. You'll need a current passport. And because you're underage your parents will have to give their consent. In fact,' she handed the envelope back to me, 'can you ask them to sign at the bottom, underneath your signature?'

I nodded, hoping it wouldn't be too difficult to obtain a passport. No, the thing blocking my trip would be Dad. He would never sign.

15

Nothing and nobody was going to stop me from going abroad with ENSA. But how could I go? I didn't have a passport. If only I could persuade Mum...

I telephoned her.

'Where abroad?' she asked, her voice faint.

'Somewhere in the Middle East. They're not allowed to tell us and we're not allowed to say, even if we knew...which we don't,' I finished lamely.

'I'd like to hear more about who you're going with,' my mother said firmly. 'Who's in charge?'

'Miss Long. There are ten of us. Dancers and singers and an acrobat and a comedian. And Hal, the pianist. I'll be perfectly safe, Mum. Miss Long is a dragon even though she hardly comes up to my shoulder. She won't let any harm come to me.'

'I'll write to her first,' Mum said. 'There's time for her to write back. I would need reassurance. There are several questions I want satisfactory answers to. If all is as I would expect, I won't stand in your way as you seem to be set on going. But I'll be worried sick until you come safely home again.'

'I haven't even gone yet!' I tried to laugh. 'Will you telephone me as soon as you hear from her?'

'Call for you, Kitty,' Barney shouted up the stairs.

'Coming.' I flew down and grabbed the receiver.

'Kitty?'

I recognised her voice immediately. 'Yes, Miss Long.'

'I've heard from your mother. She's given her permission for you to join the troupe when we go abroad.'

'Oh, Miss Long...' I didn't know what to say. I felt strange. Out of my depth. Alone. But I was so excited it didn't matter. I was finally going to do my bit. And now I wouldn't have any trouble asking Mum to sign for my passport.

'You'll need to know what to pack,' she said, 'and you'll also need some inoculations so you'll have to see the doctor.'

I hadn't thought of this. One thing I hated was needles. But even a needle wouldn't have the power to stand in my way.

'It will be warm,' she went on, 'so I suggest some light daytime clothing and thicker cardigans and jackets – it gets very cold at night. But you'll be given a proper list of things to pack.'

How could I tell her I didn't have the money to buy new things?

'Will that present a problem?' she said, after a silence where I couldn't think of what to say. 'Kitty? Are you there?'

'No, there won't be a problem.' The lie left my lips easily but I had no idea how I'd fulfil any list.

'Good,' she said. 'I'll see you on Wednesday at the Theatre Royal, Drury Lane, for a rehearsal, and we'll run through everything then.'

'What time shall I come?'

'Be there at half-past ten.'

Where could I get any summer clothes? The windows of the London department stores displayed the new summer season and I'd often stop and stare, wishing more than anything that I could buy just one lovely dress. But clothes, like everything, were becoming more and more expensive and there were rumours that material was next on the list to be rationed. Then I had a brainwave. Joyce. She was about the same size as me. I hadn't seen her since that awful night at the pub and it was time for me to get my roots touched up anyway.

I waited outside the shop at six o'clock that evening, and finally she came out, swinging her shoulder bag.

'Joyce,' I said, smiling at her.

'Oh, it's you, Kitty. Long time, no see.'

She sounded a tiny bit sarcastic but I decided to take no notice.

'Joyce, can we go somewhere…have a cup of tea or something?'

'Sounds mysterious.' Joyce's eyes lit up. 'Who is he?'

I shook my head. 'It's not a man. I just want to ask you something.'

The nearest place was a seedy café opposite. It was grim inside – dark and none too clean. I thought of Annie's Tea Rooms. No wonder it was so popular with its spotless tables and home-made cakes. This place was horrible. I tried to drink the cup of grey-coloured oily tea without retching.

'Come on, then. Tell me.'

'Oh, Joyce, guess what?' My face broke into a grin. I couldn't help it. 'I'm going abroad.'

Joyce's mouth dropped open. 'You're kidding.'

'I'm not. I'm joining ENSA.'

'What's ENSA?'

I felt rather smug that I knew about something Joyce didn't, for a change.

'It stands for Entertainment…' I couldn't for the life of me remember what the initials stood for. 'Well, anyway, it's entertaining our troops. They go all over England and abroad.'

She stared at me. 'Aren't you a bit young to be going abroad on your own?'

'I shan't be on my own. Mother Hen in the shape of Miss Long looks after everyone.'

'I see.' She didn't look as though she did see. 'Whereabouts are you going?'

'They won't tell us. It's a security thing.' I looked straight at her. 'Joyce, promise you won't say anything if I tell you where I *think* it'll be.' Joyce nodded. 'No,' I said firmly, 'say "promise".'

'I don't know why it's such a secret.' Joyce sounded a bit sulky.

'Because "loose talk costs lives",' I reminded her. She was silent. 'Joyce?'

'All right, I promise.'

'I only *think* this, mind you, so I'm not giving anything away, but it might be Egypt. I heard on the wireless yesterday that the British found out the Germans were getting ready to invade it.' My heart thrilled with fear. 'And where's the most likely place?'

Joyce shook her head. Considering she was older than me, she didn't seem to know much about the world.

'If I'm right, it'll be Cairo,' I said.

'Where's that?'

'It's a city on the edge of the desert. Where the pyramids are,' I explained.

As I told her the little I'd learned, my pulse raced. I'd forgotten about the pyramids until this minute. We'd talked about them in Bible Study and I remembered at the time thinking how wonderful it must be to actually see them instead of peering at the fuzzy black and white photographs. But Joyce was fiddling in her handbag and I realised she'd lost interest.

'I'll be singing to the troops,' I said.

Joyce's head shot up. Ah, now I had her attention.

Her eyes widened. 'Oh, Kitty. All those men. Can I go with you as your hairdresser?' She giggled.

'I wish you could.' I laughed too, then suddenly had a thought. 'Actually, that's not a bad idea.'

'Are you serious?'

'Would you really come?'

'Course I would,' Joyce said, agog. 'Your roots need touching up now, and they will again in a few weeks. How long are you going to be away?'

'I'm not sure. Miss Long said a few months, but she said it could be up to a year.'

'Blimey. Well, there you are, then. They won't want you looking awful for a whole year.' She caught my eye and winked. 'And the other women will need their hair doing too. Oh, Kitty, please put in a word for me.'

'How old are you?'

'Twenty-one.'

'So you won't need your parents' consent.'

'I wouldn't anyway as I don't have any parents. They died two years ago in a car crash.' Joyce regarded me steadily. 'It's just me.'

'How terrible for you.' I laid my hand on her arm. Poor Joyce. This would be a perfect opportunity for her to have some fun. 'Yes, of course I'll speak to Miss Long. The other thing is, do you have a passport?'

'Not on me,' she laughed, 'but I'll make bloody sure I get one.'

We arranged to go to the passport office together.

Part of me was delighted that Joyce wanted to go with me and I'd have a ready-made friend, as so far I only knew Hal and Miss Long, and I doubted I would ever feel completely comfortable in that formidable lady's company. To have a girlfriend would be wonderful. But the other part of me – the horrible part – wished I hadn't mentioned it to Joyce, and that I was embarking upon this adventure on my own. I tried to weigh up the pros and cons and decided that Joyce won, hands down.

16

I was glad I'd encouraged Joyce to apply to ENSA. Even if Miss Long didn't think she'd be suitable, Joyce was wonderful at getting the two of us fitted out with lighter clothes and shoes, all from her customers who passed things on to her when they bought new ones. She also let me in the hair salon after the stylists had gone home to cover up my roots.

I told Miss Long about Joyce at our next rehearsal.

'Miss Long, have we got a wardrobe mistress, and someone to do hair and make-up coming with us?'

'Why do you ask, child?'

'I have a friend who's a hairdresser and she said she would love to come if you didn't already have someone.'

'Naturally we do, but Irene who I thought would jump at it prefers not to be sent abroad. She has children, so I suppose it's more difficult with her husband in the forces.' Her brown gaze fell on me. 'Who is this friend of yours?'

'Her name's Joyce. I met her when I'd only been in London a few days.' I decided not to say she was still an apprentice. She was on her last year, after all. It wouldn't be long before she was qualified. 'She's a marvellous hairdresser.'

'Hmm.' Miss Long fiddled with her own strawberry-blonde locks. 'I could do with a trim myself.'

'I'm sure she'd be pleased to do it,' I said, hopefully.

'Maybe I'll let her do Grace's hair and see how she does.'

How rotten. Grace, one of the dancers, had the thinnest, frizziest hair which stubbornly went its own way. It never looked as though it had seen a hairbrush, let alone the inside of a hairdresser's. But Miss Long would never allow Joyce loose on her own locks until she'd seen and approved Joyce's handiwork on someone else.

'Shall I arrange it?' I asked eagerly.

'We'll see,' she said. 'Let me talk to this Joyce first.'

At twenty-past six the following evening we were both outside Miss Long's building. Joyce was almost hopping up and down with excitement. I looked at her and felt mean that I wished she wasn't wearing quite so much jewellery, quite such large earrings, and quite so much red lipstick. But that was Joyce. I just hoped Miss Long would see her for what she was – a generous girl who loved having a laugh, who was not afraid to work hard and who would prove herself a skilled hairdresser. Maybe not being qualified quite yet would save ENSA money.

It was a cool April evening and we sat round the fire as Miss Long snapped out one question after another. Joyce answered really well and Miss Long seemed impressed. That was, until Joyce said, 'Would you like me to do something with *your* hair, Miss Long?'

It was the way Joyce said it. And her expression. As though she couldn't wait to get her hands on such an unsightly head of hair. I hid a smile. Joyce wasn't going to be intimidated by Miss Long or anyone.

Miss Long hesitated. Then she gave a little nod to herself, her lips pulled together in a decision. 'No, not me,' she said. 'But you might like to do something with Kitty's. Get rid of that awful bleached blonde. By her roots that were all too obvious the other day, she's a brunette,' she gazed hard at me as though I was someone she'd never seen before. Then she turned back to Joyce. 'That would far better suit her natural colouring. Really, I don't know what her mother could have been thinking to allow her to ruin it.'

I didn't know where to look. Nor, I think, did Joyce. We didn't dare catch one another's eyes. I coughed into my hand to smother a nervous giggle and heard Joyce say:

'Good idea. I'd be delighted to work on Kitty's hair. Mind you, I think it's a lovely colour. Blonde is all the rage, what with all the glamorous film stars—'

'Yes, yes, I know,' Miss Long interrupted. 'But see what you can do. We already have one blonde singer in the troupe and I don't think she'd appreciate being upstaged by a younger and prettier girl.'

For some reason I blushed.

'By the way, we're six women in the group and four men,' she went on. 'Eleven with you, which should keep you busy. That is,' she gave Joyce a stern look, 'if I find you suitable.'

She reached for her handbag which stood beside her chair and took out a gold cigarette lighter and a small flat box. She flipped the lid open and took out what looked like a black cigarette, then lit it. When she was satisfied it had taken she leaned back in her chair and inhaled. No one spoke. The room was silent except for the crackle of the fire. I knew Joyce was as much on edge as I was. Miss Long formed her lips into an O and made a breathy noise from the back of her throat, as though she was puffing air on to a pair of spectacles to clean them. Then she lazily blew the smoke out into a perfect circle. Another ring followed which she somehow sent through the centre of the first one. Joyce and I watched, fascinated.

'Can you cut men's hair, too?' she finally spoke.

'Oh, yes,' Joyce said eagerly, 'they're easy.'

'Mmm.' Miss Long took another drag. 'Let's see what you manage to do with Kitty and I'll make a decision. In the meantime, I would suggest you arrange for a passport if you don't already have one.'

'What will my wages be...that is, if you take me on, Miss Long?' Joyce added hastily.

I felt myself holding my breath. Trust Joyce. Even I hadn't been told.

'The same as everyone,' Jennifer Long said. 'Ten pounds a week.'

Our jaws dropped simultaneously. *Ten pounds.* That was a fortune.

'Now, if that's all…' Miss Long rose from her chair.

We were dismissed.

'Ten pounds!' Joyce squeaked when we were out of earshot. 'I barely earn that in a month. I'm definitely up for Egypt, or anywhere else they care to send me.' She looked at me. 'What's the matter, Kitty? You've gone a bit quiet.'

'I'm so cross,' I said. 'I love my hair.'

'She's certainly a dragon,' Joyce said, grinning, 'though a pretty one. Good job you'll have me around. You'll need me for a bit of light relief.' She grabbed hold of my arm. 'Come on. We're going back to the salon.'

'I'm not letting you dye my hair back again.'

''Fraid that's exactly what I'm going to do,' she said, stealing a sly glance at my hair. 'It's the only way I'll have any chance of getting the job…and I'm not giving up ten pounds a week without a fight.'

Two and a half hours later we emerged. I was back to very dark, almost black, close to my natural colour. It was strange after the weeks of being as blonde as Sally Gray, but when Joyce had set it, dried it and combed it out I quite liked it after all. She'd cut a few inches off and parted it in the middle so it fell dramatically on each side of my face.

'With your full mouth and dark blue eyes you look just like Hedy Lamarr,' she said admiringly.

She'd touched up her own mousy hair with golden brown, but because it was so late and everyone had gone home, there was no one around to cut it. She normally wore it in a victory roll, and had an answer ready if Miss Long asked why she hadn't altered her own hairstyle.

'I'll tell her that once it's done it's out of the way and I can concentrate on everyone else and make *them* look glamorous.'

We hung on to one another, laughing at her cheek.

'So when are you going away?' Barney asked me that evening when Joyce and I had gone our separate ways.

I felt guilty as I hadn't mentioned any of this until I was positive I was going.

'Week after next.'

'As soon as that?' A look of disappointment crossed his face. 'I was hoping—'

'I think I'll skip supper and go to bed,' I cut in before he could say something more. 'It's been a long day with one thing and another, and I'm tired out.'

Upstairs I lifted my suitcase down from the top of the wardrobe, knelt on the floor and opened the lid. Miss Long said for us not to take much as we would have to lug it ourselves to various venues, as she called them. Joyce had given me a sly glance at that. She was sure she'd be coming with us. Miss Long said sometimes we'd only be one or two nights at each place so there was a lot of travelling about. I'd spent the previous day washing and ironing all the clothes Joyce had given me, and now I tried to judge whether the case was big enough for several weeks. Presumably there'd be some kind of washing facilities. Also, I didn't know what items you couldn't buy that we'd need to stock up on.

I heard the doorbell ring and Barney's heavy footsteps. Then a familiar voice. I ran down the stairs.

'Diana!' I said. 'I'd almost given up hope seeing you again.'

'If it isn't Kitty with her hair back to normal.' Diana's face broke into a smile. 'I wondered if you'd still be here.'

'You've only just caught me,' I said. 'I've got a job with ENSA.

130

I'm going abroad soon, singing to the troops.'

She gave me an incredulous stare, then shrugged off her jacket. 'My, you have been a busy girl. Have you told your parents?'

'Yes. They're not very happy about it,' I admitted, 'but they know it's what I want to do.'

'Where are you going?'

Was this a test? I looked into her eyes. She raised an eyebrow.

'You know I'm not allowed to say anything,' I said. 'We don't even know the exact day we're leaving – only when to report.'

'That's a pity.' Diana looked disappointed. 'I've found someone willing to teach you to drive. You'd then be eligible to join the FANYs.'

I couldn't believe it. One moment even Lyons' tea shop didn't want me and in the next breath there were two interesting jobs on offer. Diana saw my face.

'I'm too late to recruit you, it seems.'

'I'm so sorry, Diana, but it's what I've set my heart on. I'd still like to learn to drive, though.'

We talked some more about general things, and what would happen to Mrs Parker's house, and I gave her Mum's address so we could keep in touch, but I noticed Diana didn't say any more about driving lessons.

The following day I had a letter from ENSA saying I was to report on Thursday morning at the Theatre Royal, Drury Lane, nine o'clock sharp to be fitted for my uniform. Uniform? Why? After all, I hadn't joined up with any of the forces. My mind now flew to the smart WRNS and WAAFs I'd seen around London. Maybe wearing a uniform wouldn't be so bad. It would certainly solve part of the clothes problem. I read the letter further.

After you have been fitted for your uniform you will go to the doctor on duty who will vaccinate you against yellow fever, tetanus and typhoid.

Ugh. I didn't like the sound of that. But better the needle than being ill in a foreign country. I wondered if Joyce had heard whether Miss Long had offered her a place on our tour.

Although tired from queuing for a few vegetables and a bit of meat, I decided to call into the hairdresser's on my way back to Mrs Parker's. Two girls were talking to a woman at the reception desk, and all of them looked up as I came in. I saw Joyce at the back of the room sweeping up clumps of hair from the last customer. She waved and smiled, then put a finger to her lips. She nodded and grinned. Yes, she'd been accepted all right, but hadn't told anyone.

'Do you have an appointment, miss?' the woman on the reception desk asked.

'No. I just wanted to have a word with Joyce.'

The woman frowned. 'We don't allow friends coming in and talking to the girls. They've got work to do. There's no time for chatter.'

'Shan't be a mo, Kitty,' Joyce called as she put her broom down and stepped up to the desk. She glanced at the clock, then let her gaze fall on the receptionist. 'I've already worked an hour overtime today, Mrs Lane, and two hours yesterday, so I'd like to pack up for the day, if that's all right.'

The woman didn't seem to notice Joyce's sarcasm but I smiled to myself. I wondered if Joyce was being brave in front of me or whether she was naturally bold. Whichever it was, the receptionist said, 'Very well. Just be here on time tomorrow. Your timekeeping isn't so hot first thing.'

'Yes, Mrs Lane.'

Joyce winked at me and I hovered by the door, waiting for her to take off her overall and get her things together. It took Joyce all of two minutes before we were outside, arms linked, laughing at poor Mrs Lane who was doomed to be behind a reception desk in a hairdresser's throughout the war while we were off to foreign places to do our bit.

'I heard from Miss Long this morning before I went to work,' Joyce said excitedly. 'I'm in.'

'I knew you would be. Did you have a letter from ENSA as well?'

'Yes. I have to report on Thursday for the uniform and vaccinations.'

'Me, too, but I'm not keen on the needle.' I pulled a face.

'You'll live,' Joyce said matter-of-factly. 'But what I didn't realise was that we had to wear uniforms.' Her mouth turned down at the prospect. 'I prefer my own clothes. Everyone looks the same in uniform.'

'You're lucky,' I told her. 'You've got lots of nice things. I'm quite glad. A uniform will stop me having to worry about whether I'm wearing the right thing...and a uniform can make you look quite attractive.'

'With your natural dark hair you'll always look glam,' Joyce laughed.

We'd been told that all ENSA people were automatically of officer rank, which pleased Joyce and me no end, though we couldn't really understand the point of a uniform when we weren't soldiers or nurses.

'Why do we have to wear uniform when we're really civilians?' Joyce bluntly asked the surly chap when it came to our turn to collect our uniforms.

'So you don't get arrested as spies,' was the surprising answer. Joyce and I looked at one another with raised eyebrows. Surely he was exaggerating. 'Friggin' Jerry,' he went on, almost spitting out the words. 'If you get captured and you're in uniform at least they'll treat you properly. If you're wandering around in your frocks, they'll think you're up to no good...an excuse for them to pull the trigger.'

I glanced at Joyce. She looked worried and I felt a shiver of apprehension.

'Don't think it's never happened.' He rubbed his forehead. 'It's a bloody possibility, pardon my French. This posting's not a walk in the park, y'know.' He glared at us. 'There's a war on. It can be dangerous where you're going, particularly for women. And don't you forget it.'

He emphasised the word "women" with a twist of his mouth as though he didn't approve at all. Looking us up and down he turned his back and picked out two sets of clothing and tossed them on the counter. Then he reached up on a shelf and pulled down two hats which he plonked down next to the uniforms. I picked one up. It was a smart peaked cap with a badge showing the letters ENSA pinned above a long flat bow. Joyce held up a short-sleeved jacket nipped in at the waist with a belt. There was a khaki short-sleeved shirt and a tie, but instead of a skirt was a pair of shorts, almost to the knee. Hmm. I wasn't sure about those. But at least I now knew we were definitely being sent to a hot country. When I wore these clothes I'd be in another world. My heart did a double somersault.

'You'll find boots and shoes in the next room,' he said. 'Try them on, make sure they fit and take one pair of each. Then report back to me and I'll show you where to go for your vaccinations.'

We were to go back the next day for the second one, the nurse said as she plunged the needle in.

My arm ached for several days from that one, and of course whenever I knocked into anything it was always on that spot.

17

We hadn't yet been told if we were going to the Middle East by air or by ship, but I didn't care which. It would be an adventure just getting there.

'I know I'll be sick if we go by boat,' Joyce said when we were making lists of all the things we needed to take. 'Dad once took us on the ferry to Calais and I was sick all the way. And that was only a two-hour crossing.'

She'd actually been to France. My dad had never taken us anywhere. She must have seen my expression.

'It was only for the day,' she laughed. 'He was a mean old bugger most of the time.'

I was astonished. I'd half envied her for having two wonderful parents, and even though they'd died too young, it somehow seemed romantic that they'd died together. But in her way she'd probably had just as difficult a time with her father as I'd had with mine.

'You've never told me much about your mum and dad,' I said.

'Mum was always off with some man or other,' she said, then laughed at my shocked face. 'Dad was okay in his way, but he would get in terrible jealous rages when Mum disappeared again, as she did quite frequently. Then he'd get drunk. He was driving with Mum and I suppose he was shouting at her and...' her eyes suddenly filled, 'he crashed the car. They were both killed...instantly.'

'I'm so sorry, Joyce.' I went over to her and put my arms around her. She gave me a quick hug in return.

'It's all right,' she said. 'Let's get on with our lists.' She ran her eyes over hers. 'Do you think we'll be able to buy bunnies in the land of the pyramids?' I had no idea what she was talking about. 'Sanitary towels,' she said, laughing at my immediate flush.

'I hadn't thought of that,' I said, my mind full of glamorous dresses and shoes and soft floaty scarves. 'We don't even know exactly how long we'll be away. Miss Long was a bit vague when she first said we were going somewhere in the Middle East. And it's still only my guess that we're going to Cairo.'

Luckily, ENSA sent us a list of all the essentials to take and what we could and couldn't buy when we were in wherever we were going. It still only told us it was the Middle East, but we were relieved that "bunnies" were definitely on the "could buy" list.

There were several false starts until one day, when I'd given up hope it was ever going to happen, we had a call from Drury Lane to say we'd be leaving in two days' time at four in the morning. I could barely contain my excitement. I'd be seeing other countries. Singing to the soldiers. Maybe even finding a proper boyfriend.

We still hadn't been given any more information, or even told what station we were leaving from, but at the allotted time a bus, its windows all blacked out and ENSA printed on the front where the final place name usually was, came to collect us. Along with a sleepy, grumbling Joyce, I struggled to load my luggage like the rest of the troupe.

Finally, we were on our way. The rumour was, we were going north to Liverpool docks, so it looked as though we would be going out by ship. Hal said we were going to St Pancras. The train was already waiting, and it didn't take more than a few moments before we'd filled the two compartments. Just as the whistle went off some officers piled in and had to find space for their boots between our two rows of legs and shoes. They were very cheerful with their chatting and bantering as they heaved their kit above our heads.

Yawning from such an early start, and to keep me awake, I began to hum "We'll Meet Again". One woman who I'd not met before, with hair even blonder than the colour Joyce had first dyed mine, darted me a look of contempt. I took no notice, and in fact started to sing the words. Joyce joined in, a little out of tune though it sounded like clever harmonising, and incredibly Jennifer Long began to sing with us. I bit back a smile as the blonde woman turned to her, and I noticed her mouth was all nipped in with disgust. The four officers grinned at me, and joined in too. Pretty soon we were swapping sandwiches and sharing drinks and chatting about everything, including our programme with ENSA.

It was an odd journey, vaguely reminding me of the one I'd made from King's Lynn to London, which now seemed a hundred years ago. We had plenty of starts and stops with no explanations, but after several hours we eventually arrived at a port.

'We're in Liverpool,' one of the dancers said excitedly. 'I recognise it. My gran lives here. So we'll be going from Albert Dock. Gran and Grandpa used to take us kids down to the quayside for a treat if it was a nice day.'

In less than an hour we were guided onto a troop ship, the bulk and colour of a giant whale.

A quiver ran through my body right to the soles of my feet. My voyage, as I secretly called it, had begun.

PART III

The Desert

18

Cairo

May 1941

It was as though I'd stepped into Mum's oven.

It had taken us nearly a fortnight to get here – a mixture of train, bus, ship and plane – and we were all exhausted. There'd been a few spats between some of the members of the troupe but I was thankful not to be involved. I'd had enough to worry about trying to cope with the trots on a ramshackle bus to Tunis, the most unpleasant and embarrassing experience I'd ever had.

'I know what it's like,' Lionel, the long thin acrobat told us as he stopped the bus for me for about the tenth time, or so it seemed, that horrible day. There couldn't be anything left in me to expel, I thought, as I squatted miserably behind a thin, dead-looking tree on the side of the road, sure that everyone in the bus was peering out, watching me.

Before that, the troop ship we were on had zig-zagged over the Atlantic to escape the U-boats. We were all handed life-belts which we were under orders to have with us at all times. They called them Mae Wests and although at first I found it a nuisance, it almost became a friend. It made a marvellous extra pillow or cushion when I broke the rule and inflated it ever so slightly. The alarm went off several times during the voyage, and Joyce became almost hysterical as we whipped on our life-belts to the point where I wished I'd never suggested she come with me. But then it would all die down...until the next time.

Poor Joyce was sick whether we were in calm seas or stormy – it didn't seem to make any difference, just as she'd warned me. There was nothing I could do to help her except wipe her forehead with a cold flannel and give her sips of water and just be there with her. We missed the whales which the captain had shouted over the megaphone for us to watch, which was a pity, but I told her we'd catch them next time around on the way home. She looked a ghastly white as she whispered there wouldn't be a next time for her. She'd never be able to make the crossing again. From Gibraltar we sailed to Algiers. By this time Joyce looked skinny and still very pasty, but as soon as we were on land, to my relief, she began to recover her old sparkle.

Two days later we had that rotten bus ride where it was my turn to be ill, and when Jennifer finally told us we were to be based in Cairo.

On the plane Joyce and I could hardly contain ourselves. We gripped one another's hands, giggling with terror, as the plane made a dash along the runway, then roared up into the sky. Strangely enough, even though at times it was bumpy, Joyce didn't even feel sick. Flying through the night was a thrill. We both loved whooshing along in the sky until it finally made its descent over a city glittering with stars, where we rattled and bumped to a halt in Tripoli. There we stayed overnight in a clean hotel – heaven, as for once our bed didn't move.

The next morning we flew to Cairo.

The heat and smell was like nothing I had ever experienced. I looked up at a sky the exact colour of Frankie's eyes, but the sun was so fierce I had to look quickly away, only to be dazzled again by all the white buildings, and the glittering dust swirling round them.

How strange everything was, yet this was normal to the people who lived here. Normal life – but as abnormal to me as it could possibly be – and I was thrilled.

But the stench. A burning smell reminding me of when the bombs dropped in London. I couldn't identify it. And another overpowering one of wee mixed with strong unidentifiable spices which made my nostrils tingle. Hal grabbed hold of my arm.

'Stay close,' he said. 'They're not used to women on the loose.'

'Who aren't?'

'The Arabs, of course.'

'Aren't women allowed out by themselves?' I looked around. Come to think of it, I hadn't seen any women in the street on their own. Without exception they all had a man, either young or old, by their side. 'After all, they have the vote now and—'

'Not here they don't. It's all to do with the Muslim religion. Egypt is a man's world, and don't you forget it. We're here in their country and we have to respect their customs and not criticise them.'

Well, no one was going to stop *me* from going out by myself. Why would these Egyptian women put up with it? Now, after what Hal had said, his hand on my arm annoyed me. I didn't exactly shrug him off, but I sort of turned, pretending I was looking around, making sure we were all there, so that he was forced to release me.

We made a straggly line towards the row of taxis. Drivers jumped out of the first half-dozen cars, all of them clad in white robes, looking as though they'd wrapped Mum's freshly ironed sheets around them. I watched, fascinated.

'You want good hotel, sir?' The first one touched Eddie's arm. Eddie was one of the dancers, tall, slim and graceful. I was looking forward to seeing him dance.

'We have an address of our hotel,' Eddie told him. 'The Victoria.'

'You show me.' The driver practically snatched the piece of paper from Eddie's hand and peered at it with his hooded eyes. 'This no good.'

'Well, that's the hotel where we're booked in.' It was Jennifer

Long's firm voice. So small and frail-looking, with her strawberry-blonde hair, looking doll-like against the magnificent Egyptians. She didn't even come up to this driver's shoulder.

The driver took no notice of her at all. He didn't even glance her way. It was as though she hadn't spoken. As if she simply didn't exist. I stood, open-mouthed, wondering who would win.

'So would you be good enough to take us?' Jennifer asked.

The driver still ignored her.

'Well, we'd better ask another driver,' Jennifer said firmly. She turned towards the taxi behind.

That was enough to make him take notice.

'Very good, lady.' He looked so crestfallen that he had to take an order from a woman, I wanted to laugh. 'I tell my brother and cousin. They are also drivers. We take everyone.'

19

Every time I thought about the evening I was afraid I was going to be sick. My stomach had been churning for days and Joyce had complained of an upset tum, as she called it. We'd only had two rehearsals since we arrived but when I'd approached Jennifer Long two days ago she'd dismissed me impatiently.

'We've no time to give you any special attention,' she said. 'Can't you see we're all busy?'

There was nowhere to practise quietly either. The others in the group were friendly but were trying to perfect their own act. It was all right for them. They were experienced.

Lucky Joyce. I licked my lips that felt as dried up as the desert I'd glimpsed from the filthy taxi window. She hadn't got to perform. She just had to make sure everyone's hair looked nice. I glanced at myself in the mirror. Maybe I should get Joyce to add a bit more colour to my pale cheeks. Miss Long had asked Joyce if she could help with make-up as well, and Joyce said she'd have a go. I couldn't help smiling. I didn't think it was quite the answer Miss Long was looking for.

Come to that, Joyce hadn't appeared for a while so I thought I'd go and find her. It would be good to have a chat – take my mind off things.

'Have you seen Joyce?' I asked anyone within earshot. Most of them shook their heads, but Eddie said the last time he'd seen her she was heading for Rhoda's room.

Our quarters were in a plain-looking building on two floors. Rhoda shared her room with two other dancers who had all been friendly to me but they kept mainly together.

I knocked on the door but there was no answer. I wandered over to the make-up room in a building not much bigger than a large shed. A woman with a headful of pipe cleaners was sitting on a chair reading a magazine; Joyce was waving a hairdryer over her head.

'Hello, Kitty,' she said. 'I'll be with you in a minute.' She winked at me and pointed the dryer above the woman's head and pulled a face. I wanted to giggle.

The woman looked up, saw it was no one who interested her in the slightest, grimaced, and went back to her magazine. I recognised her. She was the woman in the compartment when we were in the train and I'd started singing and Joyce and Jennifer Long had joined in. I remembered her look of contempt. She must be the blonde singer Miss Long had mentioned.

I found out later from Bob, the comedian, that her name was Madeleine. He called her a *prima donna*. I'd have given anything to ask him what that meant but I didn't feel I knew him or any of the others enough to show my ignorance. But by the tone he used, I didn't think it was much of a compliment.

Joyce switched off the dryer and went over to one of the cupboards where she took down a bottle. She winked and pointed to Madeleine, shaking her head in warning. 'I'll tell you later,' she mouthed.

Another hour crept by. Then another. I went into the canteen and had a cup of tea and a couple of dry biscuits. I couldn't have eaten anything else if you'd paid me.

''Fraid it's only a makeshift stage tonight,' one of the stagehands announced. 'So be careful. I'll reinforce it more tomorrow, but there's never enough time on the first day.'

Three of them had been busy for several hours but I hadn't liked to stand around watching, even though it was fascinating to see a stage gradually taking shape. I was too aware I'd be in the way, especially when I heard Joyce being shouted at earlier on. Not that she'd taken much notice. She didn't seem to have the same concern as I did, trying to keep on the right side of everyone. I was terrified of putting a foot wrong. I kept telling myself I'd be better when I'd got the first night over with.

My stomach was still growling when I slid into my dress. Joyce had chosen it from the two I'd brought with me, donated by her generous customers. I only hoped they'd fit. We'd barely had time to look at them in London before we had to pack them. This one was royal blue with a silver trim on the bodice. I'd never worn anything so glamorous and it made me look older. Exactly what I wanted.

'Very nice,' Joyce said approvingly, coming into our room. 'It suits you. Brings out the blue of your eyes. If that's possible,' she laughed. She tilted her head on one side and hesitated. 'It's a bit baggy on the hips but maybe we can pull it in with some safety pins. You need to show off that lovely figure to those lonely soldiers.'

The snooty blonde woman, Madeleine Grant, was apparently the star of our show but I'd never heard of her. She was scheduled to open and close the concert. One day that would be me, I vowed. The singer everyone waited for. 'To bring the house down' was the expression I'd heard one of the girls say. But I had no time to dwell on such fantasies. I would be going on stage in a few minutes, following Madeleine, and was sick with nerves.

Jennifer Long stepped out first on to the makeshift stage.

'Hello, everyone,' I heard her greet the eager soldiers. 'It's wonderful to see you all and we hope you'll enjoy the evening. *We're* certainly going to enjoy ourselves.' There was a chuckle from the audience. 'To get you right into the mood Bob is going to entertain you for a few minutes while we wait for the star of our show.'

Bob came on and right away I could hear the audience laughing. They sounded a nice audience and I relaxed a little. Even from the sidelines I could hear everything clearly though I didn't understand most of the jokes. After ten minutes or so he finished to lots of clapping and whistling, and with bows and smiles and thank yous he trotted down the steps to where Miss Long and Madeleine and I were standing. Madeleine had completely ignored me while we'd been watching the act.

'And now I want to introduce you to someone you've been waiting for…here she is,' Jennifer made a sweeping movement with her arm, 'Miss Madeleine Grant.'

Some kind of magic swept over me. Maybe it was the still, warm night air, so different from England, and our troupe performing under the stars, or maybe it was the whistles and shouts of the soldiers. Whatever it was, I was happier than I'd ever been in the whole of my life.

Madeleine began to sing. I didn't know the song. For one thing it was in a foreign language. Straining, I tried to understand the meaning. It seemed to be about a gypsy girl who was flirting with an invisible someone. She was wearing a flared skirt which looked as though it had been made with every piece of leftover material and patched together, and a white off-the-shoulder blouse, gathered at the neckline. Simple flat white sandals showed off her neat slim feet to perfection.

I looked down at my dress. Suddenly I felt ridiculous in the royal blue, down to my ankles, and the glittering silver bodice… a child who was playing dressing up. Oh, if only I'd chosen the other dress. The cream one with the shorter, fuller skirt and pleated V neck. It was much more appropriate for my age and where we were. Joyce and I had got it completely wrong. I felt one of the safety pins at the back of the dress begin to pull and my eyes stung with embarrassment. But seconds later I was enraptured by Madeleine's song. She began to swing her slender hips, giving the impression she was moving across the platform, tossing back the blonde hair and challenging the audience with her flashing eyes. Hal's accompaniment reached a crescendo as Madeleine held a red rose to her breast, the other hand encircling the microphone as though it was a part of her, it looked so natural, her voice rising to a thrilling high note which made the hairs stand up at the back of my neck, until she came down two notes lower, like the trilling of birdsong. She laughed a mirthless laugh, and tossed the flower out to the cheering soldiers. I shivered and saw my arms were covered in goose pimples.

How could I possibly go on after such a magnificent performance?

The crowd whistled and stomped and shouted for more, but Madeleine simply bowed several times and tripped as lightly as one of the dancers to the side of the stage where Tony was waiting with his arm held out to steady her as she climbed down.

Tony had been standing by me while I was waiting for Madeleine to finish her song. He'd already told me he would give me an introduction. For the millionth time I wished I'd had more rehearsals. My stomach began to turn over and I tasted bile in my throat. He must have felt me trembling as he squeezed my hand and said, 'Are you ready, Kitty?'

I nodded dumbly, swallowing, and watched him spring up the steps.

'Thank you, ladies and gentlemen. You'll hear from Miss Grant again later in the show. But for our next song...her first time on stage...please put your hands together for Miss Kitty Townsend.'

The sound of clapping, far away...

'You're on,' Miss Long said from behind me, her breath coming quickly. 'Go on, Kitty. Don't hang around. They're waiting for you.'

She didn't say it unkindly but the words were frightening.

I forced myself to step on to the stage and walk up to the microphone.

The clapping died away. I looked out to the audience, hoping to see a friendly face, but everything was a blur. My heart pounded with fear as I drew in a ragged breath. I hesitated...became confused. I could hear some faint notes from the piano but they meant nothing to me.

Kitty, you have to start.

My jaw felt tight. I tried to move it from side to side to loosen it, then thought how stupid I must look. I smiled but my nerves were so taut I must have looked like a wildcat baring its teeth. Dear God, why had I thought I could do this? My knees began to tremble and I thought they would give way beneath me. I took a deep breath, filling my nostrils with the warm spicy air, trying to calm myself, then heard the echo of Jennifer's commanding voice in my ear and I blew it out again.

I clutched the microphone, sweat from my fingers trickling down the stand, and parted my lips. Hal played the introduction again and this time I recognised the song – "I'll Never Smile Again".

I opened my mouth. To my horror, all that came out was a squeak. It was far worse than that first time when I'd had to sing for Jennifer.

Come on, Kitty, you can do it.

I tried again. This time I reached the note. It sounded pure to my ears. Dizzy with relief I sang the first few phrases but suddenly my mind went blank. I stopped in mid-sentence. I couldn't remember what to do next. What the words were. Or even where I was.

I froze.

The audience froze with me. After what seemed like hours, I heard mutterings. In the dusk I could see some of the soldiers making the "thumbs down" signal as they looked at one another and even twisted their necks to the row behind. I could hear feet banging against the wooden benches, and I heard the rumble of their voices. My face, which must have gone as white as the moon, was now on fire. I turned to rush out.

Then, from nowhere, came the most beautiful voice I had ever heard. It seemed to float from the back, over the heads of the soldiers. It was my song; the melody was the same but the words were different. As I stopped, half turned from the audience, my body seemed to come alive. The same tingling I'd felt when Madeleine sang her gypsy song began on my scalp and shivered down my neck, but this time it followed every bone down my spine, along my arms, to the tops of my legs…I couldn't think…couldn't breathe. I swivelled round to face the soldiers who were now silent, all eyes facing me. The voice that made me feel like melting wax finished the verse. Instinctively, I joined in the second verse, he in the strange language, and me in English. Our voices harmonised perfectly. '… *until I smile at you.*' I didn't want it ever to end. We finished on exactly the same note to wild applause. I stood for a few moments to let it die away, relishing the cheers of the soldiers, knowing I would never forget this night. I had sung under a desert sky lit with stars which were straight out of *Arabian Nights* with an unknown soldier who I would never meet. But who could he be?

I stumbled off the stage in a dream, the velvet voice from the back filling every cranny in my head until I thought it would burst.

'Kitty, I want a word with you,' Jennifer Long put her head round the door of our room where we girls were taking off our make-up. 'In my room.'

The jar of Pond's cold cream had done the rounds, and as the newcomer I was last to take my share. I was too busy pulling a face at the orange swirls in the pot from the last girl's fingers to register at first.

'Kitty! Did you hear me?'

'Sorry, Miss Long. I'm just finishing taking off my make-up. I won't be two ticks.'

She was bound to be pleased that what could have been a disaster had turned out wonderfully.

'So, Kitty,' Miss Long began, when I stood in front of her. 'What happened?'

The tone was sharp and I stepped back in surprise. There was no point in trying to pretend.

'I-I...it must have been nerves,' I said, completely at odds. 'I just forgot what came next. But one of the soldiers helped me. As soon as he started, even though it was in German—'

'Italian,' she cut in. 'He's an Italian prisoner of war. And he's not a soldier, he's an officer – and a high-ranking one. Nevertheless,' she glared at me, 'he's the enemy – the same as the Germans.'

So the man with the golden voice was Italian.

I felt a bit better. After all, my own father was half-Italian. 'Well, I didn't know that,' I began, defensively. 'I'm sorry. It won't happen again, I promise you.' I pushed down the stab of disappointment. Just my luck. A prisoner of war.

'Your inexperience certainly showed you up. We have to keep up the standards. Madeleine was most upset.'

'Why was Madeleine upset?' I was genuinely puzzled.

'Because,' Jennifer Long looked at me as though wondering how to put it, 'one bad slip like that makes the whole show seem amateurish. And Madeleine's a professional, through and through.'

'I was all right as soon as that soldier...I mean, officer,' I faltered, remembering his glorious voice, 'sang with me. Even though he was singing in another language I remembered the words then.' I managed to keep my eyes fixed on hers. 'I thought the two different languages sounded lovely together.'

'I'm afraid, Kitty, you're in no position to comment.' Miss Long impatiently swished back a strand of her amazing hair.

I had the most awful sense of foreboding.

'Madeleine says that as long as your name's on the programme she won't be singing,' Miss Long continued. 'And as you're aware, Kitty, *she's* the name – the big draw – the one they all want to see.'

I couldn't believe my ears. I badly wanted to say that I doubted the men would worry about whether we were famous or not, so long as we could make them forget for an hour or two. But why on earth did Madeleine have it in for me? What had I ever done to her?

'You're going to kick me off the show, aren't you,' I said, the words tumbling from my lips, 'before I've even had a proper chance?'

Jennifer Long was silent. She wasn't being deliberately unkind, I was sure, but I couldn't understand why Madeleine was calling the tune on who should be in the programme and who shouldn't. I'd always understood that it was Jennifer Long who was in charge.

'Please tell me, Miss Long,' I said, my eyes brimming. 'I'd rather know the truth.'

I braced myself, waiting for the blow.

'I'll speak to her again, Kitty, but don't hold your breath.'

20

Ruggero

When Madeleine Grant swept on to the stage in her gypsy skirt, grabbing up the folds of material so it showed off her slender calves and ankles, and began to sing the seductive "Habanera" from *Carmen*, Ruggero shot up in his slumped position, his eyes wide with surprise and anticipation.

Her voice was such a shock after the comedian – who he hadn't found one bit funny and whose accent grated on his ears – that for a few seconds he imagined he must be dreaming. As he'd watched the British soldiers flinging their heads back and laughing uproariously at the weakest gags, he realised how different their sense of humour was.

He hadn't wanted to come to what even the Tommies called "Every Night Something Awful". Ruggero's motto, drummed into him by his parents, was that if you didn't or couldn't do something really well, you shouldn't do it. Simple as that. And if you couldn't look at the best art, listen to the best music, or read the best literature, then it wasn't worth bothering with. But tonight some of the officers had insisted he go with them, and quite frankly he'd been too depressed to argue. He'd thought maybe it would do him good to break the monotony. But the comedian had made him slip down even further into the gloom.

The gypsy woman began to sway, her blonde hair following the curve of her body, falling almost as low as her waist. It was quite the wrong colour for Carmen but somehow it didn't matter, and for a minute or two he forgot where he was. Forgot he was in a prisoner-of-war camp. Forgot he and thousands of his fellow men had been captured by the British only weeks ago. He'd just been thankful all the rumours about the way the British treated their prisoners were true. There was no sign of torture or solitary confinement or lack of medical care or inferior food, so far as he was aware. The British eked out the rations in the same proportion to everyone. It was their famous sense of "fair play" he'd often been told about. Thank God for it.

The woman's voice was good for her gypsy part. Not as powerful as any of the singers he was used to, but then this woman wasn't an opera singer. She was up to her limit and needed that microphone. He shook himself. Who was he to criticise? He was lucky to hear something from *Carmen* at all. She was a little too thin for his taste but she used her body well; her arms and hands moving above her head, then at hip level, to seduce an invisible Don José, all the while swaying her bottom. It was almost too much for him. How he missed having a woman. He felt the familiar hardening, and squeezed his eyes shut so all he could hear was her voice, but flicked them open again. He couldn't resist watching her. She certainly knew how to put the song across.

He clapped even more loudly than those around him who were making catcalls and stamping their feet. He wouldn't go that far but he had to admit he'd enjoyed it. As her voice swelled to hit the last high note, '...*si je t'aime, prends garde*', and finally dropped down to finish on the home key '...à *toi*', he felt his shoulders relax and the frown smooth away from his forehead. How he missed his beloved opera.

He would have been content to leave there and then. He didn't need to hear anyone else, but he couldn't move – he was pressed so tightly in his seat by the others. If there was a fire... *Dio mio*, it didn't bear thinking about. "Carmen" bowed several times to all sides and corners of the audience, and disappeared. It was then he noticed another figure in the dusk. A young girl had tiptoed on to the stage waiting for her turn. She looked tall, though it was hard to tell at this distance. But for all her height she had no stage presence. In fact, by the way her hands clenched and unclenched he was sure she was terrified. He recognised the introduction the pianist played and braced himself, quite certain her voice would not be a match for the woman who'd sung the "Habanera".

He was right. The poor girl couldn't begin, she was so nervous. Not that he blamed her. All those hundreds of men watching. She was far too young to have experienced this kind of an audience. She couldn't be more than sixteen. Oh, God, she'd started the song again, maybe hoping she'd remember the words this time. But there was something unusual about her voice. Some quality...high and pure...the slight tremor...though that was probably nerves.

He hummed softly, hoping she might somehow pick up the notes from across the heads of the soldiers, then smiled at his own foolishness. *Dio mio*, she'd stopped altogether and was just standing there in the centre of that makeshift stage like a frightened bird.

He opened his mouth. He only knew the song in his own language. He didn't know whether it would help her or finish her off completely. For a few bars he was so engrossed that he didn't realise the girl had picked up the words again, her voice increasing in strength. He should stop now, let her finish the song on her own. But he couldn't. His musical ear knew her voice blended perfectly with his own.

21

Kitty

'I couldn't believe you suddenly dried up, but in the end you were bloody marvellous,' Joyce said later that night as I rushed past her. 'Hey, wait. What's got into you?'

I ignored her and fled to our room. She had to help with wardrobe and unpin hair and generally tidy up, so I had some moments to myself. I sat on the edge of the bed, my head in my hands. Tears squeezed through the narrow slits between my fingers. My mind reeled. What would Miss Long do with me? Would she force me to go back to England? If she did, how could I face everyone at home? The "I told you so" from Dad. Now I'd had my first taste of the stage I was determined never to forget my words again. But could I convince Miss Long?

Did Madeleine really have such power? Was she bluffing? Would she really bow out of the programme if they let me stay? The only person I felt I could ask was Hal.

'She's a bitch,' he said. 'She's done this sort of thing before. You're competition for her.'

'Me? Competition? With *her* voice?'

'You're younger and prettier for a start, and you've got a glorious voice if you use it properly. More unusual than Madeleine's. Richer. Much more powerful. You don't even need a mike. How about if I give you a few tips in performing? That is, if you don't get shoved off right away.'

'I'd be really grateful,' I told him, blushing with his compliments even though I was squirming inside just thinking about being "shoved off".

Maybe if I didn't say anything more about leaving, Miss Long might forget all about it. I was wrong.

'So, Kitty, I've made a decision,' Jennifer Long said, having kept me on edge all through the next day. 'You can stay with us but no singing. You'll be useful helping with the cooking and cleaning up each evening. I don't want any arguments,' she said firmly as I opened my mouth to protest. 'Be thankful I'm letting you stay in Cairo.'

A tiny part of me rejoiced that I wasn't being sent home in disgrace, but when evening came I knew I'd feel heartbroken not to be singing.

'Won't you please give me one more chance?' I begged, knowing my future rested on her answer. 'I promise I won't let you down.'

'It's more than my life's worth,' she said.

She left me sobbing my heart out.

Cooking and cleaning. I doubt I'd have volunteered for that, even if it *had* meant going to Cairo. My whole body seemed to go into a slump. I didn't have my usual appetite; I couldn't get enthusiastic about the show. I missed my mother terribly. Everything had gone wrong.

The worst thing was when I was sent to Madeleine's room to clean it. I felt so humiliated and angry this woman had the power to put an end to my singing. But I was determined not to show it, even for an instant. I wouldn't give her the satisfaction.

'Mind you do a thorough job,' she said with a curl of her lip, when I arrived with an assortment of dusters and a mop. 'I'm off to a rehearsal so I'll leave you to it.'

She gave one of those false smiles that kept well away from her eyes. I just nodded, too furious to speak in case I ended up putting a bruise on that smooth pale face of hers. It was a relief when she'd gone.

As I dusted and polished and swept, feeling like Cinderella, I couldn't help thinking about the Italian prisoner of war who'd sung with me. I wanted to know who was behind the voice but of course I would never find out. Somehow that thought made me feel empty. Then I "pulled myself together" as Dad would say. I reminded myself he was the enemy. I wouldn't ever be able to speak to him. But it didn't stop me imagining what he looked like, what kind of a person he was, how he was coping with losing his freedom. And more than anything I wanted to hear his voice again.

The only thing that stopped me from going mad was Hal, who gave me performance tips during my lunch breaks.

'The voice is there when you're not nervous,' he said, 'but you've just got to learn how to put a song across.' He stood up and began to sing "The Nearness Of You". He used his face, his arms, his whole body, all the time fixing his eyes on me. 'Like that,' he finished, sitting down at his piano. 'Find some guy you could fancy in the audience and sing just to him. Reach out to make him fall for you.'

'There's no point now,' I said bitterly.

'Someone always gets sick,' Hal said firmly. 'They'll need you to fill the gap.' My heart lifted just a little. 'Okay, do it again, and this time make me believe you're mad about *me*.'

The following morning Joyce rushed into our room as I was about to leave to help Bert in the kitchen. I wasn't interested in cooking but at least it was doing something that the troupe could enjoy, and was better than mindless cleaning. I wished I'd taken after Mum who loved cooking. She'd be pleased I was learning as I always steered clear of the kitchen when I was home.

'Kitty, you won't believe it but Madeleine won't be singing tonight.' Joyce was panting as though she'd been running.

My heart leapt. 'What happened?'

'She's been sick. Must be something she ate. She's got it both ends.'

Hal was right.

'Dear-oh-dear.' I beamed at Joyce. 'Do you think Jennifer will let me go on in her place?'

'No idea,' my friend smiled. 'But someone's got to give the boys a song. And if it's not going to be Madeleine, it might as well be you.'

'Have you seen her?' I asked.

'Yes. Remember I told you I was supposed to be doing her roots this morning. I barely recognised her when she came to the door. She looked awful. Sheet-white. Eyes dull. Hair a sight. She said she was too ill for me to do her hair.' Joyce looked at me and chuckled. 'She *must* be ill to say that.'

'Has she eaten anything different from the rest of us?'

'I think she went out with one of the chaps last night for a meal after the show. Heaven knows what they give you in those places with all that weird music. I'd be afraid to try their stuff when you have no idea what they put into it. Bert told me they eat dogs and cats and rats as a matter of course.'

'Ugh.' I made a face, not really believing it.

'So I'd rather stick to *your* crummy dinners,' Joyce added, ducking as I pretended to cuff her.

'What do you think I should do?' I asked her, all serious now.

'Talk to Miss Long, of course,' Joyce said. 'She's the one in charge.'

But I was in for a disappointment.

'I'm sorry,' Miss Long said, sounding genuine, although it didn't help me. 'I can't take the risk. Madeleine would be furious if she found out you'd sung in her place, and I can't be sure you wouldn't forget your lines again and embarrass us all.'

'But, Miss Long,' I protested, 'surely I deserve another chance. I've had my audition to get into ENSA and you wouldn't have passed me if I wasn't any good.' I hoped this would be enough to flatter her into changing her mind.

'I can't go back on my word to Madeleine. I'm sorry, Kitty. That's all there is to it.' She turned abruptly on her heel and walked away.

I stood there without moving. What hold did Madeleine have over Jennifer? Why did she seem to be so completely in awe of the woman? I was determined to get to the bottom of it. If I didn't I could see my future going straight down the drain.

Half an hour later I found out why Madeleine had got me off the programme. Hal had half hinted she was jealous but it was Lionel who gave me an extraordinary explanation. I was trying to smoke a cigarette outside the kitchen door when he came along, showing off and grinning as he performed one cartwheel after another, finishing with a backward somersault. He was just like a jack-in-the-box.

'Caught you,' he said, his bright-blue eyes crinkling with laughter as they spotted my cigarette. 'Those fags will ruin that lovely voice of yours.'

'It doesn't matter,' I said, choking on the third puff. 'Joyce gave it to me. She knows I'm upset that I'm not allowed on the stage anymore. Madeleine's instructions.'

'Oh, yeah, I heard something about that,' Lionel said, peering at me. 'Bloody shame. Well, I'm not surprised. She's good and jealous.'

There it was again.

'Why should she be jealous of me?'

'Can't you guess?'

'No.' I was puzzled.

'She's a dyke.'

'What do you mean?'

Lionel grinned. 'Don't you know what a dyke is?'

I stubbed the rest of the cigarette under my foot, feeling incredibly grown up and incredibly childish all at once.

'It's a woman liking another woman,' he said, watching my face closely.

I thought of Joyce. We liked one another. What could possibly be wrong with that?

'I still don't understand,' I said.

'A dyke's a woman who hates men. Or at least doesn't find them attractive. But she's attracted to other women...for sex, and all that,' he finished, patting his head, the hair of which was already thinning though he couldn't have been more than twenty-five.

My stomach clenched. I'd never heard of such a thing.

'What did you call her again?'

'A dyke.'

'What a horrible word.'

'No more than "queer". Which is what they call men who like other men.'

So men could be that way too? I shook my head. It didn't make any sense at all.

'But how do they—?' I stopped. I couldn't go on. I didn't want to know.

Lionel chuckled. 'We won't go into that,' he said. 'You're far too young. But I'll let you into a secret.' He bent his head low and put his mouth against my ear. I thought at first he was going to kiss me, and I was about to tell him I didn't fancy him that way. But to my surprise he said, 'Don't tell anyone or it'll cost me my job but...' He paused and looked around him. Seemingly satisfied there was no one about, he said in an undertone, 'I'm one.'

'One what?' I gaped at him.

He looked at me with impatient eyes. 'I've just explained. A queer.'

'Do you hate women?' I asked, more for something to say than anything else. I was truly shocked.

'Not in the least,' Lionel said. 'In fact, I adore them. I just don't think of them as sexual beings. But if I did...' He broke off and looked at me, his eyes roving from my head down to my feet. Then he roared with laughter. 'Well, duckie, you wouldn't be safe with me.'

I couldn't help laughing.

'Coming back to Madeleine...' Lionel said.

I'd almost forgotten her with trying to digest all this stuff about women liking women and men liking men.

'Oh, yes.' I swallowed. I was still upset and bewildered by Madeleine's attitude towards me.

'She's jealous,' Lionel said, patting his head again, 'because Jennifer likes you and Madeleine's scared she'll lose her.'

I stared at him. *Lose* her? 'Do you mean Madeleine and Jennifer are...?'

'Yes, that's exactly it,' Lionel nodded. 'Madeleine and Jennifer are having an affair, and Madeleine can see how gorgeous you are, and she's worried that Jennifer will fall for you.'

It really was too ridiculous to contemplate. Yet somehow it fitted.

At least I could understand why Jennifer felt forced to carry out Madeleine's instructions to dismiss me. Jennifer hadn't wanted to, I was certain. But she couldn't antagonise Madeleine else she would risk losing her love. And Madeleine wouldn't have any cause to be jealous of me now, because being a cleaning woman or kitchen assistant hardly put me in a glamorous light.

Oh, it was all so stupid. I could never like another girl in that way so neither of them had anything to worry about. But knowing that wasn't going to get me my job back.

22

I made a pact with myself. I *would* sing again. That's what I'd joined ENSA for. It certainly wasn't to be on kitchen duty. And when the opportunity came I'd be ready. I wouldn't forget my lines, I wouldn't be consumed with fear, or intimidated by the other singers. I told myself I was every bit as good as Madeleine. I just needed to gain confidence and Hal had offered to coach me.

Hal was an attractive man. His hair, always looking as if it had just been shampooed, had a hint of grey at the temples which actually made him more appealing. And his intriguing green eyes. You couldn't help looking into them. Bit wasted on a man, really. He was what we called "lanky" in Norfolk. He'd been so kind to me since Madeleine had put her boot in, and my singing was improving under his green eye.

'Hal, could I practise later on today?' I asked him at the first opportunity. He'd just come from a rehearsal himself.

'Sorry, Kitty, no time today,' was his disappointing reply. He saw my face. 'Maybe tomorrow.'

I had to be content with that.

The day after I'd asked Hal for a singing practice Jennifer Long came to the kitchen. She stood in the doorway watching me and the two cooks, but mostly me, without saying a word. I pretended I didn't see her and carried on scrubbing down the pine table with a vigour I didn't really feel. If I said anything it would be rude and I didn't think it would take much to give her the excuse to send me home. Finally, she said, 'Kitty, when you've finished, I'd like a word with you.'

What did she want now? More rotten chores to do, I supposed. Before I could reply, Bert said, 'You can go now, Kitty. We won't be needing you until five o'clock.'

I thanked him and followed Jennifer Long out of the door. I still hadn't said a word to her.

'We'll go to the studio where we can be more private,' she said, the words flying over her shoulder.

Rhoda and the two other dancers were changing into their outdoor shoes ready to leave and Miss Long waited until they'd gone, talking to me about nothing much and me nodding back.

When they'd disappeared she turned to me, but before she could open her mouth I couldn't resist asking, 'How is Madeleine? Is she feeling better?' I didn't allow a trace of sarcasm in my enquiry, though Miss Long narrowed her eyes.

'I think she's making some progress,' she said. 'But I don't want to discuss Madeleine.'

A picture of her and Madeleine cuddled up in bed together flew across my mind. Jennifer was so pretty it seemed a waste that she didn't have a nice husband or boyfriend.

'...so you can come back.'

'I'm sorry, Miss Long, I was miles away.'

'You can sing to the troops again.' She sounded almost apologetic.

It took me a few seconds to take in what she was saying.

'Come and sit down.' She took my hand and pulled me on to one of the upright chairs. 'Maybe I've been a bit hasty taking you off the programme. And now Madeleine's not well we're two singers missing. So if you'd like to come back this evening—'

'*Like to*,' I burst out. 'I'd love to.' Then I remembered. 'I'm on kitchen duty this evening.'

'Leave that to me,' Jennifer said. 'I'll let Bert know.' She looked at my happy face. 'It's all settled then.'

165

'Oh, yes,' I breathed. Then I couldn't resist it. 'And you're not worried about what Madeleine will say when she finds out?'

Jennifer gave a hint of a smile. 'I'll deal with her.'

I went out of the studio practically skipping with joy. I was going to sing tonight and no one would stop me.

First of all I needed a new song. One that wasn't too difficult so I didn't get overcome with nerves like last time. I'd been given another chance and I didn't want to muff it. I had an idea of one but I'd need to ask Hal if he thought it suitable for my voice and if I could practise it.

I found him on a bench in the garden on the other side of the studio having a quiet cigarette.

'Hal,' I said, running over to him, 'I've got some wonderful news.' I sat down by the side of him, breathless. 'I'm back in the show. Miss Long has just spoken to me.'

'Hey, that's swell.' Hal pulled in a deep drag on his cigarette and looked at me, his green eyes twinkling. 'It worked then.'

'What do you mean?'

'I had a word with Captain Travers. Asked him to give you a break. Jennifer's feeling guilty, I know, but can't bring herself to do anything about it. But Travers can. He told her the boys felt bad and wanted to give you another chance.'

Tears sprang into my eyes. Dear, dear Hal. What a friend. And Captain Travers, too, whoever he was.

Hal glanced at his watch. 'We'd better do some practising. When are you going on?'

'Tonight. Oh, Hal, I'm nervous again.' Just thinking about the disaster the last time made my legs run to water.

'You'll be great. C'mon, kid, let's run through a couple of numbers.'

He jumped up and I followed him back into the studio. Immediately, he began flicking through some songbooks.

'Hal,' I said, 'there's a song I'd like to sing. My mother sometimes sings it.' Hal raised his eyebrow in question. '"You Made Me Love You". Do you know it?'

Hal began fingering the keys, and I went straight in.

Hal stopped. 'Let's begin at the beginning,' he said, turning towards me. 'I don't have the music but I know it pretty well. And, Kitty,' he hesitated, 'sing it for one person. Sing it to me. And sing it as though you really mean it.'

He gave me a couple of bars again, then nodded. I was ready.

When I'd finished Hal looked up and gave me his slow smile, and I grinned back.

'Wonderful,' he said. 'It sounds as though you're really familiar with it which is good. You need to go on that stage and sock it to 'em. What are you wearing?'

I stopped. Not the dress I'd worn that first fateful time. I remembered how uncomfortable I'd felt in it. I was truly grateful Joyce had lent me the two evening dresses, but how I wished for something new – something made especially for me.

'I don't know,' I said, miserably, the excitement draining away. It would have to be the cream which I'd privately thought was too bland.

'Jennifer'll find you something, don't worry.' Hal looked at his watch. 'Got another song? You need at least two.'

'What about "Love Walked In"?'

'How about something new?' He turned over some pages in his songbook and said, 'Aha. This could have been written for you, Kitty. It's called "Bewitched, Bothered and Bewildered".' He began to play, humming the tune, and singing the introduction.

'I've never heard it.'

Hal ignored me. Then he started to sing the melody,

'I'm wild again, beguiled again…'

I peered over his shoulder and hummed while he sang the verses. By the end of the song I'd pretty much got the music in my brain.

'All right, Kitty, away you go,' and he gave me my introduction.

I loved the words. And oh, the song sounded so damned good the way Hal played it. Even to my own ears my voice was assured. I only hoped it wouldn't fail me tonight.

'I knew it,' Hal said, looking up at me and smiling. 'It's your song. Now sing it again.'

If anything, it sounded even better.

'That'll do you,' Hal said when I'd gone through it a couple more times. 'Just make sure you learn the words of "Bewitched" because there's no need to practise either of them anymore. They'll sound fresh if they're not over-rehearsed.'

The desert was all sun and light one minute and before you could say Jack it was as though a black curtain had fallen. A tall British officer with fair hair stood at the side of the front row looking up at the stars. He had his back to me so I couldn't see his face. The rest of the men were busy chatting and laughing and giving each other friendly pushes and nudges.

I stood trembling at the side of the stage again. It was like the repeat of a bad dream. I wished I'd never heard of ENSA. Fragments of phrases flitted through my brain but they were all from different songs and nothing to do with the two Hal and I had chosen. I was going to make a fool of myself again. The officer who'd been staring at the sky had moved right into the front row. He caught my eye and winked. Somehow that little gesture gave me the courage to put my foot on the steps leading to the stage.

'So please give a big hand to the lovely Miss Kitty Townsend.'

There was a thin sound of clapping and a few boos. Some of them had more than likely been in the audience last week. I felt my cheeks go warm. Hal was at the piano. He looked my way, gave his slow smile, and nodded.

I opened my mouth. To my horror I began the second verse.

Oh, please. Not again. I felt the blood rush to my face. Oh,

Hal, what should I do? Carry on? But what happens when I get to the *real* second verse? I stood, frozen, my legs shaking, my fingers curled into fists at my side.

Tears of anger and misery stung my eyes. Hal half rose from the piano and turned towards me. 'I'm sorry, Kitty, I didn't realise I'd started playing the second verse,' he said in his deep tones. He gave me such a wink I couldn't have missed it. 'I'll play the first verse this time.'

There were some loud chuckles from the audience.

'Th-thank you for being patient,' I stuttered into the microphone. 'I've never sung this song before…but my mother sings it.' I looked straight out at the audience. 'I miss her.'

There were a few cheers.

I took in a breath and started again.

'*You made me love you…*'

A hush swept through the crowd and I felt a power well up inside me. I was sure they were listening to the words, and to me. My voice carried over to the lonely soldiers.

'*…you know you made me love you.*'

I let the last notes dangle in the velvet air.

There was a thunderous stamping of feet which frightened me. Had I got it wrong again? But when I glanced over to Hal he was smiling, both thumbs raised. I grinned back.

'More!' they shouted. 'More!'

Hal played the introduction to "Bewitched, Bothered and Bewildered" and this time I was ready. I tried to keep my eye on the fair-haired officer but it kept straying to the man sitting next to him. He had dark wavy hair brushed back from his forehead and a mouth which looked as though it would break into a smile at any moment. His eyes were fixed on me, and for what seemed like forever our eyes locked. It was as though he was looking deep into my soul. My stomach gave an odd quiver. I saw his mouth lift at the corners into a half-smile but I didn't smile back. But what had Hal said? That it was a good trick to find someone who looked friendly in the audience and to sing to that one alone as it made the song more personal.

I'll choose him.

At that same moment the fair-haired one looked towards me, his expression open and friendly. Perhaps I ought to focus on both men. Mum always said there was safety in numbers.

I sang the introduction and with my confidence building I fairly sailed into the tune.

'*I'm wild again, beguiled again...*'

Before I'd even finished the line I heard the words fly back to me – so softly in Italian, just like the last time. I caught my breath. I'd found the man who'd sung with me that first disastrous night. But this time the voice didn't come from the back. It was much closer. He was the Italian officer – a prisoner – sitting in the front row. I wanted to smile at him but my lips wouldn't work. I wanted to let him know I recognised his voice. But how? My legs were shaking but there was nothing I could hold on to. I managed to finish the song and stood there, my eyes glued to him, my mouth full but unsmiling. As though he knew how tight my breath felt, how hard my heart beat, he smiled at me instead. Really smiled. It lit up his face and made his eyes sparkle like the stars above us. I fought to breathe. It was as though all the wind was knocked out of me.

'Thank you, Miss Townsend,' said Tony, stepping up from the sidelines, but his words were drowned in the whistling and clapping and shouting.

All I could do was nod to the two men at the front who were staring up at me, then look over their heads to the rest of the crowd who were still giving me thunderous applause. My head was spinning. I gave a quick bow, and rushed off the stage before the next act came on. All would have been well if I hadn't caught my foot in the wire of the microphone and missed the top step. I flew headlong, my arms flailing, the shouts of dismay from the audience bursting in my ears.

I heard pounding footsteps across the wooden stage and opened my eyes.

A warm voice. 'Are you hurt?'

I must be dreaming. It was the Italian officer. But it wasn't a dream. I could smell the lemony scent of him, the warmth of the night air around him. I couldn't tell if I was hurt or not, but before I could say anything he lifted me up and carried me off the stage as though I was as light as one of our dancers. He shouted for someone to bring a chair.

'Do you feel pain?' he asked when I was seated.

'I-I don't know,' I said, reeling more from the closeness of him than the shock of falling.

'You have bad knee and little bit on hands,' he said, bending down and taking my hands carefully in his own. He peered at the grazes, then let them go. 'I don't think enough to worry. Can you stand? That way to make sure nothing is broken.'

Gently, he pulled me to my feet.

I tottered a few steps, feeling his arm firm around my waist, but my knee was so painful it bent under me. With his help I hobbled back to the chair, feeling his warm, strong fingers on my skin.

'That knee needs attention,' came the strident tones of the British officer who'd sat next to him. The Italian officer stepped aside while the British one wiped my knee with his handkerchief. I saw the blood oozing. Feeling dizzy I squeezed my eyes shut.

'We need to get her to a medic.' The words sounded blurry in my ears. 'Get it bandaged.'

'I bring her.'

My heart leapt. I opened my mouth to thank him but the English one cut in.

'No need, Colonel Andreotti – it's on my way.'

I caught the gleam of disappointment in the Italian's eyes but

171

he gave a brief nod, then a quick glance at me, and abruptly turned.

I must remember his name. Andreotti. I murmured it under my breath. Andreotti. But Italians were the enemy. I chewed my lower lip and resolved not to have any more fantasies about him.

Concentrate on the good-looking, fair-haired officer. The one on our side. But even though that was the sensible thing to do, it didn't stop me from being determined to find out all I could about Colonel Andreotti.

23

Ruggero

Ruggero Andreotti seethed as he walked back to the quarters where he lived with Travers and a couple of other officers. To be told where to go, what to do, at what time to be back from a lower-ranking officer was barely more than he could take. The worst of being a prisoner. But at least he'd managed to keep his temper in check.

But the girl: Kitty. He would have given anything to have taken her to the hospital to get her leg seen to. He would have told her how he'd loved singing with her. But why should she give him a minute of her time when she would have been given strict instructions not to fraternise with the enemy? How could he even contemplate any kind of friendship? He was a prisoner and nothing could change it.

Still fuming at Travers, he stomped his way along the hall, unbuttoning his jacket as he went through to the communal sitting room.

Ruggero poured himself a brandy and sat in one of the chairs, making a face as he felt the metal framework beneath him. He turned the glass round and round in his hands, swirling the dark golden liquid, then put his nose in the glass and sniffed. Not bad, though he'd have preferred a decent wine. He took a deep swallow.

Then a feeling of unbearable guilt and pain swept over him, causing his throat to ache and his stomach to heave. How could he even *think* of the merits of brandy and wine when his fellow Italians were being maimed and killed at this very moment he was sitting here in the lap of luxury, compared to what they were being exposed to, poor devils. He squeezed his eyes shut but it didn't stop the agony, thinking about those four men who knew the danger of a failed assassination. Four brave men. His friend, Piero. All of them Jews. That was their crime.

He slammed the glass down on the table in front of him with such violence some of the liquid splashed over the rim.

It was only because of his new promotion that he'd been so lucky. The British treated him courteously at all times, except maybe the cocky Captain Travers. They'd even allowed him his beloved records, though Travers made a big thing of walking out every time he put one on, which was rare. Ruggero closed his eyes again, picturing the Tommies going through his possessions when they'd first been taken as prisoners. They'd pulled out his precious handful of opera records, mocking him, then tossed them on one side in scorn, so that only the paper sleeves stopped them from becoming scratched. Remarkable they hadn't found the thin slips of paper he'd tucked into those sleeves, making sure nothing peeped out through the hole in the centre. He would hand them over in his own time. First, he would have to work out who he could trust to interpret his actions in the way he wanted. He grimaced. Obviously, no one trusted him at present. He sighed and leaned back in the chair.

His thoughts turned again to what was happening to the lives of decent men and women at this moment. Not only to the Jews in Poland and Czechoslovakia but all over Europe. He put his hand up to wipe the cold sweat that had broken out on his forehead, shuddering at the idea of Italy being swept into Greater Germany. Only yesterday Travers had told him the news that Belgrade had been bombed so relentlessly by the Germans it had already fallen with hardly a whimper. Ruggero wondered if Great Britain would be next on the list of horrors.

He'd heard some shocking stories about torture and starvation in the occupied countries and no human contact. It would send you mad. How this whole bloody war was going to end, heaven knew.

But one thing he knew for sure – Hitler would be rubbing his hands together in glee that the Germans wouldn't have to feed or clothe or shelter thousands of 'sub-standard' Italian soldiers who had been captured by the British in the desert. A heavy price for the British to pay. Ruggero blew out his cheeks.

The British needed to win some battles now so there was a chance Italy might actually capitulate. That was Italy's only hope as far as Ruggero could see.

He swore under his breath and got up, pacing the room. He must say something – hand over the precious pieces of information without any further delay to somehow persuade the British where his loyalties lay. He'd been interrogated when he was first captured but because of his rank it had been brief with so many other officers to attend to. Now it was time to act.

He heard the front door open, then slam shut. Moments later his minder appeared.

'I'll join you,' Travers said, striding to the cupboard in that overconfident way the British had. As though anyone who wasn't British had drawn the short straw, Ruggero thought irritably. He watched as Travers poured out a half-tumbler of brandy and took the armchair opposite.

Why hadn't Travers mentioned Kitty? Told him she was all right? But the captain's expression was thoughtful – as if he had a far greater weight on his mind than some slip of a girl. Well, he'd have to speak first.

'Did someone see to Kitty?'

'Kitty? Oh, yes,' Travers answered in an absentminded fashion. 'She'll be fine. Just a scrape. No need to worry.'

Why did he say there was no need to worry? Was he trying to tell me my place? Keep my eyes off Kitty. Be damned if I will.

He was about to challenge Travers' remark when he felt the captain's gaze upon him, alert and focused.

'I can't fathom you out, Colonel Andreotti. Your soldiers seem to respect you more than you might deserve.' Ruggero raised his eyebrows. 'Yes,' Travers went on. 'I've spoken to a few of them. You were right in the middle of things in Rome, so it seems. One of Mussolini's puppets.'

'What is puppet?'

'Someone pulls the strings and you act according to how they want you to.' Travers' lip curled.

'I have never been puppet,' Ruggero retorted angrily. 'Why do you say that?'

'It's obvious. You're in Mussolini's circle. You'd never be able to act independently. Oh, yes, you've given a few hints you're anti-fascist – easy to say in your position – yet there you were, kow-towing to that pig. Frankly, I don't believe a word you say.'

'Believe what you like.' Ruggero's temper bubbled to the surface. 'We Italians never wanted war in Europe. This was Hitler's idea.'

'Yes, I agree. Italy was in the wrong place at the wrong time,' Travers said, downing the rest of his brandy. 'But that's no excuse, I'm afraid, old boy. Your friend Mussolini wants the power just as much as Mr Hitler.' He looked at Ruggero over the top of his glass. 'So what game are you playing?'

'Game?'

'Yes. Toadying to Mussolini.'

Ruggero frowned. He wished his English was as good as his German. What on earth was toadying? He waited for Travers to say something more.

'Give me one good reason why I should believe these hints you're dropping.'

'I'd prefer to speak to Colonel Thornton, if that's all right with you.' Ruggero couldn't keep the sarcasm from his tone. 'In fact, I would appreciate if you could make me an appointment to see him as a matter of urgency.'

24

Kitty

The following morning when I got out of bed my knee was still sore but it had stopped bleeding. I'd be able to sing that evening. I needed to be careful though. If they thought I was accident-prone they might think I'd bring the troupe bad luck.

Jennifer, as I called her in my head, came flying into our canteen, hair swishing, as though she had some sort of wind machine behind her. Joyce and I were snatching a coffee break – if you could call the stuff that came out of a bottle "coffee" – before I gave Bert a hand.

I'd missed the camaraderie in the kitchen and told Jennifer I'd like to continue to do a few hours each day. After all, Joyce was kept busy all day sewing, repairing, colouring hair, helping with make-up and wigs, but all I was doing was rehearsing after lunch for a couple of hours. She seemed pleased I hadn't grown all bitter and twisted, and I think that had helped my case in allowing me to sing again.

Jennifer plonked herself on the chair next to Joyce.

'Have you heard the news?'

Joyce and I looked at one another and shrugged.

'It's unbelievable.' Jennifer's eyes gleamed.

'What is?' Joyce and I said in unison.

'Alice Delysia's joining us.'

'Who's she?' Joyce's eyebrows rose comically.

'She's only one of the most famous singers ever,' Jennifer said impatiently. 'She's known all over the place. Leads in musicals... comedy...and she can sing anything – songs, opera, you name it.' She made a tutting sound and shook her head as though she couldn't believe we were so ignorant. 'She's French. And never call her Alice – which, by the way, is pronounced "Aleece". She is *always* Miss Delysia.'

As if that explained everything. But I couldn't help catching some of her enthusiasm. Maybe she'd give Madeleine a run for her money.

'I've never heard of her,' Joyce said bluntly.

'Nor have I,' I put in.

Jennifer threw us a withering look. 'Well, she's at the top of her profession. Anyone who's anyone knows her.'

'Does Madeleine know her?' I couldn't resist asking.

Jennifer's face clouded. 'Well, Madeleine knows *of* her, if that's what you mean.'

Jennifer, I was sure, knew perfectly well I was being sarcastic. But her tone had given her away. It didn't sound as though Miss Del...Del....whatever her name was, was going to be welcomed with open arms by Madeleine. It sounded as though A*leece* was a far bigger name.

'Have *you* met her?' Joyce asked.

'No, but I can't wait.' Jennifer pushed her hair back from her forehead with her delicate hands. 'I've heard her recordings. She's extremely funny. Goes a bit close to the bone sometimes.' She broke off with an unexpected chortle. 'But the boys love her.'

Aleece sounded a lot of fun.

'When's she coming?' I asked.

'Tomorrow.' Jennifer actually beamed at us, a rare sight. 'Well, I must go and see that the studio is all clean and tidy and set out right. Not that she'll need much rehearsing, mind you.'

She left Joyce and me sitting at the table, trying hard to stifle our giggles.

178

'Poor old Madeleine,' Joyce said. 'I'll spend a bit longer with her today. Try to find out exactly how worried she is about this Alice...or rather, Al*eece*.'

We couldn't help laughing.

'But she's not "poor old Madeleine",' I said, becoming serious and getting up from the table. 'I think she's absolutely horrible and I want nothing more to do with her.'

Joyce crinkled up her eyes until they were like slits and made a "miaow" sound. I had to smile.

'Must go, Joyce,' I told her, putting down my empty cup. 'Got your lunch to cook.'

I couldn't wait for the evening when I would hear how Miss Alice Delysia put a song across, as Hal called it.

A tallish slender woman with short dark curls and a mouth the colour of a pillar box swept on to the stage in a gorgeous turquoise beaded gown as though she were at a grand ball. I completely forgot I was in a rough camp on the edge of the desert, thousands of miles from home. From those first moments she held the audience in the palm of her hand.

With a delicious gurgle she said, 'I'll start with a poem...to explain how I feel about...' she paused dramatically, '...*men.*'

Already the men were beginning to chuckle. She cleared her throat four times. I counted. I wanted to learn every secret of this famous woman I'd never heard of, and I was sure she didn't have a cold or anything. The throat-clearing must be part of her act. I couldn't take my eyes off her.

'I like a man...

I like 'is face, I like 'is place...'

She speeded up, sounding almost breathless.

'I like 'is...' She paused for several seconds.

'Well, *in any case...'* another pause, *'I like a man...'*

She gave a high-pitched giggle and the men roared. I felt myself go red as I remembered Barney and me in Diana's bed. I was sure that's what she was referring to.

'Oh, I like a man...

Oh, yes, I do...

I like a kiss, not once but twice...

Oh, no, no, no, no, no, no, no...

I like 'im big, I like 'im strong

And when the winter comes along...

I like a man.'

She practically sang out the word "man", waving her arms to the crowd as though she were embracing them all personally. Her speaking voice was seductive and I could only imagine how the soldiers felt as they listened and shouted and whistled.

'And now for a song.' Miss Delysia waited until the cheering died down. 'I sang zis one at ze London Pavilion. I 'ope you enjoy it.'

I was watching a real professional. Much more so than Madeleine. More than anyone I'd ever seen. I drew in a breath as though her song rested on my concentration.

She cleared her throat again and opened her mouth. Her accent was just as strong when she sang.

'If you could care for me

As I could care for you...'

She swooped up very high on the last two words, then brought her voice down an octave. It was extraordinary. Her voice was high and clear and rich. She continued to do the strange swooping with her voice. I loved it. She ended her performance with another song which at first I thought was just funny.

'Oh, do it again...

I might say "No, no, no," but do it again...'

She strode up and down the stage and I could see the soldiers' eyes follow her every movement.

'You know if you do, you won't regret it

Come and get it...' Here the audience laughed.

'*Please do it again. Oh, please...*' her voice rose almost to a shriek, '*do it again.*'

She stopped abruptly, laughing, giggling, holding out her arms to the lonely men. Their clapping practically burst my eardrums. But when I heard the soldiers stamping their feet and calling out, I realised Miss Delysia definitely meant more than simply asking a man to kiss her again.

I stood there in the darkness, rigid with envy, admiration, insecurity, and such happiness that I was actually here listening to someone so different, so utterly confident, so incredible.

'One more song,' came the shouts.

'*D'accord*!' Miss Delysia said, still laughing. Then she stopped dead, her smile fading. The audience immediately hushed. Again, she cleared her throat and momentarily closed her eyes. Then fluttered them open. This time her voice was softer, more intimate.

'*The badge on your coat will be close to my heart*
It will always remind me of you.
All the time we're apart...'

I didn't hear the next bit. Tears were falling down my cheeks though I had no idea why. Maybe I was missing Mum. Or was it the father I never knew? Instinctively, I felt he would have loved the song. I closed my eyes. If only...I shook my head. I mustn't think like that. "If only" were words that meant nothing. It was done. Dr Alexander Townsend – my real father – was dead.

'*I love you, love you, more and more each day*
The badge will be my memory
Till the day you come back to me.'

The applause made the stage vibrate. I could feel it from where I stood at the side, tears now streaming down my face.

'You are very kind,' she laughed, bowing her head in little bobs, as she strode up and down the stage so she could engage every single soldier. I'm sure they all thought she was singing to them alone. There was more wild applause as the men leapt to their feet, cheering.

'Too kind. You are too kind.' She smiled at them. 'Zank you so much.'

To rapturous applause she tripped daintily off the stage at the other side from where I stood.

Through a fog I heard my name being called. Something inside had sprung to life, and I didn't even notice my sore knee as I practically leapt up the steps on to the stage with a new belief in myself. I waited while the audience finally quietened down after Alice Delysia's mesmerising performance.

I was singing with a full heart. Singing with every fibre of my being, hands reaching out to the soldiers – boys and men – as though my song might be the last they ever heard. I finished with the "White Cliffs Of Dover" and beckoned them to join in. They did. Their voices sounded strong and true, and when the song ended, to my astonishment, soldiers were standing up and shouting and clapping; then others were following suit until every man was on his feet. I'd heard of standing ovations, and as I walked off the platform, my cheeks were flushed with excitement that I'd touched the nerves of those brave men. This time my tears were tears of joy. For once, I felt I'd made a difference.

Someone was breathing heavily behind me. I looked round. Madeleine. Her undeniably pretty face was contorted and her eyes were blazing as they pierced into my own.

I was determined not to let Madeleine unnerve me. Why did she hate me? I didn't have "the hots", as Joyce called it, for Jennifer Long, so what was the matter with the woman? But under her furious stare I dropped my eyes first and just said goodnight. She stood there perfectly still, her blonde hair almost silver in the moonlight, but I was certain she watched my back until I was out of her sight.

I was already in my bed, hands behind my head, trying to sort it all out, when Joyce came in.

'Well, what did you think of our Miss Delysia?' she asked immediately.

182

'I adored her,' I said, not hesitating a second. 'I'd love to tell her how much I enjoyed her performance, but Hal says she was whisked off to one of Cairo's posh hotels.'

'No wonder Madeleine's nervous.'

'Why should she be? She's got a lovely voice...even though it's not so high as mine,' I couldn't resist adding.

Joyce grinned. 'You were the best you've ever been. Probably annoyed the hell out of Madeleine. But I'm not talking about that. I mean Alice's personality. Wasn't she amazing?'

It was even more amazing the next morning when Lionel knocked on our door and handed me an envelope with my name on. I turned it over in my hand. It had been sent by a courier from the Artemide hotel.

'Who on earth—?'

'Why don't you open it and see,' Lionel grinned. 'And do it in front of me. I want to know too.'

I carefully opened the envelope and pulled out a sheet of expensive notepaper – the kind that had a watermark.

'Read it out,' Lionel commanded.

'Dear Miss Townsend,' I began. 'I hear your songs last night and think how charming you are. You have a voice that improves with more training. But your dress is hideous. I have several dresses and am sure one suits you perfectly. If you like to take coffee with me tomorrow, Wednesday, at 11.30, I will send a taxi. Perhaps you let me know. I look forward to our chat. Alice Delysia.'

I had to read it through three times before I could take in that this was my chance to actually speak to the famous Miss Delysia in person. Then I blushed to read she thought my dress hideous. I'd worn the royal blue one again. But if I was able to borrow one of Miss Delysia's dresses...well, I should think myself as good as... well, as good as Madeleine, for a start.

'So are you going?' Lionel broke into my thoughts.

'No, I don't think I'll bother,' I said with a straight face.

'What! Are you mad?'

I couldn't stop laughing. 'Of *course* I'm going. Do you take me for a complete idiot?'

25

The taxi was twenty minutes late. I really didn't think it would turn up, but in the end a shabby-looking black car pulled to a stop where I was waiting just outside the camp gate, getting hotter and hotter. I was getting used to things not working in the same way as at home. The heat was smothering and when I stepped into the back of the car it was even worse. Besides, it had some kind of strong animal smell like goat, but I was too excited to make any kind of fuss and it wouldn't have been any use anyway.

'You okay, missie?' The taxi driver twisted his neck round to me, with no apology for being late.

'Yes, thank you,' I answered, as I tried to make myself comfortable on the stained fabric seat.

'We go,' he said, and slammed down the accelerator.

We roared off. Grabbing the door handle to stop myself from keeling over, I took in the blur that was Cairo. Compared to King's Lynn – a strange comparison, I grinned to no one – it was a madhouse. The taxi's windows were rolled down because of the heat, but it let in the boiling air. The noise outside was a jumble of men's loud voices, animals braying and barking, and two screaming cats fighting to the death. Children rushed in and out of the traffic selling anything from fly swatters to melons, mindless of the dangers. Donkeys were patiently jostling with taxis and there was a sprinkling of private motor cars, many of the drivers suddenly braking and shouting out to friends on the streets and honking their horns. It made me feel quite ill to look at such a scene, and yet it fascinated me at the same time.

Spicy aromas wafted up from large wicker baskets where traders had set up crude stalls, some of which overflowed into the road itself. The traders were calling out their wares; not dissimilar after all to the market in King's Lynn. I couldn't help grinning, longing to share all this with Joyce. But amongst all the seething chaos stood elegant buildings, banks, theatres, night clubs, hotels and restaurants.

The driver drew up outside a grand building with the solitary word "Artemide" emblazoned across the entrance.

The foyer looked the size of Liverpool Street station. Shaking with nerves I walked over to the reception desk and told a man in the hotel's uniform that I had an appointment with Miss Delysia. He looked surprised, then asked my name.

'I'll call Miss Delysia's room.'

He spoke briefly on the telephone, then turned to me and said someone would take me up.

In the lift was a young uniformed boy who took me to the fourth floor. When we stopped he pointed to a door opposite. I couldn't have missed it because it had her name on a small plaque outside. Maybe that would be me, one day.

I knocked, and immediately Miss Delysia herself appeared.

'It is nice to see you, Kitty. *Entrez.*' She gestured me inside.

Her room was beautiful. There was no sign of a bed so I assumed she had more than one room. How wonderful to be so famous. She sat me down and rang a bell.

'Coffee for two, *s'il vous plait,* and some sweet cakes.' She swung round to face me. 'Now, Kitty, I want you to sing a song.'

I gave a start of surprise.

'What—'

'Sing what you like. Zere is no piano but it is better. I can hear you wizzout distraction.'

I hadn't expected this at all so I wasn't prepared. But Miss Delysia had more or less ordered me, so that's what I had to do.

I sang a couple of my usual songs, and was encouraged to see Miss Delysia nodding her head every so often, and smiling.

'Bravo,' she said when I'd finished. 'You have 'eart.' She pounded her chest and laughed. 'Many peoples sing, but many peoples have no 'eart.'

I wondered where this was leading.

'Tell me about yourself,' she demanded, when the waiter disappeared after leaving a tray with the most enticing smells. She poured out two delicate china cups of coffee and handed me one, then offered me the plate of small sweet cakes. I couldn't answer for a moment; I was too busy letting the honey drip down the back of my throat and savouring the precious mouthfuls.

'I want to sing more than anything in the world,' I began. 'Professionally, like you,' I added. She laughed. 'But Miss Long took me off the programme when I made a mess of it, and although I've been allowed to sing again, it wouldn't take much for me to be sent back to the kitchen.'

'Why did this 'appen?'

I told her about Madeleine. She was silent for a few minutes and I was curious to know what on earth she was thinking. She suddenly said, 'Madeleine has not right to say who goes on ze programme. It is for Jennifer Long to make decisions. I speak to Jennifer to make sure it does not 'appen again.'

'Oh no, Miss Delysia, please don't do that,' I blurted, horrified it would cause another load of trouble. 'Madeleine has got it in for me for some reason and I don't want to make it worse. She's already furious that Miss Long said I could sing again.'

'Because she is insecure,' Miss Delysia said. 'But leave to me. I promise not to make worse.' She looked at me. ''Ave you ever been to the opera?'

I shook my head. I'd always wanted to but it was out of my

league. And they regularly took place in London which was too far from King's Lynn to go in one night.

'We go togezzer,' she said. 'I introduce you to a magic world. We go zis afternoon.'

'I'm not wearing the right clothes,' I said, at once thrilled but anxious, remembering Mum telling me how everyone had been dressed up very fancy when she and my father went to the opera.

'You are all right as you are,' Miss Delysia said. 'It is just dress rehearsal. No one will be in evening clothes.'

'What time will we be back?' We had a show tonight.

'If we are late Madeleine can do by 'erself,' Alice Delysia chuckled.

If I was late it might get me into Jennifer Long's bad books again, but the chance to be with such a famous person was too wonderful to resist.

'It doesn't look a bit like an Egyptian building,' I said, my eyes almost on stalks as I stood looking with awe and instant love at the dramatic colonnaded façade which was the Royal Opera House.

'It isn't.' She smiled at my obvious delight. 'It's an Italian architect. Maybe Italian built. Is wonderful, no? And so is *Aida*. I must tell you, it is sung in Italian. Ze composer, Verdi, was Italian. And opera sound better in Italian. English is no good for opera.'

'What is it about?' I asked her, feeling apprehensive that I'd be watching something for several hours and not understand a word.

'We go in to find our seat and I explain.'

I followed Miss Delysia through the entrance where she spoke to a uniformed man, who finally nodded. Two minutes later we were sitting in what she called a royal box. The seats were of a crimson velvet and deeply padded. As soon as I sat down I felt wrapped in luxury. We were quite high up and although it was a side view of the stage I was sure we'd be able to see everything perfectly.

'So,' Miss Delysia said, pulling off her gloves and settling into her velvet cocoon, 'ze story is of an ancient princess from Ethiopia, called Aida. She is captured by ze Egyptian army but Rhademas, who is leader of ze army, fall in love wiz her. But ze pharaoh has a daughter, and zis daughter is also in love wiz Rhademas. She screams to Aida zey are rivals. Rhademas refuses ze daughter because he loves Aida. But zey are only 'appy for short time. He is called traitor. Zen ze daughter, I forget her name, she say to Rhademas she will set him free if he forget Aida. He say he cannot. So ze pharaoh order Rhademas to be buried alive in ze rocks. Aida find him and she die in his arms. Zat is end.'

'Oh, that's dreadful,' I said, a shiver of horror creeping up my back. I'd really only understood the last part. It was difficult to follow the story with Miss Delysia's strong accent.

'It is same wiz many operas,' she explained. 'Zey nearly all have bad ending. Everyone die, or sometimes just ze woman or she commit...what you call it?' She made a stabbing sign with her glove to her chest.

'Suicide,' I said.

'It is always very much emotion. Don't be surprised if you cry.'

I wasn't sure I wanted to sit through something so mournful, but we were here and the theatre was beginning to fill. I looked about me. Just as Miss Delysia had said, no one was in their finery so I didn't feel awkward, though I'd loved to have seen all the beautiful evening dresses and flashing jewellery when it was the real performance. But the glittering interior of the theatre more than made up for the plain clothes of the small audience. I thought about how my father was half-Italian. Maybe that was the reason I felt drawn to anything to do with Italy. It was in my blood. Tears threatened me. What would my father think if he could see Italy at war with England? Italy was part of his homeland, and England was the country he'd chosen to spend the rest of his life in after meeting my mother.

For an instant I saw him clearly. A lovely tall man with black wavy hair. And the two of us would make up songs and sing together. I remembered his clean smell when I nuzzled into his neck, safe in his arms. When I didn't have to question his love. How could I have accepted that another man was my father? When had the changeover happened? After all, I was almost four when he died. Surely that was old enough not to forget. But I don't ever remember saying to Mum that when Dad came back from America he wasn't my father. Maybe because he was Frankie and Harry's real father they had no problem calling him Dad, and I just followed suit. With Dad being so jealous of my father, he probably forbade Mum to tell me about him. And to keep the peace, which is what their generation of women seemed to do all the time, she must have obeyed him. Then I thought of Mum's flashing eyes when she was extra cross and I smiled. She wouldn't take any nonsense from Dad, no matter what it cost her. And yes, I was like her. But what traits had I taken from my real father?

At that moment I vowed I would find my father's family. And even though I was still angry that his mother had refused to acknowledge my mother, I needed to find out about her after this terrible war was over. I'd have to be patient – not easy for me – but one day I might get some answers.

I also had to remind myself that Italy was Britain's enemy. My mind wandered to that other Italian. The one with jet-black wavy hair and twinkling dark brown eyes, and a mouth just made for singing. And kissing. I smiled in the darkness. What would it be like? My scalp prickled just thinking about him. An Italian prisoner of war. The enemy. But I couldn't think of him like that. Dear Joyce had found out his name, though she refused to tell me how. I whispered it to myself. Ruggero.

The lights dimmed. The orchestra started up. At first they made odd clashing noises for a minute or two, sounding awful, but the next moment the curtains swished back and there was ancient Egypt in all its golden glory. A massive pyramid was surrounded by

190

soaring pillars carved with men dressed only in a short white cloth tied round their waist, some of them wearing the head of a strange-looking animal. Pairs of eyes in the faces of golden gods stared blankly down on us, and the theatre lights bounced off the temple looking for all the world like the setting sun. It was as though the stage was on fire.

At first, the music was gentle and haunting. It wasn't long before a man dressed in a sort of kilt-length skirt, wandered out on to the stage and mimed some expressions that I couldn't understand. But when he finally began to sing I somehow knew that he was uncomfortable and worried about his position. His voice reminded me of Ruggero's. But minutes later all thoughts of anyone or any misgivings I had evaporated as I listened to the most heavenly singing.

'What do you think?' Alice handed me a lemonade at the interval.

'I love it,' I managed to stutter.

She laughed. 'I knew you would.'

And when Aida, the pretty Ethiopian princess sang, I was well and truly captivated.

When it finished – all too soon – I wiped away the tears I'd shed for poor Aida. Miss Delysia turned to me and smiled, her own eyes brimming over.

It had been a perfect day. Except for one thing. Miss Delysia had forgotten about the dress.

26

Ruggero

'Thanks, Captain Travers, that'll be all.' Colonel Thornton nodded a dismissal.

'Right, sir.' Travers saluted again and disappeared.

'Take a seat, Colonel Andreotti.' Colonel Thornton gestured to the one chair. 'One thing before we start,' his eyes flicked over Ruggero's face, 'you're a bit young, aren't you, for a lieutenant colonel?'

'I came in the army as a captain. But quickly got promotions. It's not so difficult in war.'

'Hmm.' Colonel Thornton looked thoughtful. He let a few seconds roll by. 'So you wanted to see me?'

'I come straight to the point,' Ruggero said, keeping his gaze firmly fixed on the colonel. 'I want you to know that I am not a fascist. My sympathy – loyalty – is with the Allies. That is, the British.'

'Yes, I hear you told Captain Travers you're anti-fascist.' His cloudy-grey gaze drilled into Ruggero's eyes, and Ruggero had the uncomfortable feeling Thornton was trying to dig deep into his soul. 'Before we take this further I need to know more of your background,' Thornton continued. 'You were a close adviser to Mussolini, were you not, before you were sent to Egypt? Would you like to explain exactly your position and what kind and level of advice you gave him?'

Ruggero breathed out. 'I've told one of the other colonels all this before.'

'But you haven't told *me*.' Colonel Thornton's features stiffened.

'Tell me your background before the war. How you got to be in Mussolini's circle if you didn't agree with him. How you weren't found out. I need to be clear about things.'

'I was his translator, not adviser…as I'm sure you know,' Ruggero began. 'Mussolini doesn't read and write well in German, though he can speak it – after a fashion. But I raised the suspicion.'

'Go on.' Thornton leaned forward on his desk, steepling his nicotine-stained fingers.

'I brought together a group of resisters. Then I planned an assassination to kill Hitler and Mussolini at the same time – when Hitler was coming next to Rome.' He was gratified to see that he had Thornton's full attention. 'We planted four snipers in the crowd. They had Nazi uniforms so they look like Hitler's security and will not be recognised by other Italian workers loyal to Mussolini. I had to give the sign. Then the four would raise their rifles and shoot. But a fire started in the room at the back of where Hitler and Mussolini were standing – no one found why – and smoke poured on to the balcony. You could not see who or where to shoot. But they shoot anyway. Hoping. But the bullets went astray. Hitler's bodyguard had a small wound to his arm. Nothing more. All four Italian resisters were caught and tortured and executed.'

Ruggero's eyes stung at the thought of his friend, Piero. Not only him, but his whole family had been executed. His voice trembled. 'How could I be supporter of Mussolini? Him and that madman, Hitler.'

'Good God,' Thornton said, his eyes narrowing and leaning even further forward.

'Hitler insists…insisted there is a spy in Mussolini's circle.'
'And is there?'

'He thinks I am involved,' Ruggero continued, 'but he could found no evidence. Hitler tells Mussolini I am hiding…no, I mean,' he paused, fumbling for the English word, 'protecting someone or some people.'

'And were you?'

'Yes. So Hitler is suspicious of me. He wants me shot. Mussolini has to show he has taken serious action. And I'm of least important as a translator. He decide it best to train me as front-line officer and orders me to Egypt. You know the rest.'

'Would you be prepared to work for the British?' Colonel Thornton suddenly asked, his voice hardening, his eyes sharp.

'That is what I want to talk about. It is what I want for a long time.' Ruggero welcomed the relief flooding over him as he spoke the words. 'And apart from the fascists, it's the same for most Italians. They don't want to fight the British. Our two countries have always been friendly. My people don't have their heart in this war. And most of them hate the Germans.'

'Excellent.' Thornton offered him a cigarette and lit them both. 'That's the impression *we* get. Maybe it won't be long before they finally wake up.'

Ruggero nodded as he gratefully inhaled.

'But before we take this any further,' the colonel went on, blowing out a thick funnel of smoke, his flinty eyes boring into Ruggero's, 'you need to convince me of your motives, and that you are truly on the side of the Allies.'

'You will have to trust from all I have told you. One officer's word to another.'

'Not good enough, I'm afraid.'

'Maybe this will convince you.' Ruggero put a file on Thornton's desk and opened it. He took out a sheaf of papers and handed them over.

'What's all this?' Thornton frowned as he leafed through them. 'Why are they in German?'

'They're straight from Hitler's office,' Ruggero said. 'I have the translations in the folder. Some of the information is...' he fumbled for the word, 'stale, but some tells his next plans. Of much interest to the Nazis is the American submarine – the *Reuben James*.' He caught the colonel's eye across the desk. 'Do you read German?'

Colonel Thornton's voice cooled. 'No. I don't.'

Ruggero forced himself not to show any smugness. 'Then you will need these.' He pulled out some more papers from the other side of the file. Colonel Thornton pushed his glasses back up on the bridge of his nose with his forefinger and began to read. Once or twice he raised his eyebrows. 'Hmm. *Most* interesting,' he murmured almost to himself. A minute or two passed before the colonel looked up. 'And it didn't occur to you to hand this information in straight away?'

Ruggero shook his head. 'It might be taken the wrong way.'

'How do you mean?'

'It could be used against me – incriminating evidence.'

'Hmm.' Colonel Thornton tapped his pen on the desk a few times and read a little more. Ruggero waited, determined not to allow his impatience to get the better of him. Surely the colonel would believe him.

'I'll keep these, if you don't mind,' Colonel Thornton said, putting them all neatly together. He pinned them with a large paperclip.

Ruggero nodded his consent. 'Do you now believe I am sincere?' he couldn't help asking.

'From one officer to another we must trust one another,' came the instant reply. Colonel Thornton actually broke into a half-smile. 'By the way, where did you hide these papers?'

'In the sleeves of my records.'

Thornton nodded. 'Fair enough.' He cleared his throat and Ruggero was sure he was trying to give himself thinking time. 'In the meantime,' Thornton took off his glasses and polished them with a snow-white handkerchief, 'I want you to do something for me. Jennifer Long, the woman who looks after the entertainment group – cousin of mine, actually – asked me for a favour – told me about a certain little songbird here. She tells me the girl likes opera and wants to learn. Has a great future.' He put his glasses back on. 'Well, Jennifer wants her to have Italian lessons. Give her a chance for a singing career when this bloody war is over. It's the least we can do.' He looked straight at Ruggero whose eyes steadily met his.

'Who is it you want me to teach?' Ruggero's fingers gripped the sides of the chair.

Colonel Thornton picked up a glass of water and took several deep swallows.

'It's a Miss Kitty Townsend.'

27

Kitty

'Colonel Thornton heard you went to the opera with Alice Delysia and loved it.' Jennifer waylaid me as I was leaving the canteen after breakfast.

'How did he know that?'

Jennifer smiled casually. 'Don't spread it around but he's my cousin. I told him.'

'I don't understand.'

Bad enough to have Jennifer and Madeleine's beady eye on me, let alone Colonel Thornton's. I wondered what on earth was coming next.

'I asked Basil...Colonel Thornton if one of the Italian prisoners could be spared to give you Italian lessons.'

'But why?'

I didn't understand. Surely Colonel Thornton had more important things to do than arrange for an ENSA singer to have Italian lessons.

'Kitty, you're young. Your voice could easily be classically trained. You already have an operatic voice but you need to know what you're singing about. Opera is usually in Italian. I wanted you to take advantage of your time here and learn the language. I think you will be very pleased one day – when you're building your career.'

I swallowed my astonishment. 'What did Colonel Thornton say?'

'He said he'd like to think that one day when you're famous, he helped in some small way.' Jennifer's face was serious. 'You might as well do it with good grace.'

'I don't want to sing opera. I'd never be able to do that. I just like singing the songs I sing.'

'Don't be a fool, Kitty. You've got your whole life in front of you. Take this opportunity. You may never get another chance.'

I wasn't sure I wanted to study a foreign language. It sounded like a lot of hard work to me. I could think of lots of things I'd rather do than sit and learn a load of words that meant nothing to me. And then I caught myself. *Don't be so stupid, Kitty.* Of course I would do it. If I ever had the chance, I'd be able to speak Italian to Ruggero Andreotti. He'd be so surprised…and I hoped impressed.

'When do I start?'

'Today. Two-thirty. In the officers' mess. Colonel Thornton said you can have a quiet hour or two without being disturbed.'

Two-thirty and I was walking towards the officers' mess. It was a long, low building with a corrugated roof and small-paned windows, and although the ENSA group had officer status and were allowed in, we never used it. We preferred the friendly canteen. The door had been a cherry-red colour once, but now the paint was peeling off. I couldn't hear a sound from inside. Unsure what to do I stood there, wondering if my new teacher was already there. I hoped he'd be patient. I'd never learned a word of any foreign language before and felt nervous. He'd probably think I was an idiot if I didn't learn quickly enough. And where would I practise? Would I have a book to take back to my room? All these questions buzzed through me as I tapped lightly on the door.

It opened. And my mouth opened. In my wildest dreams I'd never imagined it would be him, a lieutenant colonel, giving me Italian lessons.

He stood there smiling at me. 'It is nice to see you, Signorina

Townsend,' he said, and stepped to the side to make way for me. 'I am Lieutenant Colonel Ruggero Andreotti. When we are here you may call me Ruggero.'

'I don't understand...'

He gently put his hand on my waist and nudged me inside. 'Didn't Jennifer Long explain?'

'Yes, but—'

'Maybe we should not question more. Come and sit. We will get to work straight.'

'Straight away,' I corrected. If he was going to teach me Italian I'd help him brush up his English.

'Straight away,' he repeated, his warm brown eyes twinkling.

There were two glasses of water on the table, and a notepad and pencil.

'I want you to write things down to learn again when you have time. It would be better if I had a lesson book to give you, but I did not know I will be helping a beautiful young English singer with her Italian.'

Such a compliment said with such a tender smile, my mouth went dry. I couldn't answer. My legs were so wobbly I was relieved when we sat down.

'We start with simple everyday words,' he said, smiling at me. I wanted to look at him forever, his face fascinated me so.

He named various objects around the room such as "door" and "window" and "table" and "chair", making me repeat the Italian words several times until I got closer to the pronunciation. It was almost impossible for me to concentrate. I was so conscious of him sitting close to me, his hand occasionally brushing mine as he used them to emphasise a point. Every time it happened it was as though all the nerve endings in my hand were exposed and tingling. I wanted more than anything for him to kiss me. Once his eyes trained on my mouth and I was sure he was thinking the same thing. After half an hour he got up abruptly.

'I think that is enough for today. Too long and you get tired and forget.'

My heart fell with disappointment. Jennifer had definitely mentioned an hour or two. Just as I was about to tell him I wasn't tired at all and could easily do another half hour he said, 'I have something special for you.'

He walked over to a side table where there was a gramophone. There was a small stack of records by the side. He studied one or two labels, then pulled one out of its jacket and put it on the turntable.

'Listen carefully. It is all in Italian but you will feel the emotion.'

The introduction to the piece began. And then the most glorious female voice filled the fluorescent-lit room.

'It is the Contessa's aria from *Le nozze di Figaro*,' Ruggero whispered, then glanced at my puzzled expression. '*The Marriage of Figaro*. Mozart.'

It didn't mean anything to me although I'd heard some Mozart with my mother. But nothing like this. A woman's voice sailed out of the gramophone and I saw Ruggero close his eyes, the muscles in his face relaxing as though he were dreaming. My own eyelids drifted downwards. I'd never heard the song before and I couldn't understand a word, but it spoke to me. As her voice trilled up and down the notes my body thrilled in response, just as it had when I'd seen *Aida*. But this was more intimate. There were no distractions of other people around. Only Ruggero and me to listen. Tears squeezed through my closed eyes and ran down my cheeks. I didn't bother to brush them away. I didn't want to make any movement to break the spell.

And when her voice throbbed to its heady finale I reluctantly opened my eyes to find Ruggero gazing at me, a half-smile pulling at the corners of his mouth.

'Do you like?'

'I liked it very much.' My voice sounded shaky. 'I liked it more than very much.'

He nodded, as though that was the answer he expected.

'It was you, wasn't it, who sang with me that first time?' I drew slightly away so I could see his expression. 'When I forgot my words.'

'I couldn't help myself.' He smiled at me as though reassuring a child. 'But you recovered...I mean, remembered the words soon after.'

'Because you gave me confidence,' I said. 'I'll never forget that evening. I was so nervous. It was my first time on stage. I wondered who was singing. Who had such a wonderful voice.'

'And I thought the same for you,' he said. 'Your voice can be trained for opera. That is why it is important you learn the language. Then you can sing with your whole heart.'

My whole heart was beating so hard I was sure he could hear it. Nothing would quieten it down. And from that moment I knew I would do my very best to learn his beautiful language. And one day I would sing opera.

'It is time for us to go, Kitty,' he said, saying my name for the first time.

I didn't want to go. I wanted to stay. Just to look at him. I couldn't take my eyes off him. Couldn't drag them away. The way his brown eyes sometimes flashed golden. The shadows under them. From worry and sleepless nights? The cleft in his chin. His lips. I wanted to feel them on my mouth more than anything I'd ever wanted in my whole life.

And then his hands pulled me to my feet and his arms tightened around me. It happened so fast I was hardly aware of his movement. Our eyes were on the same level. His held a question. And then he stepped back.

'You are very young, Kitty.' He traced the outline of my face with his fingertips and I felt my cheeks grow warm.

He'd been about to kiss me. I know he had. I could have wept with frustration.

I think Ruggero hated leaving me as much as I hated leaving him. But my senses leapt knowing from now on it wouldn't be so difficult to see him. It was as though we had Colonel Thornton's blessing to have some privacy. I didn't think to ask why. We fell into a routine. When I arrived at the mess hall Ruggero would give me a quick kiss on the cheek, the sort you'd give a friend you hadn't seen for a while, but never anything more.

We'd get down to studies right away. It was slow to begin with and Ruggero was not the most patient teacher; he often became irritable if I didn't pick it up immediately. But I'd laugh in his face and kiss his cheek and make him laugh too. And gradually I began to hear with my ear the sheer musicality of the language and to love getting my tongue around the words.

'You are beginning to sound like a real Italian, Kitty,' Ruggero laughed.

I lived for those lessons.

'As you have been very good I will play you some opera,' Ruggero would say, his eyes gleaming.

I heard arias – as I had been instructed to call them – from Verdi, Bellini, Mozart and Puccini, and adored them all. Once, when it was particularly sad, he reached for my hand, his fingers winding through mine, stroking the fingertips. And then he opened his eyes and searched my own as though asking a question. Time stopped. He shook his head. And when I plunged into the depths of despair that nothing would ever happen, he squeezed my hand and kissed it.

And once he kissed the palm, then curled my fingers around it as though to hold his kiss there forever.

After every lesson finished he ended with one particular song, nothing to do with opera.

'It's called "Bella Ciao",' he said, the first time he sang it to me. 'Listen carefully to the words. You know some of them now. It is a special Italian song, Kitty. Know that I think it important and true.'

By the time he repeated the chorus I could hum along, and was determined to learn every word. If it was important to Ruggero then it was important to me.

'Tell me how you understand this song,' he said on our fourth lesson.

I couldn't help counting them. I wanted them to go on forever and be lost in his smiles. The twinkle in his eyes as he kissed my cheek. Hearing him say, '*Buongiorno*, Kitty. I'm so happy to see you.' I knew it wouldn't be long before it would come to an end and I wouldn't see him for twenty-four more hours, so I'd mumble something back, but I couldn't stop the thought that he still hadn't kissed me the way I wanted him to. All this was jumbling through my mind as Ruggero patiently waited for me to answer.

'The tune is happy but I think the words are sad,' I said, hesitating. '*Bella ciao* – it means "goodbye, beautiful", doesn't it?'

Did it mean he would say goodbye to me one day?

'Yes, it does. But it is not all sad. It is a song of hope.' He looked at me. 'But you do not ever sing it where there are people as long as we are at war. Do you promise?'

'I promise,' I said, not understanding why a shiver ran down my spine. If only Italy hadn't joined in the war. If only the Italians had been on *our* side. But if they had I would never have met him. It gave me a peculiar feeling.

After that we'd sing the song together, and just like that first night when I froze with terror and he helped me, our voices blended perfectly.

The tune of "Bella Ciao" was so catchy I used to hum it softly around the camp. Once when I thought Joyce was safely out of the way and I was in our quarters I began singing the words. At first I didn't see her as I was in the bathroom singing away. She immediately wanted to know what the song was, but I just mumbled it was something Hal had played. It wasn't just the song I was determined to keep to myself, it was my time spent with Ruggero.

It was our secret and too precious to share.

It was our fifth lesson. We were coming to the end of our allotted time when Mike Travers came in, making me jump. We'd never been interrupted before.

'Colonel Thornton wants you for a few minutes. Just to clarify something.'

'Excuse me, Miss Townsend,' Ruggero said, sending me a wink which Mike couldn't see. I hid a smile. 'I will be back to finish.'

When they'd disappeared I skimmed over the notes I'd taken and the Italian book we were reading, wishing it was a children's book to make life easier. But all I could think of was Ruggero. What did Colonel Thornton want to speak to him about? Moodily, I went over to the gramophone and picked up one of the records which was already out of its cover, obviously the one he was going to play at the end of our lesson. As I was taking it out of the sleeve I heard a faint rustle of paper. Flattening my hand I felt inside and pulled out a thin piece of paper folded in two. Feeling guilty snooping into Ruggero's personal possessions, and with my heart throbbing in my ears, I was just about to unfold the sheet when I heard footsteps. There was no time to put the paper back where I'd found it. Without thinking I hurriedly dropped it into my handbag.

The door opened.

I looked up and caught my breath. His eyes were full of desire. My heart started pounding as he pulled me to my feet, just as he had that first time. But today was different. He held me close against his chest and I could feel his heart thudding against my breasts. His hands were in my hair. 'Kitty.' It was a whisper. And then he groaned as he tipped my head back, cradling it with one arm to steady me while he kissed me. My lips parted as his tongue slipped into my mouth, warm and exploring, caressing my teeth, my tongue, then licking each of my lips in turn, until my whole body quivered and the place between my legs tingled with longing as I felt him hard against me. I tried to speak but he stopped me with more kisses until I thought I would faint. Until finally he drew away. I clung on, my arms round his neck, my trembling legs threatening to collapse from under me. As though he knew, he gripped me with both arms and looked deep into my eyes.

'Dearest Kitty.' His voice was unsteady.

'Ruggero, I—'

'Hush,' he said, covering my lips with his fingers. 'Do not say a word. We do not want the colonel to have the suspicion.'

And then he kissed me again.

I told myself I'd remember those kisses for the rest of my life. But they wouldn't be enough. I wanted him to go on kissing me forever.

Joyce was chatting away when I got back to my room to get ready for supper and the evening's performance, but I couldn't take in what she was saying. Nor did I have the chance to look at the piece of paper. What it might contain. I didn't want to open it. It might be a worried letter from his mother – or much worse, a girlfriend. Whatever it was, it must be important for him to have hidden it. In the end I decided to give it back to him, unopened, the very next time I saw him. After those kisses I wanted to be completely honest with him. I could only hope he would believe me that I hadn't read something so private.

28

Ruggero

The door closed behind her. Ruggero sat down heavily on the nearest chair. He no longer knew himself. If anyone had asked why he was so attracted to young Kitty Townsend he would not have been able to answer. Her age, for one thing, was against her, as far as he was concerned. She must be ten years younger. He had no business to be encouraging her. He'd seen the signs on her face that she liked him. Her shining eyes when he opened the door to her, as though she lived for that moment. Her flushed expression when he came near. Her voice, always nervous at first, then becoming more self-assured when they talked. Her beautiful dark blue eyes fixed on him. The way she'd run her fingers through his hair just now. Or had it been him caressing *her* dark hair that tumbled to her shoulders? He couldn't think. It was as though they'd been one.

He hadn't wanted her to leave. He'd almost begged her to stay. But though his body ached for her, anything more between them was impossible. It made no difference that the two of them were desperate for an end to this senseless slaughter so people could go back to their lives in peace; he was just another prisoner of war. He closed his eyes but the vision of her was as clear as if she were standing before him, her lips parted, responding to his kisses, just as she had only minutes ago. His body trembled with desire. She hadn't acted like any schoolgirl. No, Kitty had been all woman. He felt himself hardening as he imagined making love to her. Touching her. Feeling her skin warm against his. At first the shock, and then the perfect knowledge of being inside her. He shook his head in despair. At her age she'd be a virgin. And the last thing he wanted was to hurt her.

He tried to calm himself. Not think of the physicality of her but herself as a person. Her sense of fun and adventure. Her openness when she spoke of the horrors going on in the world. How he longed to be open with her too. Tell her his fears for his beloved Italy and how he'd plotted to get rid of Mussolini and Hitler but it had all gone dreadfully wrong. No, he must keep his mouth shut. It was too risky to say anything until he started officially working for the British – if he ever did. One word leaking to the wrong person... Mussolini had long arms. But Ruggero would tell her the first minute he could that he was on the British side. His face broke into a smile. He didn't have to explain anything. She knew anyway. She knew he wasn't the enemy.

Darling Kitty.

The sheer joy she brought to the soldiers each evening with her heavenly voice. It was one of the things he loved most – her passion for music and her love of singing. How she adored listening to his records. She was beginning to sing some of the arias in Italian, just quietly, but always perfectly in tune.

Elisabetta's take-it-or-leave-it attitude to opera had always been a deep disappointment to him. But he'd learned you can't force anyone to be crazy about it the way he was. The music either reached your soul or it didn't. She had other qualities, he reasoned. She loved him – at least she swore she did – was loyal, she came from a good family, and without doubt would make a wonderful mother. She'd even admitted, laughing a little self-consciously, she was just passing the time until he asked her to marry him. Which he'd intended to do once this bloody war was over.

Until he'd set eyes on Kitty Townsend. And his initial spark of interest when he'd seen her on the stage that first night, rigid with fear, had fanned into a raging fire.

But how could he explain that to Elisabetta? Tell her that just like the song he was bewitched. He knew he'd fallen head-over-heels in love with the young English singer. But it would destroy Elisabetta.

29

Kitty

The following morning Joyce and I were discussing the merits of Alice Delysia, particularly how she had the men eating out of her hand with her naughty songs, when Jennifer stormed in, as usual without knocking.

'We have to leave tomorrow.' She sounded agitated.

'No!' I practically shouted.

Jennifer glared at me. 'You don't have any say in the matter, Kitty.'

'Where are we going?' Joyce said.

'I can't tell you until we get there.' Jennifer's eyes travelled round our untidy room. 'You need to pack up and be ready to leave by six o'clock sharp.'

'What, six in the evening?' Joyce said innocently.

'No, you silly girl.' Jennifer's eyes snapped on Joyce. 'Six in the *morning*. So you'd better get the lights out sharpish tonight. You'll need all the sleep you can get. Things are hotting up around here and they think it's too dangerous for ENSA to stick around.'

'I don't want to go.' Panicking, I pushed the words out.

Ruggero. Oh, Ruggero. I can't leave you now. Please let something happen that I can stay.

'You have no choice.' Jennifer's eyes were sharp with curiosity, as though she could see how churned up I was.

'Are the Germans coming?' Joyce asked.

209

'We're not supposed to talk about it,' Jennifer said, her eyes darting towards the door. 'But,' she lowered her voice, 'they say Rommel is on his way.'

Joyce's eyes widened with fear.

'When—?'

'That's enough.' Jennifer put the palm of her hand up to stop our questioning. 'I don't want to hear another word. Just be ready to leave by six.'

'Oh, Joyce, I can't bear it.' I sat on the bed covering my eyes with my fists after Jennifer left.

'It's the Italian, isn't it?'

I nodded dumbly.

'Don't worry too much, Kitty.' Joyce came and put her arms round me. 'Lionel says they often go to a smaller camp for a while and then come back.'

'But this sounds more permanent if they're expecting Rommel,' I said, my voice choked. 'I'll tell them I'm not well. And it'll be true. I feel sick. They'll have to leave me behind in the sick bay.'

'Don't be a pin-head,' Joyce said. 'Miss Long will see through that immediately. People are already gossiping about you and Ruggero. Saying no matter how high-ranking he is, you have no business talking to the enemy.'

'I wish people wouldn't keep talking about Italians being the enemy. I hate it, every time I hear it,' I burst out.

'This war won't last forever, Kitty. And if you two are meant to be together one day, you will be.'

But however much I denied it, he *was* the enemy. Together with Germany his country had declared war on England and France. They were against everything I believed in: fairness and loving your neighbour. All that my mother had taught me; all we'd been taught in school. I had no business to be falling in love with him. But my heart said something different.

*

210

It was still dark when Joyce and I and the rest of the troupe stood outside the canteen waiting for the army lorries to pick us up. Madeleine had her arm through Jennifer's and she was whispering something in Jennifer's ear. There was no sign of Alice. Lionel and Tony and Eddie had already loaded the stage and the piano, and all the other paraphernalia. It was just the case of getting the humans on board.

The air felt cool to my cheeks. Stupidly, I looked around, searching for a dark head. Only a few men in overalls were about at this time of the morning, running towards and away from a couple of small aeroplanes. A few mosquitoes were half-heartedly buzzing around our heads, bloated from sucking our blood the night before, no doubt, but other than that it was quiet except for our whispers. We'd all been ordered not to speak or ask any questions.

As friendly arms hoisted Joyce and me up the back of one of the lorries, with me wincing as my sore knee bent, I caught a glimpse of Madeleine's shapely legs as she pulled them into the front seat where she'd secured a place beside the driver. She would, I thought. As long as she was comfortable, to hell with the rest of us. I hadn't forgotten her blazing eyes as she'd sent daggers through me after I'd finished singing that night. She was all set to get rid of me at the least opportunity. A picture of Alice Delysia flicked into my mind. What would Miss Delysia do in the circumstances? Laugh, most probably, and not take a blind bit of notice. I resolved to do the same. And then I thought of Ruggero and the smile faded from my face.

Our vehicle, whose engine had been revving for a minute or more, slowly began to move down the track.

The next camp made our first one look like the lap of luxury. We'd been travelling half a day over the worst roads I'd ever been on, and I was getting tired, hot, thirsty and hungry. We'd only had a bit of bread and cheese for lunch, where we'd just stopped fifteen minutes on the side of a dusty road. One of the men handed me a beer to wash down the dry sandwich, but it was so bitter I pulled a face. Ugh. Horrible. But I was thirsty and there was nothing else. I looked at Joyce. She had a bottle and was tipping her head back, her eyes closed in utter bliss.

By early afternoon the temperature had risen to over a hundred and ten degrees. I was glad of the shorts but the material felt like sandpaper against my skin. Sweat dripped off my forehead down my cheeks as though I was crying my heart out, and my mood wasn't improved when I looked at our tent and found out who I would be sharing with. Joyce, thank goodness, but also Jennifer and Madeleine bloody Grant.

At first I thought I'd be all right. Madeleine took one look at me and marched over to the men's barracks. I presumed she was putting in her complaint that she didn't want to share with Joyce and me – that we were beneath her – and would the authorities move her? She came back to us, a triumphant smile pasted over her face; that was, until Hal came over a few minutes later as she was collecting her things together.

'Sorry, Mads, that chap you spoke to forgot Alice Delysia is having that tent. To herself,' he added, mischievously. I could see he was desperately trying to hide a smile. He caught my eye and winked.

It was almost worth having to share with her to see the expression on her face.

Our stage, if you could call it that, was a few planks of wood resting on some oil drums, and we had to get changed behind the lorries. Not surprisingly, there was no enthusiasm from any of us. We were all worn out and I suppose we didn't have our hearts in it. In spite of that, we did our best, but were thankful when the programme – shorter than usual – came to an end and Joyce and I could fall on to our camp beds. This was after flapping the sheets and inspecting them for creepy-crawlies. Madeleine was nowhere to be seen. Come to that, nor was Jennifer.

*

It was only a few days later when we were bundled back in the lorries and bound for Cairo again. I couldn't contain my excitement. I wondered if Ruggero had been told that the ENSA troupe was on its way back. Did his heart pound at the thought of seeing me – the way mine did? Our Italian lessons would start again…his lips on mine…

But he wasn't to be found. I looked for him in every audience, sure that I'd spot him, even amongst such crowds. But he never appeared and I began to wonder if anything had happened to him. If he'd been sent away – or worse.

How could he have disappeared in such a short time? My heart was splitting in two and my singing became more of a duty than a joy.

And then after five days, when I'd almost given up hope, Jennifer handed me an envelope when she caught up with me after breakfast. My pulse raced as I tried to appear nonchalant.

'Oh, thank you, Miss Long.'

'Normally I would not be acting as postman between prisoners of war and our group, but I believe this is from the Italian officer who gave you lessons. I expect it's to tell you when they are to resume.' She looked me directly in the face, giving a warm smile and patting my arm. 'You're not a bad kid, Kitty. And you've got a voice. It's magical. Just don't throw it away over some man.' With that she strode off.

I watched her retreating back for a few seconds, too shocked to move. Jennifer was actually aware she was giving me a letter from an Italian prisoner. And she'd smiled as though she was not upset about it. As though she'd almost approved. My eyes dropped to the envelope. My name, Signorina Kitty, was written in a different hand from an Englishman. I liked it. A firm strong hand but with a natural grace. I looked about me. No one near. I ripped it open and pulled out a sheet of plain white paper.

Tuesday.

Kitty, I am sorry not to give you your lesson for some days
but hope to continue them. Do not answer this. We will meet
us soon.

R

I read the note three times, desperate to find something, just a hint, that he'd missed me, wanted to see me…but there was nothing. And then I shook myself. If the note had got into the wrong hands it might have been awkward.

I couldn't bear to think how long it might be before I saw him again. When I'd have to pluck up the courage to confess I'd taken out that piece of paper from one of his records. My heart faltered. Suppose he didn't believe that I hadn't read it. But who was it from? Probably not from his mother after all. Something much more personal, much more important. I felt sick in my stomach. A girlfriend who loved him? Who he loved in return? I bit the inside of my lip. Should I open it? But no, I couldn't lie to him if I read it. I'd have to tell him. He'd be furious. And he'd never trust me again.

What about if he'd already missed it? He'd suspect *me* before anyone.

'The Red Cross are giving a ball to raise money this Saturday,' Joyce announced that same evening. 'We've all been invited. And ENSA doesn't have to entertain. There'll be a band and we can just enjoy ourselves for a change.'

'They'll still be calling out for their hair and make-up to be done,' I said.

'I shall ignore them. I'm going to be off that day as well, whatever Jennifer says.'

'We need to decide what to wear then,' I laughed, linking my arm through Joyce's. Not for the first time did I think how glad I was to have her here with me. She made everything seem fun.

Rhoda and the other two dancers kept themselves to themselves. Hal was lovely but as he reminded me, he was much older than us, and Lionel was in his own world half the time. Besides they were men and didn't understand half of what Joyce and I talked about. And Jennifer Long was like a second mother so you couldn't make a friend of her. In a strange way, I felt closer to Alice Delysia than any of the others.

I wished with all my heart that I had a beautiful dress to wear but Miss Delysia had forgotten her offer to lend me something pretty. I wouldn't feel my best in the awful blue or the washed-out cream, but it couldn't be helped. And did it matter? I couldn't dance anyway. No one had ever taught me. I'd look foolish watching everyone else. The more I thought about it the less I wanted to go.

This second time in Cairo our troupe was billeted in the National Hotel. It was certainly an improvement on the previous two places. As usual I was sharing with Joyce, but this particular morning I was on my own, doing my breathing exercises, ready for tonight's show. Just as I was bending down with my nose almost touching the carpet, there was a knock at the door.

'Ah, you are in.' It was Alice Delysia, her face wreathed in smiles.

I was so surprised to see her that it took me a few seconds before I invited her inside. She laughed at me as she swept in as though making her stage entrance. I noticed she was carrying a large bag.

'It's lovely to see you, Miss Delysia,' I said, feeling a little overwhelmed that this star should have come to my room. What on earth did she want?

'I have zis for you,' she said, and whipped open the big canvas bag. She pulled out a soft parcel wrapped in tissue. 'Take it,' she said, and laid it in my arms. 'I forgot to give it last time.'

I tore the paper off. There lay the most exquisite dress. Wonderingly, I picked it up. It was a light shiny material, maybe silk, the colour of lemons, with a pleated skirt which would sweep the floor, and a swathed top of a paler lemon with shoulder straps. My heart beat fast as I pictured myself in it.

'Oh!' I held it against me as I walked over to the mirror. The dress shimmered back at me; it was going to look wonderful. 'It's the most beautiful dress I have ever seen.'

'I'm glad you like it,' she said, chuckling. 'It is for the Red Cross ball.'

'I'm not going.'

'You *are* going to the ball, Cinderella,' she grinned, 'in the yellow dress.'

I laughed. You couldn't argue with her. 'I'll be very careful, Miss Delysia,' I promised. 'I won't eat or drink anything so I don't mess it up.'

'Eat and drink what you want.' She gave her high-pitched giggle. 'It's yours.' I stared at her unbelieving. 'You will fill out ze bosom better than me.' She glanced at my chest and I felt my face go pink. 'Do not be embarrassed, *ma cherie*. They are asset. And call me Alice. I would like zat.'

She offered her cheek as I moved to kiss her. 'I'll never forget your generosity,' I told her. 'Never. Thank you, Miss…thank you, Alice, I mean Al*eece*.'

She smiled. 'That blue one was terrible for you. It made you look nearly as old as me.' She laughed. 'I 'ope you enjoy to wear zis one.' With that she was gone and the room somehow dimmed a little.

Joyce came in minutes later.

'You've just missed Alice,' I said.

'Oh, it's *Aleece* now, is it?'

I blushed.

'What did she want?'

'She gave me this.' I took the dress out of the tissue paper and once again held it up against me.

216

Joyce's eyes widened. 'Good gracious. You'd better look after it.'

'I'm going to,' I said. 'It's the most beautiful dress I've ever seen, let alone owned.'

'You mean she *gave* it to you?'

'She didn't think the other one fitted me very well.' I left out what Alice had really said.

'What a shame you won't have the chance to wear your favourite blue one at the Red Cross ball, because if you did you'd hurt Al*eece's* feelings for not wearing the yellow one.' Joyce kept her face straight until we caught one another's eye and burst out laughing.

I thought Saturday would never come. But it did.

'You look sensational, Kitty.'

'Do you really think so?' I couldn't believe the transformation.

'Nah, I'm lying. I'd change it for the royal blue glittery one, if I were you.'

We chuckled.

'You look lovely, too, Joyce,' I said, and meant it. She was in an emerald-green dress which I hadn't seen before. It had a full chiffon over-skirt which flattered her curvy body, and the colour was perfect for her new red hair.

'It was Doreen's, one of my customers. She's put on weight and couldn't get into it anymore.'

'Keep eating the cakes, Doreen,' I said, even though I'd never met her. We screeched with laughter.

The dance was in full swing when we arrived. Nearly all the men were in uniform and several girls were making a beeline for the officers. Immediately I felt awkward. Maybe I was still overdressed. None of the women wore anything half as lovely as mine. Then I spotted Alice Delysia and she winked. She was in bright red with a floaty blue and green scarf, and looked like an exotic bird. I smiled back.

'Dance, miss?' A young man in officer's uniform came up.

'I don't know if I can,' I said. 'This is my first dance.'

'Let's give it a whirl.'

After he'd trodden on my same foot three times and apologised over and over, I told him I'd like to sit the next one out. Gallantly, he took me back to where I'd been sitting chatting to Joyce, but her chair was empty. Looking round I spied her on the dance floor with a tall sergeant.

'May I have the pleasure, Signorina Kitty?'

I thought my heart would stop beating. Then I gathered myself together.

'I'm surprised to see you here.'

He gave me a mischievous smile. 'They let me out for the evening so I have come to found you.'

Ruggero Andreotti held out his hand and I took it. Without saying a word I let him lead me on to the dance floor. In my nervousness I gabbled before we'd even started.

'I can't dance,' I said, as he laid one of my hands on his shoulder; the other he grasped with a firm hand. He was the same height as me in my heels, and because he held me so closely I noticed again how his mouth turned up at the corners, that his nose curved like a Roman emperor and his golden brown eyes teased and twinkled. Immediately, I faltered and he pressed his hand on my back even tighter. 'I've tried but I must have two left feet,' I stuttered.

His smile widened showing gleaming white teeth against the tan of his complexion. 'Then you have never danced with an Italian,' he said, drawing me against his solid chest. 'You just follow…like this,' and he whirled us both away.

The joy of being held tight to him again after so many long days. To catch the very breath of him, smoky with his last cigarette, but he himself smelt as fresh as a newly cut lemon.

The band was playing a song I was very familiar with, but no one was actually singing. I found myself humming gently to "You

Made Me Love You", then realising what I was doing and what the words meant, I stopped. My face grew hot as it occurred to me that he might think I was being fast.

'Don't stop.' His voice was soft in my ear. 'I like it. But I like it even better when you sing.'

We drifted in what felt our own world. There was no war. No camp. No prisoners. No Madeleine. No anything to bring us back to the real world. He felt it the same as I did, I could swear, by the way he held me ever closer.

Ruggero kept me near him as we danced to the next two songs, then with his hand on my arm he guided me to an empty chair on the other side of Joyce who'd returned with her sergeant.

'I will come and found you again soon,' he promised.

I forced a smile, but all my effervescence suddenly went flat. I nodded and watched him disappear into the crowd. In one breath I was shaking with happiness that I'd matched my step perfectly with his. I *could* dance, after all. But why had he left me so abruptly? I definitely didn't want to stay where I was, playing gooseberry to Joyce and her sergeant. I mumbled something about going to the powder room but Joyce and her new friend were already kissing.

Ten minutes passed before I was back in the ballroom. And there was Ruggero, hovering near Joyce's table, holding two drinks. As soon as he saw me he came towards me, his face looking as though it had somehow been lit from inside. It gave me a fuzzy sensation.

'I have a glass of wine for you,' he said. 'Only I am not sure you are old enough for alcohol.' He winked and I laughed.

I took the glass and clinked it against his. 'I think I can manage.'

He took a deep swallow of wine, then took my glass and set them both on the table behind him where Joyce and the sergeant were still snogging. 'I want very much to dance with you again,' he said, and my body gave a surge of joy. 'And I have not said before how beautiful you look. The most beautiful woman in the room. I mean it.'

My heart turned over.

'This is a new dress?' His arms were firm around me as he waltzed me into the centre of the dancing couples.

'It's new for me. Miss Delysia gave it to me – to keep.' My voice was unsteady.

'You look like a ray of sunshine. It is made for you,' he whispered.

Just as the band finished three more numbers I noticed Madeleine, who was at that moment dancing very near us, throw me a look of pure venom. I sent her a wide false smile and she looked away, her lips curling in contempt.

Was it because I was dancing with the enemy? Or because I was in the arms of the most handsome man in the room? Quite honestly I didn't care what she thought. I was only aware of Ruggero. Several women threw me envious looks, though I hardly noticed as I gave myself up to the feeling of Ruggero's jaw against my cheek, his fingers gently pressing on my back, his warm breath on my neck. The music stopped.

'May I have the pleasure of the next dance?'

It was Mike Travers. I didn't want to be anywhere but in Ruggero's arms but he practically pulled me away. Ruggero smiled but it didn't reach his eyes as he released me.

'You like our prisoner of war, don't you?' Mike Traver's tone was a little put out as he twirled me round.

'Don't call him that,' I protested. 'He *does* have a name.'

'Yes, an *Italian* one. Don't forget…he's the enemy every bit as much as the Krauts.'

'I *do* know that, Mike. And I wish you wouldn't keep calling him "the enemy". My father was half-Italian.' I raised my voice and a few couples looked round curiously.

'Our boys are dying – being shot at by the Eyeties as well as Jerry.'

I hadn't heard the word "Eyetie" before but guessed it meant the Italians. It sounded horrible and Mike didn't endear himself to me one bit by using it.

'And I don't think Andreotti can be trusted.'

'*I* would trust him.'

I probably shouldn't have blurted that but I couldn't help it. We danced the rest of the dance in silence. Mike thanked me rather stiffly.

'Time Andreotti and I made for home – if you can call it home.' Mike cocked his head towards Ruggero who was standing close by watching us.

Ruggero's eyes narrowed. 'You go, Captain Travers. I will be here for...' he glanced at his watch, 'oh, maybe another hour or two.'

'Orders are we stick together.' Travers' mouth tightened.

'I'm hardly likely to run off into the desert,' Ruggero retorted. 'If I did you'd soon come and get me.'

'It's time for me to go,' I said, not wanting him to see I was embarrassed on his behalf. 'I have kitchen duty in the morning.'

'And then you will sing tomorrow night.' Ruggero spoke the words so softly I didn't think Mike heard.

'Yes. I will sing tomorrow night.' I repeated his words as softly.

'And do you sing for me?'

'Yes,' I said. 'Only for you.'

That night Joyce was late coming to bed. I took off my make-up, thinking about Ruggero. I was falling in love. And I was sure he was falling in love with me. I felt a glow of happiness. And then I remembered something, and a ripple of jealousy and fear almost choked me. That sheet of paper. It *must* be from a girlfriend, else why all the secrecy? Did he still love her?

Without thinking I jumped to my feet and grabbed my bag. My fingers scrabbled for the piece of paper I'd tucked into the zipped compartment. Heart thumping in my ears I unfolded the sheet. No flourish of writing. It was typed. That couldn't be right. I peered at it and couldn't understand a word though I knew enough to know this wasn't Italian. Then I spotted the word *U-Boot*. I'd overheard Hal only the other day talking to Lionel about the successes the Germans were having chasing our ships with their U-boats. This must be the German word. But why would Ruggero have a letter or report or whatever it was in German?

30

After lunch I excused myself from kitchen duties with a headache. I put it down to the wine I'd had last night, but I knew the real reason. I hadn't slept all night. All that hammered through my head was that Ruggero might be working for the Germans. What other reason could he have? He obviously didn't want Mike or Colonel Thornton to see the sheet of paper.

And then I shook myself hard. Drew in a deep breath and slowly let it out, as though to prepare for singing. What could I have been thinking? Ruggero a traitor? There had to be an explanation. I loved him. He was not the enemy. Whatever anyone said. With relief I decided to go back to the hotel and try to have a couple of hours' sleep when Jennifer hurried over looking pink and breathless.

'Colonel Thornton wants to see you, Kitty,' she said. '*Pronto.*'

'To see *me*?'

'Yes. I expect he wants to know how the Italian lessons are going.' She looked at my doubtful expression. 'I suggest you go straight away. He's not the type that likes to be kept waiting.'

'I don't know where to go,' I said.

'Luckily, I do.'

I spun round to see Mike Travers strolling up. He took my arm. 'Come on…I'll take you over.' He glanced at me and grinned. 'Don't worry. He's not an ogre.'

Even though Mike's words were supposed to be reassuring my

heart felt as though it was ready to jump out of my chest.

'I need to comb my hair. I can't go in looking all hot and sweaty. Just give me a few minutes.'

'Sorry, Kitty. The old man won't wait for anyone. I've got strict instructions to bring you over right away.'

My knees were hardly holding me up by the time Mike knocked on Colonel Thornton's door. We entered, and after all the saluting, Mike left me to it. My heart now pounded so loudly in my ears I was sure Colonel Thornton could hear it.

'Sit down, Miss Townsend,' he said in a fatherly tone. 'Don't look so worried. I want to know how the Italian lessons are coming along.'

So Jennifer was right. That's all it was. He leaned towards me and his air of authority was so powerful, like a wave rolling across the desk, it made my brain reel. The piece of paper burned in my handbag and I was sure he knew I had some incriminating evidence against Ruggero. It was as though he was willing me to hand it over. He knew it was there. I gripped the sides of the chair. Mustn't say anything for him to suspect I was protecting my love. I had to put him off.

'Um...I'm improving, I suppose.'

'You don't sound as though you're enjoying them much.'

'It's difficult when I've never learned another language before,' I said, desperately making things up as I went along. 'Sometimes I think I've remembered a phrase and then when I want it it's gone completely out of my head.' I gave him one of my best smiles.

'I want them to continue,' he said.

I was so sure he'd been about to say the opposite he completely took me by surprise. Why would he want that? He studied my face and I became unnerved under his piercing look. I put my hand up to my head, trying to smooth my unruly hair.

'I'm sorry I look so untidy,' I managed. 'Mike...I mean Captain Travers...didn't give me a chance to put a comb through my hair.'

'You look lovely,' he said surprisingly. 'A lovely, fresh, natural girl.'

What on earth did that have to do with Italian lessons? I began to feel uneasy.

'Let me ask you, Miss Townsend,' he began, coming round his side of the desk and taking a chair next to me. He swivelled it round to face me. 'What do you know about Lieutenant Colonel Andreotti? Your Italian teacher.'

'N-not much. Why?'

'I believe you are quite smitten with the chap.'

I felt the heat crawl up my neck to my cheeks. It was as though I was somewhere else. What had he seen? We'd been so careful to keep away from the window when we'd kissed. Italian lessons were all very well but kissing the enemy. Oh, God. What punishment did he have in store for me? For Ruggero… I hid my hands behind my back so he couldn't see them tremble.

'It's not true,' I blurted out.

'But didn't he help you to remember your lines by singing the same song during your first performance?' He leaned closer to me and I could smell the stale smoke on his breath.

By this time I was shaking hard. Was he trying to get me to say I'd fallen in love with the enemy? It would be all over then. I *had* to convince him otherwise.

'You have my feelings all wrong, sir. It's Mike Travers I like…love.' I threw in the last word for good measure. If the colonel thought I was in love with an Englishman, we wouldn't be punished.

Colonel Thornton raised his eyebrows. 'Hmm,' he grunted, as though he didn't believe one word. He stared at me. I tried to show I wasn't intimidated but after a few seconds I had to look away – anywhere but at him. There was an awkward silence. What was he waiting for? I was sure he could see right through into my skull. 'That's as maybe,' he tapped his fingers on the edge of his chair, reminding me of Harry, 'but it doesn't matter in the least. In fact it's almost better.'

I couldn't see what he was getting at. He was starting to scare me. And then his next words filled me with fear.

'Make him fall in love with you by *pretending* you've fallen in love with him.'

My mouth fell open. I couldn't speak.

'Miss Townsend?'

'W-why?'

'To help me make a decision.'

A decision to punish him? On what charge? My mind whirled. I gripped the sides of the chair in panic. It was as though I'd waded into the sea and could no longer feel the seabed. *Turn round. Go back to the safety of the shore. Oh, Ruggero, what have I done? Do something, Kitty. Say something. Save him.* But my head felt like concrete. I stared at my shoes.

'Kitty?'

My head snapped up. He'd called me "Kitty". He was using his father tone again. Mustn't say anything I shouldn't.

'Y-yes, sir?'

'Will you do this for me? It's important to us.'

'I don't understand why.'

'Find out about him. Where his loyalties lie. Ask him questions. But not too directly – at least, not at first. Then when he becomes more sure of you and begins to talk in a more intimate way,' Colonel Thornton cleared his throat, 'you'll find out a lot more about him than we could, because you won't seem to be a threat.'

Something clicked.

'You want me to *spy* on him?'

'That's a bit strong.' Colonel Thornton shifted slightly in his chair. 'I need to know his thinking. He's offered his services but we can't take any chances. I need to be absolutely certain he's on our side. And if he thinks you're in love with him,' he paused and looked directly at me, 'he might let down his guard.'

I sat there barely taking in what he was asking.

'I don't see how I can help,' I said, cold sweat dripping down my back. Then I raised my eyes to Colonel Thornton's face and saw his grim but watchful expression. This was not a game. 'I'm not experienced. I wouldn't know what to say...what information you're looking for...' I was stuttering with nerves.

'Your very naivety would work for you, rather than against, I believe,' Colonel Thornton smiled, 'especially as I understand he's already taken with you. He'd be suspicious of someone older and more experienced but he won't be on his guard with you. No, it shouldn't be too difficult to make some casual enquiries when he's not expecting it – I think you know what I mean – and report back. Make it a challenge. But make sure you win.'

What would Colonel Thornton say if I told him I didn't have to pretend to love Ruggero? Colonel Thornton was trying to warn me that Ruggero could be pretending to be on our side. No, it wasn't possible. Ruggero would never be a spy against the British.

How do you know that? What about that piece of paper you found, written in German? Maybe he's in contact with the Germans. It sounds ridiculous but why did he hide it in there? You don't know him at all. You've fallen in love and you see only one side of him.

Thoughts flew back and forth in my head. I had to be very careful not to give anything away of my feelings where Ruggero was concerned. I needed to put Colonel Thornton off the track... convince him he'd got it wrong. Lie as I'd never lied before because I was only too well aware of how bad the consequences could be. Something terrible could happen to Ruggero.

'I'm sure you're mistaken,' I said with all the confidence I could muster. 'I really don't know anything about him personally. He's a good teacher and that's all I know. But thank you for giving me the opportunity of having Italian lessons. I'm sure one day they'll come in useful.' I came to my feet.

'I haven't finished yet,' he said, and recoiling at his stern face, I promptly sat down again. 'Like it or not, Kitty, I've been keeping an eye on you. And as I've said, I believe he has feelings for you and I want him to think they are reciprocated.' I must have looked blank. 'That you return his feelings,' he added.

'I know what reciprocate means,' I snapped, then went bright red as I realised who I was snapping at.

'I will, of course, give Andreotti even more freedom to meet you,' Colonel Thornton said, slyly, as though he knew I was lying, 'but you must convince him that you've fallen in love with him so he tells you things he wouldn't normally divulge. Information we'd never prise out of him. You need to dig down – right into his soul. And give me some answers.'

'I can't spy on him.'

As if I hadn't spoken, he continued, 'And if you carry this out successfully you will be doing your bit for the war effort. We must all do our bit if we are to have any chance of winning this bloody war – excuse my French.'

So this whole thing about Ruggero giving me Italian lessons to help my future career had been a ruse.

'I don't want to get involved in anything like that. I came to Cairo to sing to the troops, not to spy on them.'

'He's the enemy, Kitty, in case you've forgotten.' His voice had cooled. 'And remains so unless I'm absolutely sure he's on our side. I have some important work for him. But I need your help to clarify his position.' He stood up and held his hand out to me. 'Think about it seriously.' He stared down at me and I squirmed under his gaze. 'I would ask you not to mention any of our conversation to *anyone*. Just remember you're bound by the Official Secrets Act even though you haven't yet agreed to help us...yet.' He emphasised the word "yet". 'I'm giving you forty-eight hours to think about it.'

*

I was too upset to rehearse that afternoon. All I could think of now was that piece of paper. Since my interview with Colonel Thornton it had burned in my bag and was all I could think about. If only I knew what it said. Would it incriminate Ruggero? If only I'd never seen it. But I had.

Hal came to find me in the canteen sitting on my own, drinking a cup of tea which tasted as though it had been brewed yesterday, and wishing for the first time that I could take comfort from lighting up a cigarette.

'My head's splitting,' I told him. Mum used to say that when she had one of her bilious headaches. Thinking of Mum made the tears roll down my cheeks.

'Come on, Kitty,' Hal said, taking out a huge white handkerchief and handing it to me. 'Dry your eyes.'

I hardly heard his words, my head was so full of Colonel Thornton.

'Kitty, I saw your face at the ball last night. Shining with happiness when you were dancing with the Italian, and looking bored stiff when anyone else asked you. The thing is, Kitty...' he patted my hand in a brotherly way, 'you're in love with the guy, but I'm afraid he's not for you.'

'I don't love him...' I had to keep up the pretence.

'It's not true, Kitty, and you know it. But here's a warning. Loving an Italian, people are bound to talk and you can't blame them. They see you as fraternising with the enemy. And you're so young, you won't be able to handle it.'

I did know that fraternising with the enemy was the worst possible thing a girl could do in this damn war. The very word "fraternise" made me feel sick when it was directed to Ruggero, and if Hal and the others only knew, it was the exact opposite to what Thornton had requested me to do. I didn't care what the others thought about me, but how could I spy on the love of my life?

*

I trailed around the camp, jumping every time I heard an explosion and gunfire. Men were shouting and running, practising their manoeuvres, so to keep out of their way I dashed over to the kitchen where I made myself another cup of tea. It was too early for any of the cooks to begin the evening shift, so I sat at the big work table, a knot of anxiety forming in my stomach, furious with Colonel Thornton for putting me in such a position and furious with Ruggero for hiding what was obviously an important piece of paper that the colonel was sure to be interested in. I drained my cup and decided to go for a proper walk. I needed to think about Colonel Thornton and what I was going to say to him. I certainly didn't want anyone's company. Barely wanted my own.

Fifteen minutes into the walk I had to use my hand to shield my eyes, wishing I'd brought my sunglasses. I hadn't realised how close the camp was to the desert. It looked strangely alluring, giving me the kind of feeling I had when I was high up anywhere and tempted to throw myself over. The smooth silkiness of the sand seemed to draw me in; the strange patterns the sand made which Hal had told me were formed by the wind; the stubs of spindly bushes springing out here and there, almost apologetic, as though they knew they didn't really belong in the pristine sandscape. Well, I wouldn't venture far, and I'd look behind me every few minutes to make sure the camp was well in sight.

The light breeze became stronger, and I stood awhile fascinated by the shifting patterns as the wind tossed the sand this way and that. But it wasn't five minutes before the wind suddenly threw up whirls of sand in front of my face. I had to blink to stop any grains from getting in my eyes. Stupidly, I'd come without a hat but at least I was wearing a soft scarf, so I pulled it well over my head and put my hand up to cover my mouth. I tried to peer into the distance but I couldn't see anything through the sand. Reluctantly, I turned back.

Even though it was still hot I felt a cold shiver run down my spine. The camp had disappeared. Sand swirled everywhere, like a moving wall. I hadn't walked far. Telling myself to keep calm I set off in what I thought was the right direction. Except it wasn't. I walked for maybe half an hour. Any moment I'd see the outlines of the canteen and the soldiers' sleeping quarters – but there was nothing. Only sand. No sound except the wind whipping up more sand.

The sky began to turn a sickly yellow-grey and I could feel the air cooling every minute. I looked at my watch but the wind was so fierce I couldn't focus for more than a moment. It must be about five o'clock. I opened my mouth to call out but it was a big mistake and I spat the sand out, almost choking in the effort. The only thing was to go back to where I'd been and start walking in a different direction and pray it was right.

The same thing as before. I couldn't work out how long I'd walked in each direction, which made me feel even more disorientated. There was still nothing and no one in sight. Prickles of fear crawled over my scalp and I could feel my heart pounding in my chest. Hal had warned me of desert storms. I hadn't taken much notice at the time, thinking I wouldn't be so stupid as to go out walking in the desert on my own. And now I'd done exactly that.

No one knew where I was. Tears began to roll down my cheeks, mixing with the sand grains. How long would it last? How long would it be before anyone missed me and came out looking? There was sand and more sand whichever way I looked. I stood there shouting and screaming but there was no answering call. I was going to die. Only seventeen and all through my own stupidity. I began to shake. I crouched down in the sand, burying my head in my arms, and sobbed with terror.

I lay curled up like this for what must have been several minutes, until finally I sat up, sniffing like a child, and tried to clear my brain. If I dissolved in panic I wouldn't stand a chance. I had to think. What was it Hal had told me? If I ever got lost in the afternoon, I should turn my back away from the sun – or had he said look towards it? 'And don't call for help,' he'd added. 'If no one's about, all the shouting in the world won't do any good except dry your mouth up.'

What an idiot I'd been not to remember his warning. I swallowed hard, but the next time I tried there was no spit to swallow. I wondered how many hours I could survive without water.

Start walking again. Try to work out another direction from the two you've already taken.

Trudging through the sand, one hand covering my mouth, my scarf slipping down my forehead, I forced myself to keep putting one foot in front of the other. I couldn't be very far away, I kept reassuring myself. And the second time I'd tried to find the way back I'd definitely gone in another direction, so chances were I was still within half an hour's walking distance. I decided to stick with this route. Wishing I had some Vaseline to soothe my lips, I whispered to myself, 'Third time lucky, Kitty. Please God, let it be third time lucky.'

But after what felt like ten hours but was probably no more than ten minutes I stopped. My chest hurt with a mixture of exhaustion and rising terror. I took in as deep a breath as I could. Hal's advice could go to hell. I wrenched my scarf down and screamed as loud as I could. 'Help! Please help! HEEEEELP!'

I thought I was going mad. My brain seemed to swirl with the sand. I pulled my scarf further down my face until it practically covered my nose. What was the use? Oh, Mum, I'm going to die and you don't even know where I am. I could feel my heart beating fast until I thought my chest would explode before it fell back into slow motion. It must be the end.

As I closed my eyes, all I could think of now was Ruggero. At least I wouldn't have to make any decision about spying on him.

31

I was still breathing. I opened my eyes and managed to stand up, fear making me dizzy. I blinked. What was that grey blur? I pushed one sandy foot in front of the other, not daring to hope. The grey blur became a hazy outline of something. And as I got a little nearer my heart beat wildly with joy. It was the camp. I could recognise the shape of the canteen, the barracks, could just make out some people walking about. I wasn't going to die after all.

Ben was the first person I bumped into when I stumbled into the camp.

'Good God, Kitty, we were about to send out a search party. Where the devil have you been?'

I sobbed out my story to him in jerky half-sentences.

'You need to sit down.' He grabbed hold of my arm as I practically keeled over, I was so drained with the fright. Luckily for me he was a heavily-built man and I was glad of his strength. He propelled me to the kitchen and sat me down, then handed me a glass of wonderful water. 'Don't gulp it down too fast,' he warned but I ignored him, it was so delicious.

'That's better.' I gave him a weak grin as he took the empty glass.

I got up to go but he put a hand on my shoulder and pressed me down.

'Stay right there and wait until I make you a cup of tea,' he ordered. 'You look like a ghost. In fact, I think you need to see the doc.'

'No, I'll be fine…really.' I glanced at my watch. I'd been gone no more than two hours but it seemed like a day. I suddenly remembered to ask him, 'Who said I was missing?'

'Joyce mentioned she hadn't seen you for a while and we were worried as soon as the sandstorm began. They can hit before you know it.'

I couldn't even answer. My throat still felt dry. It didn't feel possible to say anything more. But after I'd drunk the heavily-sugared tea, which tasted like the best drink I'd ever had, and eaten a couple of Rich Teas, I assured him I'd be fine. I rose to my feet and this time he didn't try to stop me but held out his hand.

'I'll get someone to take you back to the hotel.'

'Thanks, Ben, but I'll be all right now, honestly.' I looked at his nice open face, full of concern for me. 'Thank you for being so kind.' I reached up and gave him a quick kiss on his cheek.

'Joyce!' I called her name when I finally stumbled back to our room, shivering with cold, but still breathing in lungfuls of relief that I had found the camp. There was no cheery answer from Joyce. Our performance had been cancelled because of the storm, thank God, so she wouldn't be getting the singers ready. So where was she?

All I longed to do was tear off my clothes, have a quick wash, and pull a clean nightdress over my head, then roll between the blessed sheets. I opened the bedroom door, stupefied with nervous exhaustion. Stared. My beautiful yellow dress was spread out on the bedcover. Why? I'd left it hanging in the wardrobe. Why would Joyce take it out and lay it on my bed? Did she think it needed ironing? I came into the room shutting the door behind me. I'd ask Joyce not to touch my clothes in future. My dress was too precious to be handled by all and sundry. Yet…something was odd. I rubbed my eyes. Blinked. Rushing over, I snatched up the dress, but only a slice of material came away in my hand.

What...? I stared down at my beautiful dress. My hands were shaking so much the shred of fabric I still clutched was fluttering like a captured bird. Faint with shock I tried to work out what had happened. But it was all too obvious. Someone with a pair of scissors had broken into our room and deliberately hacked my dress to pieces. It was as though someone had murdered it.

There was only one person who was capable of something so vile. Someone who hated me.

Madeleine.

Tears poured down my dirty cheeks as I gazed, disbelieving, at what she'd done. How could anyone destroy something so beautiful? I grabbed some pieces and bunched them in my fist in a burst of fury.

Joyce came flying in. 'You're back. Oh, thank God. No one knew where you'd gone!' She stopped dead as I let the thin pieces of material loose from my fist where they fell in a trembling heap. 'What—?'

'Madeleine,' I said without hesitating.

She dashed over and looked down at the bed, letting her hand trail over the silky pieces. She turned to me, her eyes wide. 'How do you know it was her?'

'How do I bloody know?' I rounded on Joyce as though she were the culprit. She backed away, her eyes startled. 'Because she bloody hates me, that's why. She wants me to suffer.' My voice rose. 'She's furious because Alice likes me. She must have heard that Alice gave me the dress and set out to destroy it at the first opportunity. Well, she's succeeded,' I finished through gritted teeth.

Joyce's mouth opened and shut.

'I'm going to find her,' I said, suddenly making up my mind.

Joyce put out a restraining hand. 'No, don't do that,' she said. 'It won't do a scrap of good. Leave it until the morning. You look done in. Where've you been anyway? We were all worried sick.'

'Bar one,' I couldn't stop the bitter tone. 'Madeleine would have cheered if I'd never come back.' I proceeded to tell Joyce what had happened. She looked more and more alarmed.

'You were jolly lucky to have found your way back,' she said, forcing me down into the easy chair. 'You could have come a cropper. Whatever were you thinking of?'

'I just wanted a bit of time on my own,' I said, lamely. How I wanted to tell her about my interview in Colonel Thornton's office. But I pressed down the urge. Something must have shown in my face because Joyce shot a curious look at me. 'I was so careful not to go far,' I gabbled on, 'but it's confusing in the desert, especially when the sandstorm got up. And all the sand looks the same.' I forced a laugh, trying to reassure both of us that I hadn't really been in deep trouble.

'Well, thank God you're back safe and sound.' Joyce gathered up the pieces of my dress and shoved them into a laundry bag. 'This is despicable,' she tucked the bag out of my sight in our wardrobe, 'but I'd rather the dress be in ruins than something had happened to you.'

Bile came up in my throat as I watched her movements and I swallowed it back, feeling I would choke. She looked at me anxiously, then turned down my bed.

'Get undressed and get in,' she ordered. 'I'm going to get you some soup or whatever's going. You must be starving.'

I obeyed without argument but was asleep before she had time to bring me any supper.

Incredibly, I slept for twelve hours. Finally, Joyce shook me awake with a cup of tea. I'd never drunk so much tea but everyone seemed to think it was the magic cure for everything.

'Come on, lazybones,' she said, setting it down on my bedside cabinet and plonking on the edge of my bed. 'Everyone's up in arms over your dress. They're treating it like an Agatha Christie mystery. Shows how little excitement there is around here.'

I shot up in bed. 'Well, I'm glad you think it's exciting,' I said. Then a thought struck me. 'Did you tell them what happened?'

'Course I did. Wouldn't you have?'

I felt a little peeved that she'd been gossiping. I'd wanted to tell people in my own way. I'd wanted to watch their expressions when I told them in case I could pick up a clue as to whether they knew something. Now it was too late. A sly expression stole over Joyce's face.

'I told them your dress was ruined but I didn't say *how*.'

'What do you mean?'

'I just said it had been damaged, but I didn't say it had been cut with scissors.'

'I can't see what you're getting at.'

'Don't you see,' Joyce said, looking at me as though I was an idiot, 'if we keep quiet that someone had actually used scissors to cut it up, the person who did it might let it out by mistake.'

'Did Madeleine say anything?' I asked.

'No, she wasn't in the canteen this morning. No one's seen her which is even better. She won't know what's been said. In fact, I think we can play a little game with our friend Madeleine.'

Glancing at our alarm clock I pushed back the bedcovers and shot out. 'Oh, is that really the time? I must go. Got a rehearsal with Hal at nine-thirty.'

Finally something to think about besides Madeleine...and Ruggero.

But I couldn't pretend I was safe for much longer. Colonel Thornton was an impatient man. He'd want an answer no later than the forty-eight hours. And time was running out.

Just when I had fallen in love with Ruggero and I was sure he had feelings for me, I was asked to spy on him. And if he found out he'd never forgive me.

*

Later that day Jennifer gave the whole troupe another night off, saying the storm had badly damaged the stage and they'd have to practically rebuild it.

'We'll stay in our room and I'll try out some new hairstyles on you,' Joyce said. 'And we can listen to the news for a change.'

She switched on the wireless and fiddled about with the knobs until she'd tuned into the BBC.

'A considerable portion of the German garrison in Crete was evacuated today because of an outbreak of plague,' came the smooth clipped tones of the British announcer.

'Serves the buggers right,' Joyce said, jabbing a hairpin into my scalp. 'Best news we've had for days. Hope they all catch it and die a horrible death.'

'Hitler has launched a surprise attack on the Soviet Union.' The announcer's voice had acquired an unmistakable bounce. He went on to say it was good news for the Allies as Russia would now be on our side against the Nazis. I couldn't hesitate any longer. I *had* to help with the war effort, whatever the cost.

Even if it meant Ruggero ended up hating me.

The following morning I was back in Colonel Thornton's office.

'Have you decided?'

I nodded. 'I'll do it.'

'Good.' He tapped his fingers on the desk, regarding me. 'Make him believe you mean every word you say to him. And don't go getting lost in the desert again,' he added, a smile creeping across his face. 'We don't want to lose our little songbird.'

'I'll do my best, sir,' I muttered, my head lowered to hide my anger.

The only person, I now realised, who could prove Ruggero's loyalty was me.

32

My ruined yellow dress was only the beginning of a series of bad luck. Jennifer gave me a dressing down about leaving the camp on my own, which I know I deserved but I still felt resentful. Lionel had an accident the next day on his one-wheel bicycle, landing on his back and landing himself in hospital. Madeleine caught influenza and wasn't to be disturbed. Was that so she didn't have to face me asking her about the dress? But all that was on my mind now was *should I, shouldn't I?* where Ruggero was concerned. I know I'd agreed to do it but my stomach was in knots of anxiety. Once I started there'd be no going back. It would be the most terrible act of betrayal to myself, let alone Ruggero.

To cap off the perfect day, we performed under a deluge of rain that evening and the royal blue dress was soaked. By the time I changed and joined Joyce and Tony in the canteen they were finishing their supper.

'It's the way ENSA keeps shoving us around,' Joyce was saying. 'We've only just got back to Cairo.' She turned to me. 'Bloody annoying.'

'What is?' I asked, cutting a piece of my beans on toast.

'Jennifer's just told us we're leaving again tomorrow night.'

In a way it was the best news. I wouldn't have to spy on Ruggero. But I couldn't stop my stomach from taking a dive. 'Why? Where are we going?'

'They won't say. You know they never tell us anything.'

239

'I'll leave you girls to it,' Tony said, getting up and taking his tray. 'Got the stage to dismantle.'

Did Colonel Thornton know our ENSA group was leaving? Would he order me to stay? No, I was under a signed contract and under the care of Jennifer Long, and she would never agree to leave me behind.

'What's up with you, Kitty?' Joyce asked when Tony had disappeared. 'You look as though you've just discovered you've eaten a rat.'

'My time of month,' I mumbled.

'You never have any problem there,' she said, her eyes on my face. 'Come on, it's something more.'

'I hate all this packing up.'

'You'll see him again,' Joyce grinned knowingly. 'Jennifer told me the move is only temporary – the boys where we're going haven't had any entertainment, poor loves, but she said we'll be back in a few days. They're not even packing up all the theatre gear.'

Although Joyce's words cheered me a little, the turmoil inside me refused to go away. I wished I could tell her about Colonel Thornton. She'd probably be impressed at first. Think it was a lark. And then she'd come back with some cynical remark that I was being used. That the colonel obviously didn't have a daughter my age, because if he did he'd never suggest such a thing. She'd ask if I'd thought about the danger I'd be putting Ruggero and me into. But of course I couldn't say a word.

Every time anyone mentioned the Italian POWs it was always derogatory. What cowards they were, how they always tried to get the easy life, singing opera and drinking wine.

I did say once that it was a good job they were such cowards. If they were as cruel as the Germans there'd be even more innocent people killed. They went a bit quiet after that.

'How far did they say it was – this mystery place we're going to?'

240

'About three hours by jeep.'

I groaned. Lionel had told me going by jeep was a hundred times worse than going by coach. And he would really feel it with his injured back.

'I've come to tell you we're moving camp again tomorrow,' Jennifer said. She'd come into our room five minutes after Joyce had left.

I nodded. 'Yes, Joyce just said.'

'Be ready at six o'clock sharp.'

'We will be.'

'You don't seem your normal self,' she studied me. 'Are you all right?'

'Yes. Just tired.'

It was more than being tired. I felt drained.

'Probably from your scare in the desert. For God's sake don't do anything so stupid again. You had us all panicking.' She saw me flush and paused. 'By the way, I was very sorry to hear about your dress. Do you have anything else to wear?' Her eyes wandered to where I'd left the blue dress after I'd squeezed out the water. It looked as limp as I felt. 'Your blue one looks as though it's had it.'

'I don't have anything else.' I'd given up on the cream one. For some reason I didn't feel like a real singer in it, it was so drab.

'I'll see what I can do,' she said, turning to me. 'There must be something in wardrobe that'll fit. You should have at least two decent dresses anyway.' She hesitated and caught my eye. 'The way Joyce was talking it seemed as though it'd been damaged on purpose.'

'Yes, and I know—' I began. Then stopped. What was the use? If I said I suspected Madeleine, Jennifer wouldn't believe me because she loved her.

'What were you saying?' Jennifer demanded.

'Nothing, really,' I muttered.

'Show it to me,' she said. 'I'm sure it can't be that bad. Rhoda is marvellous at invisible mending.'

241

I almost said it had gone much too far to be mended. Then I remembered. I mustn't give anyone any hint that it had been deliberately cut with scissors.

'It's quite badly torn,' I said. 'Alice...' Jennifer shot a look at me and I swiftly corrected myself. 'I mean Miss Delysia will be awfully upset.'

'I'm sure. It was most kind of her to lend it to you in the first place.'

'Oh, no, she *gave* it to me. Said it was mine to keep. It was the most beautiful thing I've ever been given.'

Her eyes flicked once more to the blue corpse. 'I'd better go and find you something to wear tonight.' She disappeared.

Her offering was a ghastly lime green number which made me look bilious. She said it had come from wardrobe and had belonged to another singer who apparently was very posh.

'And very short and very old,' I almost added.

33

Cramped in the jeep again, the smell of oil and the stink of people's stale sweat in my nostrils on another of those long dreary journeys, I couldn't stop thinking of Colonel Thornton. It churned over and over in my mind now I knew I'd have to go through with it. I was terrified to do or say the wrong thing, terrified Ruggero would suspect me and hate me, especially if I gave Colonel Thornton the German paper. I still hadn't made a decision what to do and when I thought I had, I changed my mind again. I tried to shake off these dismal thoughts as one of the jeeps drove up alongside us. Madeleine was sitting in her usual position by the driver.

The ruined dress. I'd run through my mind everyone else and always came back to Madeleine.

It definitely wasn't Joyce. She was my friend, and anyway she wasn't the jealous type. Neither was Jennifer. And although Jennifer hadn't always been kind to me, I always thought she was honest. It wasn't one of the dancers as I was no competition for them. And it couldn't be Alice because it was her dress.

The jeep screeched to a halt behind Madeleine's and four others.

'What fuck is going on?' Our Egyptian driver hopped out.

I craned my neck and saw him and Madeleine's driver in some kind of argument. They were both waving their arms around and looking towards our jeep. Then the other driver opened the door where Madeleine was sitting. He must have said something to her as the next moment she got out. Well, she almost fell out, the step was so high. Then to my amazement she sauntered over towards us, the edges of her long white trousers brushing the sandy road.

'Any room up there for me?' she called.

Joyce looked at me and shrugged. 'We might be able to squeeze you in at the back. Why? What's happened?'

'Something about picking up another driver,' she said, hoisting herself up. She stopped and looked at me, her lips curling into a sneer. 'Oh, *you're* in this one. I thought you'd be in the kitchen jeep with the rest of them.'

I hated the way she called the lovely kitchen crew "the rest of them". They were the very ones who made her nice meals. Maybe not gourmet, but at least they didn't ever poison anyone – unlike the Cairo place she'd once eaten in. But I held back my temper.

'Just keeping Joyce company,' I answered almost humbly. I sensed Joyce stifle a giggle. It was the right moment to play the game. Trying to keep my voice reasonable and friendly I said, 'You're looking very attractive today, Madeleine.'

She shot me a look of deep mistrust. 'Thank you,' she said in a mock gracious fashion.

'You always look just like a model. It must be wonderful to be so famous and wear such beautiful things.'

Joyce turned away, pretending to cough. Madeleine shifted in her seat.

'I wish I had nice dresses for when I sing.' I paused for effect. 'I did have a beautiful dress which Alice Delysia gave me.'

'I don't know why she lent it to you in the first place,' Madeleine started.

'People keep saying that,' I said with a mirthless laugh. 'She didn't lend – she *gave* it to me.'

'Then she's more foolish than I gave her credit for.' Madeleine took out her compact and applied more lipstick on her already coated lips. 'You obviously can't be trusted.'

I opened my eyes wide with pretended innocence. 'What do you mean?'

'Well, you didn't look after it. Everyone knows someone broke into your room and cut it to ribbons.'

'No one said anything about it being cut to ribbons,' I said in a cool voice. 'Joyce only told people it was torn.'

Lionel, spread out in the back seat, twisted his head towards us.

'That's right,' he said. 'I was there when Joyce came into the canteen and said there'd been an accident with your dress. She never mentioned anything about it being cut up.'

A flush started from Madeleine's neck and flooded her cheeks. 'Well, that's what I assumed had happened,' she snapped.

'Why would you assume?' Joyce put in. 'Unless you were the one who'd "cut it to ribbons", using your own description,' she added.

Madeleine rounded on me, her eyes flashing with anger.

'Don't think you can pin this on me,' she said. 'I was nowhere near your room when it was supposed to have happened. In fact...' she stopped as though giving herself time to think, 'you probably did it yourself, so you could cause trouble and blame me. I know you hate me.'

'We'll let Miss Long decide,' I said. 'And Joyce and Lionel are witnesses.'

'Jennifer won't believe anything like that about me,' Madeleine said. 'But try it if it gives you satisfaction.'

And with that she closed her eyes and pretended to go to sleep.

From then on our journey was silent. Joyce had dropped off minutes after that conversation, snoring in a kind of rhythm with the jolting. But I could swear Madeleine wasn't as calm as she made out by the way she kept biting her lip and opening her eyes to glance at me when she thought I wasn't looking.

*

'Lionel's reported her,' Joyce called out as she undid the flaps of our tent and crawled in.

We were lucky enough to have the tent to ourselves. Two of the dancers were supposed to have shared with us but they'd all gone in the one tent. I imagined Jennifer and Madeleine were together. I wished Alice had come with us but she was still in Cairo.

'Who to?' I asked.

'Jennifer, dopey.' Joyce flopped onto her sleeping bag. 'She's bound to send her home in disgrace after that.'

But there was no talk – or hint – that Madeleine was going home. She sang to the soldiers as usual, though I got the loudest cheers. Maybe because she sang from the operas and I sang songs which most of them knew, or had heard their mothers sing. I think the words resonated more with them. But every time I finished my songs I could feel Madeleine's eyes boring into me, or she'd catch my eye and with a disdainful look, deliberately turn her back. I tried not to take any notice.

It was a horrible little camp and we all felt sorry for the soldiers who had few comforts and were so far away from civilization. They were so pathetically grateful to attend our shows and I was glad we were there to bring them a little bit of home. But it didn't stop me from joining in the clapping when Jennifer announced we were about to go on the move again.

I could have wept with happiness – we were going back to Cairo. And Ruggero.

Except now, Colonel Thornton would expect me to start getting some results.

It was like coming home. The stink of outdoor toilets, the smell of spices, the noise of people, the cries of children and taxi drivers, the traffic, the donkeys, the beggars, the strange whining music, the filth, the men's spotless white robes and flashing teeth to match – all this now felt like home. And I was near my love again.

Soon we were back in our old hotel, even in our old room, and it was like nothing had changed. My heart leapt as I saw a small bunch of roses had been placed on our little table where we used to have tea. A note was propped up against the vase. Joyce ran over to grab it.

'It's for you,' she said.

'Don't sound so surprised, Joyce.' I took the paper from her inquisitive hands, my own trembling with excitement. I hadn't dared to think I'd hear from him again so soon. I ripped it open.

My dear Kitty

My eyes flew to the ending.

With fond wishes
Alice Delysia x

'It's from Alice,' I said to Joyce without looking up.

'I know who you wished it was from,' Joyce chuckled. 'But be grateful. She's taken to you for some odd reason and she's very influential.'

'Why should she put herself out for me?' I asked Joyce the question that had crossed my mind from the beginning.

'Search me,' Joyce laughed. 'But believe me, I'm right. That's what comes of being four years older. You get to know these things. Fame equals money equals power equals influence. Maybe you remind her of herself when she was young. You and that quick temper of yours. You want to make the most of her.'

'It sounds awful, put like that.'

'Well, you know what I mean. She's in a position to help you get on in life if you're really serious about your singing.'

'I am serious,' I said, 'but I don't want to use people in that way. I want to prove myself, not rely on someone giving me a step up.'

'Then I'll wave at you as I ascend the ladder of opportunity.' Joyce waggled her fingers in a mocking manner. 'Anyway, why don't you read the letter.'

'I have,' I said, hoping to irritate her.

'What's she say?'

'It's an invitation...to a party...this evening. Apparently there's no show tonight—'

'Party?' Joyce squealed. 'Am I invited too?'

'No mention of your name,' I teased.

She grabbed the note from my hand. '"Please do bring your friend Joyce",' she read out. 'Well, if that's not an invitation, I don't know what is.' She flicked down. 'Oh, my goodness, it's in her posh hotel. I've been longing to see it.'

I hardly listened to her. My mind was buzzing, hoping against hope that Alice would have invited Ruggero, even though it was supposed to be strictly for the British.

Joyce began putting my hair up. She'd already daubed eyeshadow on my lids, stroked pencil on my brows, and coloured my lips. I'd grumbled a bit, but secretly I felt honoured as she'd refused to do Madeleine's or Jennifer's, saying she was too tired from the journey.

'You look more grown-up,' Joyce said, standing back, admiring her work of art as she stuck another pin in my hair. 'I wonder who'll be there.' She stopped abruptly, the kirby grip in the air. 'Do you think Ruggero will go?'

'No, twit.' I hadn't forgiven her for calling me dopey. 'It's only for British officers.'

If Ruggero wasn't going to be there I couldn't work up much enthusiasm. But I couldn't say that to Joyce; she was so excited to be going to a party and I didn't want to spoil it for her.

I put my hands on Joyce's shoulders as she sat on a stool,

peering closer in the mirror to trim her eyebrows.

'You're getting better every day at this make-up lark, Joyce. I just wish you had more of a selection in evening gowns.' I looked at the royal blue and the lime green. In awfulness, there wasn't much to choose. 'At least the blue fits me better since it got such a drowning.'

'Not that Ruggero would notice what you're wearing – if he manages to get himself invited, that is.'

34

I couldn't spot Alice immediately as there was such a crowd of people gathered in the Metropole salon. People's shoulders and feet jiggled to the beat of jazz which a small band on the stage was playing. Clouds of smoke wafted over our heads. There couldn't be more than forty women against easily two hundred men. Joyce and I looked at one another and grinned. We wouldn't be short of dancing partners. Two of the nearest officers stepped over to us and pointed out some empty chairs.

'Can I get you girls a drink?' one of them asked. He would have been quite good-looking if he hadn't been so plump.

'I'll have a gin and orange,' said a voice behind me.

Not Madeleine again. I couldn't seem to get away from her.

'Yes, of course.' The plump chap turned to Joyce and me. 'And you will have—'

'The same,' Joyce said hurriedly before I could open my mouth.

Madeleine narrowed her eyes at the two of us. A triumphant smile hovered on her lips when she looked me up and down in the unflattering green number Jennifer had donated to me. I willed her to move to another group but it seemed she wanted to annoy me. Until sixty seconds later when she suddenly left us and rushed over to the door. My eyes followed her and I saw why.

'Captain Travers,' she cooed. 'Long time, no see.' She threw her arms round him and kissed him smack on the mouth. Even from this distance I could see the smudge of red she left. She laughed.

And then my heart jumped. Ruggero. He was here, after all. Madeleine smiled at him and he said something back to her I couldn't hear, then raised his head as though he knew I was watching. His smile was warm and special. He began to walk towards me, but another officer stepped in front to talk to him. My heart sank in disappointment.

'I've been looking out for you, Kitty.' It was Mike Travers, gazing at me appreciatively. 'Glad you're back. I've missed you. Would you care to dance?'

He was a good dancer, though not as good as Ruggero. We talked pleasantly enough but there was no spark for me.

'Are you Ruggero Andreotti's keeper?' I asked him when we were clapping and waiting for the small band to start the next song. I tried not to make it obvious I was glancing over his shoulder, searching for Ruggero.

'You might call it that,' he laughed, looking down at me, his arm still round my waist. 'I have to keep him on the straight and narrow. Why do you ask?'

'It's interesting, that's all, that a prisoner can have such freedom.'

Mike chuckled. 'It might look like freedom to you,' he said, 'but Andreotti wouldn't think so. It's only because he's a high-ranking officer that he's not behind bars.'

I smiled, pretending he was joking.

To shift my gaze I looked about me and spotted Alice talking to Ruggero and Madeleine. Well, I could hardly have missed Alice. She looked sensational. Only *she* could have got away with it. Her dress was a simple white sleeveless crossover at the top with a red and blue striped band of material hanging over one shoulder and down her back, which I thought was clever, the whole combination being the colours of both the British and the French flags. The skirt was also white and equally simple. It was plainly chosen so that everyone's attention was on the chicken on top of her head.

Not a real one, of course, but a hat made to look exactly like a full-size lifelike chicken about to cluck at any moment and lay an egg. I loved watching everyone's reactions. Some pretended it was perfectly normal to wear something so bizarre on top of your head, but others looked on in amazement or horror.

I noticed Ruggero's mouth quirk with amusement, which presumably was the effect Alice was after. Madeleine hovered on the sidelines of the conversation (what woman could be any competition for a charming Frenchwoman who wore a chicken on her head?) and although they weren't exactly ignoring her, she appeared out of her depth and wasn't saying much.

I thanked Mike for the two lovely dances, and pretending I hadn't noticed his forlorn expression, went to find Joyce. She saw me first.

'Alice has a plan,' she whispered. 'She told me to tell you so it doesn't look as though she's whispering to you in front of the others. It mustn't look obvious about you and the Italian—'

'His name's Ruggero,' I hissed.

'Yeah, well. Anyway, the plan is – Mike is really keen on you and Alice is going to make a play for Ruggero. Then suggest—'

'She's what?' My mouth fell open stupidly.

'It's to fool everyone, dippy, especially Madeleine,' Joyce said. 'Just let me finish.'

I let her finish.

Dear Joyce. It wouldn't have worked if she hadn't cast her eyes on one of the British officers and cheekily asked him to dance. They were getting on famously and she'd given me the thumbs up over his shoulder that he'd take her back to camp. So I was free. And Ruggero was only a few feet away, a determined look on his face. My heart somersaulted and I tipped back the gin and orange too quickly. My head began to swim but Ruggero was beside me in a moment and put out a hand to steady me.

'We must talk,' he said urgently.

I looked straight into his eyes and thought I might melt under his gaze. All I could do was nod.

'Come with me.' He put out his hand.

I'd almost forgotten Joyce's plan and was just about to put my hand in his, but luckily Alice glided up to us.

'Ruggero, darling. I 'ave something to speak in private. Could we perhaps go somewhere?'

Ruggero looked surprised, but I suppose like most men he was fascinated with the attention of such a woman as Alice. He gave me an apologetic smile.

'I will dance with you soon, Kitty?'

I nodded and watched them go outside. Mike followed after them and a few minutes later he came back.

'Would you like to see the pyramids, Kitty?' Mike sounded a little breathless. 'They're spectacular in the dark.'

'How will we get there?' I asked innocently.

'By car. Miss Delysia has the use of one. And a driver.' He sounded awestruck.

'Is Alice coming too?' I said.

Mike nodded. 'In fact I have to drag Andreotti as well as I need to keep an eye on him. In any case, Miss Delysia seems to have taken quite a fancy to him.' He glanced at me. 'Do you mind?'

'It would be a shame to waste the petrol if we don't all go,' I said, smiling.

The car Alice had produced was huge. Mike told me it was an American Packard and that I wouldn't see too many of them around Cairo. And when I did see one, I could be sure it was a VIP inside. I stared at Alice again with even more admiration.

'Mike, you are verrry tall. You sit with Smen in ze front. Ruggero, you may sit between two beautiful ladies.'

'I will be honoured.' Ruggero winked at me and I suppressed a grin.

The driver, Smen, leapt out of the car and opened the rear door furthest away from us. Bending low so as not to disturb her chicken, Alice swept in. Smen rushed round to the side where I stood with Mike and Ruggero. Mike climbed in the front and Ruggero the rear. He shifted a little towards Alice, making plenty of room for me. Then he held his hand out and I took it, and settled into my place by his side.

Night came silently and swiftly in the desert. It was nearly pitch black when we arrived, though the moon picked out lights in the distance. We all piled out of the car. And there in front of us were three giant triangles growing out of the sand, one looking as though it was overlapping the other, although that was probably the angle we were staring from. They were magnificent, but almost unreal.

'The pharaohs' tombs.' Ruggero sounded excited.

The four of us walked towards them. After twenty minutes or so, when we were much closer, Alice's voice rang out.

'Go on, everyone. Ze pyramids, zey are very powerful but I cannot walk in zeze shoes.' She held up a sandal with an extraordinary high heel. 'I will go back and sit in ze car wiz Smen.'

A few seconds passed. I held my breath and looked at the two men, willing Mike to speak. Mike looked sulky.

'I cannot let you do that,' Ruggero said gallantly, though I sensed a reluctance in his tone. 'I will walk with you.'

No, no. That wasn't how it was planned. I caught Alice's eye. She must have seen my desperation.

'Mike, darling, I want to practice my terrible English. You take me and we talk, no?'

Mike glared at Ruggero. I waited, breathless. After a few seconds Mike extended his arm to Alice. She threw me a huge wink over her shoulder as she put her hand in the crook of Mike's arm. I couldn't help smiling as he marched her off. She was looking up at him and chattering, her chicken hat nodding in agreement.

'Would you like to walk nearer the pyramids?' Ruggero looked at me. 'If you can manage,' he added as he glanced at my feet.

'I can manage.'

I shivered slightly in my thin dress, wishing I'd brought my cardigan. Desert air temperature drops fast.

'Let me put over you,' he said, wrapping his jacket around my shoulders. It smelt of citrus and tobacco, and it was as though I was already folded in his arms. I wanted to breathe it in and never stop.

We began walking again, our strides matching exactly.

I'd seen photographs of the pyramids but no photograph gave any idea of how enormous they were, or even hinted at the atmosphere of the starry desert sky, or the moon shining down on them. But even the pyramids didn't stop me from being aware of Ruggero's arm lightly round my shoulder, keeping his jacket from slipping off me.

We stopped. The pyramids were close enough to see their rough stone texture. How far one was from the other. The hugeness of them... I'm really not sure what I was expecting. But nothing like this. We walked up to the nearest one.

'Put your hands against it and close your eyes,' Ruggero whispered. Before I could move he stepped behind me and reached over my shoulders, placing his palms against one of the great blocks of granite. I closed my eyes as he'd instructed. 'Feel, Kitty,' he said. 'Feel with your hands those ancient peoples who built them. And the king who was buried in this one.'

I stretched out my hands, touching his at the same time, trying not to think of his skin brushing mine and concentrating on 'those ancient peoples'. What did they look like? What work did they do, besides building pyramids? What food did they eat? There were so many questions. It felt that time itself was buried inside the tomb along with its king.

'They are five thousand years old.' Ruggero's voice was filled with awe as he softly spoke the words.

I couldn't begin to picture that amount of time. And through it countless wars had been fought, people living and dying, many races trying to survive side by side, empires built and crashed... In that moment I wished I'd paid more attention in history class. Here we stood in the middle of another war, Ruggero and I, two insignificant people, admiring those ancient Egyptians who'd imagined and built these great tombs.

I turned to him. He was watching me instead of looking at the pyramid. Our eyes locked.

'Do you have someone waiting for you at home, Kitty?'

He'd never asked me that. I shook my head.

I was inches away from his mouth.

Kiss me, oh, please kiss me. Kiss me now. It's been so long since you kissed me.

As though he'd read my mind he pulled me towards him. He took my face in his hands and turned it oh so slightly, so that his lips met mine, softly, warmly, and it didn't feel as though we were two people, two bodies, but just two mouths meeting and kissing and exploring. Excitement rippled through my body.

With a sigh he put me gently from him.

'Oh, Kitty, I didn't mean to – I'm sorry. I tell myself after that first time I must not do it again.'

'But I *wanted* you to kiss me.' His kiss had been even more wonderful this time. My whole being throbbed with longing.

'But I want more, Kitty. I'm a man and you are a very young girl. And I never want to hurt you.'

He gazed at me and I gazed back, loving the shape of his face, the proud Roman nose, the way his nearly black hair waved, the way his eyes had darkened in the desert night, the way his mouth looked after all the kissing. Inviting. Wanting more.

'You're so beautiful,' he said, his eyes never leaving my face. 'My little Kitty. I couldn't help.' He pulled me to him again and stroked my hair back from my forehead. 'Come. We climb a few steps.'

My shoes were not the right ones either, even though the heels were half the height of Alice's. Stones slipped beneath me as I dislodged them, but so long as I was gripping Ruggero's hand, I was walking on clouds. At one point he went ahead, then turned to lift me up.

'We sit for few minutes.'

He sat down, pulling me close beside him so I could feel the warmth of his body and the stones we were using as a seat, still hot from the relentless all-day sun. And then he turned to me and kissed me again. Oh, the joy of his mouth on mine. And then his hand found my breast underneath his jacket which I still had tightly wrapped around me, and I felt his fingers stroke me. I heard him groan as he kissed me again, his hand still there, so warm on my breast it was as though it was actually touching my bare skin. And then he drew away again.

'Kitty, you drive me crazy.' He shook his head as though in disbelief. 'You make me think things I must not.'

I couldn't answer.

We sat in perfect silence, holding hands. I wished more than anything I had refused to let Colonel Thornton persuade me to spy on him. But then I would never have had this chance on my own with him. At least that's what I told myself to stop from feeling so guilty.

'Look at the stars, Kitty. You will never see them so bright anywhere.'

'Why is that?' I craned my neck upwards. Ruggero was right. They glittered and winked and sparkled. Millions of them.

'Because there is no smoke from chimneys or cars or trains. The air is pure.' He turned to me. 'Breathe it in, and you will see.'

I breathed the desert air in and out, slowly and deeply.

I will never forget this night for the rest of my life.

We sat in silence until Ruggero broke into my little reverie.

'We should return. Travers and Alice will ask what has happened to us.'

I just hoped Alice was entertaining Mike.

'Have we time to see the Sphinx?'

Ruggero shook his head. 'Next time,' he said. 'When we come back.'

I didn't think there was much chance of that happening.

'Let's stay a few more minutes,' I said.

'Just five,' he agreed, looking at his watch.

He asked me about Alice. 'I never heard of her before she comes to Cairo. She is remarkable.'

'Do you think she's beautiful?' I asked.

'Oh, yes.' He looked at me teasingly, his eyes now golden in the moonlight. 'But not half as beautiful as you.'

I told him how kind she'd been to give me such an exquisite dress, and then I blurted out the rest of the story.

'I think this situation sometimes bring out the worst in people like Madeleine,' Ruggero said finally when I'd finished.

I gave a start. I hadn't mentioned Madeleine's name.

'It *was* Madeleine, wasn't it, who cut your dress?'

'Yes, I'm sure of it.' I looked at his face, shadowed in the night. It was a strong face...a dear face...the most handsome face of any of the men here, I thought. 'But how did you guess?'

His eyes suddenly flashed. 'Keep away from her. She has said bad things about you. She is very jealous because you are beautiful and you have a beautiful voice.' He kissed me on my forehead. 'But she will not stop at this.'

He took out a packet of cigarettes from his pocket, shook two out and offered me one. I took it even though Hal had warned me against it. Ruggero lit both of them. I inhaled and immediately began to cough.

'I do not think you are a natural smoker,' he said. 'Don't do it if you don't like. It is bad for the voice.'

'It doesn't seem to have been bad for yours.'

He laughed. 'I am not a professional singer like you.'

I was glad to give him back his cigarette.

'How old are you, Kitty?' His eyes held mine. 'The truth.'

'Twen—'

'Don't give me the lie,' he said, in a tone coated with impatience.

I had a glimpse of what he was like as an officer and hoped he couldn't see me turn pink. Colonel Thornton's face swam before me. If Ruggero was impatient at such a small fib, what would he be like if he found out I'd betrayed him?

'Nearly eighteen,' I said under my breath, but he heard.

'You're even more young than I think,' he said softly. 'I see I have to wait for you to grow up.'

No, I wanted to argue. I'm not too young. I only know I love you and I always will. But I couldn't say any of those words. I'd promised Colonel Thornton I would make Ruggero fall in love with me. The trouble was, I never thought in my wildest dreams I would be forced to do something like this for the war effort.

'What I don't understand,' I started, steeling myself to carry this through, 'is that you are the enemy.' I saw him flinch. 'Yet you seem to be allowed to go around quite freely.'

He gave a short laugh but there was no humour in it.

'Oh, Kitty, how I would love to tell you everything. If you think about, I am not free at all. Just I have privileges because of my rank. But Travers is never far away.' He looked at me, his eyes searching mine. 'You must not worry. I promise we will see ourselves after this bloody mess is over.'

'What about Mussolini?' I said. 'Do you agree with him?'

I didn't know how else to put it. Only that I had to understand for myself, let alone Colonel Thornton, where Ruggero stood. It was as though I'd thrown a bucket of water over him.

'I do not agree with him on many things.' A wary expression crossed his face.

'Do you *like* him?'

'Of course I don't like him. He is very ambitious and it makes him cruel.'

'Exactly like Hitler.'

'Not *exactly* the same.'

I gave him a sharp look. Why was he sticking up for Mussolini? Was there any substance to Colonel Thornton's doubt? I felt sick inside. Had I made a terrible mistake with him? Surely it wasn't possible.

'Mussolini does not like Hitler much but he has to pretend, so with his help he achieve what he wants.' Ruggero held my gaze.

'What about Hitler then? What's your opinion of him?' I asked, my voice wobbling.

'How can you ask such things of me?' Ruggero studied me and I squirmed under his glare. 'They are both men I am against.'

'Yet the British have arrested you,' I persisted.

'Because I'm Italian.' Ruggero sighed, as though he was explaining to a child. 'To them I am the enemy. But there are many Italians like me who do not feel sympathy for Hitler and Mussolini. They want a peaceful life. They do not like to fight.'

'Have you ever met Mussolini?'

Ruggero's face hardened. 'I cannot talk of such things.'

'Surely there's no harm in telling me if you've met him or not,' I said, irritated with myself as much as him. I didn't think Colonel Thornton would be very impressed that I'd not even got an answer to this. I answered for him – to goad him into agreeing or not. 'Well, you must have, else you'd tell me.'

He took my hand and pulled me up. 'Come, Kitty. It is many more than five minutes.'

By his eyebrows drawn tightly together until they almost met over his nose, I instinctively knew he didn't want me to continue this turn in the conversation. But I had to find out some information without Ruggero being suspicious. I was in a hole with no experience for anything like this.

Ruggero wasn't a fascist. He was on our side, I was certain of it. Yet by his reaction to my question I was just as sure he'd met the famous Mussolini. Maybe even worked with him. A tingle of fear crept over my scalp. How could he if he was on the opposite side? And if it was true and Mussolini found out, that dreadful man would decide on a punishment which would show no mercy. I shuddered.

'We go before you catch a cold,' Ruggero said.

We climbed carefully down to the desert floor and made our way slowly back to the waiting car.

Joyce was all agog the next morning but I just said Ruggero and I had walked over to look at the pyramids which looked very beautiful in the moonlight.

'Did he kiss you?'

'I'd rather not talk about it.'

It was true. If I told Joyce how much I was in love with him, I wouldn't stop. I'd have told her everything.

'Oh, well, suit yourself,' Joyce said.

I'd hurt her feelings but she didn't stay around for me to tell her I was sorry.

Alice asked me the same thing two hours later, but this time I was more practised. On the way back from the pyramids all she'd been able to do was squeeze my hand and give me another huge wink. She caught me now as I was on my way to the studio and asked if I'd had a nice walk with Ruggero. I told her it was lovely and thanked her for her part in taking Mike off.

'Oh, *ma cherie*, I am so 'appy for you. 'E is 'andsome, is 'e not? But you *must* be careful. 'E is Italian which make 'im the enemy.'

That word. How I hated it.

'But when this evil is *fini*—' The roar of an aeroplane drowned her words. She shook her head, for once unsmiling.

When I thought about it later I realised I'd never get any valuable information from Ruggero in exchange for a few kisses. My insides trembled at the thought of what I would have to do next to extract the kind of information Colonel Thornton demanded.

35

'Colonel Thornton wants to see you again, Kitty,' Jennifer told me the next morning as I was coming out of the canteen.

It wasn't Mike this time who came to collect me but a hefty middle-aged staff sergeant. There was an exercise going on which was deafening. He just gave me a rueful grin and announced me as we entered Colonel Thornton's office.

'Sit down, Kitty,' Colonel Thornton instructed, and I sat on the opposite side of his desk. 'How are you getting on? Do you have anything to report?'

'Not much, sir.' I fingered the edge of the desk for something to do with my hands.

'You were with him alone on Thursday night, were you not? Looking at the stars.'

He made it sound a very silly thing to be doing and not at all what he had in mind.

'Yes, sir.'

'And?'

'I-I er...' I swallowed and took a deep breath as though I was going to sing full-throated. 'I tried to find out his thoughts on Mussolini. Where he stood politically...and everything,' I finished lamely.

'Well?'

'He wouldn't tell me exactly. Just said he didn't like every-thing...anything Mussolini said or did.' I looked straight at Colonel

Thornton. 'I asked him if he'd met Mussolini but he said he couldn't answer. But I'm certain he's not a fascist,' I blurted.

'I'd like to be as certain as you.' He hesitated. 'I wonder why he felt he couldn't answer. Probably didn't want to incriminate himself.' He twiddled his pen between his fingers. 'You haven't given me much to go on, Kitty. I hoped you'd get more. Do you like him enough to allow him to have sex with you?'

My eyes flew wide. My lips stayed clamped together. How could I tell him I wanted Ruggero to make love to me more than anything in the world? But not at the instructions of Colonel Thornton. My pulse began to race. I had to keep a calm exterior or this whole thing wouldn't work. If Colonel Thornton suspected I loved Ruggero he wouldn't believe anything I said. He'd just think I was protecting him.

'Is there a problem?' he asked.

My stomach clenched. I couldn't speak.

He threw me a cool look. 'Would it be your first time?'

'I don't have to answer that.' I flinched under the colonel's scrutiny but I held his gaze.

'You do. I wouldn't want you to be in any trouble with your family. If you're a virgin I won't ask you to do this. It wouldn't be fair – even in war.' The headmaster expression again. 'You're very young still.'

'Well, it should please you to know that I'm not,' I said, in a level tone. 'So I'll do it, if you really think it necessary.'

'Excellent. I will see that you are given the necessary protection.'

I didn't know whether he meant a person like Mike protecting me from any trouble my association with a prisoner of war might cause, or if he was talking about birth control. I didn't dare ask. He seemed to have it all sewn up anyway. I just wanted to get out of his hateful office before I completely embarrassed myself by bursting into tears.

'And Kitty,' he went on, eerily reading my mind, 'make sure he

263

uses something. You don't want to get in the family way.'

Oh, how callous he'd made it sound. My stomach tightened with anger. When Ruggero and I made love – and I had no doubt in my mind that we would – it would be the most wonderful experience I would ever have, no matter how long my life was to be.

'Well?' Colonel Thornton tapped his pen on the desk impatiently.

'Er, yes,' I mumbled. He must have asked me a question but I hadn't heard him.

'I will arrange with Jennifer Long that you have some time off tomorrow. Sooner the better. One never knows in war when one is going to be posted. You might not be here long.'

I waited all day to be given my instruction. In the end nothing came. Half relieved, half disappointed, I went on stage in the evening to sing but I couldn't put any heart into it. I was too nervous and couldn't wait to get off the stage, find Joyce and get back to our hotel.

'Kitty.' The merest whisper floating in the dark.

I swung round but could see no one. It came again, so quiet I thought I must be imagining things. He'd been on my mind all day, waiting, reliving Colonel Thornton's words. To act as though my life depended on it. As far as I knew, it might be.

'Kitty.' And he was beside me, helping me on with my shawl against the cool evening.

I heard him chuckle. 'Travers said I could have the evening to myself. He's gone to town for a few hours. So I've come to see you.'

In spite of my shawl I shivered.

'Come, Kitty. We can have some private time together.'

You don't realise this has all been planned, I wanted to scream, but I meekly let him escort me over to where he and Mike lived.

It was very strange going into his quarters, just him and me.

'What about the others you share with?' I asked.

'Working the night shift,' he said. 'There's no one to bother us. Travers knows about us and said he is going out for a night with the boys.'

I was surprised. Mike had so far done everything to discourage us. This must be Colonel Thornton's doing. My heart hammered with nerves.

Ruggero's bedroom was surprisingly warm. One of his fingers caught the edge of my breast as he removed my shawl and draped it over a chair and I felt a flood of wanting run through me – so strong I was sure he must have sensed it too.

He looked at me standing there watching him, fascinated with the strangeness of it all. 'Come here,' he said softly, and I slowly walked towards him. He drew me close.

His kiss was quite quite different from when we were in the shadow of the pyramids. Warm lips found mine, caressing the whole of my mouth, until I moaned with aching for him. I forgot to breathe. The inside of his mouth tasted of wine and I thought I would drown in that kiss, so soft and gentle at first, then strong and firm and passionate. In the end it was he who had to draw away. He held my head in his hands and looked deeply into my eyes. For those few moments I forgot all about Colonel Thornton but now I could hear his voice in my ear saying I would have to go all the way to make Ruggero fall in love with me.

'Kitty, what are you thinking?' he asked. 'You look far away. I want you to be here...with me...now.'

I blinked. He was so in tune with me he'd guessed I was worrying about something. I had to shut my mind off. Our time was precious and I didn't want to think of anything that might spoil it.

'Ruggero,' I said, 'please kiss me again.'

And he did.

'I want you,' I kept saying over and over, not caring that my senses were alert to this very opportunity cleverly presented to me so I could get more information from him. Everyone be damned.

'Oh, Kitty,' he groaned, his mouth in my hair, kissing my neck. 'Adorable Kitty. I want you too. But I mustn't take advantage of you. You are so young. This has to be enough.'

But I'd already begun to loosen his tie.

He undressed me as I lay on top of his bed, whispering how beautiful I was. He caressed every part of my body, all the while stopping to kiss my lips again before his fingers explored further... my nipples, my breasts which he bent to kiss...and then his hand was across my stomach, circling gently, until finally he found the tender folds between my legs. Quivering with wanting, I raised my pelvis to let him push his finger in as deeply as he could.

'Please!' I shouted, but he took no notice. Instead, he gently removed his finger and then his face was close to mine again. His eyes had turned dark brown. He eased me over so I lay on top of him. Instinctively, I sat up to put my hand around him to help him enter me. He shook his head.

'Caress your breasts, Kitty. Make your nipples hard.'

I did what he asked, as though I was the lover to my own body. It was strangely erotic. I heard him pant. Just as I thought I would die of desire he took hold of me and pulled me underneath him again.

Never had I known such joy as when Ruggero entered me. I clung on to him, our bodies slick with perspiration, and he pulled my legs around his back, and I heard myself moaning, and his lips were brushing my ear.

'I've waited a lifetime for this,' he whispered.

Instinctively, I raised my pelvis to his.

'Don't move, Kitty.' He pressed me even tighter against him so my breasts were hard against his chest. He began to move, deliberately at first...each thrust gentle, giving me time to watch his face...then I felt him quicken, become stronger...

'Ruggero...I...'

'Come with me, Kitty.' His breath came in short gasps. He was faster...and faster...

My head was spinning.

'NOW!' he commanded.

I felt the thrust of him deep inside my body.

His muscles tensed. His eyes locked with mine. My body burst with wave upon wave of exquisite tingling and shivering, floating on a cloud high above in our own private world. Someone called his name from far away. We were there forever until at last I sighed with the release of all that pent-up emotion and longing and love. We stayed locked together. And then Ruggero very, very gently removed himself. He rolled on his side, bringing me round to face him, putting my hand on his chest so I could feel the beating of his heart, and we couldn't help laughing and pulling each other closer with the craziness of what we had just done.

And then I saw a serious look cross his face and I held my breath.

'I love you, Kitty. I love you and I always will. We will be together always.'

'I love you, too.'

I was happier than I'd ever been in my whole life.

Afterwards, we lay quietly, smiling and very pleased with ourselves.

'I am not the first with you, am I?'

I hesitated. I was sure he'd asked the question more out of interest than jealousy. 'No,' I said. 'But you'll be the last.'

How would I know that? I was still months away from my eighteenth birthday. But I'd never felt more certain of anything in my life.

He pulled me to him – little pulls that took me closer to him until not even a feather could have slipped between us.

'Kitty,' he said, suddenly breaking the spell by moving me away a little, 'after the war you must come to me at home. In Napoli – Naples. The family name you know is Andreotti. The house is called Palazzo Andreotti. Everyone knows our name...it's old family. If

I am not there, my sister, Daniela, will know where I am. She will help you. I don't want us to lose each other.' He kissed my forehead. 'Do you remember it, Kitty?'

'I'll remember,' I answered. 'Palazzo Andreotti. It's easy as it's your name.'

I would lock it in my memory.

And then I remembered. Remembered why I was here. What I had to do. To say. But Ruggero beat me to it.

'I want to know everything about you,' he said, stroking my hair. 'Tell me about your mamma and papa, and sisters and brothers. What sort of house you live in. Where you go to school? I want to imagine you as a child. Tell me all.'

'I have a mum and dad…but he isn't my real father,' I added quickly. 'I only just found out. And you'll never guess. My real father was born in Rome. His mother was Italian.'

Ruggero sat up and propped himself on one elbow, looking at me with surprise, his eyes twinkling with delight. 'Really? You realise that makes you almost Italian?' He chuckled. 'How did that happen?'

'It's a long story. I'll tell you one day. Not now.' I kissed him quickly on the lips. 'I have a sister, Frankie, and brother, Harry. We live in Norfolk…' I hesitated. I wanted Ruggero to know my mother had been in service so he could never accuse me of any pretence as I was sure he came from what Frankie and Harry would call a "good family". 'Near a big country house,' I went on, 'where my mother used to work, called Bonham Place.' Ruggero nodded for me to go on, not seeming to worry that my mother must have been a servant. 'Frankie and Harry both joined up but I don't know where they are.' I kissed his bare shoulder this time. 'Now it's *my* turn to ask questions.'

His face closed up immediately. 'I have nothing interesting to tell you.'

'You asked me if I have anyone at home and I told you I haven't. But you haven't said if you have a girlfriend.'

'There is someone.'

My body stiffened. Of course there was. Someone as handsome and wonderful as Ruggero wouldn't be without a girlfriend. Oh, why had I asked such a stupid question? If I didn't know, then I couldn't be hurt.

'Our parents have wanted us to marry since we are children.' Ruggero laughed and twisted a lock of my hair around his fingers. 'She is a lovely woman. And maybe if I had not met you...'

'What is her name?'

'Elisabetta.' He kissed me. 'Do you remember what I said to you after we make love?'

I was silent.

'I said I love you and I always will. And we will be together always. Nothing has changed. You would not like if no girl had ever liked me.'

It was true. I'd think it was rather odd.

'Tell me about your family,' I said, kissing his earlobe. It was time to change the subject.

'Ah. I have a mamma and papa and one brother, Lorenzo, and my sister, Daniela – the same as you.'

'Is Lorenzo in the forces?'

'Yes.'

'Where is he stationed?'

'Kitty, listen.' He pinned my arms down, not hard, but firmly, his eyes black. 'I am prisoner. Not free to speak on anything. You must know that. So why are you asking me all these questions?'

'Whose side are you on?' I blurted out the words I'd told myself I'd never ask.

Ruggero went completely still. Anger flared in his eyes.

'What are you saying? You ask me this sort of nonsense before. I don't like it. It means you do not believe what I stand for. No, Kitty, I'm not a fascist. I'm not a Mussolini lover. I'm not a Hitler lover. I'm not a communist. I'm a peace-loving Catholic who just wants to be set free. Go home to my country before it is in ruins. But before that, I want to help the British. Do anything to help bring this bloody war to finish.' His eyes burned into mine and I flinched. 'Is that good enough for you, Kitty? Are you satisfied? Will that be enough to tell Travers?' He gripped my arms even tighter.

I was trembling. 'What has Mike Travers got to do with anything?'

'Has he asked you to question me?' Ruggero's voice was suddenly laden with suspicion.

'No, of course not,' I said, thankful I could be truthful about that, at least.

'Then who has?'

I froze.

'Kitty.' He shook me slightly. 'Who has? Was it Colonel Thornton?'

I couldn't even blink. I just stared at him, rigid with fear.

'You haven't answered.' He threw off the bedclothes and with his back to me got dressed. Tears poured down my face. Without turning round he said, 'So because you don't say, I know it must be him. He asked you to spy on me. And you have agreed.'

'It wasn't like that,' I stuttered.

'Well, you have some more things to tell him now,' Ruggero said bitterly. He shook out a cigarette and lit it, then drew deeply before blowing out the smoke in a stream. 'I would not like you to mention my brother. Can you at least promise me that?'

'Ruggero, I'm sorry, I...'

I couldn't think, couldn't speak. I couldn't promise anything to Ruggero. I'd already promised Colonel Thornton I would find out as much as I could. But how could I explain that to Ruggero?

Feeling sick at what I'd done, and Ruggero's unforgiving expression, I jumped up and got dressed, fumbling with the fastenings. He didn't say another word and neither did I. He opened the door and I left, crying my eyes out.

'He swears he's not on Hitler and Mussolini's side – not a fascist. Not a communist. Just a Catholic who wants the war to end before it's ruined his country,' I said to an alert Colonel Thornton who looked at me with those all-knowing eyes.

'What about his family?'

'He has a brother and a sister.'

'The name of his brother,' Colonel Thornton snapped so that I jumped.

'Um, Lorenzo.' I'd said it. Ruggero had asked me not to. He'd never forgive me. But it couldn't hurt just to tell the colonel his name. And I knew nothing more about him anyway.

'Lorenzo Andreotti.' Colonel Thornton took time to light a cigar. 'What is this Lorenzo doing in the war?'

'He's in the forces.'

'Which one?'

'I don't know. I asked where he was stationed and Ruggero got suspicious of all my questions.'

'Hmm. You were obviously getting too close. The brother will almost definitely be a fascist if he's in the forces.' Colonel Thornton rose from his desk and strode over to the window, his back to me so I couldn't see his expression. Then he turned.

'Anything else?'

'Only that he said, "I want to help the British – and the sooner the better."'

I thought I'd embellish it a little so there was no doubt about Ruggero's loyalty.

Colonel Thornton sat down at his desk again. 'Well done, Kitty. Good work.' He looked sharply at me. 'Did you have to go all the way to find that out?'

I steeled myself. I wasn't going to discuss the most wonderful lovemaking from the most wonderful man with Colonel bloody Thornton.

'I tried. But he asked how old I was. When I told him I was only seventeen he just said we mustn't get carried away as I was very young and inexperienced where men were concerned, and he didn't want to do anything to me I'd later regret.'

I was pleased to see the colonel's eyes narrow at that. Maybe it was something he hadn't expected from a prisoner, but I'd already decided what to say to put Ruggero in the best light possible. 'He was very definite,' I rambled on. 'There's no question he's on our side.'

Colonel Thornton frowned. He looked across the desk at me, then smiled. I sat there feeling nervous, wondering if he believed me. 'Just remember what I said. You must never discuss any of this with anyone. *Ever.* Understood?'

I nodded.

'Understood?' he said, louder this time, as he half rose from his desk.

'Yes, sir,' I said.

I was still smarting from Ruggero's questions and his sudden temper. Before I stopped to think what I was doing I reached into my bag and drew out that piece of paper. Without a word I handed it to Colonel Thornton. I caught a flicker of surprise in his eyes as he took it from me and unfolded it. I watched as his eyes skimmed over it, wondering if he knew enough German to understand the message.

He looked up. 'Where did you get this?'

'At the last Italian lesson Colonel Andreotti gave me.' My voice shook at the enormity of what I had done. Immediately regretting it I bit the inside of my mouth, but it was too late. He nodded for me to continue. 'It was in the sleeve of one of his records. I found it when he left the officers' mess. You'd asked to see him and I thought I'd put a record on while I was waiting. We sometimes listened to opera after the lesson…' I was gabbling.

'Thank you, Kitty, for trusting me with this.' He slipped it into a file.

'Will he get into trouble?'

'I hope not.' Colonel Thornton's face was a mask.

Nausea clawed at my stomach. 'All he wants is to help the Allies,' I said, willing the man to be convinced.

'I hope you're right.' He half rose from his desk as a sign the interview was over.

Furious with myself for ever agreeing to question Ruggero, I stood up. I couldn't undo it now. I'd known I was taking the risk of spoiling anything we might have had in the future. But I'd been dragged into it. I'd have to carry my guilty secret forever.

And then I heard Ruggero's words as though he were standing in front of me: *I want to help the British*. And I knew without any doubt – in spite of that German paper – he was on our side.

36

Ruggero

'Radio Cairo calling. This is Radio Cairo.'

Ruggero glanced at the typed script in front of him on a wobbly oak table which had to make do as a desk. No matter how many empty cigarette packets he'd stuffed under the leg that appeared to be the culprit, the desk still wobbled and he'd have to try another leg. He adjusted his earphones and shifted on the hard seat, trying to ignore the malevolent figure of Captain Travers silently watching, ready to listen to his every word to make sure he didn't stray from the script. Ruggero wouldn't have minded almost anyone else but it galled him that Travers was practically fluent in Italian and had been given the job. Momentarily he closed his eyes. This was not a game. It was the first broadcast to his countrymen, both in Italy and as far afield as Libya, and he had to get the tone right. He cleared his throat.

'*Saluti*!' he began. '*Ascoltatemi, amici mei!* This is Carlo, one of your fellow countrymen, speaking. I will be talking to you most days. You are not going to like what I have to say but you must listen very carefully. You have been duped. I have been captured by the British along with thousands of Italians. I am broadcasting to you not from my country, but from a place of our natural allies. Remember Garibaldi's Curse.' Ruggero paused, and took a drag of his cigarette. 'In case you have forgotten, let me remind you.

'England is a great nation, at the front of human progress; an enemy to despotism, and the only safe refuge for the exile, friend of the oppressed. If ever England should require the help of an ally, cursed be the Italian who would not step forward in her defence. As a Liberal and a lover and admirer of my country I am not sorry to see Benito Mussolini, the savage persecutor of Italian Liberals, the assassin of Matteotti, the treacherous conqueror of Abyssinia, the brutal oppressor of the Arabs of Libya, the cowardly Jackal of Europe, marching to destruction with the curse of Garibaldi on his head.'

Ruggero glanced at the sheet of paper. Even though it had been written by someone else, the words could have come directly from his own heart.

'Think with your hearts and act with your heads. The Germans cannot win. Torture and the killing of innocent people and children cannot win. But with our help the British will fight this evil and succeed. If we sit back and do nothing, Germany will take over our beloved country. Do you want that to happen? To be under the Nazi boot for the rest of your lives? If you survive, that is. And do you want your children brought up as little Nazis? Speaking that harsh guttural language? Of course not. Wake up, I implore you. Until tomorrow, fellow countrymen. This is Carlo, signing off. *Arrivederci.*'

The broadcasting light dimmed and as it went out he heard Travers get up from his chair and leave the room. Thank God for it. Ruggero leaned back in his seat, rubbing his neck which felt stiff with tension. Whether these broadcasts would do any good or not, who knew? Ruggero pursed his lips and blew out a long sigh. But one thing was clear. He was working for the British. And that was what he'd wanted ever since he'd first stepped foot into Mussolini's office. He lit another cigarette and closed his eyes.

The image of Kitty. Her innocent face. Her beautiful dark blue eyes. Surely she'd believed him when he'd told her he wanted to help the British? He should have told her more. That he'd been part of a plot to assassinate the two bastards. But he'd hesitated for fear he'd sound like some schoolboy on an adventure and she'd never believe him. His brain whirled as he tried to remember every detail of his conversation with Thornton, and Kitty's questions so soon after they'd made love. How could he now believe anything she said? She hadn't answered when he'd accused her of spying for Thornton. But surely Thornton would never have let him loose on Radio Cairo, even with Travers sitting there, if he'd had any doubts at all about where his loyalties lay.

But it didn't answer the most important question – had Kitty meant it when she'd told him she loved him? Or was it all a trap? It couldn't be. He was so certain she'd meant it. He'd never felt so certain of anything else in his life.

'Presumably you realised Kitty only pretended to fall in love with you – and make sure you fell in love with her?'

Ruggero froze to his seat.

'Hasn't she been asking you a lot of questions lately?' Travers lazily lit a cigarette, his eyes intent on Ruggero's face. 'Weren't you suspicious that the two of you managed to have some privacy so Kitty could fuck you – to put it bluntly?'

Ruggero flinched.

'Yes, it was the colonel himself. Colonel Thornton asked her to question you. See if you were a fascist – Nazi lover – call it what you like. Little Kitty was chosen for the job. She was told to make you fall in love with her. And the only guaranteed way to do it was to make sure you had sex with her. That's when your tongue would loosen...in more ways than one.' He winked.

Ruggero shuddered in distaste.

'And a damned good job she did, too, as you fell for it – or rather for her—' Travers broke off, grinning. 'Gave her all the information the colonel needed to be satisfied you're with us. That's why you've been put on to Radio Cairo – working for the British, as you appeared so keen to do.'

Rage swept through Ruggero. Travers made it clear he would still treat him as the enemy no matter what. Ruggero wanted to punch the Tommy's head in. Take that smug look off his pasty face. He half rose from his chair, his hand in a fist, then sank back down. Any show of violence towards Travers and he would ruin everything. He was a prisoner of war, and there was nothing he could do – except keep to his word and help the British.

And forget he'd ever met Kitty.

37

Kitty

I'd heard nothing from Ruggero. Or Colonel Thornton, come to that. Maybe he'd had what he needed from me. I was fed up with everything and beginning to hate the camp. I was only alive when I sang. But Ruggero was never again in the audience and that hurt me most of all.

A week crawled by. And then one afternoon I saw Ruggero and Mike walking towards me as I was on my way to the kitchen to help out. Ruggero looked tired and my heart went out to him. I was about to ask Mike if he would let us have a few moments alone but Ruggero beat me to it.

'Signorina Townsend.' His mouth was tight as he nodded and made as though to walk on.

'Ruggero, I want to explain.' I touched his arm. It was rigid. He deliberately turned so my arm fell away. 'Please let me speak. Mike would you—' I gave Mike a beseeching look which he chose to ignore by pretending to look elsewhere.

'There is no need for explaining.' Ruggero's voice was ice. 'I completely understand. You were doing your duty.'

'I didn't tell Colonel Thornton that we—' I broke off. Ruggero had already sidestepped me and strode off, Mike a few paces behind. I stared after them, tears burning the back of my eyelids, humiliated and hurt. Mike turned but I ignored him as I stood there stupidly in the heat of the afternoon, frozen with shock. Ruggero couldn't have made himself any clearer. He didn't believe I really loved him. He thought I'd deliberately set a trap. Who had told him? Surely it wasn't Colonel Thornton. That didn't make sense. The only other person it could have been was Mike.

And now Ruggero hated me. I couldn't blame him. I would have felt the same if he'd pulled such a dirty trick on me. Except mine wasn't any trick.

I loved him with all my heart and body and soul. And I would go on loving him for the rest of my life. But he would never know.

I trudged over to the kitchen, tears spilling down my cheeks.

The rumour flew round the camp that we were moving on. This time I was relieved. I thought I might feel calmer about Ruggero if I was away from him. Weeks had gone by. Sometimes I'd see him in the distance, usually with Mike close by, but he never looked my way. I couldn't stand much more of this.

'It's going to take some getting used to,' Jennifer said at breakfast that morning, mopping up her egg yolk with a piece of bread.

I'd just walked in. 'Where are we going then?'

She looked surprised. 'Don't you know?'

'No, and neither does Joyce. She told me we were packing up again, and didn't know any details.'

'We're going to India.'

A piece of bread stuck in my throat. I started coughing and Jennifer passed me a glass of water. Somehow, I managed to squeak, 'India?'

This was terrible. I'd never see him again. Never have the chance to make up. Even with my not very good geography I could see how impossible it would be. I stared at her almost accusingly.

'You said we'd be here for months – maybe even a year.'

Jennifer sighed. 'It's a shame as I think we're doing a damned good job for the soldiers, poor devils. Now there'll be nothing to take their minds off the war.'

All I could think of was letting Ruggero know my new address. I couldn't – *wouldn't* – lose contact with him. But how could I get it to him? We'd be lucky if we were told where we were going until we'd actually arrived.

India. If I'd never met Ruggero I'd have been so excited. I'd always wanted to travel. But this news which would take me away from my love was a crushing blow.

I needn't have worried about no address to leave Ruggero. Madeleine came to our room after the show that night and said there'd been a change of plans. We were moving the day after tomorrow, but not all the company.

'Jennifer's changed her mind,' she said with a smirk, directing her remark to me. 'Everyone's going except you two – the two newcomers. India is for the experienced members.' She turned and left us with our mouths hanging open.

I didn't know what to think. Ruggero would probably be able to find me easier if I was back in England than somewhere in India. But I felt upset that Joyce and I were being tossed out of the troupe through no fault of our own as though we'd done something wrong. Joyce wasn't bothered one way or the other. She never really got excited by the desert as I did, except of course the time when I was lost. No, Joyce's main fear was the thought of travelling by ship and being seasick the whole time.

'Quite honestly I shan't mind going home,' she confided, 'though I've lost my job at the hairdresser's.' Then she thought a bit. 'I did like dancing with all the blokes, though. I'm going to miss all that.' She looked at me. 'Don't pull that long face, Kitty. You can never have him.'

I thought and thought about Jennifer's decision not to allow Joyce and me to go with the rest of the troupe to India. It didn't ring true about our being too young. We'd proved ourselves in the desert. We'd mucked in – done more work around the camp than Madeleine ever had. In fact she'd not lifted a finger, not even once. We didn't grumble about our conditions. So why…? I decided to have a word with Hal.

'I did hear, Kitty, and it's too bad,' Hal said, sympathetically. 'But nothing is going to change Jennifer's mind.'

'Madeleine's behind this again, isn't she?' Hal was silent. 'Isn't she, Hal?' I touched his arm. 'Please tell me the truth.'

'Well, I did hear something,' he said reluctantly. 'She's spread the word that you're fraternising with the enemy – "having it off with one of them" was how I believe she put it – and if you were, then probably Joyce was too. She's persuaded Jennifer to get you both out of the camp and out of ENSA as swiftly as possible.'

I stood there, dumbstruck. I just couldn't believe what he was saying. What lengths Madeleine had gone to get rid of me. If only I could tell her it was the very opposite. I'd been asked to spy on Ruggero. What would she have said if I'd told her that? She must have seen me go over to the officers' mess, or even over to Mike and Ruggero's quarters, and put two and two together. Then dragged poor Joyce into it. This time she was successful.

'I know you're not and most of us feel the same, but it's the old story. I believe Lionel had a word with you about the two of them so you know the position with Jennifer. She'll do anything to please Madeleine.'

'Thank you for telling me, Hal.'

I couldn't even tell Hal what the truth was, but he believed in me anyway.

I left him, tears streaming down my face with the injustice of it all. I told Joyce about it but all she said was that Madeleine would get her comeuppance in the end.

Any moment I thought Jennifer would appear to tell me I was not allowed to sing on the last night. But if she let me go on stage I knew what I was going to do. I was not going to leave Cairo under a black cloud.

I practised for ages in my room. Having heard the song so many times I could sing it by heart. I'd told Hal I didn't need any accompaniment that evening and he could have the night off, and said Madeleine had agreed with me. He knew that last bit was a fib, but he smiled and said he didn't feel that well anyway and could do with the rest.

'Hal, the microphone seemed to be playing up last night.'

He frowned. 'In what way?'

I stared at him, my face innocent.

'Oh,' he winked at me, 'I'll have a word with Tony. Maybe he can fix it.'

I needed some kind of flower so I had to ask Joyce if she'd seen anything around the place. She produced one from the hair and beauty cabin.

'What's it for?' she asked.

'My last song tonight.'

Madeleine always began and ended the show. I stood in the darkness as near as I could to watch her as she walked on to the stage to her usual round of applause. I saw her look across to where Hal always sat at the piano, to give him the nod that she was about to begin. She went as still as a shop mannequin. Then she frantically turned her head this way and that, peering through the darkness. But there was no Hal and no piano. I watched as she hesitated. The audience started to mutter. A few stomping feet. It reminded me of what happened when I'd forgotten my lines. The noise became louder.

'What are you waiting for?' someone shouted from the back. Other voices joined in. After about a minute Madeleine put her right hand up as though to still the noise. Even at this distance I could see the fingers of her left hand curl and uncurl.

'Looks like I'll have to sing without any pianist tonight,' she announced.

No response from the audience. Madeleine tapped the microphone and repeated her message. But there was no amplification whatsoever.

This time Madeleine grabbed the stand and banged the microphone on the stage floor, shouting that it wasn't working. Probably no more than the front three or four rows could have heard her. The audience started to yell,. You could certainly hear *them*. I heard Joyce chuckle in the darkness and dig me in the ribs. She had a big grin on her face. Madeleine began to sing, but without the microphone her voice was lost. After a few more moments she threw her arms up into the air and marched off the stage, her face aflame.

'Where the fuck is Tony?' she said, looking wildly around for him.

'Language, language.' Joyce shook her head in mock horror.

Madeleine glared, then turned to me. 'Let's see how *you* get on with your wonderful voice and no Hal and no microphone to help you.'

'Why don't you stay and watch?' Joyce said.

'Oh, I will. She's bound to make a perfect fool of herself as usual, and I want to be around when she does.'

I swept up on to the stage with the confidence of a star and waited for the applause to die down. I pretended Ruggero was there on the front row gazing up at me with love in his eyes. I'd sing to him alone. No one else mattered. Humming the first bar in my head to get the pitch, as I'd done in my room so many times, I began the opening notes to the "Habanera" from *Carmen*. My voice, to my ears, sounded quite as powerful as any of those opera singers I'd heard with Alice as I put my whole energy and soul into the song. My hips swayed in time to my inner rhythm and I tossed my hair with my hand, enjoying the freedom of not having to stand up close to the microphone. I moved right across the stage; I became the sensuous gypsy girl. I held the rose between my teeth for a few moments, and at the end I flung it into the audience and heard the shout of delight when one of the soldiers caught it. My song ended.

All was silent under a starlit desert sky. And then a noise like thunder. It was deafening. Soldiers stood up and whistled. 'More, more,' they shouted. I nodded at them, smiling, and belted out two more songs, ending with the "White Cliffs of Dover", where the soldiers joined in at full power.

When I stepped off the stage to the cheers and roars of "encore", more drained emotionally at the thought that Ruggero wasn't there than having to sing so loudly, Madeleine was waiting for me.

'How *dare* you sing my song?' Her eyes were challenging as she clutched at my bare arm.

I flicked it away as though it were a desert fly. It was hard for me to keep my tone reasonable. 'If you *had* sung it, of course I wouldn't have. But I know how the soldiers love that particular one.' I kept my eyes locked with hers. 'And I didn't know that you could *own* a song.'

'Fuck you.' She flounced off, then stumbled as her heel caught in the sand.

'You certainly showed her,' Joyce said, but I couldn't enjoy the trick I'd played. Madeleine's hostility meant nothing. I was too eaten up with misery to relish my moment of triumph.

Joyce had the good sense to leave me quietly alone before she finally came to bed. I lay there on my back, the flat pillow doubled under my head, going over and over our last time together. I couldn't understand why he thought I'd been acting. Didn't he remember our love-making? Couldn't he tell I'd given my heart to him?

I heard Joyce creep in and get undressed and slip into bed and still I couldn't drift off. I pushed my face into the pillow to muffle the sounds.

'Don't cry, Kitty,' her voice floated across the darkened room.

I spotted Mike striding towards the games room the following day. Desperate to let Ruggero know what had happened, I'd written him a note with my home address and had it ready in case I saw one of them.

'So you and Joyce are going back to England?' Mike said. I nodded. 'I'm sorry to hear that, but I'd like it very much if you would write to me.'

'No, that's not possible.' I stared at him, knowing he'd spoken to Ruggero about me.

He shrugged. 'Can't blame me for asking.'

'One thing. Would you please give this note to Colonel Andreotti?'

A dark look crossed his face. 'You really shouldn't be writing love letters to a POW,' he said finally, not looking me in the eye. 'You've been used as a pawn but you're too young and naïve to realise it.'

I gave a start. So it *was* Mike who'd told Ruggero. Maybe even boasted that Colonel Thornton had confided in him. I badly wanted to blurt out what I suspected but I had to be nice, or he'd never give Ruggero my note. Tomorrow I'd be on my way home. I pretended not to understand what he was talking about.

'Please, Mike,' I said, thrusting the envelope into his hand. 'It's only to thank him for the Italian lessons, and that I'll try to keep them up.'

He nodded. 'Safe journey home,' he said, kissing me on the cheek.

I tried to blink back the tears as we waved to the other entertainers who had come to see us off. Lionel was coming home with us as his back was still playing up and he didn't feel he was doing justice with his act. Madeleine wasn't there, of course. But Jennifer was amongst them. She kissed us both in turn but I didn't have the same enthusiasm. I still felt she could have stood up to Madeleine. Not do everything that woman said. Everyone else hugged and kissed us. I gave a special hug to Bert and Ben in the kitchen, but most of all, dearest Hal. I squeezed him the tightest.

'Remember all I've taught you,' he said as he warmly hugged me back, his eyes surprisingly moist. 'You're gonna go places, young

Kitty. One of these days I'll be reading in the newspaper about your appearance on the London stage.'

'I'll never forget you, Hal,' I choked, and meant it. 'Thank you for all you've done for me, and being my one true friend.'

'Wouldn't have had it any other way,' he said thickly.

'And thanks for last night,' I whispered.

'Brought her down a peg or two, didn't it?' He winked.

'We'll miss you both,' the ENSA troupe shouted as the bus pulled away.

I wanted to believe them. But all I could think of was that a ship would be taking me further and further away from Ruggero.

The troop ship was packed. One soldier told me the ship was built to take six hundred people and we were over two thousand. Even a crude calculation would tell anyone we'd be as closely packed as baked beans in a tin, with few comforts.

There wasn't a spare foot of space you could escape to. It was dirty, noisy, the food was poor and not enough of it, and on top of that Joyce was immediately seasick. I steeled myself to get through the rest of the voyage, dreading every mile that took me away from my love.

Queuing for breakfast next morning I saw someone so familiar I thought my eyes were going to pop out of my head. Frankie! She was balancing a cup of coffee and a bread roll and walking towards a packed table in the 'Officers Only' area. A man squashed up and made room for her. What was Frankie doing here? She was a Wren but I had no idea she was in Cairo. I wondered why I hadn't bumped into her before now, but guessed the reason was that ENSA was small fry compared to the rest of the camp.

'Porridge or egg and beans?' someone serving asked me. I blinked.

'Egg and beans,' I said, turning back again to make sure it really was my sister. It was Frankie, no doubt about that, although I could tell, even with her back to me, that she'd lost weight. Well, I was an officer too, and in my uniform. I stuck my chest out and smiled. It would not be out of place for me to sit with her. I made my way over to her table.

'Is there room for me, Frankie?'

She looked up, her eyes flickering in astonishment. My smile faded. Horrified, I stared at the huge dark circles under her eyes, a face so thin you could see all the planes and angles, her golden hair pinned in a bun which would have been more suitable on an old woman.

'Kitty! What on earth are you doing here? We knew you were in Egypt – well, we guessed as much, but what—' It was her turn to stare at me. 'Are you going home?'

'Yes,' I said, squeezing into a tight space by the side of her. 'The others are off to India. Me and my friend Joyce have been sent back as we're the youngest and apparently we're not experienced enough to go with them. I should have thought we'd proved ourselves with some of the things we put up with in the desert.' I stopped, remembering the Official Secrets Act. I studied her profile. 'But what about you? Why haven't I seen you? How long have you been in Cairo?'

Frankie twisted towards me and gave a little grimace. 'Sorry, Kitty. Not allowed to talk about it.' I noticed her hand tremble as she picked up her cup of coffee. 'I'm on sick leave.'

'What's the matter?'

'Bit of nerve trouble, that's all.'

'What do you mean?'

She shook her head and clamped her lips together. I knew that stubborn look. I'd get nothing more out of her.

We became separated after that, but once I glimpsed her amongst the crowds and mouthed to her, 'Are you being sent away again?'

She shook her head. 'Hospital,' she mouthed back.

The voyage home was miserable. The sea wasn't that choppy, but some days I was just as sick as Joyce.

'I don't understand it,' I moaned, when I forced us both up on deck to get some fresh air. 'I didn't feel a bit seasick coming over. Maybe I'm not such a good traveller as I thought.'

'Oh, I think you are,' she said, her face still green-tinged from her last bout as she scrutinised me. 'You're only sick in the mornings.'

I stared at her. She nodded. And then it dawned on me.

PART IV

Disclosure

38

King's Lynn

November 1941

I stood on the doorstep, trembling from cold after the desert temperatures, my stomach churning, praying Mum would appear.

'Kitty, darling!' Mum said, throwing her arms around me. 'Why didn't you let us know?'

'I didn't have time,' I said, my voice dull.

She gave me a sharp look and pulled me inside.

'Just you sit there. You must be worn out with such a long journey. I'll put the kettle on.'

Dear Mum. Her answer to any problem or pain. I watched her retreating back. Really, she wasn't old yet, but her hair had a few more streaks of grey than when I last saw her. She worried me.

'I thought you might be over at the tea rooms.'

'Not today, darling. Mollie's there with a couple of village ladies. They made me have a day off,' she laughed. 'They must have had a premonition you were coming home.'

I smiled back, trying to gather my thoughts. How was I going to tell her about the baby? That the father was an Italian prisoner of war. That there was no hope of my ever seeing him again. That I'd been asked to spy on him. That we'd had a terrible row. All my worries jumbled together. My lips tightened as I thought of Dad. What he'd say. His disapproval. Then I remembered he had no say. He wasn't my father. But was Mum strong enough to fight him?

Mum poured out the tea and handed me a cup and one of Mollie's home-made buns.

'What is it, Kitty?' she said, looking closely at me. 'You can tell me. Whatever it is, I'll understand.'

I opened my mouth but no words came out.

'You're going to have a baby, aren't you?'

I could have fallen through the floor. 'How did you guess?'

'It's in your face, darling, and your blouse is a little snug,' she said, reaching over and taking my hand.

She leant over and kissed me. I closed my eyes for a few moments, savouring the faint lavender scent of her. She said nothing. When I opened my eyes she was still studying my face as though considering what she should say next.

'Oh, Kitty, you're so very young. Do you want to talk about it right now?'

My dearest mother. She hadn't accused me or said I would bring disgrace to the family. All she was worried about was how I felt. I burst into tears and she came round my side of the table and hugged me. I clutched her to me, not wanting to ever let her go.

'Does he love you?'

Her words made me want to die. 'I thought he did,' I said, unconsciously putting my hand on my stomach. Tears trickled down my cheeks.

'Take your time, darling.' She got up to get me a handkerchief. 'Who is he?'

'I-I met him in Cairo. He's an Italian prisoner of war.' I raised my face to her to see how she was taking that, but her eyes were only dark with concern.

'I don't understand,' Mum said. 'How were you able to fall in love with a prisoner?'

I was so glad she assumed I loved him.

'Because he was a lieutenant colonel he was allowed special

privileges. He...' I swallowed, and started again. 'He came to our show the first night when I had an attack of nerves. He sang with me. He—'

'Does he know about the baby?' Mum asked, gently taking my hand.

I shook my head. 'I only realised myself on the ship,' I said, and burst into fresh sobs.

'I think you must write to him, darling. It's his child. He has every right to know.'

I didn't answer. Couldn't.

'Is he married?' she said eventually, her hand pushing my hair back from my eyes.

'No,' I sobbed. 'We had a terrible row.' I put my head in my hands remembering Ruggero's cutting words.

'What did you have a row about? It couldn't have been that bad. All young people have arguments. It's natural when they're getting to know one another.'

'This was no argument, Mum.' My voice was muffled. I looked up, tears still running down my cheeks. 'I was asked by the colonel at the camp to spy on him.'

Now I was back in England I could hardly believe what I'd done.

Mum's eyes widened in dismay. 'Why on earth would a colonel ask an innocent untrained young girl to spy on a prisoner? It's far too dangerous.'

'His name is Ruggero. And it was to find out whose side he was on. If he was on our side—' I stopped abruptly, remembering I was still under the Official Secrets Act.

By the look on Mum's face I had to tell her the truth.

'I didn't find out anything I didn't already know. He *is* on our side, Mum. Just like my father would have been.'

The merest shadow of a smile crossed my mother's face at the mention of him.

'I just don't know what to do.'

'We'll come through this together,' she said, pulling her mouth firm, seeming to have made a decision. A determined look flashed into her eyes. 'And the baby, too.' She paused and smiled at me. 'My first grandchild,' she said, a tender look now softening her face. 'But you must write to Ruggero. It's only fair.'

My dear mother. No recriminations. Just reassuring me that everything would work out. And then I remembered.

'What about Dad?'

'Leave him to me,' Mum said. Her expression was pure steel. 'I shan't tell him just yet.' She looked at me, her eyes full of love. 'But I want you to think again about writing to Ruggero. Whatever has happened between you both, he deserves to know he's going to be a father.'

In my heart I knew my mother was right. I started the letter to him so many times and crumpled them up. In the end I decided it wouldn't make much difference how I actually told him. It was the news itself that was important. I started again.

Letter dated 15th November 1941

Dear Ruggero,

I'm sure Mike Travers told you that Miss Long sent Joyce and me back to England when the rest of the ENSA group went on to India. I didn't have any chance to say goodbye but I gave Mike a letter to give to you with my home address as I thought that was the safest. I'm living with Mum and Dad at the moment while I sort myself out.

I was very sick on the voyage home and Ruggero I have to tell you something has happened that you should know. I'm having – or rather, we're having – a baby. Yes, I was as shocked as you must be reading this letter but all that keeps going through my head is our last meeting. You never gave me a chance to explain, so all I can say is how sorry I am.

Even now, I hope I'm doing the right thing.

I miss you.

All my love,

Kitty

I wouldn't re-read it or I would start altering it again. It would have to do. But as I looked in Mum's chiffonier for an envelope I broke down again.

Several weeks went by. Every day I looked and hoped there'd be a letter. Maybe Ruggero had been sent somewhere else. But they didn't normally move POWs around as far as I knew. Maybe I was "out of sight, out of mind". Then when I remembered his touch, his lips kissing mine, murmuring little words in Italian, and our lovemaking, I couldn't believe I meant nothing to him.

Frankie was sent straight to the Norfolk and Norwich Hospital as soon as our troop ship reached England. Mum and I went to visit her every fortnight. It was quite a journey from King's Lynn with the buses not always running on time, but then one wonderful day she was allowed to come back with us. The matron said they could do no more for her and that she was vastly improved and well enough to go home. Frankie looked much better although she was more subdued than I remembered.

Harry was due ten days' leave which cheered everyone up, especially Frankie, though we didn't know exactly what day he'd arrive. Another week passed, and just as Dad said they might have cancelled his leave we heard the bell ring. Mum went to answer the door and came back, her face all aglow.

Harry looked so handsome in his uniform but thin like all the boys whenever we saw them in town. His face was resigned into angles of pain and the suffering he'd seen, but as usual he hugged me tight and kissed my forehead.

'How's my favourite girl?' he said, putting me away from him, his hands still on my shoulders.

'I'm all right,' I said.

He gave me a sharp look but didn't make any comment. Then he hugged Frankie and said he was glad to see her looking better than he'd expected. But after Mum had made all of us tea, Frankie went upstairs for a rest. She still wasn't back to her normal self.

I deliberately chose one of the upright chairs to sit on, wishing Mum hadn't disappeared into the kitchen to wash up, leaving Harry and me alone in the front room.

'You look a bit peaky,' he said. 'What's the matter, Kitty Cat? Cat got your tongue?'

It was his old nickname for me. I swallowed hard.

'Come on, Kitty, I haven't seen you for ages. I want to hear all about your Vera Lynn stuff. I bet the boys loved you.'

I never really knew when he was being flippant or teasing me. But at this moment he looked serious.

'Those lovely eyes of yours look sad. What happened out there, Kitty? Do you want to talk to me about anything?'

'No,' I answered. 'I'm just sick of the war, that's all.'

'It'll soon be over now,' he said, studying me. 'We've got Jerry on the run. But I don't think you're being entirely truthful. There *is* something bothering you. Is it boyfriend trouble?'

I stared back at him. It was on the tip of my tongue to tell Harry about the baby. But then I reconsidered – he didn't need to know yet. I'd only missed three monthlies. His leave would soon be over and I'd asked Mum as well not to say anything.

The following day I heard something that was to have repercussions on the whole family, but particularly me. I was about to ask Harry and Dad if they'd like some tea. They were in the front room and the door was slightly ajar. I'd just got my hand on the knob when I heard Harry's voice sounding most insistent.

'I'm sorry, Dad, but you're not going to control my life. I want to be a writer and that's what I intend to do after the war's over.'

'It's not what you've been trained for.'

'Thanks for spotting that, Dad.'

'No need for sarcasm. It's the truth. How will you get started, that's what I'd like to know? No one's heard of you. Unless you've had something published I'm not aware of.'

'I've been writing all my life – stories and articles. I edit a newspaper for the troops, and I—'

'Fat lot of good that is,' Dad interrupted, 'earning bugger all.'

'It's all experience so I can get a job as a reporter for the local newspaper when this bloody war is over. And start my novel.'

'Do you think that's what it takes to write books? Working on some tin-pot rag?'

'It's a start. If I'd begun sooner I could have been a war correspondent by now.'

'Driving your mother even more out of her mind than she is already.' Dad's tone was scornful.

'What do you mean?'

'Well, she's not been the most stable of people since you all left home. Sometimes I quite wonder about her.'

'What are you hinting at?'

'Oh, nothing I can put my finger on. And it's no good looking at me like that either, Harry. You don't see her every day like I do. She can be a very difficult woman with those independent airs.'

'Don't you dare speak about my mother like that,' Harry said. 'She's the best mother in the world. You talk about *me* – you've never had a proper job yourself, so Mum's money from the tea rooms keeps us all going. And at least she understands me and encourages me to follow my dream. Not against me all the time the way *you* are.'

I was just about to go in and tell them to stop behaving like a couple of squabbling schoolboys when Dad said in a strange tight voice: 'Maybe there's something you should know. Should've been told years ago.'

'What's that?'

There was a long pause. Little did they know I was only a few feet away, stone rigid, waiting for Dad, the same as Harry was.

Just when I thought Dad must have changed his mind and decided not to discuss whatever it was, I heard him say in an oddly flat tone, 'Mum is not your mother.'

What? Dad must be joking. His kind of joke I never found funny. But I still stood there, fingers gripping the doorknob.

'Whatever are you talking about?' my brother said. '*Course* she's my mother.'

'I'm afraid that's where you're wrong.'

Dad's voice now had a dead serious ring to it. He wasn't playing games.

Who would break the silence first? I imagined Harry's blue eyes flashing as he faced Dad. Could it be true? If so, who did Harry belong to? Mum had already told me about Harry being born and that Dr Townsend, my father, wasn't there to deliver him. How upset she'd been. So she *must* be his mother. I stood there, my mouth open in disbelief.

'Don't stop now, Dad.' Harry's voice was carefully quiet and I had to strain to hear his words. I knew he was trying to control his temper.

Still no reply.

'Come on, Dad.' Harry's voice was now raised in frustration. 'You can't spring something like that on me and not finish it. If Mum's not my mother, then who the bloody hell *is*?'

'You'd best talk to Mum.'

'Who *isn't* Mum.' Harry's voice was curt. 'Okay, I'll do exactly that.'

Before I could break my grip with the doorknob Harry appeared. He looked right through me as he rushed past.

If Dad was not my real father and Mum was not Harry's real mother, then he wasn't my brother at all, or even my half-brother. It seemed like the whole family was falling apart. No one was who they thought they were.

39

It was December and getting colder by the day. My eighteenth birthday was looming and I was going to have a baby. It didn't seem possible. But after the crossing I wasn't sick anymore. In fact, I felt fitter than I'd ever been. I could still do something to help the war. But what?

I decided to telephone Joyce.

'I've just joined the YWCA,' she said. 'Why don't you come with me? You won't show for ages.'

She explained it was the Young Women's Christian Association and that they provided huts on camps and aerodromes especially for women in the services when they were off duty. A kind of rest centre. Apparently, there were about two hundred of these centres in Britain and the Middle East. As soon as Joyce said "Middle East", my thoughts leapt to Ruggero. Was he still in Cairo? If not, where would they have sent him?

I still ached for him and most nights I cried myself to sleep.

Joyce and I opted for going with the travelling club vans which went to some of the more out-of-the-way camps in England. And every time I handed over mugs of tea and sandwiches and cakes to those exhausted women who worked such long shifts, some under enormous pressure, and who told us how lovely it was when we "pulled up", I really felt we were doing something useful.

Best of all there were often dances on the camps where there'd be a couple or so musicians and I'd sing. I put my heart and soul into those songs but there was never anyone special I was singing to. But when I sang, that was when I felt closest to Ruggero.

And I had a book to carry on learning Italian...just in case.

Joyce and I travelled to various camps and aerodromes, reminding us of our time with ENSA. Because we spent so much time together she became closer to me than Frankie. She made me laugh when things were grim and time passed quickly. My birthday came and went. Then 1942 and at last America came in. And just when I'd given up getting a reply from my letter to Ruggero a letter with an Italian stamp was delivered to me, forwarded by Mum. Joyce was with me as we sat on her bed.

'For goodness' sake, open it,' she said, almost as excited as I was.

My stomach was doing cartwheels. I kept thinking, if I don't open the letter I can imagine his words: that he's thrilled with my news. He's going to come and see me as soon as he's released. After the war we'll be married and bring up our child together. I hoped it would be a girl, but I expected Ruggero would want a boy. That was what most men seemed to want. But nothing mattered – only that Ruggero had forgiven me and loved me.

I smiled happily as I tore open the envelope. Some bank notes fluttered to the floor. Joyce picked them up and put them on her bedside table.

'For the baby, I expect,' she said.

I just grinned at her as I took out the single sheet of paper.

'Read it out,' Joyce demanded.

But it was too private. I wanted to soak up the words on my own.

Letter dated 12th December 1941

Dear Miss Townsend,

I'm sorry it won't be Ruggero replying to your letter.

My excitement faded as my eyes flicked to the end of the sheet of paper. It was signed Daniela Andreotti.

Ruggero has asked me to write to you to explain his position. He is engaged to a lovely girl called Elisabetta. They were always childhood sweethearts and the two families are very happy. As soon as this terrible war ends they will be married. He should have told you about her. He is my beloved brother but I don't always agree with him. I'm afraid, my dear, to him it was only a wartime love affair which could never be.

I am enclosing some money for you to have an operation as we both believe the best thing would be to bring this sad affair to an end.

I am sorry as I know you will feel hurt, but you are young and time will heal.

With sincere wishes,
Daniela Andreotti

I stared numbly at the sheet of paper. I looked inside the envelope in case I'd missed something. There was nothing more.

'Kitty! What is it? You've gone as white as a sheet.'

I handed Joyce the letter. I watched as her lips silently mouthed the words. She looked almost as shocked as I felt.

'It's illegal to get rid of a baby,' she burst out, throwing the letter to the floor. 'Oh, Kitty, I'm so very sorry.' She put her arm around my shoulders. 'Did he ever mention this Elisabetta?'

'Once,' I said, remembering. 'It was when he was talking about how young I was, and that we'd be together after the war. He'd just told me he loved me.' I burst into tears and Joyce found me a handkerchief. 'I didn't take much notice at the time. But he was obviously not telling me the whole truth.'

Joyce stroked my hair.

'So he's seen my letter,' I said, choking on the words, 'and couldn't even tell me himself.'

'He's a coward,' Joyce said, trying to comfort me, but it only made me more upset to hear him described like that, even though it was true – the man I loved was a coward. Just like Madeleine once said about the Italians. Just like every British soldier *always* said.

I'd go for several minutes, then even an hour or two serving cups of tea and chatting to the soldiers, until it would sweep over me once more – I was going to have a baby. Ruggero didn't want anything to do with me. He was in love with someone else, and I'd start to sob again. Joyce was wonderful. She did her best to cheer me up but it wouldn't be long before I'd have to go home and face everyone.

The baby was starting to show. Joyce said she would stay on and if I was honest I envied her freedom. My life would soon turn upside down and it didn't matter how many times I told myself not to be so selfish, I felt totally unprepared to look after a baby. And I'd have to face Dad.

Luckily, my darling mother had prepared him.

Dad didn't say much. I suppose Mum cautioned him. Apart from saying he was deeply disappointed in me, especially getting tied up with an Eyetie, and what cowards they were, he hoped I wouldn't be disturbing his nights with a screaming brat. He needed his sleep to earn the money to keep us all. I didn't remind him Mum had been keeping us practically single-handedly for years and was still working.

'I'll earn my own living as soon as I've had the baby.'

'What, and leave your mother to look after it?' he said scornfully. 'I don't think so, Katherine. She's got enough to do with the tea rooms.'

It was no use arguing with him. I would get a job in my own time and he wouldn't be able to stop me. But who would be there to look after my baby?

40

It was Harry who showed me a way out. He appeared on the doorstep six weeks before the baby was due, mumbling that he'd got a few days off before the next big push.

'Kitty!' He swept me in his arms. 'I'm taking you out for supper tonight. We need to do some serious talking.'

I dreaded him questioning me about Ruggero but he wouldn't take no for an answer. Harry had an old banger, as he called it, but it got us into town and he found a parking space almost outside The Rose & Crown in King's Lynn.

Inside, it was warm and smoky from the open fire, and full of people chatting and laughing at the bar, and those who were dining seemed to be in deep conversation while tucking into their food. We found a table and ordered from a sparse menu.

That done, Harry leaned forward and pushed a strand of hair out of my eyes. 'What are you going to do, Kitty? You can't go having babies without a husband.'

His tone sounded as though he was criticising me.

'The baby will have enough with me and Mum,' I snapped.

'Mum didn't tell me much about the bloke,' Harry went on, ignoring my mood. 'Said I should talk to you. And you never wrote to explain who he is. And if he's willing to marry you.'

I hated the thought of Ruggero being "willing" to marry me, as though it was his duty. But since Daniela's letter I'd given up dreaming about the two of us being married and excited at the thought of seeing our child. I didn't answer.

'Is he already married?'

'No.'

And then I told him about Ruggero. That he was my true love. That I could never love anyone else. And I told him about the letter, and the most horrible bit of all, the money. And what it was to be used for. He listened, not interrupting. When I'd finished he wiped my tears with his napkin.

'He sounds like a bounder,' Harry said. 'A wartime romance. Best forgotten.'

'I'll never forget him,' I said stonily. 'How can I when I'm carrying his baby?'

Harry looked hard at me as though wondering what to say next.

'Kitty,' he said eventually, 'there's something I want to tell you.' He paused again. 'Mum's not my real mother.'

I glanced round the room but nobody was looking our way.

'I know,' I whispered.

'How do you know?' Harry's eyes sharpened.

'I was coming to ask if you and Dad wanted some tea, but I heard you having a row and thought I'd better not interrupt. And then you stormed out.'

'So you eavesdropped?'

'It was to do with the family. I had a right to know.'

'Do you know who my mother is?' Harry's eyes narrowed.

'I suppose it's someone Dad had an affair with.'

'Oh, it wasn't just *someone*,' Harry said, drumming his long fingers on the edge of the table. 'It's our *dear* Aunt Ruby. Though of course she's no longer my aunt, she's my *mummy*.' His voice dripped with sarcasm.

I let out a gasp of horror. Aunt Ruby. Mum's sister. Since I'd heard Dad's announcement Aunt Ruby hadn't crossed my mind. That's where his auburn hair and famous temper came from. But

305

not from his aunt, as Frankie and I used to tease him; Aunt Ruby was his own mother. I blinked with the enormity of it.

'Do you realise we don't share one parent between us? We're not related at all.' He laughed, a strangely nervous laugh that I didn't recognise.

I stared at him. 'Y-you know about...my father?'

Was I the last to know about my own father? A roll of anger swept through me.

'Course I do. Known for ages. But I wasn't going to say anything to you. I reckoned it wasn't my place. Mum had to tell you herself. But it makes everything better, don't you see?' He leaned towards me, a pleading expression in his eyes. 'You've always been special to me...and now you need me...' He stroked my cheek but before I could jerk away he said, 'Why don't you marry *me*?'

I looked at my brother with wide eyes. 'Are you mad?'

'I've never been more sane. The baby can be mine as far as anyone knows, and I'll love him or her as my own. You can rely on that.'

'But...you're my brother.'

'Only in name...' He stopped, as the waiter set our plates of food before us.

'Harry, don't say something you'll regret. You're my brother. You'll always be a brother to me, whether we're related or not, and that will never change. Anyway,' I went on, trying desperately to convince him, 'we *are* related. My mother and Aunt Ruby are sisters. So we're cousins.'

'Cousins are free to fall in love. Free to marry.'

'I can't love you in that way. You'll always be my brother. And I'll always be your sister.'

It was madness. The thought of making love with him flicked across my fogged-up brain and I couldn't help shuddering. I stared down at my cold white plate, the fishcake and mashed potato and spoonful of tinned peas making me feel sick. He would expect me to be a proper wife in every way at the very least for taking on my baby. I put my hand over my stomach and felt it pushing against my fingers. It was as though the baby was telling me I ought to think about it. Harry wouldn't let me down. He was a decent man. He would make a good father. It would solve everything. Except one part – I just couldn't love him in the way a wife should. Harry would always be my brother.

'I love you,' he said, covering my hand with his. It could have been a brotherly touch but everything now had changed and it felt different. I didn't like it. 'I've always loved you. Always felt closer to you than Frankie, though I could never really understand why.' He concentrated his blue gaze on me. 'You can't have a baby on your own. Your life would be ruined. If you marry me you can hold your head up. And,' he paused as though to emphasise the final persuasive point, 'this way, you'll be able to keep the baby. If you don't have a husband you'll have to put it up for adoption.'

'Never,' I glared at him. 'I'll scrub floors if I have to, to keep her.' In my mind I'd begun to think of my baby as a girl.

'You may not have any choice. Look, Kitty, I know this is all a new idea to you but as soon as Mum told me what had happened I knew without a shadow of doubt what I wanted to do. And maybe…one day…we'll even have children of our own.'

That day will never come, Harry.

'Think about it,' he said, squeezing my hand. 'I think you'll realise it's the only sensible thing to do. And you'd make me the happiest man in the world.'

I thought about it for a week. I went to bed with it and I woke up with it. It occupied every moment – every thought. I swayed this way and that. One moment I told myself it was the last thing I wanted and the next breath I thought it was the only possible way I could give my unborn child a normal loving home. As soon as I decided to say yes to Harry I'd change my mind again. I tried to imagine myself telling Mum and Dad. And them having to explain to the neighbours. It was preposterous. And then I thought, why not? I'd never love anyone the way I did Ruggero. And he was going to marry someone else – the right kind of girl chosen by his family. I might as well face the fact that I'd lost him forever.

I told Harry I wanted to see Mum on my own. He looked a little hurt but nodded. I offered to help Mum in the tea rooms the following day.

'I don't know what I'd have done without your help today, love,' Mum said, as I wiped down the last table and tipped the chairs up. 'Especially as Mollie's coming down with a cold and I had to send her home.'

'Can we have a talk before we close up?' I asked her. 'I want to tell you something before I speak to Dad.'

'Sit down then, love. I'll get you a drink.'

'I don't want anything,' I said, not wanting to put it off a moment longer.

She sat on the chair opposite, sighing with tiredness. I noticed how pale she was and hoped she wasn't coming down with anything as well.

'Mum,' I said, 'this is going to be a shock, and there's no way to prepare you, but Harry and I are thinking of getting married.'

'*What?*' She half rose in her chair, her eyes wide, as she clutched at the edge of the tablecloth, sending the salt and pepper pot flying. I bent down to retrieve them. 'Katherine, have you lost your mind?'

Mum never called me Katherine unless she was very angry or upset.

'I know it sounds like a mad idea but I don't have much choice.' I couldn't look her in the eye. 'Harry offered. He says he's always loved me in a special way. He'll look after me and the baby as if it's his own. I believe him. I can't think of any other solution.'

I swallowed, praying she'd understand and give me her blessing.

Mum was silent. She just stared at me and shook her head in disbelief.

'Mum…?'

'I know Harry's told you that Ruby's his mother,' Mum said, tears gathering in her lovely eyes. 'I wanted to explain when I told you about your father. When I told you Alex wasn't there to deliver Harry. But I thought you had enough to think about.'

I remembered how she'd nearly broken down, and I squeezed her hand. Then a terrible thought struck me.

'So Aunt Ruby gave him up and you passed Harry off as your own?' Mum nodded. 'But that means you must have been going to have a baby at the same time or no one would have believed he was yours.'

'Yes, it's true,' Mum said.

'But what happened to *your* baby?' My heart missed a beat.

'I lost him at birth,' she said, in a voice so quiet it was barely even a whisper.

We were both silent for several long minutes.

'I know you're only cousins,' she said finally, taking my hand in hers, 'so there's nothing really wrong…but, Kitty,' she leaned across the table, 'you'll never be happy. You grew up with him. You love him as family, as a brother. You won't be able to be a proper wife to him and you'll always feel like that. A wedding certificate won't change that feeling one iota. Besides,' she gently squeezed my hand, 'it's not fair to Harry. He deserves to be happy with someone who truly loves him.'

'I'm doing it for the baby. To give it the best chance. To have two parents.'

'I know, darling. But I know you as well as I know myself. You'll be doing yourself an ill turn if you go through with this. I know Harry's very fond of you, but it's *your* life we're talking about…and—' she broke off, giving me one of her penetrating looks, 'you gave your heart to Ruggero.'

As soon as she spoke his name I burst into tears.

'Don't mention him ever again, Mum.'

'You never told me whether you'd written to him, darling.'

'Yes,' I shouted at her. 'I wrote. And all I got was a letter from his sister telling me he was engaged to someone he'd known all his life, and how happy the two families were. And that her brother only regarded our time together as a wartime love affair.'

'That might be her version,' Mum said, speaking calmly.

'Mum, it's no use...' I couldn't say any more.

'Oh, Kitty,' Mum gripped my hand tighter, 'don't rush into this marriage. It will be the worst thing you can do.'

I hadn't told Dad about my imminent marriage. I was relieved that Harry insisted upon being the one to break the news. We tackled Dad while he was sitting in his chair in the front room reading his newspaper.

'Dad, we've got something to tell you.'

'Oh, yes?' Dad put down his paper and looked at us over the top of his spectacles.

'Kitty and I are getting married.'

'What the devil are you on about?' Dad's mouth stayed open and his eyes bulged. The newspaper crackled as he pushed it aside.

'I love her and she needs a husband and a father to her baby.' Harry tried to muster a reasonable tone as his arm slid round my waist, now the circumference of a barrel.

'You're crazy, the pair of you,' Dad's voice rose. 'What on earth do you think everyone will say? Have you never heard of incest? It's not proper. It's—'

'Dad,' Harry interrupted, 'we're only cousins, as you well know, and it's perfectly legal for cousins to marry. All you're worried about is that your dirty little secret with dear Aunt Ruby will come to light. As it has to, to make our marriage legal.'

Dad's face turned bright red. 'How dare you!' he spluttered.

'I dare because it's true.'

'Listen to me.' Dad thumped his hand on the table. 'You'll be putting your mother in a terrible position—'

'No, Dad, you listen to *me*.' Harry faced him with blazing eyes. '*You're* the one who's put her in a terrible position with your dalliance with Ruby. Don't try to push your guilt on to me because it won't wash. Kitty and I are getting married and you can tell everyone what you like. But it won't alter anything.'

'Well, don't expect to see me at any wedding.'

Hedy Alexandra, my beautiful daughter, was born three days early on 10th June, 1942. She was the image of Ruggero. I could never have passed Harry off as her father. I laughed and wept at the same time.

Harry had already found a house to rent in Dereham. I was relieved we had somewhere to live but annoyed he hadn't taken me to see it before signing the agreement, as I would never have chosen to live so far away from my mother. But I supposed it was to stop tongues wagging. No one would know us in Dereham. He was surprised when I complained, and said it was one thing less for me to worry about. But I saw it as a man taking control of me. And I didn't like it. It reminded me too much of the Arabs in Cairo. And Dad. Which was understandable, seeing that Dad was Harry's father.

Our wedding night was, of course, a disaster. I refused to let him touch me in any way, except for a brief hug and a kiss on the cheek, which is what we'd always been used to doing as brother and sister. Harry hoped I would feel different now we were officially man and wife, but if anything, I felt further away from him.

'I'm sorry, Harry, but I can't.'

'Give it time,' he said, a disappointed look settling on his handsome features, 'and you'll get used to the idea.'

*

News of the war flooded in daily. Then something wonderful happened the following year, October 1943, when the Italians switched sides. From what I read in the newspaper they didn't have a lot of choice with their defeat in Greece and the Middle East and Africa. But Ruggero was no longer the enemy. That hateful word. And I still loved him. Where was he at this exact moment? Was he even alive? All this time I'd been furious with him but whatever had happened to him was my fault. I should never have agreed to spy on him. I might have sent him to his death... A lump of guilt stuck in my throat but I kept on hoping for some word.

Finally I gave up hope.

Everyone said the war was close to ending in the spring of 1945. We all knew we'd won when Mussolini and his mistress, Clara Petacci, were shot. The newspaper reported they were hung upside down at some petrol station in Milan but even though I thought they deserved everything they got, it was too gruesome to imagine. Two days later Hitler and Eva Braun, whom he'd married only the day before, committed suicide in his bunker in Berlin. All we wanted now was confirmation that the Germans had surrendered.

Today was Tuesday, 8th of May. I was in a queue at the butcher's for some mince to make a shepherd's pie, one hand grasping Hedy, the other holding a basket, when a young lad flew past the window.

'The war's over! It's over!' he shrieked.

We all went to the door and stared after him. He was running down the street screaming the words.

'How do you know?' someone shouted.

The boy stopped in his tracks. 'Jerry surrendered yesterday in France. It's just now come through on the wireless.'

Hedy and I were jostled along with the customers as they dragged us out into the street, shouting and hugging and kissing us, and grabbing the hands of their friends and strangers – anyone in sight – until I wanted to shake them. Maybe I'd have felt better if Joyce was here with me. She'd have made me laugh and insisted we celebrate. But I hadn't heard from her for ages.

I gripped Hedy's hand tighter and glared at them. Hadn't they lost anyone? Hadn't anyone they loved been seriously hurt? Or a neighbour's son killed? But all they kept screaming was, 'It's over. Thank God, it's over.'

I looked down at my daughter's dark head. Her face turned up to mine, her eyes anxious.

'Are the people angry?'

'No, darling, they're very happy.' Smiling, I bent down and gave her a kiss.

'Oh, that's good,' she said, giving me a toothy grin. 'Why are they happy?'

'Because the war is over. No more nasty fighting. So everyone's happy.'

'Are you happy too, Mummy?'

'Yes, darling.' I blinked hard to stop the ready tears.

I'm married to the wrong man and I'm so very unhappy.

A pain shot through my heart as I thought of Ruggero.

Wherever he was, whoever he was with, even if he and Elisabetta – how it pained me to even say her name in my head – if they had a child by now, he would never know that somewhere in England walked his daughter, a little girl who looked the image of him. To think he'd sent me money with his sister's letter to... I suddenly burst into tears. There was simply too much happening around me. I couldn't cope.

'Mummy, why are you crying?'

'Only because I'm happy too, darling. Sometimes when grownups are very, very happy it makes them cry.' I bit my lip and lifted my shoulders. I *had* to cope. Hedy was all the world to me.

Without going back into the queue I led her away from the

butcher's and we made our way back home through the cheering, waving crowds, Hedy giving a little skip now and again, and looking up at me every once in a while to make sure I was still happy.

The following month I had a letter from Mum enclosing a newspaper cutting. It showed a photograph of a smiling couple, newly married. I immediately recognised the woman. Diana. She was wearing a beautiful dress with a high lace collar and wide-brimmed hat. She looked just like she was – a real society lady. The column mentioned she'd been a driver in the FANY during the war, but I'd always felt there was something more mysterious about her when she'd disappear for a few weeks at a time.

Dear Diana. I don't know what I would have done without her. She'd rescued me when I'd first arrived in London as a young girl with a head full of wild notions. And her landlady, poor Mrs Parker. How horrid I'd been to nickname her Nosy. But thank God Diana was safe and looked so happy.

Things had become progressively worse between Harry and me, and I realised they would never improve all the time I kept him at arm's length. He did everything he could to show his love, and for Hedy, too, and I tried hard to be a good wife to him. One day after yet another rejection he finally lost patience.

'The only thing to save our marriage is for you to get psychiatric help.'

'Why don't you just put me in the loony bin and be done with it?' I shouted back.

It took me three years in a marriage that was never consummated and a war to end before I had the courage to make the decision to leave.

Hedy and I moved back to King's Lynn so I could be near Mum, and I took a job as a receptionist at Browns Hotel, supposed to be the best in town, but I hated it. Everyone who worked there looked down upon any other hotel that wasn't Browns. I was biding my time and providing Hedy and myself with a roof and food. Meanwhile, I saved every penny I could and made my plans.

Another three years passed. And then at last the day came when I was ready to throw everything up and take the biggest risk of my life. And I was taking Hedy with me.

PART V

Coming Home

41

Rome

April 1948

The lights dimmed. I stepped out into the spotlight. There was no stage. No raised platform. I was on the same level as the diners. They were still clattering their knives and forks but at least some of them looked up when I came out. I was wearing a bright red dress – quite daring, the way it was cut low at the front, but I needed to hold everyone's attention in order to keep my job – and I was looking forward to the evening. Smoke from several couples at the front tables wafted towards me but I was used to that. It added to the romantic atmosphere and gave me and the songs a certain mystique, or so I thought.

I'd come to Rome with Hedy in search of my father's family. Maybe my own grandmother was still alive. It would be strange if I found her and talked to her, knowing that Mum never did. Poor Mum. She'd been so upset when I'd told her about Ruggero and Daniela. It had dug up memories she'd rather forget about my father's parents. She'd been living in sin with their son and they hadn't wanted to meet her. But sometimes people change when they're older, I reasoned. War forced people to look at things differently.

I was determined to find out if any of the family was still alive.

And in my heart I also needed to be in the same country as my only love.

The journey had been a nightmare. I'd had to repeat my story over and over to any official who stared at my passport and then at me with open-faced suspicion and hostility, explaining why I was on my way to Rome. I told them the truth. The father of my child was from Naples and my own father had an Italian mother and came from Rome. They would look at Hedy with her black curls, then rattle off a load of Italian, ending in smiles and nods, realising she couldn't be anything but one of their own. Only then did they relent and let me through.

By the time we got off the train in Rome we were both exhausted and Hedy was fractious. I was almost too tired to appreciate Mussolini's railway station – all concrete and plate glass – so different from all the buildings nearby. I could only stand for a minute or two gawking, thinking of Ruggero. Finally, I was in his country, breathing the same air. My heart was unsteady as I whispered his name.

'Come on, Mummy.' Hedy put her small hand in mine and practically dragged me away.

It was already evening and I had no idea where we were going to stay. I had to find some cheap lodgings fast. My stomach fluttered, reminding me of the time when I was seventeen and had gone to London by myself, knowing full well I had no address to go to – and I'd been all right. Only then I didn't have a five-year-old to worry about. But Hedy was already an independent little miss, and I'd reckoned she was old enough for an adventure.

I asked a couple if they could recommend anywhere but my Italian was halting as it had been so long since I'd had any practice. They shook their heads and hurried on.

'Why is everyone talking nonsense?' Hedy asked, looking up at me, a puzzled expression in her grey eyes. She hadn't inherited the women in the family's navy blue ones. Mum told me my father's eyes were a lovely warm grey, like a greyhound's coat, she'd said, and she and I were both thrilled the colour had been passed on to Hedy.

Talking nonsense? For a few seconds I didn't understand what Hedy was referring to. Then I laughed. That's what it must sound like to her. It was going to be fun with the two of us. 'We're in Italy, darling. When people are in another country they talk in a different language. I'll teach you some words, but not until tomorrow. We need to look for somewhere to stay for a few nights.'

As I was speaking I glanced around and spotted a sign across the road advertising rooms. Holding Hedy tightly by her hand we dodged the traffic and reached the other side. I rang the bell. Then again. Soon I heard the sound of footsteps and the door swung open. A thin woman stood there, her wispy brown hair held back with combs. She pursed her lips as soon as she saw Hedy.

'I've come about the room,' I said in hesitant Italian.

'No children,' she said firmly and pushed the door to.

'*Per favore, signora*,' I pleaded, putting my hand out to keep the door open. 'We've just arrived from England.' I said the last part in English because I couldn't remember any more Italian, I was so dead-beat.

To my relief a beam spread across her face. 'Why you not say at beginning?' she said in English. 'I am Signora Dotti. *Avanti.*' She stood to one side and I pulled Hedy through into the dark hall before she could change her mind.

'The English save my boy in the war,' she said when we were sitting in her private room, drinking coffee. 'He would be shot by the Germans when Italy become Ally.'

She gave me a long explanation as to what had happened to her boy, mostly in rapid Italian which I could barely follow, and although I tried to show interest, all I wanted was to get to our room and sleep. We'd gone for more than twenty-four hours with barely a nap and Hedy was starting to grizzle.

'First you show me passport, then I show you room,' Signora Dotti said as she rose from her chair.

I hadn't thought about this. My name on my passport was Townsend. And I'd already told her my name was Bishop, as that's what I wanted to be known as while I was in Italy so I could carry out my investigations anonymously. As soon as Signora Dotti spotted the different name she was bound to ask questions.

'Oh, I-I'm not sure where... Can I give it to you in the morning?' I asked. Maybe she'd forget about passports by then.

She hesitated. Then she said, 'You must show me in the morning. For the police.'

She gestured for me to follow her up the stairs.

The room was gloomy but it was late in the day. Maybe in the morning it would look better. I glanced round. One small window looked out on to a wall of another crumbling building. Single unmatching beds topped by pretty patchwork covers were pushed against two of the walls making an L shape; there was a dressing-table, a single brown wardrobe and a chest of drawers. On the chest was a vase of mixed flowers standing on a white embroidered cloth, giving the room a homely touch. And all was spotlessly clean.

'*Quanto costa?*' I asked.

There were so many millions of lire I couldn't work out the English equivalent, but I was sure Signora Dotti wasn't the kind of woman to take advantage of me.

'The little one needs rest,' she said. 'I leave you, but you ask if you need something.'

Rome was a grim disappointment. Worse than London because the Italians had none of the London spirit. Ragged children and dogs and cats and rats all ran wild amongst the rubble, and the smell of decay and poverty filled our nostrils. Hedy stood, mouth open in horror, watching the scene.

'The nasty men hurt Rome like they did London, didn't they, Mummy?'

'Yes, darling, but all the soldiers have gone home now. There won't be any more fighting. No one will hurt anybody again.'

Instead of the excitement and noise and colour Ruggero had once described, it was grey and dreary. People's gaunt faces wore expressions of despair. Most of them were out of work, I soon found out, so how was *I* going to find any when I wasn't even an Italian citizen?

We'd been in Rome a week and I was soon depressed with the rain and the bombed-out buildings and the rationing. Prices had risen out of all proportion to what was on offer and I had to think twice before even ordering a cup of coffee, though I always bought Hedy a hot chocolate. We quickly got into the habit of eating our proper meal at noon, usually a cheap bowl of pasta. Sometimes, the owner would take pity on me and not charge for Hedy. We were hungry by then after a breakfast of just two bread rolls and a smear of ersatz jam Signora Dotti gave us every morning, but setting it out with such style it always looked more tempting than it tasted.

I'd gone into several bars asking for work. Anything to give me some money to keep Hedy and me for a few weeks. Waiting on tables or behind the bar; even cleaning. But there was nothing. No one was taking on a new person, especially a foreigner with a young child.

I felt friendless and hopeless, not really having a proper plan. Signora Dotti offered to look after Hedy the next day and put her to bed so I could look for a job without the worry of her, and I was happy to agree.

The following day I ambled around some of the streets even further away from Signora Dotti's immediate area, asking for work. Nothing. I arrived at a pretty square, the Campo de' Fiori, and immediately felt envious of the couples sitting at tables outside the cafés chatting to one another, laughing and kissing. Walking with my head high as if I'd chosen to be on my own, I wondered where Ruggero was, if he might even be here, and the thought made my breath come quickly. But then I pulled myself short. Ruggero would be back in Naples, married by now to his childhood sweetheart, and already with children.

The image of the happy family made me feel sick but I couldn't

323

stop my eyes from darting around the crowds where I might spot him. There were all kinds of people enjoying themselves; my own age or younger, whole families and clusters of old men all talking and laughing and tipping back their heads and drinking beer and wine and coffee. There didn't seem to be many women in sight. I supposed they were at home getting their men some supper. Could that seated man with his back to me be Ruggero? His head looked the right shape. Almost black hair, curling slightly at the neck. But then he would turn round and he was nothing like him. Each time it happened I blew out a sigh to give my heart a chance to slow.

I'll never see him again, so stop looking.

I tried to put these depressing thoughts to one side and enjoy the mild evening air when a notice outside one of the restaurants caught my eye. It said they played live music on Friday and Saturday nights.

Live music. Maybe…

I pushed the door to and went inside. It was dark. There were only three men sitting at the bar but it was still early. I asked in my best Italian if I could speak to the manager, and after a few minutes a little man with his shirt buttons bursting over his stomach appeared from behind a beaded curtain.

'I see you have live music on Fridays and Saturdays,' I ventured in my limited Italian. If only I'd had the sense to keep up my lessons. I'd always meant to. The manager nodded. 'I'm from England. I am staying in Rome. I wonder if you have a singer.'

'We only have a small band,' he said, his moustache twitching at my question. 'Mostly jazz. We don't have the need for a singer. Why do you ask, *signorina*?'

'Because I'm a singer. And I need a job. And I can sing jazz.' I'd never tried but I couldn't see it would be that difficult. It would just be like learning a new song with a new rhythm.

'I'm sorry.'

'Please allow me to sing one song,' I coaxed. 'Then you will see.'

'I'm very sorry, *signorina*, there is no work here. I can't even pay the musicians. They play for love.'

Love wouldn't pay for a roof over my head.

'Just one song,' I begged.

He shook his head and waved me out.

Everything blurred as I left his miserable restaurant. Several pairs of eyes followed me as I stumbled between the outside tables, tears held back only by sheer willpower.

'*Signorina.*' A tall, dark-haired man rose from one of the tables and lightly touched my arm. '*Qual è il problema?*'

'I'm English,' I mumbled, raising my tear-streaked face to his.

'So, I speak English.' He whipped out a crisp white handkerchief and gave it to me, then held out his hand. 'Come, come, sit down. I will try to help.'

He'd been sitting with friends, but rattled out something to them and they vanished. I sat on one of the seats, still warm from the previous occupant, and blew my nose on his handkerchief, then put my hand on my forehead where it had begun to throb.

'Tell me,' he said.

I told him I was trying to find my father's family; that I had my little girl with me, and was staying in a cheap boarding house but my money was disappearing fast with the alarming inflation. I was desperate to find work. He listened closely.

'What work are you seeking?'

'I'm a singer,' I told him, looking at him properly for the first time. He had a strong face and his beautiful dark brown eyes reminded me so very much of Ruggero's. His wavy hair was swept back showing a widow's peak and he was dressed in a navy blue suit. 'And when I saw the sign here,' I sniffed while he smiled at me encouragingly, 'saying live music on Fridays and Saturdays, I thought maybe I could be their singer. But the proprietor couldn't offer me a job. He said people were working for nothing.' A black despair came over me. '"Nothing" doesn't pay for food and board.'

'What is your name?' he asked.

'Katherine,' I said. Suddenly I didn't want to be "Kitty" any longer.

'Katerina in Roma,' he smiled, showing even teeth. He took both my hands in his. 'So, Katerina, you will sing for *me*.'

'What do you mean?'

'Here, at this table. A good Italian song.' He waved his hand around the people who were fully engaged in drinking and smoking and chatting. 'You make them sing too.'

'I don't know any Italian songs,' I told him. 'I only know English.'

'You must know this one,' he said. His smile widened. He drummed some beats on the table top and began to hum "Bella Ciao".

In an instant I was back in Cairo. Back at the camp. Back in the officers' mess. My darling Ruggero singing it to me. I remembered watching his face, his eyes moist with unshed tears every time he sang it. Teaching me the words in Italian. Telling me what they meant. He'd been trying to tell me right from the beginning that he was on our side. "Bella Ciao" was the Italian song for freedom and liberty. A rush of shame swept through me at any moments of doubt I'd ever had. And now it was too late. Ruggero had a new family.

I felt the tears prick the back of my eyes. I had no job. Very little money. And then I couldn't help myself. I started to sing the words to the stranger's humming. He pulled me to my feet.

'Sing it loud, Katerina,' he laughed. 'Sing for your audience.' He gestured towards the other diners.

I sang.

I was vaguely aware that people had stopped clattering their knives and spoons. That heads were turning our way. I began to sway my hips a little as I moved between the tables, smiling and using my hands and arms in true Italian style. I wasn't a bit self-conscious. It was as though we were all bound together in my song after the terrible war. I put my heart and soul into it. And then I heard voices from a nearby table singing with me. I turned towards them and smiled. More people joined in and I felt my voice shine with outpouring, closing my eyes on the final note.

There was a hush. My heart raced. I'd gone too far. Made a fool of myself. And then to my delight I heard the sound of clapping and whistling and cheering. I opened my eyes and there, standing in the doorway watching me, was the fat little owner with the moustache. This time he waved his arms to beckon me in.

I looked round to thank my rescuer, but he'd disappeared. I didn't even know his name. I walked back into the restaurant, wondering who he was and why he'd taken pity on me, but it was as though he'd never existed.

Signor Franco offered me a job on the spot with no wage, to sing two nights a week – Friday and Saturday – and the promise he would pay me after two weekends provided I brought in enough extra customers.

Tonight, Saturday, was my fourth night singing for nothing. This coming Friday I would be paid as Signor Franco couldn't deny that more and more people filled the dining tables on the two weekends I'd sung. Now I stood quietly, not moving on purpose, giving as strong a hint as possible that I would not be singing until they stopped talking and I had their full attention.

It was then that I saw a couple coming in at the back of the room. The man had his hand under the elbow of a slim dark-haired woman; she must have been heavily made up because I could make out her features even from where I stood with a spotlight shining on me, which I couldn't the man's. She was wearing very wide-legged green slacks – almost emerald green, as they caught the light from one of the lamps – and a tight-fitting top showing her narrow waist, with a fur stole casually slung over her shoulders. I watched, fascinated. I could see the outline of an empty table to my left. Yes, that's where they were headed.

The woman had a film-star look about her. That was until I saw her come closer. She was swinging one of her legs in a strange way, sort of out and then to the side. It was so noticeable because of the bright slacks.

Then everything happened in slow motion. Dizziness took hold as I saw the man come closer, guiding her, gripping her arm. Coming closer. The shape of him. His walk. The turn of his head as he looked at the woman. I put my hand up to my eyes, shielding them from the spotlight, trying to peer into the smoke and gloom. His features were blurry even as he got near. He wasn't looking in my direction. He was pulling out a chair for the beautiful woman, smiling down at her as she settled.

Goose pimples clung to my bare arms as my mind whisked me back to Cairo. If only he would strike a match to light a cigarette and I could see him more clearly. But the lights dimmed even further, and it was dark as night when I finally screwed up the courage to glance again in their direction. The small band began to play the opening bars of "Bewitched, Bothered and Bewildered", one of my favourites that I'd taught them, and I couldn't even open my mouth. But I had to. Friday I was getting paid.

For God's sake, Kitty, you're not that wide-eyed dope of seventeen anymore.

I cleared my throat the way Alice had taught me. But hers was for effect – to delay their anticipation. I was doing it because I was desperately nervous and playing for time.

I lost my entrance. The band played the opening bars again. It sounded so different from when Hal had played it on the piano that time in Cairo, but the strings and saxophone set their own mood. I started to sing.

'*I'm wild again, beguiled again…*'

The words perfectly echoed how I was feeling. I sang quite quietly but with my whole being, making sure I didn't allow my eyes to stray to their table. But all the time I was really singing to

328

Ruggero. And this man reminded me so... Out of the corner of my eye I could see that the man was completely still at the table, and even when his wife turned to him and smiled, he kept his gaze frontwards. By now the spotlight was so bright it was making my eyes sting.

It wasn't him. Of course it wasn't. But it looked so like him. Maybe I was going crazy.

'I'll sing to him...each spring to him...'

Who was singing? I tried to get a hold on myself. *I* was singing. Was I still singing? Two heads turned at the table on my left, their eyes directed straight at me. The man whispered in the woman's ear, then rose and walked slowly towards me. He came closer... and closer. There was a tension in the room. I saw the flare of a cigarette. It was as though everyone was waiting – expectant. And every muscle and bone and organ and all the casing of my skin felt it had been waiting for this moment.

The room was dead quiet.

I stood gripping the microphone stand, perspiration trickling through my fingers. Gently, so gently, he prised my fingers away.

'I've found you at last, Kitty,' he said.

42

Ruggero faced the audience who had by now all turned towards us. One or two chuckled. Then there were some mutterings. They must have been wondering what on earth was going on – who was this man?

He put his mouth close to the microphone and spoke in rapid Italian. I caught something about his having looked for this beautiful girl for seven years. And there she was, right under his nose.

Warm laughter broke from the audience as the lights came back on. I stole a glance at the striking woman whose eyes were glued to Ruggero. Was this Elisabetta, his childhood sweetheart? Or was this another woman? Without warning she looked across at me and I had to pretend I didn't mind this woman with the glittering dark eyes whose gaze caught mine.

'Why did you say anything about looking for me?' I hissed. 'It's none of their business.'

Ruggero smiled. 'They are Italian. They understand love.' He put his hand to his heart. 'Who do you think invented opera?' Then he took my hand in his. 'Come, Kitty, come and join our table.'

I tried to snatch my hand away but he wasn't having any of it. Instead, he gripped it as though he would never let me go as he guided me towards his table. After he'd pulled out a chair for me and made sure I was comfortable he turned and spoke to the audience again. They were so quiet you could hear a match strike, obviously preferring love intrigue than listening to a woman singing them an

English song. I was in such a state I couldn't follow the words.

'What did you say?'

'Just that you will take a short break and then you sing them another song.' He looked at my face and laughed. 'I'm sure they don't mind.' He sat down and lit a cigarette, then leaned back in his chair, inhaling deeply.

'Kitty.' But he wasn't looking at me. No longer smiling he glanced at the woman by his side. She gave a faint nod. 'I think Daniela has something she would like to say to you. But we need to go somewhere private.'

My eyes widened. So this wasn't his wife. It was Daniela, his sister. The woman who'd written that terrible letter which had ruined my life. Who'd told me loud and clear to take my hands off her brother as he was to be married to someone more suitable. Someone the family approved of. Someone who Ruggero had loved since he was a child. This was worse than if it was Elisabetta herself, as at least she was an innocent victim, as I'd been, of her unfaithful boyfriend. Nothing would alter the fact that Ruggero, the man I still loved, was married, with a family no doubt, whereas I had to provide for our daughter on my own. And now I'd managed to get a job and the prospect of a little money, I was determined Daniela was not going to poison my life ever again.

I didn't answer. I just sat there.

'Kitty?' Ruggero stubbed out his cigarette.

'So where is your wife?' I glared at him.

He looked puzzled. 'Me?' He tapped his chest. 'I am not married.'

'But—'

'Kitty, I never married.'

This was unexpected. Was he telling the truth? But it didn't alter anything.

'There's nothing your sister can say to me that I want to hear,' I said, rising from the chair. I stole a glance at her. She was twisting a beautiful ring on the finger of her left hand, her eyes darting first to her brother and then to me. She looked nervous, I thought. Almost frightened. And so she should be, I thought bitterly.

'Give her a chance, Kitty,' Ruggero said firmly, but he put his hand gently on mine as I stood there trying to break away from the two of them. His touch was like an electric current flaming up my arm. He looked up into my eyes; he'd felt it too. 'Kitty,' he said. 'Please.'

'It's very nice to see you again, Ruggero, but this is my job and I'm being paid. So if you'll excuse me...' I nodded to Daniela and rose, but Ruggero quickly put his hand on my arm, and with a light but firm pressure made me sit down again.

'I'm supposed to be singing,' I said, glowering. 'Let me go.' And I shook his hand off me. But Daniela had other ideas.

'Please help me up,' she said to her brother, and he gently pulled her to her feet. It was then I remembered she had something very wrong with her leg. 'Polio,' she said, to my unvoiced question as she turned her gleaming head towards me. 'I went in a swimming pool just after the war and the water was...how do you say...infected?'

'I'm sorry to hear that,' I said tightly, 'but I'm not interested in this conversation.'

Quick as a flash Ruggero caught the arm of a passing waiter and said something in low tones. The waiter nodded and gestured towards the back of the restaurant.

'Come.' Ruggero smiled at the two of us but it was not a smile I recognised. There was no lighting up of his features, and his eyes were wary. He held his sister's arm carefully and made a path through the diners. Then he stopped and looked over his shoulder at me with a steady look, not pleading, nor hard.

I had to follow.

It wasn't exactly a separate room, just an area towards the back partly divided by a screen. A table was already set out with three tumblers and a pitcher of wine. Four chairs were tucked into the table and Ruggero pulled one out for Daniela and settled her. Reluctantly I sat down opposite with Ruggero by my side. We could still hear the music but it was far enough away to hear what Daniela had to say.

The woman was definitely nervous. She was still fiddling with her ring and giving sidelong glances towards me when she thought I wasn't looking. But it was Ruggero who ought to be nervous, I thought. He hadn't had the strength of character to write to me himself but had made his sister do it for him. They were both as bad as each other. Oh, why hadn't I left in a dignified way as soon as I'd heard who she was?

As though Ruggero knew what I was thinking he said, 'Kitty, Daniela has wanted to tell you something for a long time.'

'It's true, Kitty,' Daniela said. 'I want to apologise.'

I hadn't expected to hear that word. 'What for?' I asked rudely.

'The letter,' she said. 'The one I should never have written.'

Ruggero was watching me, though I refused to meet his eye.

'It was best I knew the truth,' I said. 'I wouldn't want to stand in the way of true love.' I didn't bother to keep the sarcasm from my voice.

Ruggero shifted in his seat. 'Kitty, I—'

Daniela waved her arm imperiously at her brother. 'Please, *caro mio*, let me finish telling Kitty.' She looked at me and her eyes were like burning coals. 'Kitty, I never sent your letter on to Ruggero,' she said, forming the words slowly and carefully. 'Ruggero was once engaged to Elisabetta but he broke it off. He told me he had fallen in love with an English girl called Kitty, when he was taken prisoner in Egypt.' I stared at her open-mouthed. 'Yes, Kitty,' she looked at me, 'I told you lies.' Her eyes filled with tears. 'It was very bad and I will not blame you if you do not forgive me. I have not forgiven myself.'

All this time Ruggero was watching me.

'It wasn't, as you call it, "very bad", it was *wicked*,' I blurted.

Then I added, 'It's all a long time ago so why are you telling me this now?'

She pointed to her leg. 'I nearly died. I had to be in an iron lung for two years. Then learn to walk again. I had a long time to think. The man I was engaged to said he couldn't marry a cripple. I will never marry and have children. And I think of the big wrong I did to you, Kitty. So I told to Ruggero.' She threw her brother a fond look. 'I was lucky. He was forgiving.'

'Not at the beginning,' Ruggero broke in. 'I was very angry. You knew I loved Kitty. But I tried to understand. And how can it be right to keep the bitterness in your heart when it's your own family?'

'Well, don't expect me to be all-forgiving,' I said, jumping up. 'I'm sorry but I have to leave you. I have a duty to finish the evening.'

'Please have a little wine with us,' Ruggero implored, lining up the glasses and picking up the pitcher, ready to pour. 'To celebrate we have found each other.' He paused and stared up at me. 'Your hair is different. I nearly didn't recognise you, Kitty, with short curls.' His eyes twinkled.

He was trying to appear natural – to tease me like he used to in Cairo – but I just felt numb. Suddenly I was angry. I'd written to him twice. I'd rushed to see whether there was a letter from him every time I spotted the postman, and every time I'd been disappointed. No, not just disappointed. Devastated. Not a word in all these years. And although I now knew it wasn't his fault that he hadn't received my letter, *he* could have still written. Not given up. And by chance he'd brought his sister to what felt like my restaurant and expected I would fall at his feet.

'Do you know, we came to this restaurant because of you.' Ruggero looked up at me, still smiling. That smile that made his mouth turn up at the corners and my heart turn over. 'I saw the poster – an English singer called Katherine – but I had no idea it was my little Kitty. Why did you change your name?'

'It's my full name.' My voice was brittle and he glanced at me in surprise. I didn't see I owed him any further explanation so I turned and walked back to the band without another word.

Because I'd suddenly realised something dreadful. Neither Daniela nor Ruggero had mentioned that I'd been expecting a baby. Did that mean she hadn't told him that part? It had to, because surely he would have been far more upset knowing he had lost a child as a result of his sister's lies. And surely he would have asked me if I'd had a girl or a boy. Then the blow struck me. Daniela thought I'd gone ahead with the illegal operation using the money she'd sent me. So she'd deliberately not told her brother. No wonder she'd looked so nervous thinking I might tell him at any moment. My eyes swam again and I couldn't think any further. This was not the time or place. I needed to concentrate on bringing the evening to a good end so that I'd get paid the next time I sang.

Now I was more used to the dim lighting I could see some curious glances thrown my way as I walked over to the microphone, my hands shaking. But all I could hear was Daniela's voice saying she hadn't given my letter to Ruggero. That's why he'd never contacted me.

I decided to launch into one of Alice's comic songs – a fast one – to show Ruggero I hadn't been affected by his appearance, but my heart wasn't in it.

At the end of Alice's song, when the chuckles had died, before I could signal to them the next song, the band started to play another one I'd taught them. One I wished I hadn't. It was the lead-in to "Love Walked In". The lights dimmed and a hush came over the diners.

Before I even got to *and drove the shadows away* everyone rose to their feet and began clapping and cheering. I blushed, knowing they were showing their approval that Ruggero and I had at long last found one another. After I finished the song and bowed to their final clapping, I slipped through a side door and collected my jacket. One of the waiters helped me on with it but I was too tired to mutter more than a '*Grazie*'.

All I wanted to do was get back to Hedy. She was my life now.

43

Hedy was sleeping soundly in our room by the time I got back. I kissed the top of her head. Lucy, her beloved doll, was also under the sheet, her china head close to my daughter's dark one. The sight made me smile, taking away the edge of pain. I was being foolish that I'd left without saying goodbye to my love. My pride had come between us. But I blamed Daniela because there were so many private questions I wanted to ask Ruggero. And why were they in Rome? I was here to find any traces of my father, but Ruggero and his conniving sister had overshadowed all that.

Now we'd lost one another again. And Daniela was the cause of it – again.

As I shrugged off my jacket, trying to be as quiet as I could so as not to wake Hedy, I noticed an envelope sticking out of one of the pockets.

Tearing it open I read:

My dear Kitty,

I am sorry you had a shock this evening when you should concentrate on the songs. But it's best we know everything which happened to us. I am in Rome at a conference for Rome's rebuilding and staying at the Victoria Hotel. It is across the street from the Villa Borghese park, not far from the Spanish Steps. Anyone will say to you where it is.

Please will you meet me tomorrow for coffee in the lounge?

It is very peaceful and we can be private. My sister will not be there.

I will wait there all the morning. Come just when you are ready.

Your Ruggero

I scanned the letter again. It was late. I'd decide what to do in the morning. But my heart was thudding as I slid into bed.

I asked Signora Dotti if she could look after Hedy for a couple of hours so I could keep an important appointment, and pushed a wad of *lire* into her hands. She pressed the notes back into mine.

'I can do this,' she said. 'I do not want money always.'

She told me where the hotel was where Ruggero was staying. 'You can walk it,' she said.

I sent her a relieved smile and went back upstairs to dress. It was hard to make up my mind what to wear. In the end I chose a navy pleated skirt and pale-blue blouse, and a navy cardigan – sensible clothes, as a mother should wear. I slipped on the gold bracelet Frankie had given me on my last birthday and my small gold earrings. I stood at the mirror and brushed my hair, then quickly powdered my nose. My lipstick was down to the end, but I managed to scoop the last trace with my finger and smooth it on my lips. A light spray of scent and I thought I was ready. But was I?

By the time I left Signora Dotti's I was trembling from worry and fear and excitement.

I hurried as fast as I could, longing to see him…I couldn't think any further ahead. People were strolling through the park, some couples arm in arm, or with children in prams and pushchairs, or clinging on to their parents' hands. For a few seconds I wished I'd brought Hedy with me but it would have been wrong. I needed to see Ruggero on my own. Though when I saw a gracious building with the name Victoria Hotel, my heart was ready to jump out from my ribs. I stepped into the foyer and looked around, not knowing what to do. There was a strong smell of lilac and my eyes fell upon vases of spring flowers set on beautiful polished dressers and tables, jostling for space with softly-lit lamps even though it was sunny outside. Such a contrast with most of war-damaged Rome. A uniformed man silently appeared from nowhere and asked whether he could help.

'I'm meeting someone,' I said looking over his shoulder, and to my relief caught sight of Ruggero sitting on one of the sofas arranged around a fireplace. He saw me and rose, smiling.

'You came,' he said, kissing my cheek. 'Come and sit down. I'll order coffee.'

I watched him stroll across to the reception area, completely at home in the surroundings.

'It's a very beautiful hotel,' I said for something to say when he joined me.

I felt awkward. This had never happened in his company before. Ruggero didn't look completely at ease either.

'It has been restored,' Ruggero said, sounding relieved that we were on neutral ground. 'The Germans took over in the war but the owners hid anti-fascists and Jews right under their noses. Truly brave people.'

I looked around with real interest now I knew a little of its history. Many paintings covered the walls and everywhere was calm and elegant. My eyes fell on a grand piano.

'The hotel is now home to many Russian musicians,' Ruggero explained, following my glance. 'They want to be free from communism and Russia is very dangerous place to live now.'

My heart sank. We'd gone through six years of war and still there was trouble. I was silent.

Ruggero smiled and took my hand in his, caressing the fingertips. 'We have a lot to say to each other, Kitty.'

My heart began to race and I was grateful one of the waiters came over and set down a silver tray with silver coffee pot, matching sugar bowl and a steaming jug of milk. There was a plate of dainty biscuits and some toast and what looked like real jam.

'Eat something before we talk,' Ruggero said, pouring the coffee. 'You probably do not have much breakfast if you are staying at a *pensione*.'

He was right. I felt better after some food. He poured me a second coffee and as he handed me the cup his fingers brushed my hand again. That small touch linking me with him was all it needed. We gazed at each other.

'Where shall we start?' he said, his eyes warm and encouraging. He lit a cigarette. 'But first I will apologise on behalf of my sister. She was very wrong and hurt both our lives. But she did it for the best intention.' I shook my head, a tiny movement but Ruggero noticed it. He shrugged. 'What's done is done. We cannot alter anything. But we can try to make things better now.'

He inhaled deeply, then turned towards me. His voice was thick. 'You cannot know how I have longed for this moment,' he said, the smoke curling from his lips as he re-opened the packet. 'But I forget my manners. Do you smoke? You didn't used to so I forget to give you one first.'

I shook my head. 'You once said it would be bad for my throat, so I didn't take it up.'

'So you have sometimes listened to me,' he smiled and took a few more deep puffs, all the while keeping his eyes on me. 'But I feel there is something else you do not tell me, Kitty.'

'Why didn't you come to find me after the war?' I said, putting off the moment when I would tell him about Hedy. I needed to feel my way into the right time.

'I told you I would come back to you after the war.' He took my hand and gave it a gentle squeeze.

'But you didn't,' I said, my eyes welling up.

'But I did.'

My heart leapt. So he *had* tried to find me. He hadn't forgotten.

'I look for a Miss Kitty Townsend. I remember you are from this place, King's Lynn. I remember you say your mamma once worked at the big house in Bonham. So I go there and ask them about her. They tell me where she lives. At Camellia House.'

Oh, dear God. Ruggero glanced at me to see my reaction.

'Your papa came to the door. I ask for Miss Kitty Townsend. He ask who I am, and I tell him we meet in Cairo. That I love her. He says there is no one here by that name. I tell him this was the address they gave me at the big house in Bonham. He had cold blue eyes. He say, "She is a silly romantic girl. She has her own life now. A husband and a child. You must forget her." My heart is full and I know it is too late but I ask where you live. Just to see you one more time. He will not tell me, only that you are not at Camellia House. But I go back many times to the road which go to your house. I think I may see you going to visit your mamma. I go to the post office and ask about you. They don't know a Kitty Townsend.'

No, they wouldn't. They knew me as Katherine Bishop. My heart swelled. He *had* tried to find me. And Dad had stopped him. I could just imagine the scene. Dad would have been furious I was using my own father's name.

Once again, he had interfered with my life and my happiness. I pressed the anger down.

'I lost all hope.' Ruggero's eyes darkened. He turned his head to me. 'I did not find your papa very kind. Then I remember he is your step-papa. Your real papa was Italian, no?' He looked at me and smiled.

I nodded. Why couldn't it have been Mum who answered? She would never have closed the door on him. But she would have been working at the tea rooms.

'When did you go?' I asked.

'After the war. In December. It was impossible to come before then. I had to wait until I was sent back to Naples. And nothing was

341

the same at home. The house was in a terrible mess. It still is. Some Germans moved in and when they leave there was much damage. I am trying to get things back to normal. But I cannot work fast enough. Mamma died a year after I am back—'

'I'm sorry.' So I would never meet the woman who had picked out Ruggero's wife when they were children.

'I think she die of a broken heart,' he said, his eyes filled with sadness. 'Lorenzo, my mamma's favourite, he was executed at end of war.'

I shuddered. 'I'm so sorry.'

Then a flood of guilt poured over me. Dear God, had I been the cause of his brother's death?

'Ruggero,' I stopped him with my hand on his arm. 'Was that...did it have anything to do with me telling Colonel Thornton his name? That's all I told him. And that he was in the forces but I didn't know which one.'

'No, Kitty, it is nothing to do with you. He would be caught anyway. He was on the wrong side from the beginning.' Ruggero stubbed out his cigarette. He looked at me and his eyes glistened with tears. 'But you, Kitty. I think maybe your papa is right. You have met someone else. And have a child. So I think it best not to try to see you again. And I say goodbye to my love. Then Daniela was very ill for a long time. Everyone think she will die. She think so too and so she told me about the letter you write to me. I was very angry she didn't send me the letter when it came. When I ask her for it she says she put it on the fire.'

I gave a sharp intake of breath. How dare this woman—?

As though he knew what I was thinking he picked up my hand and caressed it with his fingers. Little shock tingles ran up my arm.

'She said how sorry she is, over and over,' he went on. 'But she is not so sorry as I am. Everything would be so different if she gave me your letter all that time ago. We would be together. I told her so. But it is too late. You have a new family. And Daniela needs help always, so I do what I can.' He shook another cigarette from the packet, shrugged and tapped it back in again. 'When I was coming to Rome for the conference she ask if she can come with me to make a change. And that is when I see there is an English girl singing. But not my Kitty. Still, it reminds me of you if she is English, so we enter. And there you are, little Kitty, singing that same song. And I couldn't help you this time. If I did I would cry.' Then he looked at me intently and said, 'Why did you not leave me a note before you left Cairo?'

'But I gave Mike Travers a letter for you with my home address so that Mum would send it wherever I was.'

Ruggero drew his black brows together. 'Travers did not give me any letter.'

'But he promised...'

I could almost see Ruggero's brain working. Then he gave a bitter smile. 'It is very clear. Travers did not want me to found you.'

'But why?'

'He wanted you for himself...you know he was in love with you. I told you the same once before.'

'But I never gave him any encouragement,' I protested, as the waiter came to clear our table. 'He was just a friend.'

I was upset all over again. But this time not with Ruggero. Had Mike realised what he was doing when he'd decided not to give Ruggero my letter? He was almost as bad as Daniela. It was hard to believe how the two mean acts could have had such a devastating effect on my life.

'It seems no one want to give me your letters, Kitty.' He gave me a rueful smile.

'Such a lot of unhappiness caused because they didn't,' I said.

'Are you happy now, little Kitty?' He leaned forward on the sofa, crossing then uncrossing his legs.

'As much as anyone is, I suppose.'

Ruggero gave me a sharp look at my lack of enthusiasm. 'But you have a husband and a child,' he said. 'That must make you very happy.' I was aware of him watching my face intently. 'Why is your husband not with you?'

I could tell he was not going to let it go. 'We're divorced,' I said, not wanting to explain about the annulment. I'd do that later. For now, I had to think of the best way to tell him about Hedy. Daniela had purposely left out that part of the story. The vital part. I felt a rise of anger in my throat. How was I going to tell him? I couldn't keep it from him any longer. He had a right to know. And then I remembered something. I opened my bag and unzipped a compartment. Carefully, I took out a photograph of Hedy, taken last year at Christmas. She was smiling at the camera in her cheeky fashion, her dark curls tumbling around her neck, holding Lucy.

'Here's a photograph of my daughter,' I said as I handed it to him. 'Her name is Hedy.'

He studied it, then looked at me.

'She's lovely,' he said, looking back at Hedy's picture. 'She's as beautiful as her mother although she doesn't look like you, only her colour.' He glanced at me again. 'So she must take after her father.'

Couldn't he see she was the image of himself?

'How old is she?' he asked, holding the photograph much closer, a frown appearing.

'She's nearly six now – five when the photograph was taken.'

I could see Ruggero trying to calculate the years. 'But that means...' He frowned. 'What is her birthday?'

'Look at her again, Ruggero.'

There was a long minute. He looked up; his eyes held mine.

'She's ours, isn't she?'

44

Time seemed to hang between us. I was vaguely aware of the phone ringing, gabbling foreign voices, beautifully-dressed women gliding across the foyer instructing porters where to take their luggage. One little dog trotted in front of his mistress on a long lead. But Ruggero didn't notice any of this. His eyes were glued to the photograph of Hedy.

'I presume Daniela chose to leave out that piece of information,' I said, my voice shaking.

'You told me in that letter?' He gave a long sigh. 'Oh, Kitty.' He finally looked up, and his eyes glistened with tears. 'I didn't know. You do believe me, don't you? I didn't know.'

'I believe you,' I said.

He took my hands so I was facing him.

'I was frantic,' I said, wanting my hands to stay enfolded in his forever. 'Not yet eighteen, not married or even engaged. I didn't realise until I was on the ship going home. Joyce told me why I kept being sick every morning.'

Ruggero sagged into the sofa and held his head in his hands. 'Who helped you when she was a baby?' he asked in muffled tones.

'Mum said she would take care of both of us but she had the tea rooms to look after. Dad wanted me to have the baby adopted but Mum and I wouldn't hear of it.'

Ruggero shook his head from side to side. He looked up. 'But you married very quickly.' Again, the hurt tone. 'Do you love him? Tell me the truth.'

'It's someone I've known for a very long time,' I prevaricated. 'He wanted to help me, to give the baby a name so there would be no question of having it adopted. I thought I was doing the right thing for Hedy but it didn't work and we separated.'

I deliberately kept things hazy. Now was not the time to tell him my real relationship with Harry. If I was truthful I was putting it off, dreading what Ruggero would say. Whether he'd understand. Thankfully, he was too much taken with Hedy's picture to ask for more details.

He became very quiet as he studied the photograph again. 'Little Hedy,' he said. 'Where is she?' He took my hands in his again and his voice was humble as he asked, 'When can I see her?'

'Not yet.'

Ruggero's face dropped. Of course it was natural that that would be his next wish but I wasn't ready to put myself through the wringer again this soon. I hadn't realised how drained I would feel at this meeting. It was a huge thing for Ruggero to take in – that he had a little daughter – and it was only natural that he wanted to see her straight away, but my emotions were also running at a pitch.

'Did you bring her with you?'

I could so easily have lied. But I couldn't – not to Ruggero. 'Yes,' I said.

'Then what is the problem?' A hint of frustration crept into his voice.

'I need to prepare her,' I tried to explain. 'She doesn't know anything about you. She only knows we've come to Rome to try to find my Italian father's family.'

'I understand,' he said. 'But you must also understand my position.' He got up and started pacing up and down in front of the fireplace. 'I am only here until this evening.' He glanced at his watch. 'Then I return to Napoli.'

'Can't you stay a few more days?' I asked.

'Regretfully not.' Out came the cigarettes again. He lit one and inhaled deeply. 'Papa needs my help and I promised I would be back tonight.' He threw me a look of despair. 'But there is enough time for you to let me see my daughter.'

I could tell by the way his lips tightly clamped on to his cigarette that he was not used to not getting his own way. But I wouldn't give in. I had to do what I thought was best for Hedy.

'We have to leave this evening. Daniela must be back to her job tomorrow.'

I wrinkled my nose at the mention of her name. 'Then there's nothing more to say.'

'Kitty.' He came over and sat down beside me again, and his eyes looked deep into mine. 'Please let me see her. I've missed six years of knowing her. Don't make me miss some more time.'

I didn't know what to do. And then he stroked the side of my face and my skin quivered under his touch. He pushed a thick strand of hair away from my forehead, letting the waves run through his fingers. And then he put his lips on mine and I could no longer think of anything except to melt into the warmth and familiar nearness of him. The faint smell of tobacco and lemon. His kiss.

'That is what we needed to do,' he said, when we finally pulled apart.

We were both breathing fast. He gripped my arms. 'Kitty, I want to make love to you. I've waited so long. Do you want it, too?'

It was what I wanted more than anything, but the knot I'd carried so long inside made me say, 'It's not the right time, Ruggero. I'm not ready to be hurt again. I couldn't stand it. I've been on my own too long. And if you remember, the last time we saw one another in Cairo you cut me off.' I felt the hurt as though it were yesterday and was glad to see his eyes cloud over at the memory. He opened his mouth to say something but I held my hand up to stop him. 'Besides, you only want to make love to me so I change my mind about Hedy. And that's not the right reason.'

Anger flared in his eyes. 'You know that's not true.' He paused as though wondering if he should continue. And then it came. What I'd always dreaded. 'How can you accuse me of such a thing when you pretended you loved me in Cairo and all the time you were spying on me.'

'Who said anything about spying?' I tried to laugh it off but my heart was beating hard.

'Travers, as it happens. He said Thornton asked you if you will spy on me, and you agreed. And to say I must fall in love with you and we have sex so I am weak and tell you if I am fascist...or not.'

'Colonel Thornton practically forced me,' I raised my voice. A man on one of the nearby sofas looked up from his newspaper with interest and I spoke more quietly. 'He was the head of the Propaganda department, for God's sake. Not that I understood about propaganda in those days but you didn't say no to Colonel Thornton. He promised to give us opportunities to be together. I didn't want to do it – I was horrified at what he was asking. Remember, I was very young, only seventeen. But I wanted to see you more than I was scared of the consequences of what Thornton wanted me to do. Except the consequences were more than I'd bargained for.'

'That's not how Travers told me.'

Did Mike also tell him about the German report I'd handed over to Colonel Thornton? It was so long ago but I felt as guilty as though it were yesterday. I knew I would never be completely at ease with myself or Ruggero until I'd confessed.

'Mike Travers has caused a lot of trouble,' I snapped, my guilt making me angry. But it was now or never. I'd have to own up or there'd never be any trust between us. 'Did he tell you about a letter I found – one that was written in German?'

Ruggero's eyes fixed on mine. 'No, he did not,' he answered slowly. 'What letter?'

'On our last Italian lesson – when Mike came to tell you

348

Colonel Thornton wanted to see you, I thought I'd put one of your records on. I found the letter, or report, whatever it was, hidden in the sleeve. I took it. I didn't open it for ages because I thought it might be personal, from your mum…or girlfriend.' I looked at him to see his reaction, but he gave no sign. Just kept his eyes pinned on my face. 'But one day I couldn't stand not knowing if you had a girlfriend writing to you. I had to know. So I opened it. I couldn't believe my eyes. It was some kind of typed report – in German.'

'And you think it was evidence. That I am on the side of the Germans.'

'I did think you might be at first,' I admitted, biting my lip. 'So when Colonel Thornton kept questioning me and telling me it was my duty to tell him anything I knew, I-I handed it to him. I wasn't going to,' I added, seeing a dark look come into his eyes. 'But I knew I had to take the risk and let him see I was doing my best to help. As soon as I'd given it to him I knew you couldn't be a traitor to your country. And I told him so.'

'Why did you know that?'

'Because…because I just did,' I finished lamely.

He was silent for a minute, then shrugged. 'I am glad I didn't know you took it from me. I didn't realise it was missing. I had several copies of Hitler's various plans to destroy the Allies. Thornton found them extremely useful.'

My head shot up. 'You gave him everything?'

'Except one, it seems.' A small upward turn at the corners of his mouth. 'I'm glad you have made your big confession, Kitty.'

I didn't know whether to laugh or cry. 'And you're not angry with me?'

Ruggero smiled and kissed my cheek. 'You were a child. You were asked to carry out instructions. There was a war. Though I wish you had told me at the time so I could explain.' He went serious again. 'But now I need to ask *you* some questions. Much more important than some German report.'

Relieved the worst was over, I swallowed.

'Did Thornton tell you we should make love so you can ask me questions?'

'Yes,' I whispered, my head lowered.

'Did you tell him what we did – that we made love? Tell me the truth. If you did it doesn't matter now, Kitty. But I would like to know.'

'No, I didn't tell him. What we did together was none of his business. It was too special to talk to anyone about.' My voice broke as I remembered that meeting with Colonel Thornton. 'I lied and said you wanted to have sex with me but that I was too young, so you wouldn't. You said it would have been wrong.' I raised my eyes to his, willing him to believe me.

'Did you pretend to love me?' His eyes were on me again and I knew this was the most important question of all.

'No,' I whispered. 'I loved you so much. I felt so guilty knowing that I truly loved you but I had to ask you questions for Colonel Thornton. He put me in a terrible situation. But at least we could be together, almost with his blessing. That's what I kept telling myself – to make it right. But I dreaded you would find out and hate me. Which you did.'

A smile crept over Ruggero's lips. He raised my hand to his mouth and kissed the palm, then closed my fingers over it. 'I did at first. And then I thought about you and us. Our kisses. Your eyes – how they were always full of love for me. I knew it really. But I wanted to hear it from you. Darling Kitty, I—'

But whatever he was going to say was interrupted by the waiter.

'*Signore* Andreotti?'

Ruggero looked up. '*Si, che cosa?*'

'*Una telefonata per lei.*'

Two minutes later Ruggero was back. 'It's Daniela,' he said, his face a mask of worry. 'She's had an accident.'

*

350

Daniela's accident wasn't serious. She'd slipped while trying to get out of the bath and had bumped her head. Give her her due, she insisted she was perfectly all right but Ruggero wanted to have her thoroughly checked at the hospital in case of concussion, and if she was fit enough to travel he would take her back this evening as planned.

'I'm sorry, Kitty,' he said, his hands on my shoulders. 'I must go.' He kissed me, this time a swift but warm kiss, then slipped a small card into my hand. 'My full address in Naples,' he added. 'Don't let us quarrel.' His finger lightly brushed my mouth. 'We don't want to waste more time than we already have.'

I couldn't bear it. We'd only just found one another again and now, once more we were to be parted.

'If I cannot come back to Rome very soon, maybe you will come to Naples...with little Hedy. Come anytime...anytime at all, Kitty. Don't leave it too long. Do you promise?'

'I promise.'

He nodded.

I couldn't even bring myself to say I hoped Daniela would be all right. Once again, Daniela had come between us. It was horrible of me because patently the woman hadn't had the accident on purpose. But she obviously felt she had first claim on her brother even though she'd apologised to me. I swallowed the tears. Maybe in time I'd stop feeling so bitter. And then I remembered the money she'd enclosed with that letter. And its purpose.

45

Even though my heart ached that Ruggero was leaving for Naples, I was sure it wouldn't be long before we saw one another again. Maybe a little time apart would be good for us. We both had much to think about. He was desperate to meet his daughter so I wouldn't leave it too long. In the meantime I had a mission.

I had no idea where to start looking for Signora Townsend but I had faith that if any of the family were still in Rome I'd find them. And as well as looking for my family I was determined to see something of Rome. I might never have another opportunity.

I asked Signora Dotti where I should go to find a missing person. I said it was someone I'd known before the war who had died and I was trying to find his family. She looked at me with a question in her eyes, then suggested I go to the Royal Archives. She said it was too far for Hedy to walk, so she explained how to get there by tram.

The man behind the counter at the Royal Archives tried to flirt with me instead of listening to my request which I'd practised in Italian.

'You English?' he asked finally, grinning and smoothing back his hair with the palm of his hand.

'Yes,' I answered impatiently. *For heaven's sake, can't you just do what I've asked?* I stood there without smiling back.

He stared at me openly until I began to feel uncomfortable, then angry.

'Look, can you help me, or not?' I snapped in English.

'I fetch Lorella,' he said, reluctantly. 'She know English good.'

Lorella was about my own age and smartly dressed in a suit and red and navy scarf. She threw me a cheerful smile.

'Now, tell me the name of your friend,' she said, 'and I will see if he is registered.'

'It's a "she" and the family name is Townsend,' I said. 'The person I'm looking for is Signora Townsend.'

'Her first names?'

Annoyingly, I hadn't thought to ask Mum. 'I don't know,' I told her, 'only that she was born in Rome and emigrated to Australia with her English husband and son. Then when Mr Townsend eventually died, Signora Townsend left Australia and came back here – to Rome.'

'The name "Townsend" in Rome should be easy to find,' Lorella said with logic.

'If she's not dead,' I told her, 'she'd be in her eighties by now, I should think. But she may have some family here and it's important I find them.'

But nothing came to light. The only good thing was, neither did any death certificates, which gave me hope. But if my grandmother had any other living relatives they didn't have the name Townsend. Lorella seemed almost as disappointed as I was.

I'd drawn a blank.

Signora Dotti was eagerly waiting for news that afternoon when Hedy and I went back.

'I found nothing,' I said, quickly, not wanting any more questions. But I hadn't reckoned on Signora Dotti.

'Is missing person Italian?' she asked.

'Yes, but maybe under an English name.'

'Why is that?'

'Because her husband was English.'

'Ah.' She thought for a few moments. Then she said, 'Maybe

353

police can help. They not maybe know person but tell you how to found her.'

My heart turned over. Ruggero always muddled up "found" and "find" and I never corrected him because it was so endearing. Swallowing the lump in my throat I tried to concentrate on Signora Dotti's suggestion about going to the police. At least it was something to go on.

'I'll try that tomorrow,' I told her.

She beamed and nodded. '*Buono.*'

The police were unhelpful though they made a great fuss of Hedy and were most enthusiastic, talking to one another so fast that I couldn't keep up with them. I asked where the British Embassy was. It was my last resort. I'd worked it out that my grandfather, being English, might be in their records.

I watched the all-male group of policemen conferring with one another, arguing, waving their arms around, until it was clear no one knew where it was. Finally one of them took out a directory and pounced on a name.

'You will find it at the Villa Wolkonsky,' he said, beaming with satisfaction.

I looked blank.

'On the...' he looked back again at the page, 'via Ludovico di Savoia. I show you.'

He pointed on the map and explained that I could take a bus from the Spanish Steps and it would take me within five minutes' walking distance from the building. I should tell the driver where I was going and he would call out the stop.

As soon as I saw the embassy with the Union Jack proudly waving in the light breeze I began to feel more confident. At least I would be able to understand everything and they would me. Holding Hedy's hand tightly and ignoring her whining, we walked up a tarmac drive dotted with trees towards the grandiose building.

We stood in front of the columned entrance not knowing quite what to do.

'Come on, Hedy,' I said with determination, and we marched up the steps.

A fair-haired young man stood behind the reception desk, smiling. 'Good morning, madam. What can I do for you?'

Oh, how wonderful to hear English again. I smiled back.

'I'm trying to trace someone,' I explained. 'My grandmother on my father's side, though I don't know her first name. But her last name is Townsend.'

'I'll get somebody to help you,' he said, picking up the telephone.

Two minutes later a pleasant-faced older man dressed in a pinstriped suit strolled in and gestured me over to a table with a screen half pulled round. He introduced himself as Robert Garner.

'Now, madam, tell me how I can help you.'

I repeated what I'd told the young man on the reception desk. Mr Garner steepled his fingers together, a thoughtful expression crossing his face.

'Townsend, you say. She doesn't sound Italian.'

'She was married to an Englishman who died in Australia.'

'Is she still alive, your grandmother?'

'I have no idea. My father and grandfather are both dead. But I thought you might be able to tell me if my grandmother's death is registered. Or if there is any other family I could contact.'

I told him as much as I knew, which was very little. I only had a very approximate date that my grandfather would have died, but Mr Garner said there might be enough to go on.

'Leave it with me,' he said. 'It might take a little time. Come back in...' he glanced at his watch, 'well, better make it after lunch – say two-thirty.'

I thanked him and Hedy and I made our way back to the Spanish Steps. Just as we were about to walk up them I spotted an attractive old building at the foot, and a sign on the wall between two of the windows advertising Babington's Tea Rooms. On a closer inspection I read the words "English Tea Rooms" in bronze letters, set into the stone itself. There was nothing about this place that looked a scrap like Annie's Tea Rooms. This one was much grander and not stuck at the back of a post office like Mum's, but it brought a lump to my throat. She'd be wondering if I'd found out anything about my father's family.

I had tried my best to persuade her to come with me.

'You know I can't leave.' Mum had looked troubled. 'I've got the tea rooms to run.'

'Mollie will look after it. Mum…' I looked at her intently, 'you do realise why I'm going, don't you?'

'I hope you're going to find Ruggero and introduce him to his daughter.'

An ache had crept round my heart as it always did when I heard his name.

'I'm not going to Naples, Mum. I'm going to Rome to see if I can find my father's family.'

The colour drained from Mum's cheeks. 'If she's alive I don't know if she'd want to see you,' she said, 'and I wouldn't want you to get hurt. You've had enough of that already. Why don't you leave that side to rest? Raking it up won't solve anything.'

'That's where you're wrong, Mum,' I told her. 'She was cruel not to ever want to meet you and it shows how stupid religion is when it affects your life and your family. She could've come to Camellia House and seen how happy you and her son were together. And I expect the two of you would have taken me to Rome to stay with her for a bit if things had been normal.'

Poor Mum. She looked as though she was going to burst into tears. I took her in my arms.

'I want to find her, Mum,' I said softly. 'Let her see her great-granddaughter. If she's alive and refuses to see me, at least I would have given her the opportunity. And if she's dead there may be a cousin or someone. I just want to know about my father and my roots on his side. Come with me, Mum. I'd so love you to.'

'I know, darling, but I can't,' she said, her deep blue eyes misting.

'Why?'

'You wouldn't understand, so don't press me.'

Now, here in Rome, I went over our conversation. What was it with Mum that she wasn't able to spend some time with me? It wasn't the tea rooms – that was just an excuse. Mollie would be perfectly capable of running it for a few weeks. Then it must be Dad. Maybe she thought he'd make her life a misery when she returned. Well, there wasn't time to dwell on these questions. Hedy was trying to snatch her hand away but I gripped it more firmly.

'I want to go to the toilet.'

'All right, darling. Just be patient for a moment.'

In one of Babington's windows was a clock like the one we used to have in our classroom at school, and cups and saucers and teapot laid out on a tray with a lace doily like Mum used. I bit my lip. This place would be expensive, no doubt about it. I only had my singing job at weekends and money was dribbling away alarmingly. Everything here in Rome seemed even more expensive than in England, but for once it didn't deter me. I opened the door and a bell rang to announce us. We stepped inside.

The interior reminded me of Mum's tea rooms with the beamed ceiling and oak tables and chairs, except this room was much bigger. I looked around. The customers appeared to be English rather than Italian. A waitress, similarly dressed to a Lyons' Corner House waitress, came up to show us a table and I explained my daughter needed the toilet.

'Of course,' she said, smiling at Hedy. 'Would you like to come with me and I'll show you where to go?'

She was definitely English.

When Hedy was done, we sat at one of the oak tables and the

waitress handed me a menu. My daughter shifted around on her bottom, rather like a cat, until she was comfortable. The waitress brought her a cushion and smiled at her indulgently.

'She is a very pretty little girl,' she commented.

'I'm not little, I'm nearly six.'

The waitress turned to Hedy. 'Yes, I can see you're a big girl now. What will you drink, my love?'

'Blackcurrant juice,' Hedy answered immediately. 'Please,' she added quickly.

The waitress and I smiled at one another.

'And a pot of tea for me, please,' I said, glancing at the menu, 'and I'd like the Welsh rarebit and Hedy will have a small bowl of soup. And a fruit scone, please.'

The waitress ruffled Hedy's curls and nodded.

I noticed a lady at a table further away from me, conservatively dressed in unmistakable all-black Italian fashion for ladies of a certain age in mourning, and idly wondered why she came to an English tea room. She must have felt me look, for she caught my eye and smiled, and I smiled back. But then I noticed even from a few feet away she looked confused. Her smile faded. She gave the faintest shake of her head and dropped her glance on Hedy. This time her face lit up.

'What is your name?' She directed her question to my daughter.

'Hedy,' she piped.

'How charming,' said the lady. 'Like the film star?' She glanced at me with raised eyebrows and I smiled and nodded.

She looked lonely and I was tempted to ask her if she'd care to join us. But it wouldn't do to feel sorry for everyone. I had enough to do to see to Hedy and find my family.

Hedy and I ate our lunch and by the time we'd wandered around the market it was time to go back to the embassy again. Mr Garner had left me a note at the desk.

I've searched every record possible but I haven't come up with anything. I'm so sorry and wish you good luck.

I wasn't really surprised but I'd now come to a dead end. I didn't know what my next step should be. I only knew I wanted to give myself enough time to be here where my father's mother had lived, and to think whether there were any more avenues to try.

As I suspected, the food and drinks at Babington's were very dear – because it was English, I supposed – but I took Hedy for tea every few days for a treat. The elderly lady was always sitting there. She must go every day. We'd begun smiling and greeting one another in Italian, and the other morning we even commented on the weather getting warmer. The café owners had started to put out their awnings – a welcome sight that summer was on its way.

Then on what must have been my fourth or fifth visit I noticed the lady wasn't at her usual table. I called the waitress over and asked her but she didn't know anything.

Even Hedy asked, 'Where's that nice lady gone?'

I was just about to order coffee when I happened to glimpse a stooping woman through the window who fell over in front of my eyes. It was our same lady. Warning Hedy to stay where she was, and calling to the waitress not to let my daughter follow me, I rushed outside. Some people were already helping the poor woman to her feet. They brought her into Babington's which was the nearest place where she could sit, and I noticed her face was ashen.

'Sit her at our table,' I told one of the gentlemen who'd helped her up, 'and I'll order her a coffee. She's probably in shock.'

The old lady allowed herself to be guided over to where Hedy was sitting, and sat down heavily.

'Good girl, Hedy,' I said, wiping her mouth. 'Say hello to the lady.'

'She fell over,' Hedy said to me, her eyes wide. 'I saw her.' Then she turned her small dark head to the old lady. 'Did you get hurt?'

'I do not think so…but maybe a coffee…'

'It's coming.'

We introduced ourselves. Her name was Signora Moravia. Somehow we fell into a real talk. Her English was good. She'd learned it at school, she explained, and had been to England once with her fiancé.

'But I forget everything. So I come here to Babington's to practise,' she smiled.

'But you're always alone.'

'No, not alone. I have the customers. They speak English. I listen hard for the new words. I had a friend. She like to speak English with me. She speak much better. Me, I must practise in my head.'

I laughed. 'That's one way of keeping up with a language. How I wish I'd done the same with my Italian.'

She asked where my husband worked.

'He was killed in the war,' I said in an undertone, crossing my fingers under the table. 'He was Italian. He never saw his little girl.' At least those last two things were true.

I prayed Hedy wouldn't connect what I was saying with herself but she seemed to be concentrating on her piece of chocolate cake the waitress had brought her as a treat.

'I'm so sorry,' Signora Moravia said, her eyes filling with sympathetic tears as she searched in her handbag for a handkerchief. She blew her nose. 'My glasses...where are the glasses?' Panic rose in her voice.

'Are these yours?' The waitress appeared at our table and handed them to the old lady. 'Someone found them in the street,' she said. 'I'm afraid one of the sides is broken.'

'I can't see without,' Signora Moravia said with a worried frown.

'Let's finish our coffee and find an optician,' I suggested. 'I'm sure they can mend them.'

We found one who repaired the arm of the glasses while we waited. Signora Moravia was delighted.

'It is time we eat,' she said. 'Would you like to eat with me?'

'Oh, we couldn't possibly impose,' I said, then saw her face droop with disappointment. 'Unless you're really sure,' I smiled.

'*Really* sure.' Her warm brown eyes sprang into life. 'We are only ten minutes away.'

I thought she meant a restaurant but she'd meant in her house which was actually an apartment in an elegant old building. There was no lift and I noticed she was breathless when she reached the second floor. We stepped into a narrow hall which opened out into an enormous room. One end was set out as a dining room, the other as a sitting room with a beautiful fireplace and moulded ceiling.

'Flora will give us soup,' she said as I unbuttoned my jacket.

Hedy was looking around her, fascinated, a gleam in her eyes. I bit back a smile. My daughter liked the look of the good things in life.

We sat at a beautiful polished oak dining-room table and Flora, a young woman dressed in an overall, brought in a bright green soup.

'Broccoli,' was all she said, and disappeared.

What was broccoli? Whatever it was, it was delicious. I'm sure she'd put cream in. I drank every scrap as well as finished two crisp white bread rolls.

Signora Moravia asked where I lived.

'Opposite the railway station,' I said, 'at Signora Dotti's.'

She pursed her lips and nodded. 'I know Signora Dotti,' she said. 'She is good woman.' She hesitated, seeming to consider something. 'How long do you stay in Rome?'

When I told her I'd come prepared for at least a month, maybe longer, she took me completely by surprise.

'I am old lady alone in big apartment. You and your daughter could stay with me. I practise my English. You pay for your food. Nothing for bed. You can stay short time or long time.' She looked at me slyly. 'More comfort and bigger room than Signora Dotti.'

'Mummy, I like it here with Mrs Nora.'

Signora Moravia laughed while warmth spread up my face. 'Is that how she calls me?'

'She can't remember "Moravia",' I answered weakly.

'Then Mrs Nora I am.'

At that moment Flora came in to clear the dishes, and I jumped up to help her.

'After coffee I show you a room you and little Hedy can share.' Signora Moravia beamed at the two of us.

The room, as Signora Moravia had promised, was vast. At least twice the size as the one Hedy and I were in at Signora Dotti's. There was a double bed and a small single bed, perfect for Hedy. The air smelt of lavender and when my new friend pulled back the shutters sunlight poured in. I went over to the window and asked if I might open it.

'But of course,' she said.

At Signora Dotti's place I looked out on a wall and not much else. Here, the room overlooked a small piazza with a mixture of dilapidated and bombed buildings, and gaps where houses and shops once stood. But there was life in the cafés, the waiters balancing trays as they brought drinks and snacks to the customers sitting outside in the warm spring afternoon. I noticed a couple kissing by one of the two fountains and bit back a quiver of envy.

'Is a bit of noise at night,' she admitted, 'but not too late.'

'Are you really sure you want us?' I turned to her. 'Hedy is quite a handful sometimes, even though she's a good child at heart.'

At that, Hedy did a perfect cartwheel.

'I see already,' Signora Moravia chuckled. 'But she is the one who persuades me.'

'Really?'

'Really.' Signora Moravia smiled kindly. 'It will be wonderful to have a child here again.'

*

That evening I told Signora Dotti about Signora Moravia's invitation. She'd been so kind to Hedy and me when we'd first arrived, I felt guilty, as though I'd discarded her at the first sign of a better offer.

'I really appreciate you taking us in,' I said. 'We didn't know anyone and you've been a good friend.'

'More room with Signora Moravia,' Signora Dotti beamed. 'You are well there. But bring Hedy to see me sometimes.'

I promised I would.

Two days later Hedy and I moved into our new lodgings.

Hedy was thrilled to live with Mrs Nora. I laughed at Hedy's name for her but after a few days, that's what I began to call her too.

During the evenings when Hedy was tucked up in bed with her doll, and I wasn't singing at Signor Franco's, Mrs Nora and I talked. Of course she wanted to know where my husband's family was and if I saw them regularly. I managed to skirt over it, hating myself for telling a lie. But it was too complicated and would rake up all my misery. Instead I told her about Mum and her tea rooms which were so different from Babington's.

'I would like to meet your mamma,' she said. 'And see the tea rooms. It sounds charming.'

'Maybe one day you can come to England for a holiday.'

Hedy and I slipped into the habit of going for a walk in the morning, but Signora Moravia never came with us.

'You need time on your own,' she said. 'I live here. I have seen the tourist places.'

Most afternoons we would go to Babington's for tea and Signora Moravia usually insisted on paying. 'It is the only luxury I allow myself,' she explained.

It was after we'd been with her for a few days that I came across it. Mrs Nora rarely sat in the sitting area – she had difficulty prising herself out of an easy chair and preferred to stay at the dining-room table on an upright chair for our evening talks – so I hadn't noticed it before. I was dusting, as she'd told me she could no longer afford a regular cleaning lady.

'You are not here to clean,' she'd said more than once when I used the carpet sweeper or washed the dishes.

But it was the only way I could think of to repay her kindness.

I was taking plates and cups and saucers and bowls off the dresser, privately thinking it ought to be in the dining room end so the pieces would get used. From the amount of dust it hadn't been touched in months. Photographs in silver frames were crammed in amongst all the fine porcelain china so I decided to rearrange them so they could be properly displayed. I was enjoying the job I'd created when I picked up a photograph of a dark-haired smiling young man.

Bolts of electricity shot up my arms and my eyes burned with recognition.

I was looking at my own face – but it was on a man.

46

The frame slipped through my fingers and crashed on to the tiled floor. Mesmerised, I stared down at the broken pieces of glass. Swearing under my breath as to why it hadn't fallen on one of the expensive rugs, I bent down and picked it up, careful not to let any slivers of glass cut me. The man in the photograph continued to smile with no idea he'd caused such an accident.

'Mummy, what was that noise?' My daughter flew in from our bedroom.

'Just a little accident,' I said. Hedy held out her hand as though to take the photograph from me. 'No, Hedy. There's broken glass. Don't touch anything or you'll hurt yourself. Go and fetch the dustpan and brush for me.'

Signora Moravia had gone to the market with Flora an hour or so ago so I had to wait for her to return before I could ask any questions about the man. The more I gazed at his face, his eyes smiling into mine, I was sure I was staring at my own father. The shape of his face, his mouth…nose…I was just like him, except his eyes which were lighter than mine. But he looked nothing like Signora Moravia. Fond as I was of her, she was no beauty. She had the typical dark Italian eyes, but her nose was big and hooked, and although her mouth was wide like mine, her top lip was fuller than her bottom one, making her look rather vulnerable and endearing. They were not at all like the man's lips in the photograph. He must look like his father – who might be my grandfather.

If this was her son, then why wouldn't she see Mum? She seemed such a kind, generous-hearted person, who'd taken Hedy and me in as strangers and made us feel at home. Who would do that, yet turn their own daughter-in-law and grandchild away? It simply didn't make sense.

I was in a dilemma. She would have no suspicion that I might be her granddaughter, although thinking about it maybe that was why she'd taken us in. Maybe my face had subconsciously reminded her of her son. But should I leave it like that or confront her? If I did, what would the shock do to her? She might be racked with guilt that she'd shunned my mother all those years ago and send me packing. She wouldn't want to look at me anymore. I'd be a reminder of her cruelty. But she'd be turning her back on her great-grandchild as well, and I could already see a bond forming between them.

I looked across at Hedy. She was talking to her doll and telling her she'd been naughty. She gave the doll's leg a little slap. As she raised her hand again with a determined look on her face I went over to her.

'What's Lucy done to deserve a smack?' I asked.

'She wet the bed.'

'That's only because she's not such a big girl as you.' I picked up the poor doll who gazed up at me out of impossibly bright blue eyes. 'I expect she'll learn but you must be kind and help her.'

Hedy was silent.

'What's the matter, Hedy? Tell Mummy.'

'I want Nannie.' Hedy burst into tears.

'We'll see her soon.' I put my arms around her and hugged her. 'We've come for a lovely holiday in Italy. You know how you like the ice-cream here. And you like Mrs Nora, don't you?'

Hedy nodded.

'Well, then, don't be cross with Lucy. She's probably tired. Why don't you take her to bed and have a little nap with her? Help her get off to sleep.'

I tucked them both in bed and went back to the sitting room, my mind a jumble of questions. Hedy was not really unhappy here. She missed Mum who doted on her, that was all. But I wasn't ready to go home yet. Not until I'd found out who the man in the photograph was.

An hour later I heard footsteps coming up the stairs and Signora Moravia and Flora appeared at the door. My heart did a somersault. I still didn't know whether to say anything. If I did, everything would change. I wasn't quite ready to face Signora Moravia and risk another emotional upset.

'I have some meat. The butcher say it is lamb and I know it is sheep.' Signora Moravia's brows drew together in frustration. 'But Flora, she say she make it tender.'

'I'm sure she will.'

Flora's cooking was wonderful. Signora Moravia had told me Flora was from a village outside Rome, and that she had the third bedroom along the hall from me. The girl refused to do any cleaning, except to make the beds, but that didn't seem to worry Signora Moravia much. By the size of the older woman's girth, she enjoyed Flora's food above most pleasures.

'Mrs Nora,' I began, when we'd finished supper. I wasn't going to let anything spoil such a delicious meal by telling her beforehand.

'Si, cara mia.'

'I'm afraid I've had a bit of an accident.'

'Ah. What is it?'

'I was dusting the dresser and one of the picture frames slipped and fell to the floor. The frame's all right, I think, but the glass will have to be replaced. Of course I'll pay.'

'Let me see.'

I rose to fetch it.

'Oh,' she said, as I handed her the photograph.

The shattered glass across the young man's face hadn't dimmed his smile one fraction. I waited, hardly daring to draw breath.

'Oh,' she said again, her face lighting up, 'it's my best. He is twenty-one there.'

'What is his name?' I asked, desperately trying to sound normal, though I could feel my heartbeat drumming in my ears.

'Alessandro.' She turned to me, and her eyes were blurred with tears.

My stomach turned. The name wasn't exactly the same, but it was so close, it must be the Italian equivalent of Alexander. Though it might all be coincidence. But after Mrs Nora found another frame and we'd eased the photograph from behind the broken glass and fixed it into position, I studied it carefully. I still couldn't help thinking he looked exactly as I imagined my father would look, only younger, of course. But for the time being I decided not to say anything. I needed to think. Signora Moravia, if she *was* Alexander's mother, hadn't taken her husband's name, so I decided there couldn't be any connection after all. And if she was tearful she was just being a typical mother and sentimental about her son when he was in his youth. I couldn't upset her further by prying.

Two days later the three of us – Signora Moravia, Hedy and I – were wandering through the local market when we practically bumped into a woman who had stopped suddenly. She turned and stared at us.

'Rosalia!' the woman exclaimed, towering above Signora Moravia.

She was about the same age as Signora Moravia but looked like a fashion plate by the side of her. A handsome woman and taller than any Italian woman I'd ever seen. She was dressed in black from head to toe, with matching hair swept up into a chignon, Maria Callas style, showing off her magnificent drop pearl earrings. Her eyebrows were artificially arched, and her face subtly made up, but with startling crimson lips. She beamed at Mrs Nora, though she didn't even glance my way.

'Vittoria.' Mrs Nora's voice had become oddly distant. '*Come sta?*'

The tall woman kissed Signora Moravia three times while I excused myself and walked on ahead with Hedy, letting the two of them catch up. I waited a little self-consciously several steps away for the two women to finish their greetings.

After a couple of minutes when I was helping Hedy to blow her nose, Signora Moravia looked round to see where I'd gone to. She sent a smile when she saw us.

'Come, Kitty,' she said in English. 'I will introduce you. Vittoria, here is Kitty Bishop. Kitty, a friend of mine, Signora Stephanini.'

I prised my hand from Hedy's strong little fingers and Signora Stephanini graciously shook it. Then she looked at me for the first time. Something unfathomable sprang into those cool brown eyes. She swung round to Signora Moravia who was facing me and I swear no one else would have spotted the tiny nod of her head. What was going on? Could Signora Stephanini have seen the same similarity between her friend's son and me?

'Very nice to meet you.' Signora Stephanini turned to me, not even trying to disguise her curiosity as she looked me up and down.

'You, too,' I said sweetly and insincerely. For some reason she made me feel uncomfortable.

'So you're from England.' Her eyes bore into mine.

'Yes.'

'Are you here on holiday?'

I thought quickly. I didn't know what Signora Moravia would tell her later. 'I have friends in Italy,' I said.

'Oh?' She raised one of those eyebrows. 'Where?'

'In Naples.'

'So you speak Italian,' she said as though it were a foregone conclusion, then added with a slight curl to her lip, 'or rather Neapolitan.'

'I speak a little,' I answered.

'Well, *cara mia*,' she said, turning to Signora Moravia, and continuing in English, 'it's a long time since I saw you. Why don't you bring your little friend and the child to lunch tomorrow?'

Surprisingly Signora Moravia hesitated. Then she seemed to make a decision. 'We would like that, wouldn't we, Kitty?'

'Hedy and I don't have anything else planned,' I said in a cool voice, and although Signora Moravia didn't sound all that enthusiastic either, I couldn't very well have said no.

Signora Stephanini looked down at Hedy who was clutching my hand, and smiled. This time it was a warm smile, but Hedy could charm anyone. The older woman bent down so she was on the same level as my daughter. 'What is your name, child?'

'Hedy.'

'Hedy,' Signora Stephanini repeated. 'Mmm. Unusual,' she rose with a little wince of pain, 'but very pretty.'

Hedy gave her a toothy grin. I gave the woman a tight smile.

'You will like Signora Stephanini's house,' Signora Moravia said that evening after supper. 'She has a lot of—' she curled her fingers in the air and rubbed her thumb under them. I assumed she was telling me how wealthy her friend was. 'That is not why she is friend,' she assured me quickly, 'but I know her from when Alessandro is only a baby.' Her eyes misted.

Was it...could it be my father she was talking about? I'd tried to dismiss the idea and call everything a coincidence but it didn't stop my heart from hammering at the sound of his name so close to Alexander. It still made no sense to me that this kind, lovely lady, who smiled every time she heard me call her Mrs Nora, had shunned my mother without even knowing her. The only contact Alexander's mother had made was to write to my father that she was upset he'd decided to live with a married woman. And when my father told his parents that they'd had a little girl and called her Katherine Alexandra, Mum said Alex's mother had written that she was very pleased for them, but that was the last they'd heard from her.

'She is a little difficult at first,' the old lady continued, drawing her eyebrows together. 'You must take no notice. She is not a bad person.'

Why should she be defending her friend? I hadn't given any indication that I was bothered one way or the other.

The following day at noon Signora Stephanini's maid ushered us in. I looked round in astonishment. The reception hall was huge with a marble floor. Full-length sculptures and busts lined the edges in the way Mum used to tell me about when she worked at Bonham Place. There was a broad flight of marble stairs rising to the first floor from where Signora Stephanini swept down, her hands outstretched in welcome. Hedy, who either took to someone or didn't, ran straight to her. I couldn't have been more surprised. Signora Stephanini bent down and hugged her.

Holding Hedy's hand, she kissed me on both cheeks and greeted her friend, then took us into a magnificent drawing room. It was three times the size of Signora Moravia's and though I was no connoisseur, even I could tell the pictures and rugs were of good quality; the furniture was elegant and there was so much polished silver it looked like the moon had run riot. A fire blazed in the marble fireplace even though it was a beautiful spring day.

Signora Stephanini sat us down in such deeply upholstered armchairs, I worried Signora Moravia might never rise out of hers. The maid brought in an old-fashioned child's chair for Hedy who immediately said she was too big for it and could sit on a grown-up's chair, thank you. I bit back a smile. Hedy was never in awe of anyone and said what she thought. The maid nodded and took the chair away.

All this was carried out with the utmost politeness but I sensed a kind of restrained excitability about Signora Stephanini that I hadn't noticed yesterday in the way her eyes kept darting from Hedy to me, then back to Hedy again. I pretended not to notice.

Her long thin fingers seemed restless, forever twiddling with her wedding ring as she continued to slide surreptitious glances at the two of us.

To my relief the maid brought Hedy a drink, making a fuss of her, and I tried not to think what any of this meant.

'Will you have wine?' Signora Stephanini glanced at her friend, then me.

'No, thank you,' Signora Moravia said.

'Yes, please, I would love a glass,' I heard myself answer, not looking at Signora Moravia. If she knew how jangled my nerves were I was sure she would understand.

'Then I will join you,' Signora Stephanini said.

The maid brought in a tray with glasses of sweetened lemon drink for Signora Moravia and Hedy, and chilled glasses of white wine for me and Signora Stephanini. I noticed she didn't touch hers. She spoke so fast to her friend I could only understand snippets which didn't make sense, but every so often I caught her openly staring at me. Was she trying to see something of me in her friend's son? Had Signora Moravia had a chance to tell her what she suspected, and Signora Stephanini was giving me the once-over to see if there was any merit in her friend's suspicions?

In my nervousness I drank my wine rather too quickly and felt my head start to swim. I was relieved when the maid came in to announce that lunch was ready.

The dining room was almost as grand as the drawing room. A long polished oak table took the starring role with a beautiful set of dining chairs upholstered with a deep pink and red rose pattern.

A chandelier hung over the table and when I admired it my hostess announced it was made from Venetian glass in Morano – the very best, she assured me. There were bookcases lining the walls almost as high as the ceiling and two sideboards with fancy carving. It was an elegant room, but not a place I would ever feel at ease in.

Hedy was on her best behaviour until we reached the pudding stage. Then she swung round and somehow knocked my long-stemmed wineglass which spilt in a deep puddle on the pristine white tablecloth.

Mortified, I jumped up, but Signora Stephanini waved me down again.

'I will have it cleared,' she said imperiously.

As the maid was mopping up the liquid I saw a nod of what I took to be an understanding pass between the two women. I swallowed a second glass of water, and wished I hadn't. My bladder was already complaining. I sat for a few minutes in the most awful discomfort, and when I thought I would burst with the pain, I asked Signora Stephanini if I could use the toilet.

'Gisela will show you,' she said, ringing for the maid.

A little embarrassed, and certain they would talk about me when my back was turned, I rose from the table and followed Gisela. She left me outside the cloakroom and I told her I would find my own way back. But as I was making my way towards the dining room I saw an open door and couldn't help glancing in. It was a long narrow library and seemed to beckon me. Signora Stephanini certainly liked her books. I'd only be a couple of minutes, I told myself, as I guiltily took in the carved columns and glanced at the sets of old books lining the shelves on either side of a magnificent stone fireplace held up by two female figures with uplifted arms. I stepped over to admire them, running my fingers over their limbs. How could a human make something so lifelike out of a lump of stone? It was then that I raised my head and noticed the photographs displayed on the mantelpiece. There were several of a small boy, his

373

eyes crinkled up in laughter in every photograph, but the one which caught my eye was Signora Stephanini on her wedding day. My, she had been what Joyce would have called a real "looker" in her time. At her side was the groom, his fair head tilted slightly towards his dark-haired bride. They were both looking very serious, though they weren't encouraged to smile in those days, I reminded myself. Nevertheless, they made a striking couple and I wondered if he was still alive. I'd ask Signora Moravia later. I liked the look of him. Even without the hint of a smile his eyes were kind and full of life.

I had just lifted it off the shelf to peer closer when a voice behind me spoke with the control of someone who doesn't want to allow their temper to take full reign.

'Oh, there you are. We thought you were lost.'

It was Signora Stephanini herself. I wondered how long she'd been standing there watching me.

I swung round to face her, the photograph still in my hand. 'I was just admiring your wedding photograph,' I said, then hesitated. I didn't know her enough to ask what might prove a sensitive question. But I really wanted to know, so I plunged in. 'Would it be rude of me to ask if your husband is still alive?'

'No,' Signora Stephanini said, coming right up to me and stretching out her hand for the photograph. 'It would not be rude, and no, Stephen – that's my husband – died many years ago.'

'Oh, I'm sorry,' I said, staring at his face before she took it. 'He looks a nice man.' I handed it over.

'He was a very nice man,' she said abruptly, placing it in exactly the same position as it had been before I'd picked it up. She glanced at me, her eyes lingering a fraction. 'Well, we'd better go back. Rosalia and your charming daughter will be wondering what has happened to us.'

47

Ruggero was always the first person, besides Hedy, I thought of when I woke up every morning, and the last person at night before I closed my eyes. How I longed for his arms to enclose me. And Hedy should know her father. I was feeling guilty about letting him go back to Naples without seeing her. He must be feeling terrible to think he has a daughter and hasn't been allowed to set eyes on her, I thought unhappily. I'd acted stupidly out of pride. Well, I'd give myself another week to look for my father's family but if I had no luck then I'd take Hedy to Naples. And I'd apologise.

First, I needed to ask Signora Moravia more about Alessandro. A perfect time came the following evening when for once she took me into the sitting room area where Alessandro was smiling at us from the new frame she'd found. She busied herself with a piece of crochet, hooking the needle in and out. We chatted about Hedy and how she was picking up some Italian words and how clever she was that she was using them in the right places.

'Mrs Nora,' I began, glancing over towards the dresser, 'you never talk about *your* family. Your husband and children.'

Her head jerked up and her eyes grew moist. There was such a long pause I wished I'd never started the conversation. If Alessandro was her only child and no longer alive it was a cruel question.

'I am not married,' she said finally, keeping her head bent low over the crochet.

Dear God. So she and Alessandro's father had never married. What on earth could have happened?

'My fiancé, he killed in the first war.'

'Oh, I'm so sorry, Mrs Nora,' I rushed in, 'but at least you had your baby.' I tried to soften her words, but having a baby out of wedlock would have been even more shameful in those days than when I was pregnant with Hedy.

She drew her grey brows together so they almost met over the bridge of her nose. 'I cannot have baby. Baby comes *after* wedding, not before.'

'But Alessandro—'

'My beloved Alessandro, he died.'

'Oh, Mrs Nora.' I got up and went over to her, kneeling down by her chair and putting my arms round her. Tears fell down her soft plump cheeks.

Now *I* couldn't find the words. A lump collected in the back of my throat. She stopped crying and wiped her eyes. I took her hand in mine and looked into her dear face, lined with misery.

'I'm so sorry you lost Alessandro,' I said, thinking how inadequate the words were. I was trying to work out my next question when a shriek from along the corridor brought me to my feet. Hedy! I rushed from the room, my heels clattering on the tiles.

'What is it, darling?'

Hedy was struggling to sit up in her bed, her eyes wide. I touched her forehead. It felt clammy.

'Mummy, there was a horrible man...'

'It was just a bad dream,' I told her, hugging her to me and stroking the dark silky hair. 'It's all right now.'

'I'm scared. I want you to come to bed.'

'I'll be there very soon, darling. Mrs Nora and I are having a little talk.'

'Can I come down?'

'No, Hedy,' I said firmly. 'I promise to be up in a few minutes.

Just close your eyes and think of all the lovely things we'll do tomorrow.'

'Just me and you?' Her eyes scanned my face anxiously.

'Yes,' I nodded. 'Just the two of us.'

When I returned, Signora Moravia had cleared away her crochet and was sitting staring into space, reminding me of Mum. Her head twisted round when she heard me come in, and I saw she was still tearful. She gestured for me to bring my chair closer.

'What is matter with Hedy?'

'She just had a bad dream.'

The old lady nodded and smiled at me. 'I understand now, *cara mia*,' she said gently. 'You think Alessandro mine. You think *my* son died. No, he is godson. But to me like son I never had.'

So she wasn't his mother. I stared at her, all my hopes and dreams rushing out of me, leaving me barely able to breathe. And then I heard Signora Stephanini's voice in my head when she caught me looking at her wedding photograph. *Stephen – that's my husband – died some years ago.* Suddenly, it began to connect.

'Mrs Nora, is your friend Vittoria's family name "Stephanini"?'

'No. She change it to Stephanini after her husband die and she return to Rome, because her married name is not Italian.'

'Is that because she married an Englishman?'

She studied me closely, her eyes never wavering from my own. She nodded.

'Could it...could it...' I faltered as I drew in a breath from deep down, aware of every heartbeat. I started again. 'Could her husband be...Stephen Townsend?'

Mrs Nora didn't pause. Just watched me as she spoke.

'Yes, that was his name.' Her words hovered in the air around us.

'And did they have a son, Alessandro, who became your godson?'

'Yes.' Her voice was a whisper.

'And was Alessandro a doctor in Australia?'

I trembled, waiting for her reply.

She nodded slowly, still staring at me.

I was numb. And then I felt a weight lift from my shoulders. At last I knew the truth. But I'd been completely wrong. Dear Mrs Nora wasn't my grandmother. It was her friend, Signora Stephanini, that cold-hearted woman who was the missing relative. My grandmother. Hedy's great-grandmother.

My eyes were caught in Signora Moravia's steady gaze. I was sure she'd always realised who I was. But I had to say it out loud.

'Mrs Nora, I think you know Alessandro was my father, Dr Alexander Townsend? And I also think you had a suspicion from the first moment you set eyes on me.'

A look of relief crossed her face, as though at last the mystery of the resemblance I had to her godson was finally out in the open.

'You do look like him. Except for...' she pointed her forefinger to her own eyes, 'you are blue like the midnight. His were the soft grey – just like little Hedy's.'

I was certain Signora Moravia knew I'd hoped she was my grandmother as she must have seen the disappointment on my face. I doubted I would ever feel the remotest shred of affection for Signora Stephanini. How could she be my father's mother? She was so aloof, so superior. Strange that she and Mrs Nora were such friends as they were so different. But I had a feeling they weren't the close friends they'd been when Alessandro was a boy.

Then I remembered how Hedy had run to Signora Stephanini that first day, and Hedy didn't run to everyone. It was almost as though the child knew by instinct the strange woman was her great-grandmother. And I'd seen how Signora Stephanini's face softened at the attention Hedy had unexpectedly given her.

But first I owed it to Mrs Nora to tell her my side of the story. And the best time to do it was right now.

'My mother once told me she used to look out for the postman when she lived with my father, hoping he'd brought a letter from his parents.' I took another sip of wine which Mrs Nora had insisted upon opening. 'But it never happened.' Mrs Nora's head shot up. 'Well, you could count on one hand how many times Signora Stephanini wrote, and it was never to my mother, only Alex.' At this, poor Mrs Nora's face crumpled. 'My mother's the best in the world,' I went on. 'She's so loving and unselfish and kind. I hate to think of her being hurt. And she loved my father so much she would have been hurt on his behalf as well.'

Mrs Nora looked thoughtful. 'You know,' she said, 'I believe Vittoria have regret. I see great sad in her eyes. I wish you to have known her before. She adored Alessandro. When he go to England she is happy he has holiday. Then he tell her about your mamma and Vittoria she still happy. And she want to meet who will be her daughter-in-law. She is always homesick in Australia and tell Alessandro she hopes wedding is in Italy. Alessandro, he say no wedding. Annie already married with two children. Then she is angry.'

Signora Moravia glanced at me and I nodded for her to carry on, my senses alert to hear the rest of the story.

'I tell her she must meet Annie. She like England very much so it make good holidays. Then decide. But Vittoria very stubborn. Then Alessandro write that Annie is expecting you. Vittoria's husband say now they must go to England. She say she will think about it. But they don't go. And when you are born Alessandro send photographs of you and letters for four years so she know her grandchild. Then no more letters and pictures. He don't tell her he is ill so she have terrible shock when she has letter – the first and last one from your mamma. She say he die. Vittoria don't stop crying. I can't do nothing for her, only listen. She know I don't agree. She make excuses and we never see us until you come.'

I was silent. It was all such a waste.

48

Signora Moravia was in a sombre mood the next morning but Hedy more than made up for her by chattering non-stop. Finally, I had to tell her to please be quiet – that Mrs Nora and I had important things to discuss.

'Should we go and see Signora Stephanini today?' I said. 'Explain who I am, and that Hedy is her great-granddaughter?'

I'd have to get this over with, though I was sure she already had her suspicions as well as Mrs Nora.

'*Si*. I telephone her that we come soon.' She gave me a gentle smile and struggled to her feet. She was back a few minutes later to say her friend said we should come for coffee.

'I don't say why,' Signora Moravia said, smiling, 'but only it is important.'

She sounded excited and worried at the same time.

An hour later the three of us were sitting in Signora Stephanini's drawing room drinking coffee. Hedy had run to her again, arms outstretched, and the old lady had given her the same warm welcome. It was strange Hedy knew before I did that she was part of her family. Could it possibly be that Signora Stephanini had intuitively known as well? I still refused to think of her as my grandmother.

At first I was anxious about talking in front of Hedy. Would she be upset? But she would have to know the truth sooner or later, so I let Signora Moravia take charge.

Questions and answers flew backwards and forwards in Italian between the two women who threw me glances every few seconds, and then to my astonishment Signora Stephanini burst into tears. I felt embarrassed for such a self-contained woman losing her dignity and kept my head averted. Hedy had no such reserve. She jumped off her chair and threw her arms around her great-grandmother.

'Don't cry,' my daughter said.

'Oh, *cara mia*,' Signora Stephanini said, kissing the top of her head, 'how close I came to not knowing you.'

Mrs Nora handed her friend a handkerchief and Signora Stephanini dabbed her eyes and blew her nose loudly, then caught my curious gaze. She gave me a rueful smile which I couldn't bring myself to return. I wasn't ready to forgive her so quickly. I'd seen how Mum had been affected by the Italian woman's refusal to acknowledge her. How short-sighted the woman had been, cutting her son out of her life at the same time. It must have hurt not only my father, but Stephen, her husband, terribly. Where did Stephen fit into all this mess when he and his wife were in Australia? He must have been devastated not to have had any contact with his son. Had he been too weak to go against his wife's wishes?

Then a flicker of compassion grew for this woman who was my grandmother. I pictured Signora Stephanini sitting alone in her apartment, not long a widow, opening that first and only letter from Mum telling her that her son had died. It would have been a terrible shock.

Signora Moravia excused herself, saying she needed the toilet. I pleaded with my eyes for her to stay, but she ignored me and left the room.

'So you're my granddaughter,' Signora Stephanini said, coming to sit on the chair her friend had vacated.

'I think I must be,' I muttered.

'Rosalia said you came from England to look for me.'

'I wanted to find anyone connected to my father's family,' I answered abruptly. 'I remember very little of him. I was younger than Hedy when he died. Of course I had no idea if you were still alive. But if you were—' I broke off. Anything I might say would sound rude, even hostile. Signora Stephanini waited. 'If you were alive,' I began again, 'I wanted to explain to you about my mother. How she longed to meet you. To tell you how much she loved my father...your son. You would have liked her.' I blinked back the tears, determined not to cry the way she had.

'I know now I would have loved her,' she said, wiping her eyes again. 'What can I say, except how sorry I am?' She shifted herself in the chair so she was directly facing me. 'You must try to understand how difficult it was for me...and my husband. Our boy living with a married woman in England who already had children. Who was not even Roman Catholic. Then having a child with him who would be illegit—' She broke off, her face red with embarrassment, and put her cup down, then pursed her lips as though with resignation. 'That child was you, of course. But we did not bring Alessandro up to do something like that. He was a doctor. That was all he wanted. All *we* wanted for him. And to marry someone of our own class. I'm sorry...I didn't mean to sound so blunt but that is our way'

I barely heard the excuses she made. My stomach was in knots. How dare she insinuate my mother wasn't good enough for her darling boy? But then I remembered Mum explaining what a terrible sin it was in those days for unmarried couples to live together, and even more shocking if one or both were already married. And for a gentleman to marry a servant – well, that would be enough to break any parents' hearts. And that was in England. It would be so much worse in a Catholic country.

Tears rolled down her cheeks again. 'I'm sorry,' she repeated, looking at me with dull eyes.

'It's a bit late for apologies,' I said crisply. 'You lost your son. I lost my father. Nothing we say will bring him back.'

'But maybe his death can do some good. Bring us together. Perhaps your mother—'

'My mother gave up any hope about you a long time ago,' I told her, ignoring my mother's voice in my ear, warning me not to be so cruel.

But I couldn't stop myself. She closed her eyes briefly against the raw pain I was throwing at her. It was only Mrs Nora appearing that stopped me from saying more. She sat down opposite us and raised an enquiring eyebrow at her friend, but Signora Stephanini seemed as though her spirit had been sucked out of her. She gave the tiniest shake of her head. Good. Let her stew on all that. I felt so angry and sick and hurt for my mother and I was glad when Mrs Nora said it was time to go home and get Hedy some lunch.

No matter how often I told myself not to be so immature, that Hedy deserved better from me, I couldn't disguise my deep disappointment that dear Mrs Nora was not my grandmother. That it had turned out to be that old trout, Signora Stephanini, instead. Well, if she thought I was going to fling my arms around her, tell her I'd forgiven her and we'd make up for all those lost years and be close as grandmother and granddaughter, she was mistaken.

I'd achieved my aim. I'd found a living member of my father's family – his own mother, even though I'd never feel anything towards her. Best of all I'd met my father's godmother. And that was wonderful as she told me as much as she could remember about him as a boy. Until the heartbreaking day when he must have been about twelve, she said, and Vittoria announced that she, Stephen and Alessandro were going to live in Australia. Permanently. Listening to her, I realised Mrs Nora never really got over the loss. There'd been no more children, so I had no other aunts or uncles or cousins to discover. Just the uncharitable Signora Stephanini, who nevertheless seemed eager to make amends. And if I really had no intention of meeting her halfway I should take my daughter home. But first I needed to tell Hedy that Signora Stephanini was her great-grandmother.

'I know,' Hedy said, her grey eyes serious.

'How did you know?'

'She whispered to me one time. It was our secret.'

I shook my head in disbelief. My daughter not yet six, and wiser than her mother.

But for now Hedy and I would go to Naples. It might be weeks before Ruggero managed to come to Rome, and I had been the one to leave in a huff. It was a relief to finally make a decision and I trembled with excitement, longing to see him again. To hear his voice. To show him his little daughter. We would have some proper time on our own, the three of us. I decided not to let him know we were coming. I wanted it to be a surprise, but I did confess to Mrs Nora that Hedy's father was alive and living in Naples. She took it very calmly and said she was very happy for my sake and Hedy's.

But the next morning Signora Stephanini – I would never call her anything else – telephoned and asked to speak to me.

'I am thinking,' she said.

No more than I am, I thought, my heart beating a little faster as I wondered what she was about to say.

'Rosalia told me about Hedy's father. I believe his family is in Naples. I have a brother in Naples who is very ill in a nursing home. I should like to visit him as it might be the last time. Maybe we could travel together – that is,' she hesitated, 'if you are thinking of taking Hedy to see her other grandparents, and her papa's grave.'

No! I gripped the receiver trying to think. I'd lied about Hedy's father being dead and really didn't want to travel all that way in her company pretending something which was completely untrue. And what would I tell Hedy?

But Signora Stephanini was my grandmother and she'd lost everything because of her pride and religion. She was trying hard to make amends. I'd treated her in an off-hand manner to the point of rudeness. I sighed. I knew I had to break the cycle.

'I thought I would take her there before I went back to England,'

I heard myself saying in a voice that didn't sound like my own, 'so it would work very well. It will be good for her to spend some time with you.' There was a sharp intake of breath at the other end and I resolved to tell her the truth on the way to Naples.

'Just one other thing.' Signora Stephanini hesitated, sounding unsure. 'Would you allow Hedy to call me Nonna Stephanini?' Before I could answer she added, 'I know I'm really her great-grandmother but that's...how you say...a mouthful? Or will it be too difficult for her to say?'

'No, she'd like that,' I said. 'She loves using long words.'

Her next remark caught me a little off-guard. 'And maybe one day, Kitty, you will call me Nonna too!'

We planned to go the day after tomorrow, much to Mrs Nora's delight. I think she'd missed her friend over the years and was thrilled to think that things might be coming right after all Vittoria's loneliness and grief. I wasn't quite so optimistic though I was willing to give our tentative relationship a try. I begged Mrs Nora to come with us but she didn't feel she was up to the travelling. After her fall outside Babington's I suspected she'd lost her confidence.

'Better for you and Hedy and Vittoria alone,' she said.

49

I decided not to tell Hedy my plan until the morning itself in case she was too excited to sleep.

'We're going on a long train journey today,' I said, as she was pulling on her socks. 'To Naples. You're going to see someone special.'

She looked up at me, her little heart-shaped face serious. 'Who?'

'A wonderful man. He lives in Naples and wants to see you.'

'Why does he want to see me?'

'Because he loves you.'

'Why does he love me?'

'Because...' I swallowed. 'Because he's your real daddy. Your Italian daddy.'

Her beautiful grey eyes went wide. 'Why have I got two daddies?'

'You haven't, darling,' I said, my heart going over with the thought of explaining to her. 'Daddy Harry was just looking after you until you met your real daddy.'

Please, dear God, I thought, let Ruggero love this precious one and let us all be together, no matter how complicated...how uncertain the future.

Her mouth turned down at the corners as she looked up at me. 'When are we going home to see Nannie?'

'Soon,' I said. 'But Nannie will want to hear all about your Italian daddy.' I sighed. This was so difficult to explain. 'I want you to be kind to him.' I bent down to her. 'He's been very sad lately and that's why I thought you were the best person to make him smile.'

'Why is he sad?'

'Because he's never seen you before.'

'Why doesn't he live with us if he's my real daddy?'

'Because he lives in Italy and we live in England. But we've come to Italy especially to see your great-grandmother and your Italian daddy.'

'Are you coming to see my Talian daddy, too?' my daughter demanded.

'Yes, of course, darling,' I said, helping her button her shoes. 'We're going together. And your great-grandmother is travelling to Naples with us to see her brother in hospital. And she has asked that you call her Nonna Stephanini. Do you think you can do that?' My daughter nodded. 'But not a word to Nonna about your Italian daddy. I'll tell her when we're on the train.' Hedy opened her mouth but I stopped her. 'Now, no more questions. We've got to hurry. Is Lucy ready to travel?'

'I'll get her.' Hedy rushed for her doll and came back asking, 'Does the Talian daddy love you, too?'

Her question was so unexpected I felt my skin prickle all over. Hedy waited expectantly, as though my reply was important to her.

'Very much,' I said, feeling the tears sting behind my eyes at the thought of Ruggero loving me through all those lonely years. Perhaps he'd been about to tell me so when we'd been interrupted by the waiter when Daniela had had her accident. Or perhaps I was completely wrong.

Hedy nodded in a grown-up manner as though she approved. I couldn't help smiling.

Signora Stephanini had thought of everything for the long train journey to Naples. She'd brought plenty of food and drink and a colouring book and crayons for Hedy. She read to her from a children's book in Italian which Hedy didn't seem to mind in the least, and once in a while she would dart a glance at me, sometimes giving me a wan smile. I smiled back, but automatically. As the train rumbled along I was busy collecting my thoughts.

When Hedy eventually fell asleep I told my grandmother the truth about Hedy's father. That he was still alive and I was going to take Hedy to see him.

She raised her eyebrows and shook her head, and I thought our tentative relationship seemed about to collapse. But then she gave me a genuine smile that reached her eyes.

'Poor Kitty,' she said. 'You have had a difficult time for the past years. Maybe now you will have some happiness.'

We began to chat more easily – not just about the weather and what Hedy wanted to drink, but personal things.

'Please tell me about your husband,' I said. 'After all, he's the grandfather I never knew, and Hedy's great-grandfather...if it doesn't bring back painful memories,' I added.

'I would like to tell you about him,' she said, unbuttoning her jacket and relaxing her head on the upholstered seat. 'We met in England.'

This was a surprise. 'How?' I asked.

'I was a young girl in London,' she said, a faraway look in her eyes that reminded me of my mother when she was thinking of my father. 'I went to a finishing school in London. We used to go dancing nearly every night and I fell in love with the brother of one of my English friends.' She half-closed her eyes. 'Stephen said he fell in love with me the first time he took me to meet his mother. She was making dinner – it was cook's night off and the maid was ill – and I could see she had no heart for it. I asked if she would like me to help. Being Italian, cooking was natural for me.' Her face lit up and I saw for an instant the lovely young girl she must have been. 'Stephen came to the kitchen to see if I was all right. I was wearing the cook's apron,' she chuckled. 'I remember he kept staring at me all through dinner, and how embarrassed I was when he pointed out afterwards that I was still wearing the apron.'

I smiled back at the thought of them when they were young. 'How long was it before you told his parents?'

'Not long. We wanted to marry soon and live in Italy. Stephen's parents were not happy. And then when Alessandro was born they only came here once a year in the summer. His mother did not have good health. Then when Alessandro was twelve Stephen got a position in Australia. That was of course even further away. Impossible then.' She looked at Hedy and smiled.

'We had a good life in Australia,' she went on. 'We were happy although I missed my home and my family and friends. But I made new ones. Of course I missed Alessandro when he grew up and left home. He married a lovely Australian girl but she died very young with a brain tumour. He was heartbroken and decided to become a ship's doctor. He told me later that is when he met your mother.'

She was silent for a few minutes. It was obviously very difficult for her.

'One day he wrote to tell me he was in love with an English lady and I am very happy for him. I ask when is the wedding. He says she is married with two children who he loves too. I am so upset. No wedding. Two children to look after who are not his children. But Stephen wants me to go to England to meet this girl, Annie... your mother,' she looked at me with soulful eyes, 'and I say, "How can I? She is against everything I believe." Stephen finds it hard to understand because he is not Roman Catholic. Then Alessandro wrote that your mamma is having a baby and Stephen say he will go on his own to England. And he would. And then I tell him I will go with him. He is so happy. But he became ill...too ill to travel. And I will never forgive myself for not writing to your mother to tell her we planned to come but my husband was too ill. She would have understood and I know she would write back and send photographs of herself and my son, and their little girl...you, Kitty.

Also, the two other children. It is not their fault. I start many letters to her. But I don't send them. I feel too ashamed to write so late.

'Then Stephen died. And not so long after I receive a letter from your mamma. The first one. She...' Signora Stephanini gulped, 'she...told me my darling son had died of tuberculosis. My lovely son.'

Tears gathered in my throat and I swallowed hard.

'Then after Alessandro...' she broke off and tears streamed down her face but she let them run. I waited quietly. '...I went back to Roma. And by then Rosalia, my dear friend, was not the same to me. She always said I should go to England to see my son and meet the woman he loves. So Rosalia and I don't see each other. Until we meet...met the other day. And I could not help looking at you and Hedy. You look so much like him but Hedy has his eyes. And Rosalia, she saw it too. You brought me back to my friend. And I am now happy, Kitty, because I think I have found my granddaughter and her dear little Hedy.' She leaned across and I allowed my hand to rest in hers.

Her relief at telling me was obvious but there was still the nagging feeling that my mother had lived through all those years carrying such a weight of hurt. Some things were hard to forgive.

50

The train finally pulled into Naples. This last part of the journey had been very beautiful, and while Hedy was either sleeping, munching, or reading her book, I'd spent most of it admiring the scenery and the sparkling bay when we were approaching the city. Signora Stephanini had leant back on her seat and closed her eyes. I glanced at her every now and then, wondering if I'd inherited any feature from her but I couldn't see anything. Everyone else in the carriage was asleep which gave me some thinking time. But my mind was such a jumble of thoughts of Ruggero that I didn't work out anything or come to any conclusion. Only that in a few hours I might see him.

There was a crowd of people on the platform waving madly and for a moment I looked for Ruggero. Then I told myself not to be so silly – he had no idea I was here. I helped Hedy, with Lucy gripped tightly in her arms, on to the platform. A kind-looking man lifted down both my case and Signora Stephanini's, and after we thanked him the three of us made our slow way towards the station gate.

Signora Stephanini begged me to go with her to her brother's so at least she knew we had a definite bed for the night, but I refused. I had Ruggero's address and even if I couldn't stay at his parents' house I had enough money for a few days in a *pensione*. We arranged to meet in three days' time to catch the morning train back to Rome.

'And if you do not come?' Her face was flushed and she looked less in control than I'd ever seen her.

'You must leave without us,' I said.

Her face fell. 'Oh, I could not—'

'Don't worry,' I told her. 'I have your brother's address if I need to contact you. We'll be all right...honestly.'

With a swift kiss and hug for Hedy, and a squeeze of my hand, she turned and hurried away. I waited until I could no longer see her hat bobbing above the crowd. Then Hedy's hand slipped into mine.

We were on our own.

Naples looked in an even worse state than Rome. The rubble and gaping holes where buildings had once been, the shops with little on display in the windows, the stray dogs, ribs poking through mangy coats, lifting their legs in doorways and sniffing at the piles of litter, desperate to find some scrap of food to keep themselves alive. It didn't look as though there'd been much repair work going on since the war. A sense of resignation and poverty hung over the city like a heavy black cloud. It reeked of bad fish and urine and God knew what else. There seemed to be nothing of beauty; nothing to lift the spirits. This was my first impression anyway. No one caught our eye as they shuffled past, old ladies and younger ones, dressed in black; all in mourning from losing loved ones.

I squeezed Hedy's hand when she looked around, her grey eyes wide with shock.

'The nasty people did horrible things to this town too, didn't they, Mummy?'

'They did, darling, but they've all gone back to live in their own countries. And they realise how silly they've been to do such horrible things. They promised not to do it ever again.'

We hailed a taxi and I showed the driver Ruggero's address. He simply nodded, waved us into the back seat, and roared away without even looking behind him. I had no telephone number to warn Ruggero so I crossed my fingers he would be home.

'Palazzo Andreotti,' the taxi driver said, holding open the door for us. He set our two bags on the pavement, and I gave him a small bundle of notes.

I looked across the road at Ruggero's home. This was definitely no palace. It was a tall building at the end of the street, with glimpses of the bay to the side. And though the house must have been elegant in its day it was in dire need of repair. Not only was the paint peeling on all the window frames, but there were deep cracks in the stucco on the left-hand side, and when I strained my neck back I could see missing tiles on the roof, and dangling wires. It looked unloved and uncared for and not like a proper home at all.

'Can I pull the bell, Mummy?' Hedy's face had lost its tired look. Without waiting she pulled the cord. The door opened. And there stood my love.

Ruggero's eyes widened in amazement.

'Kitty,' he said, his face lit by one huge smile but I noticed the dark circles under his eyes. 'Why didn't you tell me you were coming?' He held his arms out to me. And then he stopped.

Our daughter stared up at him, quiet for once.

'Hedy, darling, this is your Italian daddy.' I ignored Ruggero's raised eyebrows. 'Say *buongiorno* to him.'

'*Buongiorno*,' she parroted. She'd practised that one a lot in the shops we went into.

Ruggero's eyes brimmed with tears. He bent down to her but I was pleased he didn't thrust himself too close so that he frightened her. '*Buongiorno, cara mia.* Do you have a kiss for your papa?'

Hedy looked at me and I nodded. She allowed Ruggero to give her a kiss, but when he offered his cheek for a kiss in return, she took a few steps back, her eyes wide.

'She needs to get used to you.' I took Hedy's hand. 'Can we come in?'

'What am I thinking?' Ruggero threw his arms up. 'Come in, please. And warm welcome to Palazzo Andreotti.'

Cautiously, we stepped through the doorway, Hedy keeping her hand tight in mine, into an enormous hall. What a contrast to the outside of the building. I didn't expect this at all. The heels of my shoes clattered over a marble floor, once beautiful but now badly stained. A cumbersome dresser stood against the left-hand wall, empty except for a few plates and a pair of silver candlesticks. Antique chairs and small tables adorned with flower-decorated lamps were haphazardly placed, but my attention was drawn towards the far end where an elegant curved staircase with wrought-iron banisters rose to the first floor.

Ruggero led us through one of the doors from the hall into a drawing room. A fancy cornice with a pair of chandeliers adorned the ceiling, but the carpet and curtains, once a superior quality, I was certain, were faded, exuding a sad, damaged kind of air. Before I settled myself on a stained and torn sofa while Ruggero excused himself to get Hedy a drink and me a coffee, I walked over to the windows and fingered the curtains. A cloud of dust rose, tickling the back of my throat, and I coughed. The material was full of tears and holes, and worst of all, cigarette burns.

It was such a shame that this beautiful house had been left to rot.

Hedy looked around the room, eyes wide. 'Is this where my Talian daddy lives?'

'Sometimes,' I told her. 'It's where he grew up when he was a child. *His* daddy still lives here.'

'Where does his mummy live?'

'She's gone to heaven.'

'Oh.' Hedy looked disappointed and clutched Lucy a little tighter.

At that moment Ruggero returned with the drinks and Hedy's eyes followed every move he made. The three of us sat at a small table, Hedy seeming quite content, sipping her milk. When she finished she asked me if she could get down.

'Yes,' I said. 'But don't rush about. Your grandpa might be asleep.'

'He is,' Ruggero said, 'but he will arise shortly. How surprised he will be.'

Hedy vanished.

Ruggero led me over to the sofa and we talked softly about nothing important. Five minutes later we saw two small feet sticking out the bottom of one of the curtains. She popped her head out and stared at her father.

'You didn't know where I was hiding, did you?'

'I did not.' Ruggero beamed at her and she giggled.

Our daughter came out, cobwebs sticking to her clothes, and sat on the floor by my feet, attending to Lucy. Ruggero couldn't take his eyes off her. So many expressions flitted across his face. One moment he was the proud smiling father, and the next he was slowly shaking his head at her, and I knew he was trying to come to terms with having a daughter.

'Did you have a good journey down?' Ruggero asked. He still hadn't kissed me. Maybe he felt awkward in front of Hedy.

'Made bearable by Signora Stephanini,' I said. 'She brought a picnic basket with her. She hopes to meet you but at the moment she's visiting her brother in hospital.'

'Who is this Signora Stephanini?'

'It's a long story.'

'I have time to listen,' Ruggero said, lighting a cigarette.

'I would like to meet her,' he laughed when I'd finished. It was a good sound.

'Well, I go back to Rome in three days' time,' I said, 'so if you come and see me off she'll be on the platform. But if you want to know her better you'll have to come back to Rome with us.'

Hedy looked up. 'I want to see Nonna Steph. Is she coming to see my Talian daddy after she's seen her brother?'

'I don't know, darling. Her brother's not very well.'

'What do you like to do at school, *cara mia*?' Ruggero's gaze was on Hedy again.

'I like music best,' she said, skipping over to the window, then running back to where we were sitting, her little face shining. 'And I like singing in the choir. And sometimes teacher lets me sing on my own. I'm the only one in class who dares.' She gave a delighted chuckle and plonked down between us.

'So you like singing,' Ruggero said in wonder, as though his daughter had just told him she liked doing brain surgery. Hedy nodded vigorously.

'It's no surprise,' I set the cup back in its saucer, 'with a mother and father who like singing, and my own father, Alexander, loved to sing. I used to sing with him when I was younger than Hedy. I remembered after all this time. We'd make up songs. I'm sure that's why I wanted to be a singer. And I've always sung to Hedy, ever since she was a baby.'

'Oh, Kitty.' The love in his eyes was undeniable as he put his arm around the back of the sofa to enclose us both.

'Are you really my daddy?' Hedy asked, looking at each of us in turn for confirmation.

'I really am. But I lost you for a long time.' He put his hand on top of her head and she turned to face him.

'Then why are you crying now you've found me?'

Even from where I sat I could hear Ruggero swallowing hard.

'Because this is the first time I ever saw you, but I've loved you right from the beginning, when you were still a baby. When you're older your mamma will tell you all the story.'

She smiled at him, seeming satisfied. Then using her finger, she brushed the tears on his cheeks.

'Don't cry, Daddy. I'm here now.'

She sounded so wise that I felt my own eyes fill, but I blinked hard. It wouldn't do to have both her parents crying.

My eye was caught by the shadow of a figure at the doorway.

'Papa!' Ruggero jumped up to greet his father, a flow of Italian pouring from his lips, his arms waving and gesturing to Hedy and me. I wondered if he'd warned his father that he had a six-year-old daughter. I hoped he had as the shock might be too much for an elderly man.

Conte Andreotti was a small man, his shoulders stooped, and wearing clothes too baggy for him. I remembered from the newsreels how even the rich had suffered and been close to starvation. He'd lost his elder son, his wife had died, and his daughter had been severely ill with polio. I rose from my seat and slowly walked towards them. Immediately, the old man grasped both my arms and pulled me to him and kissed me on both cheeks. Then he saw Hedy who was still sitting, trying to take in all that was unfolding before her.

'Come, little one,' he said in English. 'Say hello to your grandpapa.'

I saw a look of confusion on Hedy's face but she meekly went over to Ruggero's father who simply put out his hand to shake hers. Hedy beamed. She loved to be treated like a grown-up. I breathed out a long sigh. Everything was going to be all right with Hedy's new family.

'You will stay here with us,' Ruggero said, 'but you will both share in my room and I will sleep on the sofa because there is not enough bedrooms in good condition.' He said this very matter-of-factly, without any trace of embarrassment. 'Come, I will show you both your room and then I give you a tour of the house.'

It took us until lunchtime to inspect what was, Ruggero assured me, once a palace. With Hedy dragging on my hand I found it hard to believe the house had suffered so much damage in the war, and that it had not been repaired and restored.

'It's been very difficult, Kitty,' Ruggero said, reading my thoughts. 'I didn't get home finally until two years ago, and with Lorenzo's death...' his voice became unsteady and I heard him take in a deep breath, '...and Daniela being so ill, any renovations not so urgent had to wait. Some of this damage,' he looked around the library, 'was from German officers who took over the main house. They left Mamma and Papa in just two rooms upstairs. You can't imagine what they went through. Much bomb damage and then in 1944 Vesuvius erupted. Did you hear?'

I nodded, feeling ashamed how I'd judged the state of Ruggero's home.

'It was devastating to all,' he went on. 'Worse than any bombs. Houses fell like playing cards – like as in earthquakes. Papa said he could hear the noise of walls of houses falling in a near village from here. The sky was black smoke and then ash falls. He said no one can understand who hasn't seen it. And so difficult to clean up after. They had to use the military vehicles. Many lost their homes. Many died. My parents were the lucky ones.'

'I'm so sorry,' I said, thinking how inadequate it sounded. Hedy let go of my hand and had skipped on ahead.

'But now I look through your eyes,' he said, his own now full of amusement, 'the repairs and cleaning are all urgent. I must see to it. But there are more important things than a fine house.'

And as if he couldn't wait a moment longer he took me in his arms at the top of the stairs and kissed me.

The three of us spent two wonderful days in Naples. Ruggero was sensitive to the needs of Hedy and he made sure she was part of all we did, not giving the child any cause for jealousy by taking too much notice of me. I loved him for it. After a couple of hours Hedy took his hand as naturally as she did my own and my heart leapt with joy.

'We go to see the Fountain of Neptune this afternoon,' he said, gazing down at Hedy as we walked along, our child in the middle holding our hands. 'And you can make a wish.'

'A wish, a wish, a wish come true,' Hedy sang out, to the amusement of some old ladies dressed head to foot in black.

We wandered through a busy market and along several streets, finally coming to the Piazza Plaza della Borsa. And there stood the Fountain of Neptune. Ruggero explained how it had been moved to different locations in times of various wars, but to me it looked as though it had been there forever.

'Look at the water coming out of the lions' mouths,' Hedy shouted, hopping from one leg to the other.

Water wasn't just coming from the four lions, it was pouring out of sea monsters and dolphins. A spectacular sight. Some tourists were taking photographs and one woman in a drab fawn raincoat with a despairing expression threw in a coin and stood for a few moments. Then she turned abruptly away. I hoped her wish would come true.

Ruggero gave Hedy and me a few lire. 'You throw in a coin,' he said, 'and make a wish.'

Hedy clutched the coins in her small hand and threw them as hard as her little arm let her, but it fell short of the fountain. She turned to Ruggero. 'You throw it for me, Daddy.'

He threw the coin hard and it made a tiny ripple as it sank to the bottom. Hedy danced up and down in delight. 'I've made a wish,' she said.

'Don't tell us,' Ruggero said, 'or it won't come true.'

We lingered a while longer and stopped for coffee and cake, then walked a bit further until Hedy told us her legs ached.

It was the morning of our departure. Ruggero had said nothing more about coming back with us. Pride wouldn't let me mention it again, but when he met us in the hall carrying a small bag my heart soared.

'I'm taking a little time with you, Kitty,' he said. 'Only few days as Daniela finds it hard to look after Papa too long.'

At the station the man behind the ticket counter asked me if I was Signora Bishop. When I said I was he handed me an envelope.

My dear Kitty,

I hope you have had a lovely time in Naples with Hedy's daddy. My brother died only a few hours after I reached him but at least he knew me and could speak a little. I am leaving one day later than our meeting to make arrangements to come back for his funeral, but you are a sensible girl and I know are very capable to travel on your own with Hedy.

I look forward to seeing you both upon my return.

With sincere affection,

Vittoria Stephanini

I was sorry she had lost her brother but a little relieved she would not be travelling back with us. I wanted us to be together on our own.

'Are we going back to Mrs Nora's?' Hedy asked excitedly.

'Yes, darling. I expect she's missed you.'

Hedy nodded vigorously. 'I've missed her lots.'

So had I.

Late in the afternoon we were back in Rome and after a few tram stops we were outside Signora Moravia's apartment. Hedy held tight to Ruggero's hand and my heart turned over to see his proud expression.

I rang the bell and Flora opened the door and ushered us in. Mrs Nora must have heard us as she came straight out into the hall.

'This is Ruggero Andreotti,' I said, wondering what they would think of one another. 'And this is Signora Moravia.'

Ruggero kissed her hand. She studied his face for a few moments, then gave a tiny nod. He returned it and released her hand.

'I made a wish, Mrs Nora,' Hedy shrieked, 'at the Nep...Nep... fountain.'

'Neptune fountain,' Ruggero said, grinning.

'Neptune fountain,' she repeated.

'Did you, *cara mia*? You are clever girl.'

Hedy beamed. 'I wished for—' she stopped suddenly. 'I'm not s'posed to tell.'

'Maybe you can whisper it to me later, Hedy,' Mrs Nora said. 'Then it won't count.' The old lady turned to me, smiling. 'And I have a surprise for you, Kitty.'

I followed her into the dining room. Nothing prepared me for Mrs Nora's "surprise".

'Nannie!' Hedy shouted as she rushed over to my mother and fell into her arms.

'I do believe you've grown, my love.' Mum beamed at her granddaughter. She looked over to me. 'Hello, darling. I thought I'd give myself a little holiday. And when you wrote to me I decided to come straight here. Do you mind?'

'Mind?' I said, hugging her. 'I've missed you so much. So's Hedy. It's wonderful to see you. You must have arrived just after I left for Naples.'

'So Signora Moravia told me,' Mum said. 'And I believe there's someone you want to introduce me to.' Mum glanced over my shoulder and smiled at Ruggero who was looking dazed.

'I am very happy to meet you,' Ruggero said. 'I should have met you before, but your husband – he said I come to the wrong house.'

Mum frowned. 'You came to England looking for Kitty?'

'*Si*,' Ruggero answered. 'I was so sure she is there but the man who I think is her papa, he say no, no one by that name lives there. I had no other address.'

Mum's eyes flashed. 'Ferguson has his own opinions on things. They are not always the same as mine.'

My eyes widened. She didn't usually say anything disloyal about Dad.

'But now Kitty and me have found each other.' Ruggero looked at me with such love that the two older women smiled.

'He's my Talian daddy,' Hedy squeaked. 'He was looking for me. Mummy said so.'

Lunch was wonderful. Mum and Ruggero talked, Ruggero mostly about Italy, although he listened intently when she told him about me as a child. Mrs Nora seemed perfectly content to join in now and again, her eyes twinkling every time I looked at her. Everything was going so well until Mum said, 'I wonder if you would take me to meet Signora Stephanini,' as I was collecting up the plates for Flora to wash.

I stared hard at her. How much had Mrs Nora told her?

'It's all right,' Mum said, reading my thoughts. 'Signora Moravia has explained everything…about Alex, and that Signora Stephanini is your grandmother. That you've met her a few times already.'

I bit my lip. 'Yes. I travelled with her to Naples. Her brother died soon after she got there, so she's staying a bit longer, and even when she's back she probably won't want any company right away.'

'Nevertheless,' Mum continued, her jaw set firm when she was determined to carry out something against everyone's wishes, 'I should like to meet her – when she feels ready.'

'After the way she treated you?' I blurted. 'I should have thought she'd be the last person you'd want to see. And anyway,' I said, 'I doubt if she'd want to stir things up after all these years.'

'Signora Moravia thinks I should,' Mum said, glancing at our hostess. Mrs Nora nodded. 'And I know Alex would agree.'

Her eyes glowed as though she was a young girl again. In fact, it didn't take much for me to imagine her as a young woman, falling in love with Dr Townsend, knowing she couldn't say anything and neither could he. Then his coming to find her when he heard Dad had gone off to America. Wondering if she felt the same way about him. My heart felt tight with understanding but all I wanted to do was protect her from any more hurt.

Ruggero had remained silent throughout the conversation. Hedy had pushed herself into the circle of his arms and he seemed absorbed with her and not really listening to us. But I was wrong.

'I think you must let your mamma and Signora Stephanini meet,' he said quietly. 'It give your grandmother the chance to make amends. Then she die knowing she did the right thing.'

51

Three days later Signora Stephanini's maid smiled at us in recognition when she opened the door, giving a nod of her head to my mother. Ruggero lagged behind. Perhaps it was courtesy but I wondered if he felt uncomfortable with what lay ahead. Maybe he was thinking the two women would cause an impossible scene. I knew different. Mum didn't show her emotions in company.

'Signora Stephanini is expecting you,' the maid announced in Italian.

My grandmother rose stiffly when we entered the drawing room but immediately sank down again.

'Welcome,' she said in English, then added, 'My knees are bad today. I expect it's the long train journey. I do apologise.' She looked at us. 'You have all come. I am very pleased. Make yourselves comfortable.' She beckoned my mother to sit beside her.

'Mrs Bishop,' she took my mother's hand in hers for some seconds, 'I am so very happy to meet you at last. But first I will get one sad thing over. I expect Kitty told you I have just lost my brother.'

'She did, and I was very sorry to hear it,' Mum replied.

'This is life. But he is at peace now.' She crossed herself.

I muttered my condolences as well, and glanced at Mum. She was staring at Signora Stephanini as if she couldn't believe she was finally in the same room as Alex's mother. I was glad Signora Stephanini hadn't made any pretence of kissing her. I wished the drawing room hadn't been so enormous so I could have heard them talking, but my grandmother had gestured Ruggero and me towards two comfortable chairs by the side of a wall of books at least ten feet away. Hedy amused herself spending a few minutes with each of us until she finally sat quietly at a small table with her colouring book.

Snippets of their conversation floated over, even while Ruggero was telling me about his work in Rome. They were "Annie" and "Vittoria" now. I held back a bitter smile. Signora Stephanini mentioned "Alessandro" and my mother "Alexander" several times. Once Signora Stephanini actually broke into a smile, and glanced towards Hedy. My daughter caught her eye and ran over. My grandmother gathered her in her arms and kissed her. I was ready to pounce at any moment but the two women looked over the top of Hedy's dark curls and their smiles seemed genuine. I didn't know what to make of it.

Lunch spread into two hours. I had to leave the room once to go to the toilet. In the cloakroom I combed my hair and reapplied my lipstick. There was no denying it. In spite of my concern for my mother, my eyes sparkled back at me in the mirror. I was happy again. The only man I would ever love was by my side.

When I returned to the dining room Ruggero was sitting next to my mother, their heads close as if in serious conversation. Finally, I stood up and said it was time to go. I knew it was bad manners but if I waited for my mother to stir I could see another hour sliding by, and I was impatient to be with Ruggero on my own. But he didn't move from his seat. Or look at me. What was going on? I felt rather silly standing when everyone else was still seated.

'Well,' Signora Stephanini went on briskly, 'I must return to Naples for the funeral, but it won't be for another week, and I wondered…Annie, would you do me the honour of staying with me for a few days? You would be very comfortable and I think we still have plenty to say to one another.' The older woman waited for my mother's answer, seeming to hold her breath. 'I do hope you can feel it in your heart to do so as it will help take my mind off the funeral.'

After the merest hesitation, but without even a glance in my direction, Mum said, 'I'd like that very much, Vittoria.'

'I will send a taxi for you so you can return today with your case if that would suit you.'

I turned to Ruggero. I had to look down to him as he still hadn't moved.

There was an expression on his face I couldn't work out. His mouth twitched as though he wanted to speak – to tell me something – but thought better of it. I could understand if I'd found misery there for the years we'd lost, and not knowing he had a daughter, but his eyes sparked with anger. Something had changed. What was it? Maybe he was jealous he didn't have me to himself anymore. Too many women around making plans which didn't include him. Yet I never thought of him acting in such a petty way. Well, I wouldn't rest until I'd found out what was the matter.

'Is there something wrong?' I asked.

He just shook his head at me but I noticed his mouth harden.

'I will leave you now.' He got up and barely touched my cheek with his lips. 'You should speak to your mother on your own.' His voice was so quiet I strained to hear the words. 'I will stay at the same hotel as last time.' He went over to my mother and took both her hands in his, kissing each in turn. 'I hope to see you again… soon.'

They both looked each other in the eye as though they shared something private. What was going on? Or was I reading too much into something quite innocent – that Ruggero was merely being thoughtful and wanted me to have some time with my mother?

The following morning I heard nothing from Ruggero. It was a strange silence and I was beginning to feel churned up. Something was very wrong, I was certain of it, but I couldn't think what. I tried

406

to concentrate on Mum and her impending visit to my grandmother.

Mrs Nora hadn't appeared to be particularly surprised when Mum said she'd been invited to Signora Stephanini's villa for a few days.

'It is only good,' was her comment. 'Vittoria, she is unhappy for very long time. Maybe now...' she trailed off, her eyes full of hope for her friend.

'Do you mind me going?' Mum asked, as I stood in the doorway of the bedroom Kitty and I first shared. Mrs Nora had made up a cot for Kitty in her room while Mum was staying. I watched her carefully fold a blouse and skirt and put them neatly in her small case. 'I know I've not been here long,' she looked up at me, 'but this is important.'

'I don't know how I feel,' I said truthfully, 'but I suppose it can't hurt now you've finally met one another.'

'It's what Alex and I always wanted,' Mum said simply. 'That they would meet me, and when you were born, Kitty, that they would get to know their granddaughter. Now, I think she realises what she's missed over the years, especially when she looks at Hedy. And it's strange, Kitty...Hedy has really taken to her.'

'She did, right from the beginning.'

Mum nodded. 'So we've decided it's of no use to keep on about it. It won't get us anywhere. But she did tell me she and her husband had planned to go and visit Alex in England and meet me and the children and you, of course. You'd have been about two then. But her husband became very ill and the trip was impossible. She wishes she'd written to let me know that.' She looked at me. 'But how do any of us know how we'd behave in difficult circumstances?'

At least that was something, I supposed.

'So we're going to try to start afresh. Hedy's brought us together and we can't throw it away again. She wants Hedy to come in a couple of days so she can show us both the sights. Would that be all right with you?'

'I expect it will have to be,' I said.

Mum gave me a sharp look.

'Kitty,' she said, 'I understand your feelings. I felt the same myself for a long time, though I could never share it with Alex. He was too upset himself that his mother had chosen not to have anything to do with us. But I don't think there's any reason why she and I can't be friends now we've met. I can put this in the past and so must you. Don't forget, darling, it's in Hedy's interest that both sets of her grandparents get along well.'

She was right. It was *her* decision to make and she'd done it. She was so loving and courageous at the same time. Now I needed to resolve Ruggero's sudden coldness. It pained me to the core as it just wasn't like him. And I still hadn't been able to get up the courage to confess to him about Harry's and my relationship.

'You haven't told me what you think of Ruggero,' I said, curious now we were on our own.

'He's just what you need,' was Mum's reply. 'I like him very much. Harry was wrong for you. You were brother and sister in all but blood. You could never love Harry in any other way. I thought you'd told him that.'

'Told who? Harry?'

'No. Ruggero.'

I stood staring at her in bewilderment. Then I realised the implication of what she'd said. Fury bubbled up inside me.

'Did you tell Ruggero about Harry?'

'It just came out as part of the conversation.'

'How *could* you discuss my marriage to Harry with Ruggero?' I burst out, stamping my foot like a badly-behaved child.

'Darling, I assumed, wrongly as it turns out, that you must have told him.'

My heart thudded against my ribs. How dare my mother interfere? It was so unlike her. I had to keep calm. Mum and I had never had a row – ever. No wonder he'd acted so coldly. *I* should have been the one to tell him. But Mum thought I had. She didn't realise what a coward I was.

'No, I didn't tell him Harry was my husband.' I glared at her. Her eyes were dark with anxiety. 'All I said was that I was married to someone I knew very well who offered to give the baby a name and that it hadn't worked out and we got divorced. He seemed to accept that. Now he hates me.'

'Darling, he doesn't hate you. He's just upset. He'd rather have heard it from you. I'm so sorry…I wouldn't have hurt you for the world.'

She took me in her arms while I wept.

'What did he say?' I sobbed. Mum made me sit down on her bed.

'He said the man you married must have been the one you loved all the time. But I said it wasn't true. I just thought maybe he hadn't quite understood because he's Italian so I explained again who Harry was, wanting to put his mind at rest. I told him you could never love him as a wife, because the two of you had grown up as brother and sister.' Her eyes sought mine. 'It was only then I realised you hadn't told him because he looked so shocked.' She squeezed my hand. 'Oh, Kitty, why weren't you honest with him straight away?'

'I didn't want to tell him everything at once,' I said, tears streaming down my face. 'It was a lot to take in that he was a father and had a daughter of almost six.'

'You must tell him everything,' she said flatly. 'It's haunted me all my life that I was the one who broke up Alex and his mother. It was terrible. If he'd met an unmarried woman he could have taken her back to Australia and introduced her to his parents and everything would have been normal for him. Instead, they practically cut him out of their lives, and would have nothing to do with you and me. Your English grandfather wasn't able to fight your grandmother's religious beliefs. I don't want the same thing to happen to you and Hedy.'

'What on earth are you talking about?' I demanded. 'My situation is completely different.'

'Not so different,' my mother argued. 'You had Hedy out of wedlock, the same as me. If Ruggero's parents found out their son's girlfriend had got pregnant, run off and immediately married a man who was brought up as her brother, and who acted as daddy to their only grandchild, they might well disown him. However he or you explained, it would appear to them as being incestuous. And that, to a Roman Catholic, would bring the worst disgrace on the family.'

Put like that, my mother might have something. But all the more reason for me not saying anything.

'But we weren't brother and sister and the marriage was never consummated,' I reminded her, flushing with a mixture of embarrassment and irritation. 'So there was no need of a divorce.'

'His mother and father wouldn't see it like that,' Mum said firmly.

'His mother's dead. And it's none of their damn business anyway.'

'Don't swear, darling,' Mum said in a warning tone. Then she softened. 'Don't you see, Kitty? It *is* Ruggero's business. You must tell him right away and let him decide how much his father needs to know. You mustn't have any secrets from him or it will destroy your relationship. That's what happened to Ferguson and me. He always had secrets. Nothing was ever enough for him. He always wanted more excitement. And when I found out so many things, especially about Ruby, it destroyed us.'

'I've often wondered...since you told me the truth about my father, why did you have Dad back when he died?'

'I often wonder myself,' Mum said, lowering her gaze, 'but mainly it was for you children. Frankie kept on how she missed Daddy...' Mum swallowed hard before she continued. 'She was talking about Alex, because she started calling him Daddy after

410

only a few weeks. He was a true father to her. And Harry – well, he badly needed a father, he was such a handful. And of course Dad was their flesh-and-blood father. Every child needs his father,' she looked at me and said firmly, 'and Hedy needs hers. Besides,' she bit her lip, 'we'd been happy once. No one would ever take the place of your father in my heart, but I thought at least we should give it another chance. For the sake of the whole family.'

'And was it the right decision?' I asked.

'I think it was as far as Frankie and Harry were concerned,' she said. 'But you, Kitty...' she broke off and swallowed. 'He was never right with you. You were another man's child and he knew I would never stop loving Alex, your father. He took it out on you sometimes and I never forgave him for that...or myself.' Her eyes filled with bright unshed tears.

'What about now?' I persisted. 'Are you happy now?'

'As well as anyone can be,' my mother said, suddenly brisk. She'd used my exact words to Ruggero when he'd asked me the same question. But she didn't fool me. She had that faraway expression in her extraordinary eyes, and I knew she was thinking of my father.

'Well, you can forget about Ruggero and me getting married,' I told her, almost triumphantly, even though my heart felt it would jump into my throat and suffocate me. 'He's too upset with what you told him. And besides, he's never mentioned marriage. If he did, I doubt if I would. Hedy and I are fine on our own. I don't need any more complications.'

'That's what you say, but it's not what's in your heart,' Mum said, her eyes darkening to ink-blue. 'He's Hedy's father, but more importantly where you're concerned, he's the love of your life.' She stared at me. 'Isn't he?'

I just stood there.

'Isn't he?' she repeated, her eyes never leaving my face.

I nodded dumbly.

'Then go to him,' she said. 'He needs you so desperately.'

How had she seen that Ruggero needed me? I hadn't seen that at all. Was it true?

I had to find Ruggero. Tell him myself. Tell him the whole truth.

But maybe it was already too late.

52

I ran and ran and ran. I ran until my chest ached. Until pains spread across the top half of my body so bad I thought I must be having a heart attack. And still I ran. I didn't stop until I reached the hotel. I asked the porter which room he was in.

I knocked.

Glory be. Ruggero opened the door. His eyebrows shot up in disbelief. Then a slow smile spread across his face. He just said one word but it was enough.

'Kitty!'

He pulled me in and closed the door swiftly behind him.

'Oh, Kitty, when are we ever to learn?' He put his arms round me and held me tight against him, but I pulled away.

'Why didn't you telephone?' I asked, my breath still coming in gasps.

'Because I am angry.' He held on to me. 'You did not tell me the truth. I had to hear from your mamma. Then she is upset because she thought I already know and she was just trying to reassure. Why don't you trust me enough to tell me about Harry?'

'It didn't happen like that,' I protested, trying to squirm out of his grip. 'You don't seem to understand. I was having a baby... our baby...and I would have brought shame upon my family if I hadn't got married. And the person who said he had always loved me was Harry.' I gabbled on, half crying. 'He said he'd marry me... be a father to the baby...look after us both. We'd found out we were cousins. And cousins are allowed to marry. I still didn't want to but I had no choice. I'd already had the letter from Daniela saying you were engaged to be married to your childhood sweetheart. She even enclosed some money to kill my baby. My precious Hedy. Thank God I didn't take any notice of her terrible letter and her blood money.'

I broke off again, convulsed in sobs. Ruggero put his arms round me and held me close.

'Kitty, I didn't know…she didn't tell me she sent you money for such a terrible thing.' I felt him shake his head in despair. 'I don't know what to say…only I am angry with Daniela…and very sad she do such a thing. I…'

And then I felt his tears mingle with my own.

'Daniela never showed you a copy of the letter she sent to me, did she?' I couldn't stop the bitterness.

Ruggero shook his head. 'I knew nothing until very recent. Tell me all, Kitty. Come and sit down.' He took me to the sofa, all the while murmuring that everything was going to be all right.

'The marriage was never consummated, so we didn't have to go through a divorce,' I finished, sniffing. 'It was just annulled as though it had never happened. But poor Harry hasn't spoken to me since. I hope one day he'll find someone—' My throat closed. I loved Harry as a brother but I'd hurt him terribly.

I burst into tears again at the enormity of all that had happened. Ruggero wiped them away with his handkerchief.

'Shhhhh,' he whispered. 'I'm here now. Everything is going to be all right. I understand all. You tried to do the right thing for Hedy. I don't know if I can ever forgive my sister. I should have been the one to look after you and the baby. To think my daughter might not be born.' He looked at me 'Oh, Kitty, I love you so much. And I adore our daughter. Thank you, *carissima*, for having her.' He kissed me – a deep and tender kiss. Sweeter than any kiss we'd ever had.

And then it was as though a flame burst into the space between us. He brought me to my feet and crushed me in his arms and pressed his lips on mine. We couldn't tear ourselves away. His kisses rained down on my head and neck and eyes. His fingers pulled out the pins in my hair, leaving it loose around my shoulders. His tongue flicked into my ear, driving me crazy.

He lifted me up and rushed to the bed. He laid me down and pulled off my shoes. Then he pushed my skirt up to my waist and stripped off his trousers with an urgency I'd never seen, locking his eyes with mine. And then he was on top of me, pulling down my silk knickers, and the next moment I felt the heat of him inside me.

All too soon it was over.

'Kitty,' he groaned. 'I'm so sorry. I needed to have you or I would go mad. I promise I am slow and gentle the next time. But give me a few minutes to recover.'

'I may not be able to wait that long.'

He laughed and I did too, hugging him tightly.

'I've missed you so much when you went back to England in the war.' He pulled away a little and his gaze was fierce. 'Did you miss me too?'

'So much, you'll never know,' I said, burying my face in his shoulder. 'I thought you'd forgotten me. Or didn't love me.'

'Never. I thought about you every day. I always wanted you. No one will be the same for me.'

'And every day I wanted you to see Hedy who looks the image of you. To tell you what she was doing. But I thought you must have your own family by now.'

His eyes glistened. 'We will make it all up to Hedy,' he said. 'She will never go without anything.'

'She's like me,' I said. 'She hangs on to a few precious things, like Lucy, her doll, but what she really wants is to be happy...and her mummy, too, of course.'

'I promise to make her mummy happy.' Ruggero kissed me,

then sat me up and unbuttoned my blouse. Deftly he unhooked my brassiere and my breasts fell free.

'They're so beautiful,' he said huskily, as he nuzzled them and caressed my nipples with his fingers until they hardened. He bent his lips and took one, then the other, in his mouth. His fingers found the spot between my legs and he stroked me, and I arched my back under him, all the time feeling his mouth on my skin. I wanted to tear his clothes off him, feel him, but I couldn't stop the rising pleasure he was creating inside me. My lips parted and I began to pant. I didn't know what I was doing as I clutched him to me and it was like the floodgates opened and wave upon wave of excitement swept over me. And when I felt I would burst, a shudder stormed through my whole being and I shouted his name, my heart beating out of control. I wanted the feeling to go on forever, but it gently faded and my breathing returned to normal. He was softly laughing. My face felt hot. Was he laughing at me?

'Did you ever feel that before, *cara mia*?'

'The last time with you,' I whispered, almost ashamed at such wild behaviour. 'But I don't understand what happened.'

'Something natural for a woman,' he said, smiling at me. 'The most natural thing in the world. It was wonderful to watch you,' and he let my head rest gently back on the pillow. I beamed back at him, my body glowing with joy.

And then we undressed properly, and this time his skin touched mine from head to toe. He moved inside me and I clung to him.

'I love you, Kitty.'

'And I love you, Ruggero. So much.'

53

'We don't tell my family the full story,' Ruggero said, as we lay with our arms and legs entangled.

I agreed wholeheartedly. 'Nor even to Signora Stephanini,' I added. 'She's not forgiven herself about Mum so I don't want to shake her with anything else to confess. You know, Ruggero, only Mrs Nora would understand. I could tell her anything. I so badly wanted her to be my grandmother. I really thought she was when I saw the picture of my father on her dresser.'

'She will always have the special place in your heart,' Ruggero said, his eyes on mine, his gaze unwavering, his fingers stroking my bare breast.

'What is it?' I asked.

'I keep thinking of our little Hedy.'

'We can go back to her at Mrs Nora's now,' I said. 'Do you know what our daughter said just before I left?'

'What was it?'

'She said, "When's my Talian daddy coming to see us again?"' I smiled at Ruggero. 'Then she said, "He's got black hair like mine."'

'She couldn't be any other colour with your dark hair as well.' Ruggero's eyes were full of amusement.

'You never saw me blonde.'

'Blonde?' He raised a dark eyebrow in horror. 'You used to be *blonde*?'

'Just before I joined ENSA.' I couldn't help laughing at my

seventeen-year-old self. 'I thought I looked a right glamour-puss. But Jennifer Long made my friend Joyce turn me back to my natural colour before we went to Cairo.'

'I'm very glad she did.' Ruggero brushed a strand of hair from my face. 'And how did you answer our daughter?'

'I think that's a question for *you* to answer – not me,' I said.

There was another long silence. Ruggero's gaze locked with mine.

'What is it?' I asked for the second time.

'Will you marry me, darling Kitty, and let me be a proper husband to you and a real father to Hedy?'

'It's what I want most in the world,' I said, my heart dancing.

'Does that mean "yes"?' His face was wreathed in smiles as he kissed me.

We walked back to Mrs Nora's hand in hand, unwilling to break any contact. When we got there I lifted my free hand to the knocker but the door opened before it clattered down. It was Mum with Hedy. They must have seen us coming up the street. Mum's eyes were anxious but I gave her a wide smile and a little nod.

'Mummy,' Hedy screamed, flinging herself into my arms. I kissed her and asked her if she'd been a good girl. Impatiently, she said she had, all the time wriggling to be put down. She stared up at Ruggero.

'You've come back,' she piped.

Tenderness filled his eyes as he bent down and swept her up in his arms.

'Are you glad?'

'What does my mummy say?'

'She says she is very glad.' Ruggero smiled at her.

'Then I'm glad too. Can we all live together in the same house? Then you won't ever lose me again.'

I never ceased to be amazed with my daughter. Such a little child with such deep thoughts.

'That's exactly what the three of us are going to do,' Ruggero told her, laughing and giving her a kiss.

'I've got a new doll. I'll show it to you, if you like. Lucy doesn't like her. She's jealous.'

He set her down and she took hold of his hand and led him through the house chatting to him about Mrs Nora buying her the new doll, which she'd named Nora. He turned his head to me and winked.

We went to see Signora Stephanini and told her our news. I'd seen already how she'd taken to him and was impressed with the kind of family he came from. I couldn't help a bitter smile. It was exactly that so-called noble family which had kept Ruggero and me so cruelly apart. She begged me to call her Nonna and I did. Mrs Nora couldn't stop beaming at the news that there would soon be a wedding.

'It will be like having my own granddaughter get married,' she said.

My heart squeezed. 'I couldn't love you any more if you really were my grandmother,' was all I could say, planting an affectionate kiss on her wrinkled cheek.

I wrote and told Joyce my news and to ask if she'd be my bridesmaid. We'd gone through so much together and I loved her like a sister. Poor Frankie was having treatment for her nerves again and wouldn't be able to travel to Italy.

May 23rd 1948

Dear Kitty,

It's been ages since I heard from you. What exciting news! I always thought you two belonged together even though it seemed impossible when you first met. Ruggero is perfect for you. He won't put up with any of your nonsense, haha. And Hedy now has her true father. She must be thrilled.

Yes, Kitty, I'll be honoured to be your bridesmaid. Please thank Signora Moravia for her offer to put me up. I gratefully accept. Can you tell her I'll arrive two days before the wedding to give us plenty of time to catch up, sort out your wedding dress – I take it you'll be wearing the beautiful blue dress you wore in Cairo, haha – decide on your make-up, and of course I will bring a bottle of peroxide to get you back to the blonde bombshell you were always meant to be!

I also have some news. I've just got engaged to Jim Sutton, one of the soldiers I met when we were in the YWCA giving out those teas! Who would have thought? More when I see you! Which will be soon!

Much love,

Your friend Joyce XX

I also wrote to Harry. I was sure he wouldn't come to the wedding but I hoped he would wish us luck, at least. Although I was hurt I wasn't really surprised not to receive an answer.

To Hedy's delight we planned to marry on her birthday, 10th June, when she'd be six, though Mum would be back in England by then. But Mum surprised us. Nonna had offered her the use of a self-contained apartment in her beautiful house for however long she wanted and Mum had accepted. Since Aunt Ethel had died, and Frankie had given her blessing on the telephone to stay as long as she wanted, Mum said she had nothing much else to keep her at home except the tea rooms, and Mollie could easily take them over. She never even mentioned Dad. She said it was an opportunity to get to know Ruggero and his father, and Vittoria and Rosalia. She even wanted to meet Signora Dotti and thank her for being so kind to us. And of course Hedy and I would be here.

I must say I was thrilled and asked her when we were in private what had made her make such a decision.

'You're old enough to know, I suppose, darling,' she said, her eyes glittering. 'I found a letter a few weeks ago that Dad had written to you when you first came here. I was curious so I opened it. He said if you ever came back with an Eyetie, you wouldn't be welcome in his home. Thank goodness he'd forgotten to post it and it was still in the bureau. Or maybe he changed his mind about sending it – I don't know – but something in me snapped. I burned it. He never knew I'd seen it. But I decided there and then that if Alex's mother was still alive, or any of his relatives, I wanted to meet them. And of course you and Hedy were in Italy. So here I am.'

All the time she was telling me this I kept thinking, *Oh, Mum, if only Alex had lived. You were so right for one another. And I would have had him as a father who truly loved me.*

'Welcome to Italy, Mum.' I wrapped my arms around her and gave her the tightest hug. 'I'm so happy you're going to stay on for awhile.'

'So am I,' Mum said. Her eyes sparkled with mischief. 'And so, I think, is Alex.'

We grinned at each other.

'He would have been pleased I was marrying Ruggero, wouldn't he?' I couldn't help asking. 'Keeping up the Italian tradition.'

'It would have been the best news possible, darling. And he would have adored Hedy.' Mum looked at me and those deep blue eyes were full of love. 'And he would have been so proud of *you*, Kitty.'

And as I walked down the aisle on the arm of my mother on the most glorious day in June, Hedy skipping behind, holding Joyce's hand, I had the strangest feeling my father was walking on the other side of me.

Epilogue

Rome

The Contessa Andreotti, June 2012

She takes one last look in the mirror and uses a third comb to secure some stray wisps that have escaped from the pins. She pulls a face. Then quickly lets it relax again when she sees all the wrinkles. All the lines and crevices of a life fully lived. She'll never get used to being old, seeing herself with long steel-grey hair that she plaits every day and winds into a bun on top of her head. She hates the way her head shakes, only very slightly at the moment, but she knows it's the onset of Parkinson's. So far a stick is all she needs to help her balance, but that can alter at any time if the disease gets worse – which of course it will if her namesake, poor old Katharine Hepburn was anything to go by. Thank goodness her figure is still trim. She's been so careful with her diet, particularly as she adores pasta.

It hadn't mattered at all that she was a late starter with her beloved opera. She had the voice and the determination. And she had Alice Delysia to introduce her to the right people. Dear Alice. What a friend she was right up until she died at ninety. I'm only one year off myself, she thinks, a little shocked. And she had Ruggero loving her and supporting her and making sure she pronounced her Italian properly.

But inside herself, in her mind, if she relives the past, she's still the young woman with flowing dark locks, madly in love with her handsome Italian, and eager to begin her new life with him, and their little daughter, Hedy – in Rome.

Rome, the city that gave her her chance. Where she first sang at the Teatro dell'Opera as Violetta in *La Traviata*. She remembers how proud Ruggero was. How he would tease her and insist he'd discovered her. She smiles and her face instantly lifts until she lets the smile go and her face falls back into its comfortable folds.

Life has mostly been kind. Her worst year was knowing her mother was so ill and not being able to be with her. Living in another country did that. But her mother always told her that her place was with Ruggero and Hedy, and that she'd be perfectly all right with Mollie looking after her. Dad died the year before and if she's honest she didn't feel much. But Mum – well, she'll never get over that loss.

Her only real tragedy was the miscarriage two years after she and Ruggero married. They were distraught at the time, and it was Hedy who helped them through those dark days and months with her happy nature. The Contessa smiles a sad smile as she remembers. Hedy is married and living in her grandparents' house in Naples. She and her husband have restored the palazzo as a labour of love. They have three grown-up children who have little ones of their own. The Contessa finds real joy in all the children, so maybe she'll move to Naples too. Hedy is always asking her, telling her the children need to see her more. But every time she thinks she'll sell up and go she changes her mind. Rome is where Ruggero's grave is. Where she feels close to him. Even after nine long years without him. But he'd want her to be near Hedy. He'd have told her to go. So maybe she's being silly. She should move before it's too late. There's certainly no one else in Rome to stay for.

She looks at her watch, takes her raincoat off the hook. It's time to make her way over to Babington's.

Juliet

Juliet has a lead.

She's gone into Babington's thinking it might be the sort of

423

place Kitty would go if she felt homesick. If she was still alive, that is. The smiling grey-haired woman behind the counter tells her they have many English visitors, and yes, there's a regular customer, very elderly, the Contessa Andreotti. She's English. And she used to be an opera singer. Not an international star, oh no, but known well enough in Italy, the country she made her home.

Juliet is intrigued.

'She's always here on a Friday for afternoon tea,' the woman says, arranging her cakes as she speaks.

'Do you know if she has any children?' Juliet asks.

'Yes, and grandchildren...and great-grandchildren by the look of them.'

This was interesting. A whole family.

'Have you ever heard any of their names being spoken?' Juliet prods a little further.

'Not that I can remember,' the woman's brow furrows. 'I never did learn Italian like I ought.' She pauses. 'Oh, I think I've heard her call one of the ladies, who I take to be her daughter, some strange name. It must be short for something else. Oh, what was it?'

Juliet waits, trying not to show any excitement. Please remember, she thinks.

'It's...oh, it's on the tip of my tongue. It's my poor old head these days...I'm getting old myself.' She suddenly smacks her hand at the side of her face. 'That's it,' she says triumphantly. 'That's it. Hedy.'

Juliet's scalp tingles. Hedy was the name of Kitty's daughter in that unopened letter she'd read addressed to Harry more than fifty years ago. It was an unusual name. Surely there can't be too many children called Hedy.

'Is the Countess's first name Kitty?' she asks.

The waitress shakes her head. 'I don't know,' she says. 'I've never heard anyone call her by her first name. It's always the Countess. Or *Contessa*, as they say here. But when her daughter comes to visit her they all troop in. They love it because it's English – different, you know, from what they're used to.'

It's Wednesday. She'll make sure she's here in two days' time.

Raindrops splatter down Babington's windows as the clock inside strikes three. Juliet sits at one of the tables, a pot of tea and two scones, jam and cream in front of her. She's buttered one of the scones but hasn't touched it. Her nerves are on edge and she fidgets with a strand of her long chestnut hair.

A very elderly lady is trying to open the door facing Juliet, but she's finding it difficult with a stick and her handbag. Juliet sets down the teapot she's been about to pour from and jumps up to open the door. The old lady gives a slight inclination of her head as she marches in, her walking stick tapping at her side.

'*Grazie.*'

'You're very welcome.' Juliet speaks deliberately in English, hoping this might stir the old lady into conversation.

The Countess, for that's who she must be by the thumbs-up signal from the waitress, smiles briefly, then her eyelashes flicker and she holds Juliet's gaze a full moment before sitting down without removing her hat or her long black raincoat.

Juliet gives her a sidelong glance every now and again. Can this old lady really be the Kitty her father mentioned just before he died? Was she one of his old girlfriends? Or might she be connected to the mysterious Dr Alexander Townsend? She watches as the waitress behind the counter walks over to the Countess to take her order. She hears them both speak in English. The waitress says something to the old lady who turns towards Juliet.

'You're from England,' the Countess calls across the tables.

'Yes, but I live in Sydney now.'

'How long are you staying in Rome?'

'I don't have any immediate plans,' Juliet says truthfully.

'I'm sorry, my dear, I'm getting a bit deaf. Why don't you come and sit with me and talk – that is, if you've nothing better to do.'

Juliet rises from the table and sits down with the Countess.

'Tell me about yourself.' The Countess fiddles in her bag for a handkerchief and blows her nose. She looks at Juliet apologetically. 'Bit of a cold. Such a nuisance.' She takes off her hat and puts it on the spare chair with her bag.

'Actually, I'm looking for someone,' Juliet says, watching the Countess's face closely. 'Someone my father mentioned just before he died a few years ago. And the waitress thought you might be able to help.'

'Me?' She points to herself. 'Why would I know anything about your father?'

'It's someone he used to know when he was young. A lady. She was important to him. He told me I should speak to her.'

'Did your father give a name?'

'Oh, yes, he said it a couple of times. The lady's name is Kitty.'

The Countess's eyes widen. Juliet is close enough to see that age hasn't faded their deep blue colour, the same shade as her beloved Nannie.

'So Ellie here,' the Countess nods towards the woman behind the counter, 'thought I could help you?'

Juliet wonders if she should carry on. The woman, whether she's the real Kitty or not, is rather a dragon. But the old lady, her head cocked on one side, is clearly waiting for Juliet to answer.

'Well, yes,' Juliet says. Is she on a wild goose chase? She tries again. 'She said she didn't know anyone called Kitty, but she said she knows an English lady who has a daughter called Hedy.'

A smile hovers over the Countess's lips.

'And did your father mention Hedy as well?'

'Yes.' Juliet's heart is racing. It wasn't exactly a lie. Dad hadn't actually mentioned Hedy, but Hedy's name was in the letter he never opened. 'Would I be rude if I ask your name?' Juliet is feeling bold.

'It's Katherine.'

Juliet's pulse races. Has she found this unknown woman in her father's life? She notices the old lady's head shakes slightly. Juliet wonders if she's aware of it, and supposes she is. It looks like Parkinson's.

'But I've always been known as Kitty,' the old lady finishes triumphantly, her face lit by her beaming smile. 'And I imagine your father's name is Harry.'

'It is.' Juliet says delighted. 'But I still don't know—'

'What Harry and I are to one another?' The Countess pauses. Seems to consider. Then she inhales deeply, her cheeks sucked in with the effort. 'I'm his sister. But for a time,' she watches Juliet with a steady gaze, 'I was his wife!'

Juliet sits open-mouthed. Has Kitty completely lost it?

'Let's order some more tea,' Kitty chuckles, unbuttoning her raincoat. 'It isn't quite so bad as it sounds…'

Reading List

A Dancer In Wartime by Gillian Lynne
Cairo In The War 1939–1945 by Artemis Cooper
Drury Lane to Dimapur: Wartime Adventures of an Actress by Doreen Hawkins
East With ENSA: Entertaining the Troops in the Second World War by Catherine Wells
Killing Hitler by Roger Moorhouse
Rommel by Desmond Young
The Rome-Berlin Axis by Elizabeth Wiskemann
The Villa Diana: Travels in Post-war Italy by Alan Moorehead

Acknowledgements

Terry Charman, senior historian at the Imperial War Museum –
I met Terry when my husband, Edward Stanton, and I went on
a study tour a few years ago: *Following in Churchill's Footsteps.*
I told Terry I had begun a novel set in the Second World War,
where my heroine meets the love of her life in Cairo. One evening
at Ditchley Park, Terry worked out the central plot, bringing in all
the military facts at the time, and even introduced me to a French
singer, Alice Delysia, who sang to the troops in Egypt during the
war. It was the swiftest and most valuable bit of research I've ever
managed – all for only one drink! Heartfelt thanks, Terry.

Alexander Turnbull Library, National Library of New Zealand –
I longed to know exactly what Alice Delysia's voice was like, so I
contacted them, and for 12 dollars they lent me a live recording
Madame Delysia made to the troops in Cairo in 1941 at the exact
time Kitty is there. What an entertainer! What a marvellous
character! I immediately knew she would play a pivotal rôle in my
story.

Edward Stanton and Richard Milton, writer – both great for
checking military details. The two of them have been friends
for a very long time with a keen interest in and knowledge of the two
world wars, and have warned me they will not be held responsible
for any mistakes or omissions I may have made!

Writerly friends – When I was in the beginning stages of the novel, Carol McGrath invited me to Portugal with fellow writers, Alison Morton, Gail Aldwin, Grace McGrath and Suzanne Goldring. What a fantastic week we had. They were so inspirational, and I made real progress. The following year Gail kindly offered us a few days retreat at her home. More discussion and working out of sequences and plot holes. Then there is my trusty writing group – the sparkly Diamonds: Tessa Shapcott, Terri Fleming and Sue Mackender (and me!) who meet once a month and read out, discuss and critique one another's work, as well as giving shedloads of support and encouragement. And finally, my friend and critique writing partner, Alison Morton. We read everything of each other's, acting as structural, copy and line editors – red pens poised to pounce! Wouldn't be this far without you, Alison.

The Romantic Novelists' Association – Without the RNA I doubt very much if I would ever have written such an ambitious trilogy. I have met the most kind and generous romance writers, many of them becoming firm friends!

Cornerstones – This excellent company provides a superb editorial service, and Helen Bryant Corner, the director, has given me two editors who were absolutely perfect for The Voyagers trilogy. Their expertise and enthusiasm, I believe, give the three books their final polish.

SilverWood Books – Once again, thank you to Helen Hart, director, and your wonderful team for producing another beautiful book.

A Note from the Author

If you've enjoyed *Kitty's Story*, which is Book 3 of The Voyagers Trilogy, I would love it if you could spare five minutes of your time to write a review on Amazon. They don't mind in the least whether you bought the ebook or paperback through them, but it makes an enormous difference to the author – me!

Grateful thanks if you could do this.

Also, if you would like to go on my Mailing List please email me: fenellaforster@gmail.com

Annie's Story

Norfolk, 1913

'We're going to Australia to better ourselves, Annie...'

Hearing those words from the lips of her fiancé, the dashing Ferguson, housemaid Annie's heart is filled with both excitement and trepidation at the thought of leaving England and her family to sail with him to a new life on the other side of the world. But Australia doesn't turn out to be the land of Annie's hopes and dreams when she discovers that those closest to her have betrayed her. A betrayal devastating enough to destroy all of their lives.

Then Annie unexpectedly encounters Alexander Townsend again, the handsome doctor she met on the voyage to Melbourne. Although she tries to deny it, when Annie looks into Alex's eyes she can't help wishing there might be a second chance of happiness for her. But she's a married woman with a secret nobody must uncover...least of all, Alex.

Juliet's Story

Kingston-upon-Thames, July 2005

It's Juliet's chance of a lifetime and however crazy the idea, she's going to grab it with both hands. An ex-client has offered to run Juliet's business to give her the freedom and time to sail to Australia to trace her emigrant grandparents' story back in 1913. But Juliet has a secret buried in her heart that only her late grandmother, Annie, knew.

There's a man Juliet loves more than life itself. And she's determined to find him. Her only clue is that he travelled to Sydney, but that was thirty years ago when she was just sixteen.

But when she boards the *Alexandria* at Tilbury she doesn't count on meeting the enigmatic Jack Delaney, and definitely not falling in love with him. Could his strange behaviour mean he, too, is carrying secrets?

And then an unexpected encounter knocks Juliet off her feet.

One man with eyes she's never forgotten.